CW01431482

CELESTIALS

CELESTIALS

COSMIC GAMES BOOK THREE

Wilbur Woods

Podium

All rights reserved. No part of this publication may be reproduced, stored in a retrieval system, or transmitted in any form or by any means electronic, mechanical, photocopying, recording, or otherwise without prior written permission from Podium Publishing.

This is a work of fiction. Names, characters, places, and incidents are either products of the author's imagination or used fictitiously. Any resemblance to actual events, locales, or persons, living, dead, or undead, is entirely coincidental.

Copyright © 2025 by Ville Aarne Elmeri Väisänen

Cover design by Tommypocket Illustrator

ISBN: 978-1-0394-6576-3

Published in 2025 by Podium Publishing
www.podiumentertainment.com

Podium

CELESTIALS

CHAPTER ONE

A Cut Above

Max stood tall and straight as he flew in the air. Well, technically it was Maverick doing the flying. He was showing off, doing twists and flips and all kinds of maneuvers that the former gun considered "epic." Max had to use [Tether] to keep his feet planted on the gold-and-black platform which his companion had become. Behind Max floated a giant black scythe, which he had commanded to follow him if no other instructions were given. The [Scythe of Oblivion] obliged as was its nature.

"It feels sooo amazing!" Maverick exclaimed. His voice was robust, clearly audible in the strong high wind. The cold air no longer bothered Max as it had before. The threshold that Maverick and he had crossed had made them something more than a human and his companion. They were now super-mortal Cultivators.

Max felt the Spiritual Energy course through him as he flexed his fingers. His meridians were now open wide, and they really felt like they were diamonds. Unbreakable and holding him upright. He felt taller, stronger, *better.*

Even my mind is clearer.

At first, the Spiritual Energy running through his meridians had been a trickle. Then, as Max had strengthened himself, the trickle had turned into a stream. Now it was a raging river, roaring with pure force.

Max understood that he was now a powerful creature. Something beyond humanity. And with that came responsibility beyond humanity. It had to be borne. But that still didn't stop the little boy inside Max, giddy to try out his new toy.

Maverick engaged this side of him immediately and gleefully. He flew them down, bursting through the clouds and approaching the land above where the Deathmatch had happened.

They descended further, and Max extended his hand. There was no technique. No Skill from the Framework was needed. Max's abilities with his Spiritual Energy were instinctive. He sent it toward a tree standing near the creek that cut through the plains of the area. The energy reached the tree, and Max *squeezed*.

Its trunk cracked like a gunshot, the bark and bits of wood exploding in every direction. The rest hit the ground with a thud.

Max grinned. The distance had been maybe fifty yards, the whole technique completely effortless; it had barely sipped from his well of Spiritual Energy.

"I wonder what else I can do," Max said and flexed his fingers again.

"Same!" Maverick said and hooted as he accelerated.

Max scoffed to himself. Maverick wasn't even listening. He was too enthralled by being able to fly. Max could hardly blame him. It was a trip. There was no feeling he had ever experienced equal to the freedom and power of soaring through the air and looking down on the world. He would let Maverick enjoy himself for now. With some wistfulness Max realized he would have to settle for simply being a passenger.

The disk that Maverick had become gleamed in the orange sun of Alpha Ludus. It was black and had ornate, intricate scrollwork made of gold. Underneath the disc was a long barrel, just as Maverick's previous form had had.

It seems our roles have changed and solidified. Well, his has. He has the mobility and the firepower.

Max's powers had potential. They had versatility. He could use them for a myriad of things, his imagination the only limit. With such power, choice paralysis could happen. It was actually a boon that Maverick's power set was so defined.

That leaves me with control, utility, and defense.

Max smirked to himself.

And maybe Damage too. Especially large-scale.

Max's mind returned to the memory of his obliterating the Outsider army attacking their base. He had felt a sense of power that was so deep and so profound, it was practically regal. He finally understood the strange expressions on the faces of kings and emperors etched in marble and painted in artworks of his home planet.

The sense of having absolute power. There was something ineffable about it. But it was intoxicating. Max had used that power to instate Joshua as the humans' de facto leader. He had dictated it. And there would be nothing anyone could do about it. He had power in the form of an insurmountable monopoly on violence.

If they do something to hamper the reign of Joshua, I will—

He would what? Destroy them? His own kin?

Sure, humans had been predators to one another for millennia before, but now that there were other high-intelligence species in the mix, he would really need to be careful with how he wielded his power.

Having power is dangerous. It's already affecting how I think. I need to make sure I maintain control and stay my hand when needed. Even when I'm feeling angry or greedy.

An old phrase from Earth came to his mind: *noblesse oblige.*

Or, in colloquial terms: *With great power comes great responsibility.*

Max looked back at the fallen tree. That would be the extent of his childish games. He would need to be wary. And for all of his might, in terms of the sheer scale of this vast ocean called the universe, he was more plankton than fish. The ICCB were beyond even his super-mortal status. They were veritable gods. And Max realized he coveted that level of power.

I will reach it. And I'll make sure humanity gets what it needs: safety, peace, prosperity. I will give it to them.

"You'd better make sure that's a side quest in our grand adventures," Maverick said.

"Hm?"

"You promised," Maverick said, "that you would focus on following our Dao. I'm fine with you helping humans. But you can't have your sentimentality distract you from our literal life's purpose."

Max nodded. Maverick did have a point.

"We are that which must destroy," Max muttered to himself. He felt a tug at his soul when he said that. It had been their breakthrough revelation toward super-mortal Cultivation.

"Yeaaaaah," Maverick said. "I think our scope's a little bit bigger than your dinky little human project."

Max focused his attention on his inner being, his soul, which he could now easily sense with his super-mortal senses. It urged. Demanded. It wanted both Max and Maverick to engage with it. To seek destruction.

"We aren't evil, are we?" Max said. He looked at the floating scythe behind him. It was an ominous thing, the silver blade gleaming in the orange sun, a testament to its supernatural sharpness. It had the power to not only rend flesh and bone but spirit and soul itself.

Maverick was quiet for a moment. Through their bond Max could tell he was being serious for a change.

"I think," Maverick said slowly, "that you are too bound by your human morality. And I have been influenced by it. I think we are beyond good and evil. I think it's not our place to wonder what we are. We just have to be true to our nature."

"Even if that leads to horrible things?"

"Maybe," Maverick said, and Max could feel a shrug through their bond. "These questions are too big for me."

"Right back at you, buddy," Max muttered. "But they have to be asked."

"If you say so," Maverick said. "I'll leave that philosophical bullshit to you."

"Hey," Max said, miffed, "I'm going to need your help."

"Don't wanna," Maverick said. "I don't think you're going to find a satisfying answer to whether you're a good or a bad person. Just accept your nature."

Max grumbled. The stupid flying platform might have a point. But Max would probably still be anxiously pondering the question for a long while.

Maverick sighed. "You do you, buddy."

CHAPTER TWO

Dao and Karma

Maverick landed them next to the creek at Max's request. Max sat down in the tall grass, removed his boots, and dipped his feet in the cool water. It felt nice. He sighed. Being the avatar of destruction or whatever could wait. Every warrior knows the hard-won value of peace. And damn it, he would enjoy a moment of peace right now.

Idly wiggling his toes and letting the wind caress his face, Max breathed in his victory. He had won the Deathmatch. And what a struggle it had been. The intense need to survive, Max thought, was a major driving force in his victory. He had an idea about why the lizards had fought. War was in their nature. They were violent and aggressive. And humans could be that too. But they also had a particular quality which Max had become very well-acquainted with on Alpha Ludus—they wanted to live. It was such a primal drive, it was practically as strong as Cultivation. It could move mountains. It could level armies. Just like Max had.

Well, having Cultivation sure didn't hurt there, to be fair.

"Speaking of which," Maverick said as he floated next to Max, "I know we're supposed to be chilling out and cracking a beer or whatever, but you've been doing that for five minutes already."

"Yeah . . . ?" Max asked warily.

"What's the next move?" Maverick demanded. "Do we Cultivate further? Diamond's nothing but the first stage of super-mortal right?"

Max chuckled. "Yeah, we're the bottom of the barrel, aren't we?"

"That's what I'm trying to say!" Maverick said. "You *so* get me."

"I get that you're an unreasonable ass."

"Hey! Feelings."

"We could peruse the book, I guess," Max said.

From his Inventory, he produced a large leather tome that had been salvaged from the ruins of the ancestors of the obsidian dwarves. Their High King Durum had given it to Max as a gift. Their relations had soured since then.

Max leafed through the book idly, using his [**Telekinesis**] to make it float in front of him and turn the pages as needed. Turning the pages that way was actually rather difficult, and on his first attempt, Max accidentally made a small tear on one of them, which prompted an angry tirade from Maverick.

With his super-mortal mind and ability, however, Max quickly got the hang of it. The book weighed approximately seven pounds, so having it float in front of him was a real luxury. For a person as naturally lazy as Max, not having to move a finger was pure bliss.

All those times I wanted to reach the remote from the comfort of my sofa . . . A dream come true.

"What should we look for?" Maverick asked as he hovered over Max's shoulder. He was letting out a subtle humming sound like an electric motor.

"I suppose instructions on how to continue Cultivation at the super-mortal level?" Max said and flipped a page.

"It had something to do with living according to one's Dao," Maverick said. "I remember that very well, because you are hell-bent on bringing ruin and destruction to our efforts."

"Okay, let's not get our panties in a bunch," Max said. "But you're right. I remember that living according to one's Dao increases our Karma, which translates into power or insight or some such."

"So, what you're saying is that I'm right and you're wrong?" Maverick declared.

"I'm not— Yeah, as always . . ."

"Another victory!" Maverick said gleefully.

"Are you sure you're not on the Dao of Ego?" Max muttered as he leafed through the tome, until eventually finding passages appropriate for a Diamond-stage Cultivator to read.

After some more perusal, Max finally found some familiar pages, and then he skipped a few ahead. His mind, enhanced by Spiritual Energy, could absorb and process information at a rate previously unheard of for him. Yet, Max still read aloud for Maverick's benefit:

For the Diamond Cultivator who has transcended the mortal realm, the path of Cultivation shifts from the external to the internal. No longer is the focus solely on the accumulation of power and the understanding of one's Dao. Instead, the Diamond Cultivator must turn their gaze inward, to the very essence of their being, and cultivate their Karma.

While elixirs, pills, and hard work on one's meridians and Spiritual Energy is still necessary, progress cannot be made without an approach that reaches beyond the material mortal realm.

The super-mortal realm is one of concepts, ideas, principles. For these are not like flesh, which decays. A powerful idea is the crux of a Cultivator's Dao. If someone possesses the Dao of Protection, they have to understand that they themselves are not truly immortal. For even with the long life and increasingly-difficult-to-destroy body that Cultivation bestows to practitioners, a Cultivator will most likely die eventually.

But the idea of Protection is eternal. It is through the act of understanding and cultivating this idea and living in accordance with it, that the Cultivator might enjoy a touch of something that is eternal and indestructible. The more profound the understanding, the stronger the Dao, and thus the more powerful the Cultivator.

"That's heady," Maverick said. Max could feel his alter ego proverbially scratching his chin, trying to chew on the complex concepts the book had to offer. "So how does this link to Karma?"

"It's here in the next passage," Max said.

Karma is the sum of a Cultivator's actions, thoughts, and intentions. It is the force that binds them to the heavens and the Earth, and determines the course of their existence. A Diamond Cultivator must be ever mindful of their Karma, for it is both their greatest ally and their greatest obstacle on the path to ascension.

To cultivate Karma, the Diamond Cultivator must first understand the nature of their Dao. They must ask themselves: What is the fundamental principle that guides my actions? What is the purpose that drives me forward? Once the Cultivator has grasped the essence of their Dao, they must then align their every thought, word, and deed with this principle.

This is not an easy task, for the cultivation of Karma requires unwavering discipline and self-reflection. The Diamond Cultivator must constantly examine their actions and motivations, and be willing to course-correct when they stray from the path of their Dao. They must also be prepared to face the consequences of their past actions, for Karma has a way of returning to us what we have put into the world.

But for those who persist in the cultivation of Karma, the rewards are immeasurable. As the Diamond Cultivator aligns themselves more and more with their Dao, they will find that the universe itself begins to align with them. Opportunities will arise, allies will appear, and obstacles will crumble before them. This is the power of Karma—the power of living in harmony with one's true nature and purpose.

It might seem magical or unnatural. But this is not the way. The heavens smile upon whoever aligns themselves with something so grand, noble, and beautiful as a true eternal concept. If one dedicates their life to the reverence and maintenance of the laws of the universe itself, there are boons to be gained.

So, let the Diamond Cultivator meditate deeply on their Dao, and let them cultivate their Karma with every breath. For in so doing, they will not only achieve great power but also great wisdom and understanding. And in the end, they will find that the path of their Dao leads not only to personal ascension but a stronger alignment with the universe itself. A true Cultivator is a servant and protector of reality itself.

"Damn," Maverick said. "Those are some big promises. So, if we just follow our Karma, do we get to own planets and stuff?"

Max chuckled. He found that he liked the idea of owning a planet. How conceited. Probably not in accordance with their Dao. Max wondered about the pharma CEOs and dictators of Earth. They would surely have had a Dao of Greed.

A powerful Dao, to be sure. But mine is mightier.

Dao of Destruction . . . Max leaned back on his hands. The book was vague on Karma. There might be passages further along that explained it more fully, but for now he wanted to try to understand, as that was what was encouraged. A Cultivator needed to be a philosopher of sorts.

Would wantonly destroying everything without worrying about it increase their Karma?

Max did a test. He focused raw gravity in a spot on the ground under his hand. The earth crumpled and twisted until the grass and dirt turned into a fine, black ash in a scooped-out hole.

Max closed his eyes and tried to feel something. To feel his Karma. He sat in a meditation pose.

"Ahem," Maverick said.

Max nodded. He stood up and mounted Maverick. He sat down cross-legged on the platform, destroyed another piece of earth the same way he had before, and closed his eyes. Maverick's platform hummed and his cannon blasted a rock to smithereens on the bank of the creek. Max could feel his buddy also falling into a meditative trance.

They sat for a long time in that state, occasionally destroying a piece of the nearby environment. It felt like the right thing to do. If destruction was what their Dao required, they needed to understand the nature of it.

Max had his doubts that this kind of destruction would be good for their Karma. He was fairly sure it needed to be deliberate. A destruction of a sort that would be valuable to the universe. Immediately after having that thought, something rushed into Max's spirit.

[+1 Karma Acquired.]
[World's First Achievement: First Karma]
[Reward: +2 Karma]

"Whoa," Maverick said. "Okay, that felt amazing."

"What does it do?" Max asked.

He brought up his interface and tried looking around. He checked his Status Sheet, his Inventory, and even the new interface with the new Stats he had gotten when they had ascended to the super-mortal level of Cultivation. But nowhere did he find his three Karma points.

Max shrugged. Maverick joined in.

"Any ideas?" Max asked.

"Nope," Maverick said. "I guess we'll figure it out."

"I would have thought you would be pining for any power-ups."

"I am an ascended being now," Maverick said haughtily. "That means I've developed some dignity."

"About time," Max muttered.

"Hey!"

Max got up and dusted himself off.

"Hey, Zoos," he called out. "If you're out there watching, now's a good time to chime in. I'd love some input."

It was strange that their patron species hadn't made any contact with him recently. Max felt a little silly for expecting special treatment, but he had grown used to it. The Zoos Collective overlooked billions of creatures across areas of space so vast that it made Max's brain hurt just to think about it. They were an empire led by a hive mind.

"Still," Max said, "I would have thought they would want to talk to me after my victory. They haven't teleported the other humans in, either. What gives?"

Maverick was about to answer, but right then a plastic jellyfish appeared in front of them. It was white with smooth angles, and it spoke in a digital, mono-tone voice.

Only, this time, the voice was garbled, and the hologram image was blinking on and off as if suffering from static like on an old television.

[Please . . . Wait . . . Urgent . . . At . . . Full . . . Capacity . . . Please . . . Cultivate . . . We will . . . Contact . . .]

And just like that, the Zoos hologram was gone.

"Huh," Max said.

"Well, that was rude!" Maverick said. "Where is the adulation? Where are the thanks? We—and by 'we,' I, of course, mean *me*—are carrying this little game of theirs."

"Maybe they're having some political battle with the Grays," Max suggested.

"Yeah," Maverick said, now getting serious and clearly unimpressed by Max's theory. "Sure. Let's go with that."

"Yeah . . ." Max said. "I hope everything's alright."

"You hope everything is alright for the patron species that took your planet, put you in a horrible death-game against other species against your will, forced you to live in primitive conditions, and constantly have to resort to violence?"

Max gave Maverick a look. "Why are you doing this?"

"Boredom, mostly."

Max shook his head. "Well, let's do as they told us: sit down and Cultivate."

"Max," Maverick said.

"Hm?" Max said as he took out the pouch of [**Celestial Illumination Pills**] from his Inventory.

"Where are you going to stuff my pills now?"

Max looked at his friend's new disc form. He tilted his head.

"Well, there's the barrel . . . ?"

"Absolutely not!" Maverick said immediately. "You're not touching my barrel."

Max facepalmed. "Please don't make this weird."

CHAPTER THREE

Heart to Heart

Turned out that Maverick's disc actually had a lot of compartments. It was very handy, really. Two containers opened at the sides, which were perfect for storing throwable weapons like grenades or rocks. As a [**Combatant**], Max had the ability to store any weapons or armor in his Inventory. But mundane things such as rocks, pieces of wood, and other similarly elemental things weren't storable. That was something only [**Laborers**] could do.

"I can't believe you want to stuff rocks into my awesome new pockets," Maverick complained.

"What else should we put there?"

"Something more dignified!" Maverick huffed.

They had discovered that pouring a handful of pills in there worked fine. Maverick could access them from there just as well as he could from his old form's bullet chambers.

And so, Maverick lowered himself to the ground and Max sat on him, and they Cultivated together. This was just pure, mindless work on their meridians. No insights were sought. It was better to build a balanced base as the book had suggested. Now was as good a time as any to get through the grunt work.

They worked for an hour, took a little break, popped another pill, worked another hour.

After four more hours, morning had turned into noon, and the sun was high, hot, and bright in the sky. Max idly wondered what the people under Joshua's rule were doing. He didn't feel compelled to check, to which Maverick responded with unadulterated jubilation. A rare feeling for him.

But just as they were about to sit down again, Max saw someone approach. Max recognized her immediately. It was Kat.

What does she want?

Max felt strange. He had liked Kat. In the army before all this crazy shit had gone down, he had had a crush on her. He still remembered admiring Kat when they had fought that crazy demon that had started Max off on his journey. She had been so fierce.

Now Max looked at her, like he looked at all the mortals. He wanted to keep her safe, but she was like a child or a dog. Something lesser that needed protecting.

Max shook his head.

You might be powerful, but you're still just a dude. If you don't want to become a power-mad monster, that's probably something you should keep reminding yourself.

"Hey," Kat called as she approached. "Got a minute?"

"Sure," Max said and got up from Maverick. "What do you need?"

Kat came close but hesitated. She looked at him, flinched, and looked at the ground. "I just— I just wanted to talk."

Max felt something relaxing inside him. He gave her a smile. "Sure. Sit down with me."

She nodded and some of the cool confidence returned to her features. She put her shield down and sat down next to him in the grass.

They sat silent for a while, just listening to the creek's soft roar. A tiny silverback fish jumped up to snag a dragonfly into the depths with it. Max found that, while he wasn't really feeling hungry, he could eat. He took out rations from his Inventory. A handful of beef jerky. He gave a few sticks of it to Kat.

"Thanks," she said. "Do you even need to eat anymore?"

"I'm not sure," Max said.

CHAPTER FOUR

The Collective's Request

[Max, we finally have time to speak. Unfortunately, that time is finite, and we must move with haste and only relay the most important information. Ah, Katherine. How serendipitous that you are here.]

"Can't you just call me Kat?"

[Max, we must congratulate you on your stellar performance in the Deathmatch. You have proven yourself worthy of our program against the Outsiders.]

"Against the what?" Kat asked.
Max glared at her to be silent.

[Normally, you would receive all the appropriate accolades and a myriad of personal rewards for such a feat. However, the situation has changed. Drastically.]

Max wanted to ask about his Cultivation and Karma, but it seemed like the Zoos had something else in mind entirely.

[We have been unable to contact you before this moment due to a critical attack on this solar system.]

"An attack?" Kat asked. "By who? Those Outsiders?"
Max and Maverick shared a brief "Oh shit!" moment through their bond. Surely the Zoos didn't mean . . .

[The Outsiders have discovered this location as a training ground for warriors, and they see it best to nip the problem in the bud. That is why they have sent a scouting party to this planet. It will arrive in approximately two weeks.]

"A mere scouting party?" Maverick scoffed disdainfully. "Let them try."

[The ICCB is unable to mobilize a fighting force of experienced Cultivator warriors in a timely manner to defend this location. A set of reinforcements have been sent, but they will arrive in nine to ten weeks.]

"I'm so out of the loop," Kat said.

"You patron races are super powerful, "Max said. "If it's just a scouting party, can't you just squash it?"

[Our personal efforts are diverted toward the fleet that sent the scouting party. The local mothership is engaged in combat as we speak, which is why the Zoos Collective will have limited ability to engage with the humans for now, as our attention and capacity is needed elsewhere.]

"Okay, so stop wasting my valuable time," Maverick said. "What is going to happen, and what undoubtedly heroic role do we have to play in it?"

The Zoos jellyfish was quiet for a while, as if not sure how to respond. Finally, it spoke, a slightly strained lilt to its otherwise monotone speech. Max smirked at that. Others deserved to know his pain, which was named Maverick.

[Quite. Max and Maverick, you will form the spearhead of a small strike force of elite fighters against the enemy assault. We know this is abrupt and very much deviates from the path we had envisioned for you. We had intended to groom you for power. But now it seems that it shall be mortal combat that grooms you. We ask you to take leadership, Max. We cannot force you. But know this: the Outsiders seek to destroy all life. They do not discriminate. Any living matter, they take and bastardize into their own sinister materials. Their only will is to consume everything. We want you to stop them. We want you to wear the mantle of a hero. Will you accept?]

Goddamn it. Here we go again . . .

Max sighed. Did he even have options? He was the most powerful creature on this planet, barring the patron races. Yet he barely remembered a time he had been allowed to make a choice for himself. Maybe he was carrying his responsibility better than one might have thought.

[We will give you a moment to think, Max.]

The hologram image froze and became translucent and low-resolution. Clearly it was a ghost image, with the strained resources of the Zoos diverted elsewhere against the onslaught of the Outsiders.

"Why do they call you 'Max?' It's short for Maximillian, isn't it?"

Max shrugged. "I asked them to."

"Repeatedly?"

"Oh yes . . ."

"I guess you get special treatment for being the boy savior."

Max cringed. "Never call me that again."

Kat smirked. "After finding the first chink in your armor since I met you again? Yeah, fat chance."

"Asshole."

"Pussy."

"Hey!" Maverick jabbed in. "Will you two lovebirds shut up and focus?!"

"Loveb— What?" Max sputtered.

Kat's ears reddened.

"You're right," Max said and turned to look at Maverick's disk. "What do you want to do, Mav?"

"It's simple," Maverick said. "Kick some alien ass!"

"I guess that's what we've been doing all this time already."

"But this time it's different," Maverick said excitedly. "Now we're going to be fighting *extra* aliens!"

"How is that any different?" Kat asked.

"Max, who is this puny mortal chick, and do we have to keep her around?" Maverick asked. "She's harshing my buzz."

"Your buzz is too easy to harsh," Kat said and scowled at the disc.

"You don't even have a crush on her anymore," Maverick said to Max. "What do we even need her for?"

Kat's face went blank. "You—"

Max buried his face in a hand. "Just shut up, Maverick."

The Zoos Collective's plastic jellyfish started slowly bobbing up and down, animated again.

[Have you decided?]

Max chuckled. "You make it sound like I really do have a choice. How is this going to play out?"

[Excellent. First, we will assemble the strike force. You shall be the captain of this team, Max. Of course, your companion here, being the second most-suitable candidate from the human race, will also be opted in. Two of the most powerful members of the other three representative races will also be chosen.]

"An interspecies Cultivator Avengers, huh?" Max said.

[We are short on time. The scouting party will attack soon, and more forces of the Outsiders will follow. We will have to forsake the other races to live by their own devices and focus only on the growth of you eight individuals. You will be provided with Cultivation materials, training regimens, and instruction. We will additionally update your Framework once you hit super-mortal Cultivation. In your case we will do it immediately after you have been teleported to the training grounds.]

"Update my—? What does that mean?"

[A specialized training instructor has been given to you for all additional questions. The Zoos Collective thanks you for your contributions so far, Max. But we must discuss further once the situation has stabilized.]

Max and Kat shared a look and, in the next moment, Max felt a tug at his navel.

[Teleport]

CHAPTER FIVE

The Training Facility

Max found himself in something resembling a military aircraft hangar—high ceilings, wide barn doors of stupendous proportions sliding to the sides as he, Maverick, and Kat entered the building outside of which they had been teleported to.

It was a gray building and inside were no aircraft, but sectioned areas. To the immediate left was clearly a sleeping area. Therein were eight beds placed in two neat rows. Next to each was a small desk made of metal.

A bed. I get to sleep in a bed?!

That was a rare luxury. Only during the few nights he had spent in King Durum's realm had he been able to enjoy such decadence any time since landing in this world.

Kat moaned loudly as Max pointed at the beds.

Next to that area were kitchen facilities and a single long table.

"I wonder if we'll have to cook," Kat said.

Max shrugged. In his mind, the flowchart was very simple. If someone was cooking for him, he would eat with gusto. If he had to cook himself, he would test to see if he even needed food as a super-mortal Cultivator.

Between the beds and kitchen sections were four stalls that Max presumed to be toilets.

"One for each race, I reckon," he mused.

But it was farther back in the massive hangar where the interesting stuff lay.

There was an area with what looked like a massive Cultivation array. It was a circle of stones, not unlike Stonehenge, except the stone arcs were mathematically symmetrical, and engraved with runic symbols glowing with light in varied hues of blue, green, and red. Trails of a substance that looked like aluminum or silver dust spread out from each stone, meeting in the middle of the array to form a circle.

"That thing must massively boost Cultivation speed," Max remarked.

"I call dibs," Kat said. "I need to do some catching up."

Max chuckled. "What Level of Cultivation are you, anyway?"

"Ruby Level Five," Kat said demurely.

"Not bad," Max said. "What are your insights about?"

"I— uh . . . Hey, check that out. Looks like an arena."

Max scoffed. He thought he understood. If Max weren't as powerful as he was, it would be embarrassing talking about his insights. He was a destroyer of things. How corny. Maybe Kat had something similar. He would let it slide for now and pester her about it later.

Near the giant Cultivation array was a huge pit. It was embedded into the floor, requiring a jump of fifteen feet to reach the bottom. The walls were of a slick gleaming metal, which could have been aluminum or silver. The floor was full of a bright, golden sand.

"A little coliseum for us to spar in?" Max wondered aloud as he took out a canteen of water.

"I shall call dibs on this one," Maverick said. "We will challenge all of the other seven strike-force members and defeat them in single combat. That way they will know to fear us, for we are mighty."

Kat gave the floating disk a deadpan stare. Max gave her a tired smile.

"Let me guess," Kat said. "Your Dao is about patience?"

Max burst out laughing, snorting water through his nose.

"Hey!" Maverick said.

Kat glanced a look at Max wiping his mouth and directed a satisfied snarl at Maverick.

Max ignored the two as they bickered and bantered and instead looked at the hangar's other facilities.

The next section caught his eye, and his heart jumped. It was a library. A row of bookshelves filled with tomes of various sizes and colors. They would be getting vetted information on Cultivation by the ICCB themselves. That alone would supercharge their training. It would especially help those still in a Ruby stage like Kat reach Diamond. Max had advanced so fast mostly because of the special information he had.

And more information is just what I need. I need to know how Karma works and how to Cultivate further at Diamond stage.

There was also another, larger area full of dummies made of the same shiny white metal as the other items in this facility. They were of various sizes and configurations. Max assumed they were meant to imitate some of the various Outsider monstrosities.

The last area was a big green ring in the ground. It glowed faintly and looked like it was made from glass. Max had no idea what it could be. A teleporter?

Seemed like all races in the ICCB could use teleportation spells through their Cultivation. Maybe it enhanced Cultivation practice like the Stonehenge array in the back?

Max was interrupted from his musings by Kat and Maverick finally catching up to him. Kat put a hand on his shoulder and pointed to the hangar doors. Six figures entered. Max's eyes went wide with disbelief as he saw who was walking inside and toward him with long, confident strides.

An Ishkarassi who was tall and broad shouldered, even for his own species. His proud features were those of a general or an esteemed warrior. His intense gaze found Max and he bared his teeth.

Max looked as Losshnak walked over to him. His towered over Max, his shoulders hunched forward slightly.

Max was not afraid. He was significantly more powerful. But Losshnak did resemble a fierce dragon and something akin to nervousness arose in Max. He was able to master it, however, and his Spiritual Energy stirred in preparation.

Losshnak bowed.

"We meet again, Master Warrior."

CHAPTER SIX

Old Acquaintances

Max felt the tension leave his body. Losshnak bared more teeth. An instinct told Max this was not a snarl but an Ishkarassi smile. He wasn't sure how to feel or what to say.

"Please hold no grudge, Master Warrior," Losshnak said as he straightened.

"Uh, just Max is fine. I thought I killed you."

"You did," Losshnak said. "I faced the end of all ends and found myself at the end of every warrior's path. Peace. But I was brought back by my patrons. My battles are not done."

Max nodded. He looked at Losshnak. They shared a strange bond. A bond of having fought against each other for the right to exist. Max had won that battle, but Losshnak had placed a high price on victory. Max found himself slightly resenting the Ishkarassi, but he also respected him. If it hadn't been for the break-through to Diamond stage, humans would have lost.

Then I would have been the one resurrected. We are the same.

Max extended an arm. Losshnak's eyes lit up with satisfaction and he grabbed Max's hand in a large, firm squeeze with his scaly appendage.

"You're a tough son of a bitch," Max said and gave him a small smile.

"And you are the greatest bastard I have ever met," Losshnak said and laughed. "I had never felt such deep bitterness. I thought I had victory, and you snagged it away at the last possible moment."

Max smiled, because he didn't know what else to say or do. Losshnak regarded him. Max realized he was much older than he was. Max was but a boy of twenty, but Losshnak seemed to be in the prime of his life, possibly ten or fifteen years older than him.

"What was it like to die?" Max blurted out.

Losshnak shook his head. "I will not answer this now. We must share meals, sleep under the same roof, find comradeship. I will answer this question later. I think we have much to discuss and teach one another, Master Warrior. But know this, if you fear death—"

"I don't," Max interjected.

Losshnak regarded him and scoffed. "Know this, regardless. In the end there was peace."

"Seems like it was hard-earned."

Losshnak nodded. "Only you and I know of the Outsiders."

"I think what we faced were a pale imitation," Max said.

"Yes, I think so, too," Losshnak said. Then he turned and called the other Ishkarassi to them.

"Master Warrior," the female Ishkarassi said and bowed. Her scales were lighter than Losshnak's and her tail longer and lither.

"This is my mate, Master Warrior," Losshnak said. "Meet Ashkarassa."

The female Ishkarassi gave Max a little bow, while maintaining eye contact.

"This puny human killed you?" Ashkarassa asked Losshnak in a sharp tone. "How is it possible?"

"Do not disrespect the master warrior," Losshnak growled.

Ashkarassa sneered and looked at Kat. "His mate looks even weaker."

Kat's face flushed a strong red. "I'm not—"

Losshnak struck his mate with a backhand. Max and Kat hissed in unison.

"Damn," Maverick muttered.

Losshnak stared Ashkarassa down. She spat out a glob of blood and punched her mate straight in the snout.

A dirty brawl broke out. They clawed, bit, struck, lashed, and headbutted each other, wrestling on the ground with fierce passion. Soon, that made way for a make-out session of equal ferocity. Growls changed tone, and fist striking flesh and scale turned into kisses and groans.

"What is going on?" Kat asked.

Max shrugged. "Cultural differences."

"You've seen this before?"

"Nah, but I'm not surprised," Max said. "They're violent people."

Max looked at the other members of the strike force who were now walking toward them, looking at the fight with mild interest.

So far Max had only seen humans and Ishkarassi. He had, of course, known there to be two other races, but no interaction had happened so far. He wondered which race was representing who from the ICCB.

One appeared to be warriors, just like the Ishkarassi, but vulpine in appearance. Long powerful legs and narrow hips. They were tall, easily seven feet, both the grey-furred female and the orange-furred male. Their stomachs were white, and their paws were black. Their faces were narrow and proud and their eyes sharp yellow slits, and they were clearly more interested in Max and Maverick than the Ishkarassi's brawl.

The other race was insectoid. It was impossible to say whether they were male or female. They had four black eyes with horizontal eyelids which seemed to blink constantly, four arms, and a stout, sturdy build, resembling that of a beetle. The upper arms connected at the shoulder were covered in a hard carapace and ended in brutal pincers. The two other arms protruded from their sides and were clearly oriented for utility, with three spindly fingers each.

The vulpines stopped and crossed their arms as they stared at Max and Maverick. Max gave them a little nod. The insectoids waved a hand at the humans in a surprisingly friendly manner and then sat down to watch the spectacle.

An old, instinctive part of Max wanted to make nice. Maverick sent a pulse of annoyance through their bond.

Yeah, yeah. Not in accordance with our Dao. Gonna lose Karma points or something.

Maverick was a stickler for their Dao, but considering that he was, for all intents and purposes, a weapon, it sort of made sense for him to be focused on destruction.

"I'm just keeping you on the straight and narrow," Maverick said. Kat gave them a quizzical look. Max just shook his head and laughed.

The brawl between the Ishkarassi went on for a long while. It was clear to Max just at a glance that Losshnak was significantly ahead of his mate in Cultivation, and thus could have easily overpowered her in a second.

But Max, who could now sense people's Cultivation with extreme accuracy, saw that Losshnak's meridians were only sending stray pulses of Spiritual Energy. The Ishkarassi warrior could have easily flared up his meridians and probably killed his mate with a single strike if he had wanted to.

Max turned his attention to Ashkarassa. She had just broken into the Ruby stage. Then he expanded his senses toward the insectoids and foxkin—all Ruby Cultivators or various stages. The gray female vulpine was at a higher Ruby stage, just missing an insight or two. Besides Losshnak who could break into Diamond whenever he discovered his **[Breakthrough Insight]**, she was the strongest in the group.

But Max knew that the difference between a mortal and a super-mortal Cultivator was so vast that he could sit still and destroy all of them without even trying. Wielding that kind of power was a heady thing. It gave him confidence, which was great. He really couldn't give two shits about what the glaring female vulpine thought of him. Or about Kat giving him strange looks from time to time.

But that was also the problem. He was kind of beyond giving a shit. With the power that he had, he felt detached. He had lost some of his humanity, it was true. And Maverick was right in that they should follow their Dao. But Max would need to make sure that he didn't lose out on connections with other beings.

Eventually, Losshnak let himself be toppled and Ashkarassa mounted him and raised a fist to punch him but instead snarled and got off.

"You need to stop doing that," she said.

"Then get stronger," Losshnak said.

"Tsk."

"What was that fight about?" Kat asked.

Losshnak laughed and rubbed at the spines on his neck. "In our culture, we settle disputes with fights. It is especially good for mates. This way, we stay honest with each other. No grudges, no resentment. If you feel violence, rage, or bitterness, this should be let out. If we allow it to fester, this transforms the feelings of violence, anger, and war into something ugly, cold, and sinister. This is not our way. We are proud and do not gnaw on old sores or plot revenge."

Max nodded in approval. "Makes sense."

"It is a good way," Ashkarassa admitted. "But ever since Losshnak fought in the Deathmatch, he has gotten too strong. But his nature is weak, and he lets me fight without destroying it. This enrages me."

"My nature is indeed weak," Losshnak admitted. "Just as yours is petty."

Ashkarassa gave him a toothy grin. They leaned in closer, and their tongues flicked each other. Kat flinched as she saw it.

Suddenly there was a flash of bright white light in front of them and a small gray humanoid with a large head and two large black eyes materialized in their midst. It immediately rose up in the air and stood above them, eight feet off the ground, clasping its tiny hands behind its back. It regarded them with an air of imperious boredom, only ever so briefly pausing when its eyes drifted to Max and Maverick.

"You are all here," the Gray said in a high, lazy voice. "We will begin your training immediately."

CHAPTER SEVEN

The Outsiders

The Gray regarded them all with a sneer and with a swish of his hand, they all flew up in the air and plopped down in a neat little row.

"You are here because this solar system has been ambushed by a force called the Outsiders. The reason why we took your planets and placed your species on this one was so that some of you could become a fighting force against them. Congratulations. You have done exactly that."

The little Gray sarcastically clapped his hands a few times while looking at them with a deadpan expression.

"You've happily gorged yourselves on resources we have so generously given to you. And you will continue to do so as the lowly parasites that you are. And you will do so with extreme gratitude. And this gratitude you shall use to put all your time and effort into becoming as strong as possible in as short a time as possible. The Outsider scouting party will land on this planet in approximately sixteen days."

"Ex-*cues* me," one of the insectoids said and raised a hand. He had a clicking voice that heavily emphasized the consonants. "Some of us do not possess the knowled-*ge* of these Outsiders."

The Gray cast a glare at the insectoid so sharp it could have drawn blood, and his tiny mouth twisted in a snarl as he muttered to himself.

"I will try to keep in mind that you are vastly inferior life-forms and thus need excessive guidance."

"Thank you," the insectoid said amicably.

"I will start the training with a lecture on the basic qualities of our enemy," the Gray said. "The Outsiders emerged several thousand years ago."

"Emerged from where?" Kat asked. "Another galaxy?"

"Are you under the assumption that you will receive answers to your questions earlier if you interrupt me?" the Gray asked. His voice was flat, but his eyes said that he would explode her into atoms if she bothered him again.

Kat had enough intelligence to not answer that question.

"They emerged from another dimension. For eons our scientists have postulated the existence of other dimensions. But no matter how it was observed or tested, we found no physical evidence. We were wrong."

The Gray let the words hang. Max wasn't sure if it was for the dramatic effect or because he thought they were all inferior and needed pauses to keep up. Max suspected the latter.

"The Outsiders emerge periodically from a space beyond space. We have had very little ability to be able to study their origins, but it seems they originally inhabited a negative universe. Some place and some time that can only be described as anti-time and anti-space. And they are the physical manifestation of that."

The Gray opened his hand, and a hologram appeared above him—a black glob that twisted and bubbled this way and that.

"This was their initial form. They simply appeared in space and landed on a planet. Within three months they had terraformed it. This Ground Zero planet no longer exists, as they consumed it to its very core. As they did with all of the other planets within that system. Their primary interest with any organic or inorganic matter is simple: consume and assimilate."

"What does that mean in layman's terms?" Max asked.

"You mean inferior-life-form vocabulary?" the Gray asked and shot a baleful glance at Max. "It means whatever they come into contact with, they will break down to a sub-molecular level and infuse with whatever animates them. Then they will opt to either refine the original form or simply use the material to create something they already like. These are the various forms they now take, after having existed in our universe for several millennia."

Another hologram appeared. This one was a massive catalog of creatures and buildings of various shapes. Max spotted the bat-like creature he had fought earlier in the Deathmatch. But there were hundreds more.

"As you can see, they do not discriminate. They are essentially engaging in a fast and dirty simulacrum of evolution."

"What's a simulacrum?" Kat whispered to Max. He was about to answer, but the Gray's angry glare was upon them, as well as a touch of spiritual pressure.

"They go from planet to planet and eat them. Then they pick out forms that they think might perform well for various tasks, such as combat, or consumption of material. And they refine. They consume, they assimilate, they refine, and they move on. They aren't intelligent—more like plants or simple beasts. Capturing or attempting to extract information out of them is entirely useless. However, they are a hive mind that is clearly guided by something intelligent. Those things are on their ships, but that is not your concern. You are lowly mortal Cultivators and cannot fight in space. Your concern is infantry combat against the abominations that will land on this planet during their assault."

"Why only choose us?" the female vulpine asked. Her voice was deep and regal, like that of a warrior princess. "Millions of my people are able-bodied and willing to fight."

"Millions?" the Gray sneered. "There are only thousands left of your primitive kin.

That shocked the foxkin into silence. The taller, orange male of her species put a black-furred paw on her shoulder as she shook her head in grief.

"As for your question," the Gray continued, "there are two reasons. The first is very simple. Most of you lower-tier life forms are not only useless in a fight but a hindrance. For the Outsiders, transforming things like soil, bacteria, and fungi takes time and has low yield. But complex beings are very dense in life force, which is the energy they crave. They can use other materials too, but every fallen warrior in the battle is not only a loss for us but a gain for them. They will infuse your fallen and animate them."

Max shuddered at the thought. It was like the Outsiders were specifically designed to destroy life.

"I wouldn't be surprised if they really were," Maverick muttered.

"The other reason is that we have very limited resources to expend on this planet and thus we had to choose a small collection of champions and hope it is enough. Spread our resources too thin, and we face the problem of having a hundred mediocre warriors, who will eventually just fall and thus give the enemy the resources we spent. No. having eight elite warriors was the mathematically optimal choice, as the number of combatants has to be limited, but some cooperation is needed."

"How do they fight?" the male vulpine asked.

"They swarm," Max said. Every head turned toward him. Losshnak nodded.

"The Outsiders believe quantity is a quality unto itself," the Gray said. "And so far, they have been right. Make no mistake. We would not recruit you if the situation was not dire. Overall, the war for this universe's survival is in a seeming deadlock, and every molecule they assimilate is one we will never get back. If you are overwhelmed, we will atomize this planet before they infest it."

"With all of our races on it?" the female vulpine barked. "You would render four sapient species extinct just like that?"

The Gray turned, regarding her with disdain. "It seems you do not appreciate the stakes. The ICCB does not care about your little species. There are hundreds of self-aware bipedal species in just this local quadrant of the galaxy alone. You are not special."

"How can you say that?" Kat asked and took an angry step forward.

The Gray sighed to itself and muttered something. Max shared a look with Losshnak. He kept his arms crossed and said nothing. Max wondered if he understood.

"I cannot believe I have to teach ethics to a dog," the Gray finally said. "Imagine your home being infested by ants. They are the last ants of its species. But they are eating away at the structures, and they pilfer your food. What do you do?"

"I exterminate them," the female vulpine said but added, "But that is not the same. The ants are not even sentient, let alone sapi—"

"Consciousness is a matter of complexity," the Gray said. "I do not particularly care what arbitrary line you draw for when life suddenly becomes valuable. Life is a spectrum. An ant is a very simple life form. Vermin such as rats are slightly more complex. Larger mammals even develop complex feelings and personalities yet lack self-awareness. And on and on it goes, until you reach a collective super-intelligence like that of the Zoos. Just because you were the apex species of your planet, the highest form of existence you could imagine, does not mean your arbitrary sense of what is valuable and what is not matters now. The Outsiders are a threat of such magnitude that snuffing out a few mediocre species to stop them from exponentially multiplying is a price we're willing to pay. Any other questions?"

Max nodded to himself. While the Gray was clearly a bully, that was not why he was saying these things. He was trying to hammer home the point of how dangerous a foe they were dealing with. Max was even more sure than before that the oily black monstrosities he and Losshnak had faced in the Deathmatch were pale imitations of the real threat.

"And now you must eat. We have prepared a carefully crafted diet optimized for the increase in Spiritual Energy. You will eat four times a day. We have prepared dishes fit for your species. Don't think that the meal means I'm giving you a break, however. While you eat, I will continue to lecture. There is simply too much for you idiots to learn . . ."

Max closed his eyes and groaned in pleasure. Thanks to his super-mortal Cultivation, he wasn't even hungry, but this food was so delicious, he knew that he would be licking his plate clean as surely as if he were starving.

Steak. The most tender steak he had ever eaten, coated with butter sauce, and mashed potatoes with garlic and spices as a side. The meat had a strange green tint to it, but that hardly made a difference.

"I think I'm going to cry," Kat said.

"Meh," Maverick huffed as he hovered over the table. "What's the big deal?"

No one answered him. One of the insectoid people gave him a quick glance, before going back to its bowl of something that Max didn't want to take a closer look at. Both the insects hummed and clicked with the utmost satisfaction.

They all sat at the long table in the kitchen area. Their instructor was hovering at the end of the other table, clearly waiting impatiently for his lowly students to calm down.

Max could care less about the Outsiders right now. He smeared a piece of the steak in the butter sauce, and once it was sufficiently dripping, shoved it in his mouth and closed his eyes again.

"Sweet baby Jesus, it's so good."

It went on for ten minutes, until every one of them had fully cleaned their plates and were now looking around at each other, at the kitchen, and their Gray instructor in hopes of more. None of them had had a real meal since they'd arrived on Alpha Ludus.

"I will give you seconds, but you will have to listen," the Gray said.

Everyone nodded in utmost agreement.

Soon a swarm of drones emerged from the kitchen and one of them plopped a plate in front of Max with another pound of steak and a hefty side of mashed potatoes. Max grinned.

"Focus," the Gray said impatiently.

"What is your name?" one of the insectoids asked the floating Gray. "This one is called Slargi."

Max watched the Gray. A subtle mix of emotions played on its face. The Grays were mostly expressionless, but Max had been observing them long enough by this point to detect subtle creases in their eyes and their mouth. A series of minor muscle contractions could give away emotions such as shock, annoyance, and slight flattery.

"You can call me Twozerofive," the Gray said. "But I am not your friend. I am your instructor. Frankly, all of your forms and smells are repellant to me, and your Spiritual Energy is weak."

"This one is pleasured to be acquainted, Twozerofive," the insectoid said and bowed.

"Now let us talk of the plan here," Twozerofive said. "All of you need to be brought up to super-mortal Cultivation as soon as possible. Some of you might be aware of insights, your Dao, and the eventual **[Breakthrough Insight]** which will allow you to transcend mortality. We will . . ."

Max zoned out and focused on his steak. He savored every bite and wondered if this was what he would be eating every day for the foreseeable future. Because that wouldn't be a bad future at all.

Apparently, his moans and the clinks of the fork were rather loud, as Max suddenly realized that everyone at the table was staring at him, Twozerofive with particularly murderous intent.

"Is there a reason you stopped listening?" the Gray asked.

Max swallowed a piece of buttery steak and nodded. "I'm already a Diamond-stage Cultivator. I didn't need to hear this."

"Ah, yes," the Gray said bitterly. "You are the one. Then why did you not say anything? Do you have any idea how strapped for time we are?"

"Some idea."

"Silence. Go meditate and strengthen your meridians. I will instruct you on Framework Recalibration after the lecture on insights.

Max sat down cross-legged on top of Maverick in the massive Stonehenge-like array. It activated as soon as Max closed his eyes, and they reached for their Spiritual Energy. They could tell because they were suddenly assaulted by a massive pressure. It was pure Spiritual Energy, attempting to penetrate Max's soul. Some of it seeped in, and it swirled and burned inside him like a firestorm. Maverick flew them upward and away from the formation, but he wobbled and they crashed into one of the stone pillars. As soon as they landed, they scrambled out of the formation as fast as they could. Afterward, an exhausted Max lay on his stomach next to Maverick, who was toppled over, gun-side-up.

Max could barely even sense Maverick through the bond. But he knew him well enough to know he was going through a similar experience. The aggressive, explosive energy inside of Max churned and made him convulse. He inhaled deeply, trying to take control of the energy, to make it his own. Eventually it started to settle. It still fought, trying to zip and zap all around his body, striking at his soul, escaping his meridians, so Max pushed the energy into his spirit veins.

But the churning waned by the minute and finally Max was able to wrest control of the energy and add it to the natural flow of his own Spiritual Energy in his body. He felt slightly stronger, such as when gaining an insight at the Ruby stage.

"Mmm, that's the good shit," Maverick said.

"That was close," Max said and wiped a sheen of sweat off his forehead. "I felt like I was going to burst."

"Nothing ventured, nothing gained."

"What is the meaning of this?!" Twozerofive asked as he suddenly appeared above them. The rest of the strike force were also coming toward them.

"You told us to Cultivate," Max said.

"And you just decided to use the array?" Twozerofive screeched. "On whose authority?"

"It seemed useful."

"Oh, it is," the Gray said and glared Max down. "Once you have supervision and someone can remove you from the array when you get overcharged. Do you have any idea how much Spiritual Power you'll be infusing per second?"

"Some idea, yeah," Max said and chuckled. Maverick hooted.

"What a ride," the disc said. "When can we do that again? Seems like it's a real fast and dirty way to Level Up."

"You— What?" Twozerofive said and flew closer. Max felt a touch of spiritual pressure coming from him. "You managed to control it? The Zoos Collective sure knows how to . . ."

"What happened?" one of the insectoids asked.

"None of your concern," Twozerofive snapped. Then he pointed. "See that Cultivation array over there? If you use it without supervision, you risk a very painful death. Do not do it. Especially after all of the resources we are about to pour into you."

"I dare you," Ashkarassa said and nudged Losshnak.

He chuckled and turned to Max. "What happened?"

"We tested the array over there," Max said. "Almost didn't make it. Don't do it before you're at Diamond stage."

"Noted," Losshnak said with a respectful nod.

One of the insectoids approached Max and Maverick.

"This one is called Slargi," the insectoid said and offered a hand. Max grabbed it. "And you are the one with the bounty."

"I am," Max said.

"How is it that you became so strong? We are a species with an inherent need for optimization. We were doing the same as what this strike force is doing now: compounding resources on a select few to create a snowball effect. And yet you beat us. How can that be?"

"That requires a long answer," Max said and smiled.

"To which we have no time," Twozerofive snapped. "Fine. We will have to recalibrate your Framework immediately. The rest of you will listen, so I do not have to explain myself twice. This human here shall ascend his Framework. Sit down, all of you."

CHAPTER EIGHT

Framework Recalibration

L isten carefully," Twozerofive said. "I will now instruct Subject #266830151 on how to recalibrate his Framework. You will remember these instructions and replicate them when you reach Diamond-stage Cultivation.

"Just Max is fine, thanks," Max said, and earned a wrathful glare from Twozerofive.

The Gray shoved a device into his hands. It looked like a white box with smooth, round corners and a faintly blinking blue light on top of it. It was clearly crafted by the Zoos Collective.

"You will hold this device and sit in meditation, flooding your meridians with enough power to prove to the box that you are a super-mortal Cultivator. Then the device will reabsorb all of the energy that you have acquired into your Framework. Once that energy is gone, a system wipe will occur."

"A what now?"

"The previous Framework will need to be deleted from your DNA and spirit," Twozerofive explained. "Now, this part is important, so do not fail. You will need to stay conscious. It will start slowly, but there will be pain and drowsiness. You will essentially feel like you are dying. Your consciousness will constrict. You will need to provide a steady stream of Spiritual Energy to keep your body, mind, and soul stable. The longer you can stay conscious, the longer the device will have time to decompress the data and feed it back into you as the new Framework is installed."

"What does all of this mean in plain English?" Max asked and resisted the urge to roll his eyes.

Twozerofive sighed. "Cretins . . . It means that the longer you stay awake, the more yield the previous Framework's energy will grant you. If you fall into unconsciousness, the energy cannot be fed back to you, and it will dissipate."

"Why didn't you just say that to begin with?" Maverick said.

The Gray only stared at Maverick and blinked slowly. They didn't do that very often.

Max sat down on top of Maverick with the device in his lap and closed his eyes.

"We're doing this carefully," Max said to Maverick.

"Of course we are!" Maverick said aghast. "What do you take me for?"

"Not generally a very careful person," Max said.

"When it comes to keeping our hard-earned power, I am the most careful person you've ever met."

Max chuckled. "Good."

Twozerofive came up to him and offered a large pill. It shone with a faint blue light, swirling patterns moving on its surface like slowly rotating azure galaxies.

"Place this under your tongue," the Gray said. "It will dull the pain and give you focus."

Max nodded and took the pill.

"Hey," Maverick said and opened up one of his compartments. "We need a second one."

Twozerofive blinked again and grumbled something, but soon another blue pearl appeared in his hand. Max took it and placed it into one of Maverick's boxes.

Max started slowly circulating Spiritual Energy through his meridians in a steady trickle, which he worked with Maverick, so that the energy flowed in a synchronized manner.

"What is the Framework exactly?" Kat asked.

"Next we will be talking about your Framework," Twozerofive said. "I do not know what rumors and lies you have heard from the primitive natives of the planet, but the Framework wasn't created by the ICCB."

Max quirked an eyebrow at that. Now wasn't that interesting.

"We study it, yes, and we have learned many things from it. And we have gained some control over its myriad substrates. But it was created by elder beings that have since ascended and left this reality. We simply discovered it. It is believed that they created it specifically so that any remaining species in this universe would be able to fight against a threat like the Outsiders."

"It is a magi-bio-cyber-technological weapon," Twozerofive said. "In short, it will infuse your DNA with magic and thus grant you access to an internet that exists in a quasi-reality that can affect baseline reality. Your brains are too smooth to understand this, I do not understand why you ask."

Kat shrugged. "Just curious."

Max interrupted his meditation and mulled over the Gray's words. "So, it's basically a network that gives gifts? If I sit down and Cultivate my meridians, sure my physical meridians will get stronger, but the Framework is designed to reward such behavior, so if I am connected to it, it will notice that I increased my Cultivation and give me resources to spend within its system. Say I spend points in Strength, it will expend energy to give me extra physical strength."

Everyone else turned to look at Max. The Gray stared at him in stunned silence. Maverick giggled.

"Hmph!" Twozerofive said and turned as he huffed. "Good for you for not being irrevocably stupid. Get back to Framework Cultivation."

Max smirked to himself and continued the meditation.

Max felt the device activate in his lap. It got warmer, and through his eyelids he sensed the blue light getting more intense. He felt something probing at his soul—an energy that was examining and tugging at it. Max and Maverick increased the flow of energy through their meridians.

"The Framework is, first and foremost, a training tool," Twozerofive droned on. "It provides a person with the ability to withstand Spiritual Energy. By utilizing the unique DNA methylation and genetic structure of the Framework, we can generate objects and creatures that are attuned to it. This is why you have the ability to Level Up and become physically more powerful. Because the Framework allows you to absorb and use the energy from creatures and objects that are attuned to it on a genetic level. It is an internet of DNA."

"Why is any of this important?" the vulpine woman asked.

"Because the Outsiders can completely neuter it when it is not recalibrated."

"Oh," she said and fell silent.

"That is why you will all need to become at least Diamond-stage Cultivators to stand a chance. Only a recalibrated network will work as an intranet, instead of an internet. The initial Framework has conditional power. The recalibration makes that power truly your own."

"Why is it that we cannot recalibrate now?" the other insectoid asked.

"Your body will not be able to handle it," Twozerofive said. "Diamond stage is required, or the process will be too intense and will destroy you. Many things change when you become a super-mortal Cultivator."

The cube in Max's hands started to hum softly. It began injecting its energy into his own flow of Spiritual Energy. Maverick stirred as he experienced the same. Both of them shared a nod through their bond and focused. Their trial was about to begin.

Slowly the energy seeped into Max's spirit. It was alien and seemed to have a reserve of immense latent power. When Max's soul and meridians were saturated, the latent power indeed started to unfold. It was slow at first, but it was clearly there.

Max rushed to integrate the energy, just as he had done with the massive Stonehenge array's energy. Without having had that experience, he might have been thrown off-guard. This energy worked in a slower fashion, but it was of the same nature. If Max didn't pay attention, it would overwhelm him.

Fighting against that, Max focused his mind and will, drawing upon all his Cultivation experience to date. He directed his Spiritual Energy to envelop and absorb the alien power, guiding it through his meridians in a controlled flow. The energy resisted, threatening to surge out of control at any moment, but Max held firm. It bucked like a wild animal within him, and Max could feel the strain in his meridians. They weren't aching yet, but they would.

As he worked to integrate the energy, Max felt a new sensation begin to build. It started as a vague sense of unease, of something fundamental was shifting inside his very being. Gradually, the feeling intensified into a growing pressure, as if his body, mind, and soul were being compressed from all sides.

Maverick sensed Max's discomfort through their bond.

"Steady," Maverick said, his usually flippant tone replaced by one indicating deep concentration. "This stuff ain't got nothin' on us."

Max nodded, gritting his teeth as the pressure continued to build. It felt as though every cell in his body was being squeezed, every thought in his mind compressed, every facet of his soul constricted. The pain started as a dull ache, then escalated into a throbbing agony that threatened to overwhelm his senses. And it was still increasing in intensity.

But Max refused to yield. He drew upon the iron will that had been building inside of him throughout his trials on Alpha Ludus, the unbreakable determination that had allowed him to get this far.

He had never known he had it in him. But now he wondered why he had ever doubted himself.

That helped. But the pain was getting worse. The conversation occurring around him started to sound like a nonsensical jumble of words. He could only barely feel the bond he shared with Maverick, and Max knew his buddy was experiencing the same.

But Maverick was right. They *had* this.

No, really. Why did I ever doubt myself? What is the point?

At that, Maverick sent a pulse of emotion through their bond. It was a smug tone, saying something akin to "told you so."

Well, in terms of self-esteem, I've been the sidekick this whole time, I guess. That stops now.

With a surge of effort, he pushed more Spiritual Energy into his meridians, using it to bolster his faltering consciousness. It helped. The pain didn't wane, but it became easier to handle. Max would get through this.

As he struggled to maintain his focus, he became aware of a strange phenomenon occurring within him. It was as if his very essence was being deconstructed, broken down into its constituent elements. He could feel his memories, his knowledge, his very sense of self being stripped away layer by layer. It felt like death. The circle was closing, and darkness was coming to him. A darkness eternal, a dreamless sleep. Death.

Panic rose in Max's chest, but he fought it down. He knew that this deconstruction was necessary, that it was the only way for the new Framework to take hold. He knew he was surrounded by allies. He knew that, even if the Grays were assholes, they wouldn't really let anything happen to him; he was too valuable. He knew that even if he died, the Zoos Collective would resurrect him.

But still, he feared. He feared losing himself. Feared becoming part of the darkness, an oblivion without a name or a face.

But the energy within him was insistent and the pain was increasing, taking over his mind. The energy gave him two options: surrender to death or be obliterated and ripped apart by the energy which couldn't be contained.

So, he surrendered to the process, letting go of his attachments and allowing his old self to be unmade. It felt like he was being eaten alive by shadows surging through him like hungry vultures. He tried to breathe, to guide the energy, but it was becoming hard not just to think but to even exist.

Can I . . . just let go . . .

"NO!" Maverick roared through their bond. "Soldier through. Just push!"

And then, just when Max felt he could endure no more, a new sensation began to emerge. It was a feeling of vast, incalculable power, welling up from the deepest core of his being. As the last vestiges of his old Framework fell away, this power surged forward, flooding his meridians with an energy more potent than anything he had ever known.

The pain started to fade. There was peace.

[FRAMEWORK RECALIBRATION]
Name: Max Cromwell
Cultivation stage: Diamond
Class: Spatial Sorcerer Level: 34
Combined Stat Points: 1899
[Calibrating reward distribution . . .]
[Accounting for Cultivation Path . . .]
[Identifying Dao . . .]
[. . .]
[Recalibration complete. 100% Attunement. 1899 Combined Stat points will be considered in the calculation . . .]
Maximilian Cromwell
Stage: Diamond (low)

Dao: Destruction
Karma: +1
Speed: 7
Power: 8
Control: 8

Max allowed himself a little smile as he distantly heard Maverick whooping excitedly. Then he passed out.

CHAPTER NINE

Newborn Cultivator

When Max woke up, he felt like he had slept for a fortnight. He hadn't felt tired for weeks. Not really. But not feeling tired was not the same thing as feeling *rested*.

With his eyes closed, he groaned and stretched like a lazy cat. He was on a bed. The sheets were firm but soft, and it felt like he was floating on a cloud.

Max got up and let his mind roam over his body to assess his new state.

Max's spirit and soul were *brimming* with energy. He let the Spiritual Energy flow into his fingertips. He snapped his fingers.

An explosive boom shot from his hand and tossed all the beds into the air, throwing them a few feet up, two of them landing on their sides.

"Ho-ly shit," Maverick said. "I want to try that out too! Where can I aim my cannon?"

Before Maverick could cause an inordinate amount of destruction, a stasis bubble enveloped them and Twozerofive appeared floating in front of them.

"How good of you to wake," the Gray said dryly. "I'm going to release you from this bubble, but you have to not use your Spiritual Power for now. I will finish the lesson with the others, and then you will be put into a simulation."

"How did my recalibration go?" Max asked.

Twozerofive regarded him with his black eyes. There was a strange look in them.

"You did get a notification, did you not?"

"I did, but it just said one hundred percent complete," Max said. "I assumed—"

"It has not ever happened before," Twozerofive said quietly. "I assume it is because you shared the burden between your spirits. But not even paths with animal companions . . ."

"Hah!" Maverick exclaimed. "I always knew I was special."

"Many firsts," the Gray mused, more to himself. "The Outsiders have never attacked a training planet before. I wonder what the Zoos are not telling us . . ."

Max watched the Gray, who finally seemed to snap out of it. He realized he had spoken aloud, and a snarl passed across his face. "Do not use your powers. Eat a meal and wait."

With that, the stasis was lifted and Twozerofive teleported back to the other members of the strike force, currently Cultivating in a circle formation.

Max walked into the kitchen area, his body still *thrum*ming with the new-found energy from the Framework recalibration. While his spirit felt invigorated, his physical body craved sustenance. He approached the dispenser, remembering the incredible meal he had enjoyed with his fellow strike force members just yesterday.

As if sensing his presence, the panel slid open, revealing a plate laden with a mouthwatering array of flavors and aromas. The scent of perfectly seasoned meat and fresh, crisp vegetables wafted up to greet him, making his stomach growl in anticipation.

Max picked up the plate, admiring the artistry of the presentation. The food here was a far cry from the simple, utilitarian fare he had grown accustomed to on Alpha Ludus. Every dish seemed crafted to not only nourish the body but to delight the senses and fortify the spirit.

As he took his first bite, Max couldn't help but close his eyes in sheer ecstasy. The flavors were just as incredible as he remembered—rich, complex, and perfectly harmonized. The tender meat practically dissolved on his tongue while the vegetables provided a satisfying crunch and a burst of fresh, bright flavor.

But even as he savored the taste, Max found himself more attuned to the subtle-yet-profound effects the food was having on his Spiritual Power. With each swallow, he could feel a gentle surge of energy flowing through his meridians, as if the very essence of the ingredients was being directly absorbed and integrated into his being.

It was a sensation he had noticed before but which now, with his heightened awareness and sensitivity post-recalibration, was impossible to ignore. The food wasn't just nourishing his physical body—it was actively strengthening his spirit, reinforcing the foundations of his Cultivation.

Maverick hovered nearby, watching Max eat. Idly, Max could sense a vague amusement through their bond.

"Hitting different now, isn't it?" Maverick remarked. "I can feel it feeding my spirit too."

Max nodded, swallowing another bite before responding. "It's like . . . I can feel it on a whole new level," he said. "Not just the taste but the way it's integrating with my Spiritual Power. It's ridiculous that you can get stronger just by eating."

"Doesn't surprise me," Maverick said. "These ICCB folks seem to have been doing this for a long-ass time. They have this figured out."

Max nodded and continued to eat, enjoying the way each bite seemed to further strengthen his Cultivation ever so slightly.

By the time he finished his meal, Max felt not just sated but empowered. He resisted the urge to snap his fingers and take up flight or something else similarly dramatic. He was sure he'd be using this energy for something productive in no time, anyway.

Max walked up to the strike force circle. They were all sitting silently and meditating. There was a strange three-dimensional formation around them, like a star map from a sci-fi movie. Between the bright stars, surges of white energy zipped around.

Max brushed at Kat's spirit with his. She was startled but kept her eyes closed and her mouth pursed in concentration. She looked cute like that.

And all in all, she seemed to have already gained some power.

Perhaps the star map formation helps them reach insights.

Max let his spirit brush through all of them. Losshnak's Spiritual Energy was the only formidable one. He couldn't even begin to put up a fight against Max, but he could take half of the strike force alone with ease.

The female vulpine had a sharp spirit. Her Cultivation was strong, almost as powerful as Losshnak's, but her meridians were still lacking. Max hoped for her sake that she was strengthening them and not looking for her **[Breakthrough Insight]**.

Twozerofive noticed him and nodded curtly. Then he started to float toward the large green circle in the corner of the room. The Gray stopped in front of it and a panel appeared. Max followed and watched as a swirling green portal appeared in the middle of the circle. It *thrum*med with power and crackles of lightning arced from it like whips to the side. In a few seconds, it stabilized and the arcing lightning attached itself to the green platform below it.

"This is a false dimension," Twozerofive said. "Within your primitive concept of reality, it could be called a simulation. It is a modified recording of a small-scale attack of the Outsiders on a planet. Go in there and defend against the assault. I will assess your combat ability."

Max nodded and walked up to the platform. It felt strange entering the portal. He felt a stir of trepidation but laughed it off. Maverick laughed too.

"After the bullshit with the Framework recalibration, this is hardly something worth breaking a sweat over," Maverick said gleefully.

Max nodded and hopped onto his buddy, and then his disc form floated into the portal.

CHAPTER TEN

Assault

Max and Maverick found themselves on a mountainside. It reminded him of the Himalayas. High peaks, snow, black stone, and ice. Maverick rose higher into the air to give them a bird's-eye view.

The wind was vicious and howled aggressively. If not for his Cultivation, he would have been overtaken by the cold in minutes, particularly given the loose black robe he was wearing. But to him now it felt no worse than a light summer breeze.

The sky was full of creatures—dragonflies with the arms and maws of monsters, jagged tusks protruding from their wide black mouths. On each of their bulbous heads was a sharp horn gleaming black in the pale sun of this world.

Their buzz filled the air like rumbling thunder. Sometimes they would surge down and crash into the mountainside. Sometimes a bolt of fire or lightning would strike at the swarm, and some of the oily, black insects would fall.

Max looked down.

Creeping forms of ooze that ate everything in their wake trudged by, moving down the mountains. Some were medium-dog-sized, others the size of an apartment building. And amongst them were another type of Outsider: A strange humanoid that was at least fifteen feet in height. It had eight arms and it wore a white mask with bright happy eyes and a malicious grin on its face. There were two of them waving their hands in intricate patterns, spells of dark flame and purple poisonous gas rising around them.

Fighting the horde was an army of yetis and something that looked like humans. The yetis had white thick fur and had various weapons on them—swords, spears, machine guns. They were all Cultivators.

So were the humanoids. They had blue skin, and all were completely bald, but other than that they looked exactly like humans. Max watched as two dozen of them got overwhelmed and consumed by one of the giant black sludges. All that was left of them were faint vapors of red gas, which instantly got blown away by the high wind.

A tiny swarm of the oily, black dragonflies surged down at them. Maverick swerved, did a tailspin, and started shooting at them.

The cannon boomed like a thunderbolt, and some gray and yellow energy blasted out of the cannon under Maverick's disc form.

The dragonflies zipped at Max with supersonic speed. Instinctively, he produced a barrier of gravity in front of them. It was based on his previous spell [Gravity Well], but now it was just a pure mass of gravity.

It was not strong enough to stop the charge of the dragonflies.

But Maverick managed to swerve again, and the gravity distortion managed to disrupt their flight paths enough. But when they flew past, a cloud of purple smoke puffed up around them.

Oh my good Christ, I'm so stupid.

Max immediately produced the [Scythe of Oblivion] from his Inventory. It was now a space in his soul, not a virtual dimension, Max noticed. There were other ways in which the Inventory had changed during the recalibration, but now was not the time to explore that further.

Max infused the giant scythe with his will, and it started cleaving down the dragonflies, finally giving Maverick and him some space.

Without stopping to ask questions, Maverick flew down. Max tethered the dragonflies with his gravity-distortion powers, but more of the monsters swarmed in. Max clapped his hands together, pushing Spiritual Power through his meridians. An arc of soundwaves laced with gravity and Cultivation power spread around Max and Maverick, repelling the onslaught of the dragonflies from every direction. Another cloud of purple smoke puffed up. This time Max breathed in the foul air.

Max sent out the scythe spinning wildly through the air toward the sorcerer. It moved with uncanny speed and the giant black scythe exploded against the mountainside, sending a rockfall down the slope.

Max recalled the scythe with his will and commanded it to keep attacking the sorcerer, if only to distract them.

Another black fireball hurtled their way.

Maverick moved instantly and flipped and zipped in the air as he fired his thundering cannon. All around them swarmed the dragonflies, and down below, one of the many armed sorcerers was throwing fireballs at him with breakneck speed. Another one had immediately started targeting them after Max had commanded his scythe to distract the first one.

"Max!" Maverick roared. "Do something!"

Max shook his head. His meridians were poisoned by the gas. His energy felt sluggish. But he managed to pull through. He opened his hands and then slammed them together, targeting a dozen of the dragonflies. In that moment, the dragonfly-monsters were also all slammed together. Meanwhile, Maverick fired at them. A bolt of gray and yellow energy struck the black clump and vaporized it completely, only a few wisps of charred black flying in the air.

"Yeahhh!!!" Maverick exclaimed.

Max managed a little smile. He coughed into his hand and saw a few specks of blood. Another purple cloud appeared around them. More dragonflies attacked. The Outsiders' offense was relentless.

Max gritted his teeth, fighting back the wave of nausea and weakness that threatened to overwhelm him. The purple gas was insidious, seeping into his body and dulling his senses, making every movement slower and slower.

He gritted his teeth. This was not a time for weakness. It was a time to fight. And with fighting, pain was a given.

The dragonflies were still coming, their buzzing filling the air. Maverick blasted at them, while Max weaved in gravitational waves around them, keeping the attacks away. Most of them missed by a hair. And down below, the many-armed sorcerer was readying another volley of fireballs, their malicious grin never wavering on the white mask.

"Mav!" Max shouted over the fast wind. "We need to take out that sorcerer!"

"On it!" Maverick replied, his voice strained but determined. The gun-disc spun in the air, his cannon glowing with barely contained energy as he took aim at the towering figure below.

Max summoned every ounce of strength he had left, pushing past the poison coursing through his veins. It was seeping into him, damaging his meridians. They had started to leak, and with that, every time he used Spiritual Energy, some was wasted.

Don't think about it. It doesn't matter. I still have plenty.

He raised his hands, focusing his Spiritual Power into a gravitational field around them, shielding them from the worst of the dragonflies' onslaught. Sometimes he would send a pulse out like a whip or a solar flare to smack a dragonfly down with gravity.

But for every one of them killed, two joined in from the swarm above the sky blotting out most of the light.

It was like trying to hold back a tidal wave with a paper umbrella. The insects crashed against Max's barrier, their oily bodies splattering and re-forming, relentless in their assault. But it bought Maverick the time he needed.

Maverick's cannon flared, a bolt of pure, concentrated energy lancing down toward the sorcerer. It struck the creature square in the chest, burning a hole clean through its body. The sorcerer staggered, its many arms flailing, but somehow it remained standing.

It seemed to slump and go idle. The black oily membrane sludging off it in slimy chunks. The hole in the middle of its chest smoked.

And then, to Max's horror, it began to laugh. A deep, gurgling sound that echoed across the mountainside, filled with malice and cruel amusement. The hole in its chest began to close, black ooze knitting the wound back together as if it had never been.

"It's regenerating!" Maverick cried out, his voice tinged with disbelief. "What the hell are these things made of?"

"Shoot it again!"

Maverick did, but now the blast was hit by a flash of a red energy shield that enveloped the sorcerer in a bubble of protection.

Max commanded the **[Scythe of Oblivion]** to decapitate the sorcerer. The giant spinning scythe cleaved through the red bubble, but the sorcerer slipped out, as if it had turned into nothing but shadow and smoke for a moment. It looked up at Max and Maverick, and the mask, which Max had thought to be inanimate decor, did something unsettling: the malicious grin on its face widened. Max suddenly felt very cold.

"What do we do?!" Maverick asked.

Max shook his head. All he knew was that they were fighting far above their weight.

The purple gas was growing thicker by the second, obscuring his vision and making it increasingly difficult to breathe. And the dragonflies were still coming, their numbers seemingly endless.

He tried to summon another gravitational wave, but his power sputtered and died, the poison sapping his strength. Max felt himself growing weaker, his body beginning to shut down. Maverick was still firing, his cannon a constant, reassuring presence, but even he couldn't hold out forever.

And then, the sorcerer made its move. It raised all eight of its arms, a massive fireball coalescing between its palms. Max tried to command the scythe to interrupt, but another sorcerer blocked it with a red shield. Then the same sorcerer waved its hands, and a purple cloud of poison manifested right by Max and Maverick.

They managed to escape it, but it was too late.

With a final, triumphant cackle, the sorcerer hurled the massive flaming orb directly at Max and Maverick.

Maverick dodged. Max tried to redirect the fireball with gravity. He screamed and his meridians felt like they were bursting into flames. With a massive heave, he disrupted the fireball. But his body wouldn't respond. It wasn't enough. He watched as the fireball hurtled toward them, as if in slow motion, growing larger and larger until it filled his entire field of vision.

They dodged it by a hair, but the massive fireball was not aimed at them. It was aimed at the purple cloud of poison.

The explosion was deafening. A wave of heat and force slammed into Max, sending him tumbling through the air like a rag doll. He felt Maverick's presence ripped away from him, the gun's panicked shout lost in the roar of the blast.

Max plummeted toward the ground, his body broken and battered. He crashed into the mountainside, bones shattering on impact, pain lancing through every nerve. Around him, the purple gas swirled and danced, the dragonflies descending like vultures to a feast.

With the last of his strength, Max tried to push himself up, to face his end with some shred of dignity. But his body betrayed him, collapsing back onto the cold, hard stone. He could feel the Outsiders closing in, their presence a tangible weight pressing down on him, suffocating in its intensity.

Some of the oozing forms tacked onto him and started sucking up his Spiritual Energy.

But even as despair threatened to consume him, Max felt a flicker of defiance, a stubborn spark that refused to be extinguished. He was a Cultivator, a wielder of Spiritual Power, a being who had transcended the limits of mortality. He would not go quietly into that good night, would not let these abominations swallow him without chewing.

With a roar of pure, primal rage, Max surged to his feet, his body aflame with the last vestiges of his power. It wasn't only adrenaline. Not only Spiritual Power. It was pure, unadulterated human willpower.

He lashed out with fists and feet, with gravity and force, with every ounce of strength and will he had left. He bent reality with his will, and some of the sludge attached to him exploded. But there were too many of them.

The Outsiders swarmed him, their bodies crushing and tearing, but still Max fought, a lone beacon of light in a sea of darkness. Near him was Maverick, shooting out massive pulses of energy from his cannon. But the creatures had grabbed onto him, and he could not fly any longer.

Max felt his strength waning, his Spiritual Power flickering like a guttering candle. The poison filled his lungs, his blood, his very soul, dragging him down into an abyss of numbness and despair.

And then, at last, it was over. Max fell to his knees, his body finally giving out. He thought he would be ripped apart, but the swarm dispersed around him. Only the ooze remained, pinning him to the cold mountainside, sucking his lifeforce and Spiritual Energy. Then three massive sorcerers approached.

They were like giants with slim, muscular bodies and eight arms waving hypnotically behind them. Each wore a white mask with vicious grins so wide they peeked out the sides. They laughed. It was an uncanny, alien sound, high, distant, and full of cruelty.

One of the sorcerers took a few steps toward Max and raised a fist. He bashed Max's skull into pieces with a single clean punch.

And then, silence. The simulation faded, the mountainside and the horde of Outsiders dissolving into nothingness. Max lay on the green circle, with the portal closing above him with the sound of an old vacuum cleaner. His body was intact, but his mind was reeling from the experience.

Maverick clunked beside him and whispered in a harrowed voice, "Well, damn."

It had felt so real. The pain, the fear, the desperation—it had all been as tangible as anything he had ever known. Idly, Max thought the simulation to be an excellent training device.

But most of his mind was still reeling, still trying to take in the experience. The ICCB had created a digital phantasm designed to push him to his limits and beyond.

And I couldn't even put a dent into the assault . . .

As Max stared up at the featureless ceiling, his chest heaving with exertion and emotion, a single thought crystallized in his mind. If this was what awaited them, if this was the true face of the enemy they were to confront, then they would need every ounce of strength, every shred of power and determination they could muster.

Even if every one of us reaches Diamond stage, it won't be enough.

Max knew that he and Maverick couldn't match even a single one of the Outsider sorcerers.

The war had not yet begun, but already Max could feel its weight bearing down on him, a burden as heavy as the universe itself. But he would not cower, would not shy away from the challenge. He had been in this situation before. Not with odds like this. Not with stakes like this. But he would rise up.

"We will try again," Max muttered.

Through their bond, Maverick sent out a pulse of grim agreement.

They *would* destroy the Outsider assault.

CHAPTER ELEVEN

Statistics

F irst, I must congratulate you," Twozerofive said in a tone that sounded anything but congratulatory. "All of you managed to advance a stage or two, and
Losshnak Shieldbreaker surpassed his limits and ascended to Diamond stage."

"Shieldbreaker, huh?" Maverick said.

Max respectfully bowed and nodded. Losshnak grinned and returned the
gesture. Ashkarassa huffed in frustration. Kat just sat hunched on the sofa, hands
on her knees, staring at the floor.

"I expect all the rest of you riffraff to ascend to super-mortal Cultivation
within the week," their Gray instructor said. "After you have achieved that, you
will be permitted to use the simulation so I can assess your combat capabilities."

At that, a screen appeared in midair and started playing a familiar scene. Max
and Maverick both groaned.

"This is a recording of the first attempt to fight the Outsiders. There are two
things to take note of."

Max perked up.

"First, that you will be fighting a scouting party. This recording is from a
first-wave assault force. By the time an assault force arrives, reinforcements from
the ICCB should also arrive."

"Oh," Max said. Everyone in the strike force turned to him. "So, I wasn't
supposed to beat it?"

"Of course not!" Twozerofive snapped. "To survive even as long as you did
is— Never mind!"

Max felt a giddy smugness arising in Maverick. He had felt deflated after the
simulation, but it had clearly been designed to be beyond their abilities.

"Another thing to note is that the Outsiders have a class of ships . . . well, we
call them ships, even though they are more like quasi-organic transport entities.

These ships, when they get close enough to a planet, will blanket it with a Cultivation-suppression field."

"Ohhhhh," Max and Maverick both said.

That explained so much. Max had felt stronger than before, sure. But, in the real world, he was able to throw furniture with the snap of a finger. In the simulation he had certainly felt powerful but in a vaguely diminished way.

"We do not know whether or not the enemy will be able to get a ship like this through during the scouting party's descent on the planet, but we are assuming the worst, so you will be training in the simulation as if you are suppressed. The suppression field's effect varies based on the strength of the ship using it and the Cultivator's natural ability to resist it."

Twozerofive waved a finger, and the hovering screen in the air started showing footage. Max followed it with a keen eye, his mind working overtime. Even Maverick was quiet for once as he took in the feedback. This was a rare opportunity to see how they fought and what their blind spots and weaknesses were.

As the footage of Max's battle against the Outsiders played out, the other members of the strike force watched with rapt attention. The room was silent save for the occasional gasp, murmur, or whisper as they witnessed the sheer scale of the enemy's assault.

Losshnak leaned forward, his eyes narrowed in concentration. "Impressive," he said, his deep voice cutting through the silence. "To hold out for so long against such odds . . . I realize fully now why I could not defeat you."

Max inclined his head in acknowledgment, feeling a swell of pride at the Ishkarassi warrior's praise. "Thank you," he said, then added, "These were not the same Outlanders we fought in the Deathmatch, Losshnak. Just, uh, be prepared."

Losshnak nodded. "I will keep your advice in mind. But I believe I will underperform. We all will. Just . . . know I understand why I lost to you."

"Indeed," the female vulpine said, her tone grudging but sincere. "I hate to admit it, but you fought well, human. Better than I would have expected."

Max raised an eyebrow at the backhanded compliment but chose not to comment. He knew that earning the respect of the other races would be a gradual process, one that would require patience and perseverance.

"This one is in awe of your prowess, Max," Slargi said, his insectoid features arranging themselves into an approximation of a smile. "To witness such spirit in the face of overwhelming adversity . . . it is truly inspiring."

Max smiled at the alien's earnest praise. "Thank you, Slargi," he said. "But it wasn't enough. The Outsiders just keep coming. And if they think you can handle them, well, say hello to sorcerers."

"And that gas," Maverick said, half-muttering. "It was like nothing I've ever encountered before. It sapped our strength. It didn't directly affect me, but Max and I share a bond, as he is my trusty sidekick."

The vulpine male chuckled.

Max nodded, his expression grim. "We need to find a way to counteract its effects," he said. "Some kind of protective gear, or maybe a Cultivation technique that can purge the poison from our bodies."

"There aren't any," Twozerofive said. "Some Cultivators have unique techniques to deal with the gas, but we have no universal solutions."

"So, you've just spent the last thousand years with your thumbs in your asses?" Maverick asked and earned a chuckle from the male vulpine.

The female vulpine jabbed his ribs with an elbow. "Have some dignity, Kerro."

Kerro grumbled but straightened himself.

"Perhaps a coordinated assault?" the other insectoid suggested. "If we can bring enough offensive power to bear on a single target, we might be able to overwhelm the sorcerers' healing abilities."

"Painfully obvious but correct," Twozerofive said as he paused the feed. "The sorcerers need a concentrated attack. They can heal themselves and each other."

"This one suggests focusing on evasion and mobility," Slargi said. "The more we can avoid their attacks, the longer we can stay in the fight."

"Easier said than done," the female vulpine scoffed. "Did you see how fast those dragonflies were moving? It was like trying to swat flies with a sledgehammer. Not all of us can fly."

"She's right," Ashkarassa said. "We need to find a way to even the odds, to take the fight to them on our terms."

Twozerofive scoffed but said nothing. Max looked at him. He wasn't telling them everything. If the ICCB had fought these things for thousands of years, some well-established battle patterns had to have already been made. But their instructor seemed to not want them to build on any preconceived notions.

The war is in a stalemate and they need harebrained creative ideas, I guess.

Max nodded, his eyes distant as he watched the replay. "The mountainside," he said at last. "It was a killing field, with no cover and nowhere to hide. If we can lure them into a more enclosed space, somewhere with obstacles and chokepoints, we might be able to negate some of their numerical advantage."

"A sound strategy," Losshnak said, approval in his voice. "We can use the terrain to our advantage, force them to come to us instead of the other way around."

"It does not work like that," Twozerofive said, annoyed. "They choose where they land and start assimilating biomass. They force us to move to them."

"What a bunch of bastards," Maverick said.

"Are they tactically minded?" Max asked. "Do they plan the assaults and adjust when they face resistance?"

Their instructor regarded Max silently before answering. "What do you think?"

The sorcerers' malevolent grins flashed back into Max's mind—their leisurely cruelty as they took their time to enjoy Max's death.

"The sorcerers think," Max said. "And if they can think, they can plan."

"Correct," Twozerofive said.

The others nodded, their expressions grim but resolute. They knew the odds were stacked against them, that the enemy they faced was unlike any they had ever encountered. But they also knew that failure wasn't an option. That the fate of the entire universe rested on their shoulders.

As the footage of Max's battle came to its brutal conclusion, the strike force members exchanged glances, a silent understanding passing between them.

Max had never fancied himself noble or just. And since arriving on Alpha Ludus, he had been forced to make decisions. Still, at the end of the day, he was selfish. But his Dao was clear on what he needed to do. This was his path. To destroy the Outsider threat.

"So," Max said, breaking the silence at last, "what's our next move? How do we prepare for the battles to come?"

Twozerofive regarded the group with his inscrutable black eyes.

"You train," he said simply. "You push yourselves to your limits and beyond. You master your Cultivation, your personal weapons, your powers. And you pray to the Heavens that it will be enough."

The Gray's words hung heavy in the air, a stark reminder of the fact that this was no longer a game in any sense of the word. But as Max looked around at his fellow warriors, at the determination and resolve etched on their faces, he knew that his team would fight to the last to win.

CHAPTER TWELVE

Array Training

Max sat on top of Maverick in the Stonehenge formation. Everyone was watching him, and Twozerofive was floating above the structure, holding out his hands, controlling the powerful Spiritual Energy emitted by the array.

"Are you ready?" their instructor asked.

"Hell, yeah," Maverick said.

Max nodded.

Twozerofive released the energy, and it surged toward Max.

"Losshnak," their instructor said, "describe what is happening."

"Max's body and spirit are being almost overwhelmed by the energy from this array," Losshnak said. "He is struggling for control and trying to capture the energy in his meridians."

"Correct. And what is happening in his meridians?"

Max felt another brush of Losshnak's spirit on his own. He was too focused on breathing to pay any more attention. The amount of Spiritual Energy surging through him was reaching uncomfortable levels, but Twozerofive was clearly regulating it, or it would have been even worse. Max felt something release within him, and the exercise suddenly became slightly easier.

+1 Control

Losshnak gasped. "His meridians. They are expanding."

"Correct," Twozerofive said. "And why is that important?"

Losshnak said nothing. Twozerofive sighed.

"When your Framework is recalibrated, it will start to reflect reality instead of augmenting it. All of those training wheel power-ups that you are now carrying within you—Strength, Resistance, what have you—all of those will be reverted back into pure Spiritual Power and fed back to you. The process is very similar to what Max here is doing."

Max was barely listening. The throbbing pain in his meridians was now getting intense. He breathed and tried to ignore the heavy beads of sweat dripping from his eyebrows to his cheeks.

"When you ascend to super-mortal Cultivation and recalibrate your Framework, your Stats will be condensed to **Control**, **Power**, and **Speed**. These are reflections of your true ability. The Framework measures that ability. **Power** is governed by the potency of your soul. That is where your Spiritual Power congregates. The more of it you have, the more potent techniques you can unleash. **Control** is determined by the development of your meridians. Developed meridians allow you to use your power at will. They let you determine how much power you're using, and through them, you can create new variations to existing techniques and even new techniques depending on how advanced your meridians are."

"And what about **Speed**?" Slargi asked.

"**Speed** is more complicated," Twozerofive said. "It is determined by your **Control** and **Power** to some extent. **Control** determines how fast you can engage your Spiritual Energy. You may have great amounts of it in your soul, but if you can't call upon it fast enough for it to be useful in battle, you're a worthless Cultivator. At the same time, you can also have intricate control and a talented mind for Cultivating your meridians, but if you don't have enough power behind it, you cannot create explosive movement or techniques fast enough to be able to strike at most Outsiders."

+1 Power

Maverick groaned under Max. "Tell . . . this . . . to . . . me . . . again . . . later . . ."

"I'll . . . try," Max said between gritted teeth.

Their short exchange seemed to have returned Twozerofive's attention to Max, and suddenly the oppressive pressure of the Cultivation array subsided. Max slumped and coughed out a bit of spit and bile.

"You are NOT wiping that on me," Maverick said between breaths.

"Yeah, yeah," Max said and wiped it on his robe.

Twozerofive waved a hand at Max. "Pay attention. I know none of you except Losshnak can sense what is going on in Max's spirit. Max, explain your experience with the array."

"It sucks," Max said and wiped his mouth. "It's like trying to drink from a fire hose."

"That is putting it mildly," Losshnak muttered.

"I am sure you will fare better than a *human*," Ashkarassa said, casting a sneer at Max. "They are so weak."

Losshnak growled. "Do you want another fight? The master warrior is different."

Ashkarassa rolled her eyes. "If you say so."

"The reason why it 'sucks,'" Twozerofive said mildly as he hovered menacingly over the two Ishkarassi, "is because we are low on time. You will all need to be completely comfortable with the amount of energy that this array is able to relay. If you want to fight the Outsiders' ground assault force, you need to be able to make attacks that can devastate not dozens but hundreds of enemies at once. Am I understood?"

The strike force all murmured in assent.

"Max, Losshnak," Twozerofive said. "You will come with me to the simulation. First Losshnak will make an attempt alone, then the two of you will attempt it together. The rest of you will either go to the library section or sit down. You need to figure out your insights fast."

Max watched as Losshnak struggled on in a futile effort to fight the encroaching horde. He had a very different approach to Max and Maverick. Max couldn't blame him; flying was overpowered.

Instead, Losshnak opted to join the yetis fighting on the ground, shielding them with his abilities while providing support. His abilities such as **[Holy Nova]** and **[Light Lance]** worked really well to provide support and cut down approaching hordes of slime and the small dog-like critters that were on the ground providing fast infantry for the Outsiders. The lancing bursts of white and yellow light shot down some of the dragonflies attacking their formation.

Things were actually going well. Arguably better than how Max and Maverick had fared in the skies.

But Losshnak's fate was sealed the moment the sorcerers noticed him. To Max's surprise, Losshnak's barrier ability actually did manage to block an attack of purple smoke. The shield was now massive, and it shone much brighter than Max had remembered. Inside were at least a hundred yeti warriors in rows and packs of five to ten. The shining golden shield moved as Losshnak moved.

It was nothing against the might of the sorcerers. The black fireballs that the sorcerers threw with reckless abandon destroyed the barrier in moments. It held the first one, but as immobile as he and the yetis were, they were easy targets. Two more fireballs and their whole company of a hundred warriors were incinerated. The sorcerers didn't even bother to gloat. Not that there was anything left of Losshnak. Max glanced at the blackened skeleton of his comrade for a harrowing moment before the simulation blinked out and Max found himself on the floor of the green circle.

Twozerofive *tsk*ed. "What good is a defense if it cannot hold?"

The restored Losshnak said nothing. He only sat on the floor and stared in silent contemplation. Max let him be. Twozerofive, however—not so much.

"You are too slow and weak," their instructor said. "If you cannot withstand the attacks, you have to dodge."

Losshnak only gave the Gray a blank stare and nodded.

"Cut it out," Max said. "The point isn't to fight alone. He'll be a great asset in a team."

"He was in a team," Twozerofive said dryly. "Of one hundred and eleven. Each of them is at least a Diamond-stage fighter."

Max flinched at that. There were hundreds of fighters in that simulation. *And they had died like flies . . .*

"Max," Maverick said, "I have an idea."

Max turned to Maverick, his eyebrows raised in curiosity. "What's on your mind, Mav?"

The gun hovered in the air, his form shimmering with barely contained excitement. "What if Losshnak rides on me while you fly solo using your spatial powers? We could be a mobile artillery platform, raining death down from above while you run interference and keep the heat off us."

Max considered the idea, his mind already racing with the possibilities. "It could work," he said slowly. "Losshnak's barrier could provide cover for you, while his light attacks could help thin out the swarms. And with my gravity manipulation, I could disrupt their formations, maybe even create some choke-points for you to exploit."

Losshnak looked up, a glimmer in his eyes. "A bold strategy," he said, his voice still heavy with the weight of his recent defeat. "But one that might just be crazy enough to work."

Twozerofive regarded the trio with a skeptical gaze. "Very well," he said at last. "We shall see if your little scheme bears fruit. But do not get your hopes up. It is power you lack, not a proper strategy."

Max nodded, his expression grim but determined. "We have to try something."

With that, the three warriors stepped back into the simulation, the mountainside and the horde of Outsiders materializing around them once more. Max took a deep breath, feeling the now-familiar weight of responsibility settling on his shoulders.

"Ready?" he asked, glancing at Losshnak and Maverick.

The Ishkarassi warrior nodded, his eyes hard with resolve. "Let us show these abominations the might of our pride."

"Geez," Maverick said. "I'm still unsure if you're cool or lame."

Losshnak stepped on Maverick with an unnecessarily hard stomp.

The gun wobbled slightly under the sudden weight but quickly stabilized, his form shifting to accommodate his new passenger.

"Asshole," Maverick muttered as he gained altitude. Max said nothing. He only gave Losshnak a nod of acknowledgment.

With a burst of speed, Maverick shot forward, Losshnak clinging to his frame as they rocketed toward the swarms of dragonflies. Max followed close behind, his body enveloped in a shimmering field of distorted space.

As they closed in on the enemy, Max thrust out his hands, his fingers splayed wide. A wave of gravitational force rippled outward, slamming into the dragonflies like a physical blow. The insects tumbled and spun, their formation broken by the sudden assault.

Losshnak seized the opportunity, his hands moving in intricate patterns as he channeled his Spiritual Energy. Beams of searing light lanced out from his palms, piercing through the disoriented swarms like golden needles. Dozens of dragonflies fell from the sky, their bodies charred and crumbling.

Maverick weaved through the chaos, his cannon flaring with each shot. The gun's enhanced firepower tore through the Outsiders' ranks, leaving trails of shattered chitin and black sludge in its wake. Together, the trio carved a path through the heart of the enemy formation.

But the Outsiders were quick to adapt. The sorcerers on the ground below took notice of the aerial threat, their white face masks splitting into grins of malicious glee. Fireballs and bolts of crackling energy streaked upward, seeking to bring down the interlopers.

Max saw the attacks coming and reacted instinctively. He swept his arms in a wide arc, creating a swirling vortex of distorted space around Maverick and Losshnak. The enemy projectiles were caught in the maelstrom, their trajectories twisted and warped until they careened harmlessly off into the distance.

Losshnak capitalized on the opening, unleashing a barrage of [**Light Lances**] at the nearest sorcerer. The beams pierced the creature's body in a dozen places, sending it staggering backward with a howl of pain. But even as it fell, the other sorcerers closed rank around it, their own attacks redoubling in intensity.

Max gritted his teeth, pouring more power into his spatial distortion. He could feel the strain on his Spiritual Energy, the toll of maintaining such a complex and potent force field. But he couldn't afford to let up, not with Maverick and Losshnak counting on him.

The gun and its rider pressed their advantage, diving low over the sorcerers' heads. Losshnak leaped from Maverick's back, his body wreathed in golden light as he brought his fists down in a devastating [**Holy Nova**]. The shockwave of sacred energy slammed into the sorcerers, sending them flying like rag dolls.

But even as they fell, the sorcerers lashed out with their own dark powers. Tendrils of strange luminescent white ether snaked out from their prone forms, seeking to ensnare and crush the Ishkarassi warrior. Losshnak danced and dodged, his movements a blur of speed and grace, but the sorcerers' magic was relentless.

Well, this is something new . . .

Max saw his comrade's peril and acted without hesitation. He dove toward Losshnak, his body becoming a living missile of compressed gravity. With a shout of exertion, he unleashed a pulse of pure force, scattering the sorcerers' pale tentacles like leaves in a gale. Some of them managed to extend and lash out at Max, causing immediate and severe pain. Max gritted his teeth and pushed through it.

Together, Max and Losshnak stood back-to-back, their powers intertwined in a symphony of light and shadow. Maverick circled overhead, his cannon raining down a constant barrage of covering fire. For a moment, it seemed as though the tide might be turning, that the Outsiders might finally be facing a foe they could not overcome.

But then, disaster struck. One of the sorcerers, its body broken and bleeding from a dozen wounds, raised a trembling hand and unleashed a final, desperate attack. A ball of roiling darkness, shot through with veins of sickly purple, hurtled toward Max and Losshnak like a screaming comet.

Max tried to deflect it with a [**Gravity Well**], but the sorcerer's magic was too strong. The dark sphere tore through Max's defenses like they were paper, slamming into him with the force of a runaway train.

Pain exploded through his body, his vision flashing white as he felt bones shatter and organs rupture. He fell to the ground, his limbs spasming uncontrollably as the sorcerer's vile energy coursed through his veins like liquid fire. It pushed through his meridians like water from a broken dam, completely obliterating his Cultivation.

Through the haze of agony, Max dimly saw Losshnak standing over him, his form wreathed in golden light as he poured every ounce of his power into a final, defiant stand. Maverick swooped low, his cannon flaring again and again as he tried desperately to keep the sorcerers at bay.

But it was too little, too late. The Outsiders swarmed over the fallen warriors like a tide of living darkness, their claws and fangs tearing, rending, devouring. Max felt his consciousness slipping away, his life force ebbing with each passing second.

As the world faded to black, Max still felt a sense of contentment. This was death, yes, but it was also progress.

For they had shown that the Outsiders could be hurt, could be made to bleed. They had proven that even the darkest of foes had weaknesses, chinks in their armor that could be exploited. And they had forced the sorcerers to demonstrate another one of their weapons, even if only briefly.

It was a small victory, perhaps, in the face of such overwhelming odds. But it was a victory, nonetheless. And as Max embraced the oblivion of death, he did so with a sense of grim satisfaction, knowing that he had done his damn best.

The simulation ended, the mountainside and the horde of Outsiders fading away into nothingness. Max and Losshnak lay on the floor of the training room, their bodies intact but their minds reeling from the experience.

Twozerofive stood over them, his expression inscrutable. "Better," he said, his voice devoid of emotion. "But still not good enough. You wounded one of their sorcerers, yes. But you let your guard down, allowed yourselves to be drawn in and overwhelmed."

Max pushed himself to his feet, wincing at the phantom pain that still echoed through his body. "We know," he said, his voice heavy with exhaustion and frustration. "But we're learning, adapting. Each time we face them, we get a little bit stronger, a little bit smarter."

"Let us just hope you learn fast enough. Time is short," Twozerofive said dryly.

Losshnak nodded, his eyes hard with determination. "We will not rest until we have found a way to defeat them," he said, his voice a low growl. "No matter how many times we fall, we will always rise again."

"There he goes again . . ." Maverick muttered, earning a smack from Max.

Twozerofive regarded the warriors for a long moment, his black eyes gleaming and unreadable. "See that you do."

With that, the Gray turned and walked away, leaving Max and Losshnak to their thoughts. They had tasted the bitterness of defeat once more, had felt the sting of their own mortality in the face of an implacable foe.

But they had also glimpsed the possibility of victory, had seen that even the mightiest of enemies could be brought low through courage, skill, and sacrifice. And as they looked toward the battles ahead, they did so with a renewed sense of purpose, a fire in their hearts that would not be quenched until the Outsiders were nothing more than a fading memory.

For they were the champions of the ICCB—the chosen few. And they would not rest until the universe was safe once more, no matter the cost.

CHAPTER THIRTEEN

Cultivation Theoretics

Damn it!" Max hissed after another go in the simulator. It had gone slightly better yet again. Just like the last two attempts. But it was nowhere near enough. Still, Twozerofive seemed to have softened ever so slightly. The instructor no longer regarded them as a stain beneath his shoe—more just like particularly ugly bugs.

"AAAH!" Maverick shouted. "I can't take this. Let me back in. Let's go again. I need a win here badly, man."

Losshnak only shook his head solemnly.

"That was . . . adequate," Twozerofive said as he hovered above them. "It was a completely foolish and reckless death charge, but it was a good attempt . . . I will relay this recording to my superiors, and a potential reassessment of how many resources should be allocated toward this strike force, especially you two, will be filed."

Max perked up at that. "We did well?"

Twozerofive managed a curt nod. "Considering the stage of your Cultivation . . . almost destroying a sorcerer is . . . acceptable."

Max chuckled at the Gray's best efforts at not giving them a single compliment.

"Take these," Twozerofive said, and three objects appeared to float in midair in front of them. Max picked the item up and looked at it in his palm.

It was a thin cylinder the size of a pencil and seemed to be made of diamond. Max looked up at the Gray.

"This is a [**Karma Attractor**]," Twozerofive said. "Highly valuable. It will naturally make accruing Karma easier for you. And seeing as you both have negligible amounts, it will most likely give you some directly. Consume it."

Max and Losshnak shared a look and shrugged. Max threw his head back and swallowed the device. Seeing as Twozerofive didn't explode into a tirade about how much of an idiot Max was, he assumed he was consuming it correctly. After he was done, he helped Maverick with his.

"I hate that I don't have hands," Maverick grumbled.

"I guess you're still going to need me as your sidekick for menial tasks," Max said and allowed himself a little smirk.

"I hate that smirk more."

"Love you too, Mav."

The three of them were instructed to take a small break, eat, and then continue Cultivation. Max asked if they could use the Stonehenge array, but they were promptly declined. If truth was to be told, Max's meridians still ached.

So, Max and Losshnak sat down, and a small drone brought them both a hot meal. Max's dish was some sort of creamy pasta that smelled sweet and peppery, while Losshnak enjoyed a huge bowl of grilled meat.

Max's meal was so delicious, it made him involuntarily moan. Losshnak raised an eye ridge in response. However, immediately after digging into his own food, he started grunting in pleasure himself.

After their meal was done, Maverick blurted out a question he'd been meaning to ask Losshnak for quite a while now: "Why are you so cool with us?" Losshnak turned his head and considered his answer.

"We fought, yes," the giant lizard started. "But never of our own volition. Humans never committed crimes against my people. I bear no grudge, no blood feud with your people."

Max felt the same. He didn't choose to come to Alpha Ludus or to fight against anyone. He had been thrust into this reality and since then he had been scrambling to do his best. Losshnak was basically the same. They were all just people who had found themselves in an unfortunate situation.

"But didn't it piss you off to lose?" Maverick pressed on. Doesn't it piss you off, when your wife or your mate or whatever is needling you about losing to humans?"

"Yes," Losshnak said. "And yes. Why are you asking these questions?"

"Cause I would be pissed!" Maverick said. "We fought so goddamn hard, putting it all on the line, life and death. If I suffered such an epic defeat, I would never live it down. I would have rather stayed dead than brought shame to my entire species."

"Means less now, does it not?" Losshnak said dryly. Then he turned to Max. "Your companion is a petty person, is he not?"

Max burst out laughing. He laughed so long and so hard his stomach started hurting, and breathing became difficult. Maverick growled and blasted him with a little shot from his cannon. It exploded the nearby furniture and tossed Max on the floor a few yards away, but he kept laughing. Losshnak started laughing too, most likely at the absurdity of the whole situation. Finally, Max calmed down and wiped the tears from his eyes, as he walked up to Maverick and patted the floating disc.

"A little bit," Max said.

Max and Maverick left Losshnak to meditate in order to strengthen his meridians. Meanwhile, they headed to the library. Sure, Durum's book was great—surprisingly great, all things considered. But it had been written by a player on Alpha Ludus. They needed more.

The ICCB had equipped them with all of the best knowledge at their disposal.

Or at least all of the best knowledge that they're willing to share.

Max perused the shelves. The books weren't actually there in person. It was only a hologram. But when Max touched one of the backs of the books with a probing finger, a copy of it materialized behind him on a long steel table.

"*Distillation and Infusion of Super-mortal Herbs and Roots*," Max read the title. "Quite a mouthful."

"Blech," Maverick said. "Put it away. They're gonna feed us whatever pills they deem appropriate."

"Speaking of which," Max said, "how is that [**Karma Attractor**] sitting inside of you?"

"You know fully well," Maverick said irritably.

Max did, indeed. The diamond pencil device was *heavy*. It weighed his whole body down in a very physical, intimate way. It felt like Max's stomach was drooping into his crotch. He had to bolster his Cultivation to keep his body taut.

"At least you don't have to float all the time," Maverick said.

"No one is forcing you," Max said. "Just sit yourself down on that table."

"I'm—" Maverick started in a snappy tone. "Oh . . ."

Then he descended onto the long, steel table. Max shook his head as he turned back to the holographic bookshelf, where he continued browsing for something that could help them better understand the concept of Karma. He skimmed over titles such as *The Dao of Elements: A Guide to Elemental Cultivation* and *Spiritual Beasts and How to Tame Them*, but nothing seemed to quite fit what they were looking for.

Then, a slim, black book with the title *The Foundations of Karma* shimmering in silver letters on the spine, caught his eye. Max tapped the hologram, and a physical copy materialized on the steel table. He picked it up and started leafing through the pages, using [**Telekinesis**] to make the book float in front of him.

Cultivation is awesome.

"What should we be looking for?" Maverick asked as he hovered over Max's shoulder, letting out a subtle humming sound.

"I suppose something about how Karma works and how to use it," Max said and flipped a page.

"It had something to do with living according to one's Dao," Maverick said instantly. "I remember this very well, because you are hellbent on bringing ruin and destruction to our efforts. At least ever since we got into this facility you've been focused and forgot about the other stupid humans."

"Okay, let's not get our panties in a bunch," Max said. "But you're right. I have been more focused here."

"So, what you're saying is that I'm right and you're wrong?" Maverick declared.

"I'm not— Yeah, as always . . ."

"Another victory!" Maverick said gleefully.

"Are you sure you're not on the Dao of Ego?" Max muttered as he leafed through the tome, until eventually finding passages appropriate for a Diamond-stage Cultivator.

After some more perusal, Max finally found a passage that seemed relevant. As was their habit, Max read aloud what the book said:

Karma is the cornerstone of a Cultivator's path. It is the measure of their alignment with the fundamental forces of the universe, the gauge by which their progress and potential are judged. A Cultivator's Karma is not a passive force but an active one. It requires nurturing, Cultivation, and above all, a strong foundation upon which to build.

The Karmic Foundation is the bedrock of a Cultivator's spiritual progress. It is formed through active engagement with one's Dao, the principle that guides and defines their path. Only by living in accordance with their Dao, by embodying its essence in thought and deed, can a Cultivator hope to accrue Karma and start establishing a strong and stable Foundation. In some cultures, this Foundation is called the dantian. *It is a place within the spirit where Spiritual Energy gathers. Karma is used to infuse this energy, and thus grant large amounts of Power, Speed, and Control.*

"Huh," Maverick said. "So, our Karma points are used to fuel this Karmic Foundation thing?"

"Seems like it," Max said, nodding. "And we build the Foundation by engaging with our Dao, which for us is Destruction."

He looked down at the book again, his eyes drawn to a particular passage:

The Karmic Foundation is not built through idle contemplation or passive meditation. It is forged in the crucible of action, tempered by the fires of adversity and conflict. Only by facing the challenges that align with one's Dao, by overcoming the obstacles that stand in the way of its realization, can a Cultivator hope to lay the groundwork for true spiritual advancement.

"That's heady," Maverick said. Through their bond, Max could feel his buddy proverbially scratching his chin, trying to chew on the complex concepts the book had to offer. "So, how does this link to the Karma points we got?"

"It's here in the next passage," Max said.

Karma points are the quantifiable measure of a Cultivator's alignment with their Dao. They are earned through actions, thoughts, and intentions that resonate with the fundamental principle of one's path. These points serve as the fuel for the construction and fortification of the Karmic Foundation.

As a Cultivator accumulates Karma points, they can invest them into their Foundation, strengthening its stability and increasing its capacity to support their spiritual growth. The more robust the Foundation, the more readily a Cultivator can draw upon the universal forces that align with their Dao.

Once a Cultivator focuses their will on their Foundation, they will be able to use the True Framework to dilute the Karma points into it. This is a strenuous and slow process, and it is advisable to make use of any external help, devices, and/or elixirs available.

"So, it's like a spiritual piggy bank," Maverick quipped. "We save up our good deeds and cash them in for cosmic power-ups."

Max chuckled. "In a sense, I guess. But it's more than just doing good deeds. It's about embodying our Dao in everything we do. Living it, breathing it."

He turned the page, his eyes scanning the text.

It is important to note that the accumulation of Karma points is not a linear process. The universe does not reward simple, rote actions but rather the sincerity and depth of a Cultivator's engagement with their Dao. A single, profound act of alignment can yield far greater Karmic returns than a multitude of superficial gestures.

Moreover, just as Karma points can be earned, so too can they be lost. Actions or intentions that run counter to one's Dao will erode the Karmic Foundation, weakening its structure and limiting its capacity to support spiritual growth. A Cultivator must be ever mindful of their thoughts and deeds, lest they undermine the very bedrock of their Cultivation.

"Damn," Maverick said. "So, we have to watch our step. Make sure we're always on brand with the whole 'destruction' thing."

Max nodded, a thoughtful frown creasing his brow. "It's a balancing act. We can't just go around destroying stuff indiscriminately. It has to serve a higher purpose. Align with the fundamental principles of the universe."

"And what better purpose than taking out the Outsiders?" Maverick said, his voice *thrumming* with anticipation. "They're the ultimate embodiment of all the bad stuff, the antithesis of everything the universe stands for. Taking them down has got to be worth some serious Karma points."

Max considered this. Maverick had a point. The Outsiders represented a threat not just to individual worlds or species but to the very fabric of existence itself. Opposing them, thwarting their nihilistic agenda, was perhaps the most profound act of alignment a Cultivator of Destruction could undertake.

Destruction does not need to be bad, evil, or unfortunate. Destruction is cyclical. It exists so creation can exist. There needs to be a balance.

Max felt a surge of energy inside of him. He recognized it. It was an insight. It infused him with some power, but it was not enough to push them into another stage in Cultivation. Even Maverick didn't whoop, but Max could feel a rush of excitement through his buddy with their bond.

"You're right," Max said at last, closing the book with a decisive snap. "Facing the Outsiders head-on, pitting our Dao against theirs . . . that's how we build our Foundation or dantian or whatever. That's how we take our Cultivation to the next Level."

He stood up, his eyes gleaming with a newfound resolve. They had a clear direction. Max liked that. Now the rest would be easy . . . Well, simple at least. Max liked simple. Cracking simple was a matter of time and effort. Max might have been short on time, but effort he had loads to give.

Max put the book down.

"Let's talk to Twozerofive," Max said, his voice ringing with determination. "It's time we stepped up our game. No more simulations, no more training wheels. We need to get out there and start putting our Dao into practice."

Maverick hummed in agreement, his form shimmering with barely contained excitement. "Now you're talking! I've been itching for some real action. Let's go show those Outsiders what happens when they mess with the embodiments of Destruction."

Max chuckled at that as he watched the book dematerialize. Somehow it knew Max was done with it.

Together, they strode out of the library, Max's steps full of purpose.

Maverick's gleeful empowered energy was rubbing off on Max. He grinned with anticipation.

CHAPTER FOURTEEN

Using Leverage

Absolutely not," Twozerofive said. "Are you insane? Did you not get completely obliterated in the simulation?"

"How else are we going to get stronger?"

"With elixirs, the Cultivation array, meditation," Twozerofive said blandly. "The basics."

"It will not be enough," Max said.

"We do not know that," their instructor said. "But putting yourself in danger and risking losing the most valuable member of this strike force is beyond foolish. The answer is and will for the foreseeable future be no."

Max was definitely not pleased with that answer. But he was left bristling alone as Maverick followed the floating Gray, complaining, until Twozerofive put him in stasis and teleported away.

Max sat down then and there on the floor as he waited for Maverick's stasis to expire. He sensed someone watching and turned toward the library section. Kat was there, holding a big book. She noticed Max noticing and waved. Max waved back. She seemed to want Max to go to her, but he was not in the mood to indulge that at the moment.

I'm not taking no for an answer here. Time to abuse my "golden boy" status.

"Hey, Zoos Guys," Max called. "I need a favor."

It took some time, but a plastic, white jellyfish did appear in front of Max. It had a slight static buzz to it, and the voice was a little choppy, but it was much better than before.

[What can we do for you, Max?]

"I need to be able to fight the real Outsiders in order to develop my Dao."

The Zoos jellyfish went still for a while as it relayed Max's wishes to whatever entity governed voting in the Collective. Max wondered idly how many individuals would vote on the matter, if they could even be called that. However many it took, the decision was made after a few seconds.

[We understand. Your Dao and the development of its Karma is important for your growth. While expensive, we do have the means to teleport you to a planet where there is a war ongoing against the Outsiders.]

"Nice!" Max said and made a fist. He could feel Maverick's excitement through their bond.

[However, as you are, it is impossible.]

"What?"

[While calling you a "talented" Cultivator is an understatement, you have only barely crossed the threshold of super-mortal Cultivation. If you are taken to a battlefield, you will die.]

Max slumped. The Zoos were right for sure. He had been in the simulations enough to understand how dangerous it was. But he had to do something to increase his Karma.

"How much stronger do I need to be for you to teleport me?"

[There is not enough time. The Outsiders' scouting party will land on Alpha Ludus in two weeks. The cost of teleporting you back and forth alone is . . . substantial]

"Just hypothetically. If I could advance enough in a week or so, would you teleport me to train against the Outsiders in real combat?"

Silence followed. Max figured that was good. Outright refusal meant there would be no room to negotiate. This meant they were considering or calculating. Maverick floated silently next to Max, who leaned on him, resting an arm on his buddy's disc form.

[We ran the simulations. If you can advance sufficiently, it will be worth the cost and the risk. Know this, if you attempt this, you will not rest for a week.]

"Heh, that's all I wanted to hear."

[We have informed your instructor, the Gray who calls himself Twozerofive. We have instructed him to assist you in this endeavor. He said he would be happy to cause you great suffering.]

"Excellent. Any chance if Losshnak advances that you agree to take him too?"

[No. This offer is for you alone, and it is mainly because of your rare ability to fly at such a low Level. Most super-mortal Cultivators eventually develop some form of flight, but yours is very early. It will give you maneuverability. We must reiterate that this will be extremely dangerous. We will not be putting you into a simulation or an environment with a safety net. This is a war zone you are asking to participate in. There will be no last-minute teleportation out of danger if you happen to face peril.]

"I wasn't expecting special treatment," Max muttered.

[We are almost certain you had hoped for it.]

"Who wouldn't?" Max said and smirked.

[You have received plenty. We are happy with your progress, Max. Now we must depart. The Zoos Collective has taken leadership of the ICCB, which has increased our workload by 1400%. Our communications will be sparse, but we will contact you again if you happen to reach a sufficiently high Level of Cultivation within nine days. Good luck.]

With that, the plastic jellyfish blinked out of existence, leaving Max smiling. It wouldn't be easy. It would probably mean no sleep. But Max sensed Maverick's feelings. Just as he suspected, his buddy was fired up as well. They had a chance.

Who am I doing this for?

"I'm doing this for Number One," Maverick said and hooted. "And that's me, baby! Imagine how much more beautiful my form will become if I ascend further."

"I think I'm—"

"Imagine it!"

"Yeah, yeah," Max said. "You'll be the prettiest drone carrier on the planet."

"Ok, wow," Maverick said in a serious manner. "I want to be a drone carrier! Imagine me piloting a hundred drones shooting down destruction with rockets and lasers."

"It's not entirely—"

"You're not imagining it!"

Max laughed and shook his head. "Shut up for a second. I was trying to think."

Maverick grumbled but obliged. Max could sense his buddy was imagining himself as a majestic drone carrier ship.

Why am I so fired up? Who am I doing this for? Humanity? The ICCB? The universe?

Max laughed at that one. He couldn't even fathom the threat. He might be a mighty Cultivator with insane levels of power now, but he was still just a kid in his twenties in way over his head. In the grand scheme of things, regardless of his relatively immense power, he was an infantry grunt again. Max found he didn't mind that.

"Yeah," he said slowly. "I'm pretty sure I'm doing this for myself as well. I want to see what's at the other end of this road."

"We are going to be soooo awesome," Maverick said triumphantly.

CHAPTER FIFTEEN

More Array Training

S eems like you were not happy with my answer, and you went ahead and complained to my boss," Twozerofive said dryly as he hovered in front of Max. "Not that I am known to be petty, but it will be fun to watch you struggle and fail."

Max only stared at the Gray. He could feel the immensely powerful alien's spirit only faintly. Like he was an ant trying to comprehend a mountain. But that spirit did seem irritated. Max couldn't blame the guy. He had gone full Karen-mode on him.

I'd like to speak to your manager . . .

He chuckled to himself.

"You will not be laughing soon," Twozerofive said. "And take these pills. They increase pain tolerance and the ability to strain your meridians."

Two small red pills like ruby pearls appeared in front of Max. He took them and deposited one of them in Maverick's compartments and the other one under his own tongue. Then he went and sat down in the Stonehenge array.

Max settled into the center, his body *thrum*ming with anticipation. The red pill dissolved under his tongue, suffusing his body with a strange, electric sensation. It was as if every nerve ending, every meridian, was suddenly awake and alive, primed for the ordeal to come.

Twozerofive hovered at the edge of the array, his black eyes glinting with a slow-burning anger.

"You've got guts, human," he said, his voice low. "I'll give you that. But guts alone won't be enough to see you through what's coming."

Max met the Gray's gaze, his own eyes hard with determination. "I know. But I've got more than guts."

Twozerofive snorted, but there was a hint of approval in the sound. "We'll see," he said, his fingers moving in a complex pattern. "Brace yourself."

With a final, decisive gesture, the Gray activated the array. Instantly, Max was engulfed in a storm of Spiritual Energy, the air around him crackling with raw, primal power. It was like being caught in the heart of a thunderstorm, the very fabric of reality trembling under the onslaught.

Max gritted his teeth, his body rigid as he fought to absorb and channel the surging energy. It poured into him like molten fire, searing through his meridians, testing the limits of his pain tolerance. The red pill dulled the worst of the agony, but it was still a struggle to keep from crying out as his body was pushed to the brink of its endurance.

Maverick was a steady presence at the edge of Max's consciousness, the gun's spirit intertwined with his own. Max could feel his buddy's strength, his unflagging support, bolstering his own resolve. Together, they weathered the storm, their shared Dao a beacon of purpose amidst the chaos.

Time lost all meaning in the heart of the array. Minutes, hours, days—they blurred together into a ceaseless, relentless assault on Max's body and spirit. He lost count of the number of times he felt himself teetering on the edge of oblivion, his consciousness threatening to fracture under the immense strain.

But each time, he clawed his way back, his will indomitable, his purpose unwavering. He focused his mind on the image of the Outsiders, on the nihilistic darkness they represented. He let that image fuel him. The agony mounted, but Max held the image in his mind.

+1 Karma point

With each passing moment, Max could feel his Cultivation deepen, his Karmic Foundation growing stronger and more robust. The Spiritual Energy that had once threatened to tear him apart now flowed through him like a river— raging but full under his control, his meridians expanding to accommodate the influx of power.

+1 Control

Twozerofive watched from the sidelines, his expression inscrutable. But even he couldn't deny Max's progress, the sheer tenacity the human showed in the face of such overwhelming adversity.

As the array reached a crescendo, the energy swirling around Max like a cyclone of pure, unbridled potential, he felt something deep within him begin to shift. It was like a key turning in a lock—a final, decisive click that resounded through his entire being.

His Dao, the principle of Destruction that had guided his path, suddenly crystallized with a clarity and intensity that took his breath away. It was no longer just an abstract concept, a philosophical ideal. It was a tangible, living force, as much a part of him as his flesh and blood.

Max opened his eyes, his vision suffused with a brilliant, golden light. He could see the threads of Karma that wove through the universe, the intricate tapestry of cause and effect that bound all things together. And at the center of that tapestry, shining like a supernova, was his own Karmic Foundation, a pillar of unshakable strength and purpose.

He had done it. Against all odds, against the doubts and the pain and the sheer, crushing weight of the universe's indifference, he had forged his Foundation. He had taken the first, crucial step on the path to becoming a true embodiment of his Dao.

As the array powered down, the energy dissipating like mist in the morning sun, Max rose to his feet. His body was battered, his spirit raw and bleeding, but he had never felt more alive, more attuned to the fundamental forces that governed existence.

+1 Power

Twozerofive regarded him silently. "Adequate."

"Are you kidding me?" Maverick said. "Max didn't even pass out. That's nothing short of amazing!"

Max grinned, his expression a mix of triumph and exhaustion. "Told you," he said, his voice hoarse but steady. "I've got more than guts."

Maverick zipped around Max, the gun's form shimmering with barely contained excitement. Somehow the guy still had energy after going through the same wringer as Max had.

"That was epic!" he exclaimed. "I mean, I was there for the whole ride, but I'm amazing by default. But you did it too! I have to say, not bad for a sidekick."

Max chuckled, leaning on his friend for support as he stepped out of the array. His legs felt like jelly, his whole body *thrum*ming with the aftershocks of his breakthrough. But beneath the exhaustion, he could feel a new strength, a profound sense of clarity and purpose.

"We're just getting started, Mav."

Maverick hummed in agreement, his form vibrating with barely contained energy. "Damn right. They messed with the wrong embodiments of Destruction. I wanna show those sludge slugs what true badassery looks like!"

Together they slumped back toward the kitchen where Max would have one hell of a meal. Double portion of everything. He had earned it. A minute of respite before they returned to another bout of hellish training.

CHAPTER SIXTEEN

Idiot Savant

After the meal, Max and Maverick had some downtime, so they went into the library to do some further research into how to use their Karma points to infuse their dantian. As it turned out, it was a matter of finding the accumulated Karma inside of them and strengthening their spirit with it.

Considering his training had naturally increased his Power and Control, he found his speed having gone up one tick, from seven to eight. This was indeed not a video game screen but a representation of his power. He had three Karma points to infuse into his dantian. Max decided to dump it all into Power. To fight against the sorcerers and to actually wound them, they needed firepower. Maverick, unsurprisingly, agreed.

After they had done that, Max took a look at his Stats, and back to training they went before the sweat from the previous array training had time to fully dry.

Maximilian Cromwell
Stage: Diamond (low)
Dao: Destruction
Karma: 0
Speed: 7
Power: 13
Control: 10

Max and Maverick weren't done. Oh no. Despite Max lying on the floor, wiping a dripping sheen of sweat off his forehead, he struggled up. The other strike force members watched him, awestruck. Even Twozerofive seemed to raise a curious eye ridge. Maverick wobbled as Max braced against him to pick himself up.

"Again," Max said.

"Are you insane?" Kat shouted. "Look at yourself. There is no way you can go again!"

"Take a rest, Master Warrior," Losshnak said.

"They are right," Twozerofive said. "There is no way you can take the full brunt of the array again."

Max *tsk*ed in annoyance. Maverick growled.

"Just pump us with your fancy drugs or something. We can take it."

"It's not about your tolerance for pain," the Gray said dryly. "It is your capacity to receive Spiritual Energy. We cannot artificially raise that without damaging your baseline Cultivation."

Max mulled that over for a while. His meridians ached with pain and his head was swimming. But they had to do more. They had to *grow*.

Suddenly a lightbulb went off in his head.

"I have an idea," Max said. "It's a win-win."

"Let me see if I understand," Twozerofive said as he tapped his sharp chin with a long finger. "You want the others to sit in the Cultivation array to train themselves, and you want me to route a part of that power into you and your companion?"

"Exactly," Max said. His breath was still heavy and labored, but his manner was completely confident. "They can't take the full brunt of the array, and right now, neither can I. But if you could disperse or reroute the power, everyone might advance."

The Gray hummed. For once he didn't seem hostile. "It is indeed possible . . . The array was initially designed for you to utilize once you were already stronger, but this way . . ."

There was a greedy glint in Twozerofive's eyes. Max figured if their little strike force venture succeeded, he'd be getting a promotion.

"Very good," Twozerofive said, decisively. Maverick whooped at that. "I will be back shortly. I need some equipment we do not have here."

With that, their instructor blinked out of existence, leaving the strike force to themselves.

Kat approached and smiled. "You're always so extra lately. I don't remember you being like this back in the army."

"I wasn't," Max said. "I guess I needed greater than life-and-death stakes to kick myself into action."

"Seems to have worked," Kat said and sucked in her lips thoughtfully. "How could I tap into that?"

"Huh?"

"You can't," Maverick said.

"Tap into what?" Max asked.

"Into the endless well of willpower you seem to have gained," Kat said and brushed back a lock of hair behind her ear.

"I also must know, human," Ashkarassa said.

Max and Losshnak shared a look and smirked.

"Piss off, both of you," Ashkarassa said and punched Losshnak on the shoulder.

"This one is Plarag," the other insectoid said, the one with a lighter-brown carapace. "I am pleased to make your acquaintance. I am also eager to know how to evolve my mind."

Max looked back at them all and found himself stymied. Maverick spoke up.

"Like I said, you can't."

"Why not?" Ashkarassa said irritably and snarled at Maverick.

Max tried to think.

"Why do you guys think you suck so much more than we do?" Maverick said.

"Come on, dude," Max said.

Kat and Ashkarassa both snarled at Maverick, but the jerk only chuckled.

"Was it because we just so happened to get lucky over and over again?"

"Yes?" Kat suggested.

"Yes," Max confirmed with an empathetic nod.

"Of course not," Maverick said haughtily and floated above the other members of the strike force. Max noticed a slight wobble, but it was subtle. He couldn't blame the little bastard. He himself was still out of breath. But the Spiritual Energy he had received from the array *thrum*med inside him. It felt good. A promise of power to come.

"You see," Maverick said, "we have been molded by many things. For one, our bond . . . which, of course, has benefitted Max more than me, but I am a generous god. Sure, we had some fortunate experiences, but any one of you could have had those, if you *willingly placed yourself in them.*"

"What are you saying?" Slargi asked and leaned in closer, his mandibles clicking softly.

"You can't bootstrap willpower or whatever we have," Maverick said. "The reason you guys suck is because you aren't willing to put everything on the line. To go all in. Bet it all on yourself. Have absolute faith in the choice you make and do your best."

"I don't know about absolute faith," Max said quietly. "It was more like, 'Oh crap, I don't know what to do, okay let's go with this . . .'"

"Shhh," Maverick hissed. "I'm trying to do a thing."

There were some chuckles. Max smiled sheepishly. It was nice to have a small moment like this. But he still wasn't sure where Maverick was going.

"We have been Cultivating our shared mind for months. We are powerful because we never backed down. I refused. For Max, well, forgive him, but he has a simple mind. It simply never occurred to him that he could."

Max's jaw dropped.

"See, I wasn't kidding," Maverick said, deadpan. "He just doesn't seem to understand that he can back down or quit or go do something else. He just makes a decision and sticks with it. And, boy, does it work magic!"

"It is true," Losshnak said as he nodded thoughtfully. "Decisiveness is good. But I am decisive. So is my mate. *Everyone* here is decisive, or we would not be this powerful."

"*You* don't suck as much," Maverick admitted. "But the rest of you? Blech."

Kat gave Maverick the finger. Ashkarassa bristled. The two vulpines who had been only quietly observing so far shared an annoyed look with each other. Max tried to offer them an apologetic smile, but the female vulpine only sniffed and looked away when she caught Max's eye.

Prideful, that one.

"Let me try to explain this to you," Maverick said. "I swear, you guys are all almost as dumb as Max."

"Would it be possible," Plarag asked, "for you to instruct us without the insults?"

"No," Maverick said. "I'm not a charity. And, anyway, I deserve some enjoyment from this transaction, too, you know."

"Asshole," both Max and Kat muttered. They shared a look and smiled.

"When Max decided he needed to get stronger and challenge real Outsiders, he never questioned that. He never considered if it was a good idea. It never occurred to his dumb mind. He had made up his mind, and so the next step was just about how to get what he wanted."

"Why can't we just do the same?" the female vulpine asked and scowled.

"Honey," Maverick said in the most condescending tone possible, "if you could have, you would have. You just don't have absolute belief in your decisions. Max is an idiot savant. He is pure. His will is pure. There is no doubt in his mind that he has chosen the right path, nor is there any doubt that he'll get what he wants. He doesn't reconsider, he doesn't second-guess, he doesn't think, 'Oh, this is really uncomfortable, I guess we're not doing this today.'"

Max nodded to himself. Yeah, that seemed about right. But he had never thought about it like that.

Maverick sent a sneering pulse through their bond. *Idiot savant.*

"Shut up," Max muttered to himself.

"How is this useful to us?" the female vulpine asked.

"It *isn't*," Maverick said empathetically, but he couldn't keep the glee out of his voice. "But you idiots asked."

A chorus of growls, snarls, and ugly words erupted at Maverick. He only continued to laugh and floated up higher when Ashkarassa tried to grab him.

"We asked Max," Kat said, throwing a knife at Maverick. He dodged it easily.

"Suuuuure," Maverick said. "Ask him."

That stopped the commotion, and they all turned to Max.

He really tried. He went over what Maverick had just said and couldn't think of anything else to say. He gave the other strike force members a sheepish look and just shrugged.

Ashkarassa and Kat groaned. Losshnak only chuckled and shook his head ruefully.

"We will try to keep up," the strong Ishkarassi warrior said.

Twozerofive returned shortly after and produced two pieces of rope that seemed to be made of space itself. Each piece was black, blue, and purple, with small shiny stars scattered all over the dark background. He handed one of the ropes to Max and then looked at Maverick and considered.

"Would you be interested in a mechanical arm?" Twozerofive asked.

Max perked up at that. He was paying close attention to what Maverick was feeling through their bond. He seemed conflicted. Max knew that Maverick could use hands. Hands were . . . well, handy.

Maverick might have a point on that idiot savant thing . . .

"I absolutely refuse," Maverick said and huffed. "If in my future evolutions I acquire hands, I shall gracefully accept them, but for now, my form is perfect. Why would I mess with perfection?"

"I hope your future evolution doesn't involve a mouth," the female vulpine muttered under her breath. They were all Cultivators; they all heard her.

"Honey, I don't have a mouth in this form either," Maverick said as if he was talking to a particularly stupid five-year-old. "Shall I speak more slowly so your brain has more time to process?"

Damn.

The female vulpine growled with rage. Her hands conjured up white and yellow flames. Kerro, the male vulpine, put a hand on her shoulder, but she aggressively knocked it off.

"Really, honey?" Maverick asked dismissively. "What are you gonna do? Please, do show me the full power of a Ruby Cultivator . . ."

The vulpine prepared to throw one of her fireballs. Before she could, however, Twozerofive placed her in stasis with a flick of a hand. Maverick laughed gleefully and started flying circles around the now-frozen vulpine. She glared at the gun-disc with furious intent.

Max chuckled. Their ascension to super-mortal Cultivation had made his buddy *sassy*.

"Who wants to go first?" Twozerofive asked, as if nothing had happened.

"I will," Ashkarassa said and stepped forward.

"Hold this **[Heavenly Energy Transfer Module]** to your solar plexus," Twozerofive said to Max. "And figure out what to do with your companion."

Max nodded. He didn't need to think. It was fully intuitive. He looked up to Maverick, who immediately flew down and let Max sit on him. Max sat cross-legged and pressed one of the tubes up to his stomach and another directly in the center of Maverick's platform, between his legs.

Twozerofive observed coolly and gave a curt nod after Max gave him the thumbs-up. The Gray lazily flicked a finger, and the tubes attached to both of Ashkarassa's shoulders. She was now sitting in the middle of the array.

Max braced himself. He was still tired and sweaty, and his mind was fuzzy. But it was go-time. There would be pain. But it would make him stronger. That was why they were here. And this was the best way to accomplish it.

Okay, I'm starting to understand the idiot savant thing . . .

Max could feel something of a smirk through his and Maverick's bond.

"I will turn on the array now," Twozerofive said, and the Stonehenge formation went alight.

The surge of power which entered Max was much more manageable than expected. After all, it was shared equally between all eight members of the strike force. However, all of the other members flinched at the intensity of the Spiritual Energy entering their bodies. Only Losshnak seemed to be able to handle it. Max glanced at Kat. She was snarling to herself in a focused manner, her shoulder-length hair a black and sweaty curtain on her face. She noticed Max looking and her eyes sank into deeper focus; she held her face still, despite it twitching with pain.

"I will now reroute thirty percent of everyone's energy toward Max," Twozerofive said.

"I can handle this," Losshnak said.

"Just take twenty from me," Kat said.

"Same," Ashkarassa said.

"Only twenty from us, too," the chitinous insectoids said po.

"Wow," Maverick said sarcastically. "Everyone has a chip on their shoulder suddenly, huh?"

"Can't let you two hog all the glory and resources," the female vulpine said wryly.

Maverick hooted. "Ha! You'd better not take those words back. This array is no joke."

"Focus," Max muttered. The pressure was getting harder to stand as Twozerofive adjusted the energy reception of each of the strike force members.

Max focused his mind on his meridians. The energy flowed into them, filling them up. Max realized the Spiritual Energy he was receiving was still too much, even when shared with Maverick.

"We gotta release some of this," Max said between deep breaths. Large beads of sweat were forming on his forehead.

"Easy," Maverick said and rose into the air, revealing the great cannon under his disc form. He blasted a bolt of yellow and gray energy at the wall nearby. Twozerofive cast a particularly displeased glance at Max and Maverick. Max only shrugged. He was too busy dealing with the Spiritual Energy.

Max extended his will, transforming the pure Cultivation energy into a Framework technique. With his [Telekinesis] he started picking up the pieces of rubble left behind by Maverick's destructive shot.

It helped. The expenditure of Spiritual Energy made it easier to control the remaining energy. This was an intense fight for control, straining Max's mind and spirit. However, he could clearly feel his control increasing significantly. There was something benign and pure about the energy emitted by the array.

+1 Control

But it was getting more intense by the minute.

"I will adjust again," their floating instructor said.

"C-cut me down by half," the vulpine female said.

"Same here," the male vulpine said.

"I want it down by thirty . . . no . . . forty percent," Kat said weakly.

"I can keep going another minute or two," Losshnak said.

Crap.

After Twozerofive made the adjustments, it felt like Max's body had been set ablaze. The energy flowed into him like a crashing wave. There was no control, only the Spiritual Energy assaulting him. Max released a [Gravity Storm] into the kitchen area and routed all of the energy into it. It crushed all the chairs, tables, and utility devices. Maverick blasted a fusillade of energy at the nearby wall. Max could sense through their bond that his buddy was suffering an equal amount of pain but was too proud to say anything. Max was proud too, but pain was pain. They couldn't go on like this forever.

+1 Power

But Max knew that this was all on him. If he quit now, the rest of the strike force would follow as they couldn't handle the energy without him.

There has to be a way to keep me in the game . . .

Discharging the Spiritual Energy was not a viable solution, as it required Max to exert energy and focus. He needed something more subtle. He needed to control the energy input.

Only one way I know how . . .

Truthfully, Max didn't know, but he could theorize. His was a Dao of Destruction, so destroy he would.

Max reached inside of himself and focused on the incoming energy coursing through his meridians. They were already getting strained by the excess energy, which was searing through him with mounting intensity.

Through his own core, the base of his soul, his dantian, he summoned the innate Spiritual Energy within him. Instantly realizing what Max was doing, Maverick struggled to reach his own as well. But Max sent a flicker of that destructive energy, imprinted with their Dao, through the bond. Maverick got the gist of it.

They both worked in tandem, building a subtle flow of energy, which increased into a stream. The onslaught of Spiritual Energy from the Cultivation array was a massive crashing waterfall, which became heavier by the second, but the little stream that Max and Maverick started emitting through their meridians began to work.

It started to *destroy* the energy that was entering their bodies.

+2 Karma points

Max sighed out in relief. Now the energy was getting easier to control. Max let the destructive energy he emitted surge through his meridians and consume the energy coming in from the array. The pain was easing up, now only a moderate throb. Max let himself slump and felt Maverick relaxing through their bond too.

"I think I'm at my limit," Kat said between labored breaths.

"Might we request another lowering in intensity?" the brown-carapaced insectoid asked.

Both Losshnak and Ashkarassa were grunting, clearly exhausted but not about to complain.

Twozerofive, however, wasn't looking at them. He was looking at Max with an unreadable expression in his black eyes. Max felt a probing brush at his spirit. The energy of it felt cold. The little alien smirked.

"I think we will test the limits today," the Gray said.

Suddenly the intensity of the incoming energy exploded. Max's world was filled with white-hot pain that almost made him vomit. It subsided a notch but then started to slowly increase again. Max heard gasps beside him, but they seemed to be coming from far away. Now was not the time to pay them any heed.

+1 Power
+1 Control
+1 Speed

Max acted immediately. This was no waterfall he had to push against. This was the relentless might of an ocean. Max and Maverick called upon all of their Spiritual Energy reserves and transformed it into a purely destructive force, attacking the onslaught.

There was no time to circulate the energy through their meridians and try to integrate it. A reasonable amount of water was good. Too much water was poison. This was like that.

Max attacked the relentless amounts of energy inside of him with all of his might. He lost himself in creating destructive energy and pushing it into the energy from the array, making it dissipate with his will. All the while, the pain mounted.

Max imagined he was climbing a mountain. It was raining like hell. A hail of sharp ice. A wind determined to topple him. A climb so steep, he needed his hands to help him ascend. The ground beneath him was made up of small rocks, making every step unstable. All the while, his body was being pierced by a thousand needles.

+1 Power

Every step was a struggle, each worse than the last. But Max carried on, feeling Maverick's unyielding will beside him, climbing with him, pushing onwards for the sake of his pride and vanity. They were powerful together, and Max took strength from that. He pushed with his will, molding the destructive energy, enduring the pain. Where Maverick felt vainglory and was empowered by it, with Max it was something different.

But he still tapped into it, and it gave him great strength and a will to protect. Despite Maverick's protestations, it was there and it helped him push through. Oh, there were other emotions too. Pride, just like Maverick. A sense of duty. A will to push forward, so no one could tell him what to do. Not even the ICCB. And something even beyond all that. A distant feeling, but something his heart yearned for so deeply that it could have practically sung it out.

Max yearned for freedom. Freedom to decide his own fate. Freedom not to be controlled. Freedom to do as he pleased. Freedom to choose.

+1 Control

And through that, his will solidified. It took form. The free-forming energy became a destructive *intent*. With this intent, he pushed. He pushed against the world and ascended. The pain and effort was making him exhausted. He could feel that the energy was going to overwhelm him. But he pushed against it. His will was taking form. Max put that feeling into words and they gave him the fortitude he needed:

I will destroy all that stands in the way of what I want.

+2 Karma points

Max pushed against the onslaught, the energy of an ocean attacking him. For a moment he carried it, just as Atlas had carried the globe in the old myths. Suddenly, he felt a sense of surprise from someone probing his spirit. But before he could react, the ocean crashed down upon him again, and his world went black.

CHAPTER SEVENTEEN

No Free Lunches

Max woke up in bed. He seemed to be doing that a lot lately. He supposed that was how it went if you pushed yourself to the absolute limit every time.

"Damn straight," Maverick said. "We went hard, and we Leveled Up hard."

It was true. Max had acquired substantial gains in his Cultivation. But it had come with a great cost in the form of considerable pain. Max cast a glance at Twozerofive, floating around the portal array. Max was furious at him. And he must have sensed it, because just at that moment, he turned in the air and smiled malevolently down at Max.

"The little bastard . . ." Max muttered.

It was probably for the best. Twozerofive had probably done it for the benefit of Max's Cultivation. He should be grateful, but he sure as hell didn't feel it. The Grays had been his mortal enemies ever since he had come to Alpha Ludus. The whole of the ICCB was something of an enemy. He would not be their slave, no matter what.

But for now, they were also his benefactors. That was a difficult situation to try to parse in his mind.

"You think too much," Maverick said. "Just enjoy the ride. Look at the Stats screen."

Max did. He had to admit, he disliked Twozerofive a bit less after seeing the leaps and bounds he had made in a single session with the Cultivation array.

Maximilian Cromwell
Stage: Diamond (low)
Dao: Destruction
Karma: +4

Speed: 9
Power: 15
Control: 12

Amazing! Only now Max could access none of the power the Stats screen told him he had. He felt a dull throb in his meridians and dantian when he tried, but nothing happened. It was as if he had been reduced back to Quartz stage. He couldn't even assimilate the Karma into his dantian.

Max felt a flash of panic. Had something happened? Was that why the Gray had smirked at him? But they were on the same side. Was this some trick? Had Twozerofive conspired to take Max out with the array . . . ?

"Cool it, you paranoid psycho," Maverick said. He was lying still and wrapped in some strange mixture of cloth and plastic. "This is why you're the sidekick."

"Huh?" Max said.

"Take a look at the gizmo you have on," Maverick said.

Max looked down and noticed that he was wearing some sort of device. A soft harness, like a weight vest for running. It was black but had a red crisscrossing pattern in the chest area. On his wrists and ankles were cuffs of a similar design.

"Why did they put this on me?" Max asked.

"We aren't allowed to Cultivate right now," Maverick said. "Which really, really sucks. I'm not allowed to fly. I can't even move. It's been driving me insane. Can you imagine what it's like, Max? Not being able to move?! It's sooooo boring."

"Can't say I can," Max said. "So, does this mean we can't train? For how long?"

"Uh . . . About that . . ." Maverick said and chuckled nervously.

"It's bad, huh?" Max asked.

"It was worth it, though. We leapfrogged months of training in a few minutes. However, it got a little messy. Apparently, the Zoos guys are now the Big Cheeses. They came down here and ripped into our instructor here. I wish you had been up. It was a hoot."

"It worked out for us, right?" Max said.

"It did," Maverick said. "But Twozerofive took a massive gamble on us. The Zoos guys think he did it out of malice and tried to get you killed, to blame it on a training accident. Me? Personally, I think he was impressed by us and wanted to test our limits."

"Like any good teacher, huh?" Max said and looked at the floating Gray again.

As far as his experience with the Grays went, he would be more than willing to bet that this thing with the Cultivation array had been an attempt at murder—or at least to cripple him. But they had passed out. And all of the other strike force members were too busy focusing on their own training. Twozerofive could have easily just redirected all of the energy at Max and Maverick and crippled or killed them. Instead, he had shut down the array.

"Seems to me he's just an asshole," Max said. "But an ally nonetheless."

Maverick scoffed. "If you say so."

"How long do we have to recover?" Max asked again.

"Well . . ."

"Maverick," Max said firmly, "don't screw with me."

"Technically we don't need to recover," Maverick said, speaking in a high voice. "Twozerofive said that we could *technically* take off these limiters and continue our training. It's just that we *technically* shouldn't."

"I don't like that word," Max said with mounting irritation. "Stop screwing around. Give it to me straight."

"Remember when I said we leapfrogged months of training . . ." Maverick said. "Well, it's gonna take months of recovery, too."

Max's heart dropped into his stomach.

"MONTHS?!"

"Don't yell at me," Maverick said. "I'm pissed too."

"We can't wait around for months with our thumbs up our asses."

"One of those rare moments I'm glad I don't have hands . . ."

"Why aren't you more pissed . . . and worried?" Max said. "All of our plans are screwed! What in damnation are we gonna do now?"

"What in damnation?" Maverick asked, clearly aghast. "Really, Max? The other strike force members are gonna stop thinking we're cool real fast if you talk like you're in an old-timey Western."

"I'm not in the mood for your bullshit right now, Mav," Max growled. "Why aren't you worried?"

"Heh, well, it's obvious to everyone but you, as always."

"In English?"

"I'm not worried, because you're you."

Max stopped for a second. He couldn't help but feel flattered. Maverick wasn't exactly known for his lavish praise. Then Max thought for a second and found himself pissed off again.

"Are you shoving this whole thing in my lap again?"

"Well, *technically*, I don't have a lap, you see."

"You're just going to sit around like an asshole and wait for me to fix the problem?"

"Yup," Maverick said gleefully. "You got me."

"And what if I refuse to do anything about it?"

"Uh-huh," Maverick said, unconvinced.

"Screw it," Max said. "You get to figure it out this time, buddy."

Max huffed and laid back on the bed. After a few minutes of stewing, he found that he had had enough waiting. This wasn't for him. It was driving him crazy. He couldn't just sit idly by. But damn it, that smug little bastard needed a lesson. He would have to just bide his time.

And do what exactly? I can't train.

Max thought for a moment. And then he got an idea. It wasn't a particularly great one, but it was better than nothing. Max tried to get out of bed. If he couldn't train, he would study. There was still far too much he didn't know about Cultivation for super-mortal stages. He might as well brush up on theory if he couldn't train. It would be boring. Maverick would be even more bored and drive him crazy. But what else was there to do?

But unfortunately, Max's body would not comply. He could move his hands and head. But his hips, core, and legs? Not a chance.

"How about we rest?" Maverick suggested, a smug smile embedded in the question.

Max scoffed.

"Heh, didn't think so," Maverick said.

"Shut up," Max said. "I just want to study. I'm not about to fix our problem. That's on you."

"Sure," Maverick said. "Keep telling yourself that."

"Why are you so sure?"

"Because I know you, Max," Maverick said haughtily. "You're going to get bored, you're going to want to do something about it, and then your mind will come up with some whack idea, and you'll have no choice but to execute it. That's just how you work. Idiot savant, remember?"

"Screw. You."

"You might as well start cooking up a plan to kill time."

"I'm not doing that. I'm going to study," Max said firmly.

"There is one itsy bitsy problem, though. *We can't move.*"

"Yeah, I noticed," Max said. "Do you know what that means?"

"No," Maverick said immediately. "No, I don't."

They shared a mental bond. Max knew he knew exactly what he meant.

"I think you do," Max said, allowing himself to grin. "I think you should do it."

"I don't know what you're talking about," Maverick said.

"We are going to have to—"

"Don't say it!"

Max savored the words. "Ask for help."

"Noooooooooooooooooo!"

Shortly after, Max accepted Kat's offer to carry them to the library when she came to check up on them.

"I can't believe you guys push yourselves so far," she said wistfully as she carried Max in her arms. It was a little embarrassing, but what else could they do? Maverick was being dragged on the floor by the end of a rope. His indignant expletives and threats echoed through the whole compound, until Twozerofive appeared above them, regarded them with distaste, and cast a spell that all but silenced Maverick, so now only indignant muffled noises could be heard behind them as Max and Kat spoke.

"I think I just had the perfect storm from the start. I needed to find meaning in life, and protecting humanity seemed like a motivating goal," Max said.

Kat scoffed. "Your answers are just the worst."

"What do you mean?"

"I mean, I think Maverick's right," Kat said.

Maverick's muffled noises seemed to take on a tone of smugness. Max could feel it through their bond, but even Kat could tell, because she looked back, scowled, and yanked on the rope around her hand.

"After I got my bearings and wasn't in full survival mode, I wanted to help too," Kat said. "I hunted game for the settlement, disposed of threats, even ventured to the Dreadlands to hunt for supplies."

"Just like I did," Max said.

"Yeah," Kat said. "But somehow it just wasn't the same."

"Why are you beating yourself up for it?" Max asked. "You are literally the second most powerful human in existence."

"Ahem," Kat said and nudged Max, "right now, *I'm* the most powerful one."

"Yeah, yeah," Max muttered. "Thanks for carrying us."

"What was that?" Kat asked, a smirk playing across her lips as she looked forward.

"I said you're alright, Kat."

"Damn straight I am," she said as they arrived at the library section. "Where do you want to be put down?"

"Against the wall over there," Max said.

"How will you be able to read, though?" Kat asked as she violently yanked Maverick next to Max, banging the disc against the wall before untying the rope. Maverick was still under Twozerofive's spell, and the intensity of his anger was clear despite being muffled.

"I can use my **[Telekinesis]**," Max said.

"Wait, did you even need me carrying you?"

"Maybe," Max said and smirked. "Maybe I'm just into being carried."

She blushed slightly, even though she realized it was a joke. "Shut up."

"Anyway, thanks, Kat."

"Yeah, anytime," she said. "Say, I'm not much of a bookworm. How should I go about using this library during my downtime?"

"Right now you just need to focus on your insights, namely the [**Break-through Insight**]," Max said. "There's bound to be plenty of books on the topic here. Ask Twozerofive."

"Right, got it," Kat said, her face scrunched up in thought. "I suppose I'll just come sit next to you and browse through a few books. Everyone else is meditating and expanding their meridians, but honestly, I don't need that. I need my insights."

"What is your Dao about?" Max asked.

"That's kind of like the flavor of my Cultivation, right . . . ?"

"Uh . . . right," Max said. "You could say that. What were your previous insights about?"

"Protecting people," Kat said.

"Oh," Max said and smiled. "How noble and valiant of you."

"Shut up."

"Actually, I'm impressed," Max said. "It isn't my Dao, but something like that drove me to become so strong."

Kat grumbled and gave Max a side glance as she sat next to him, hugging her knees, chin angled down in thought.

"I feel like I'm stuck," she finally said, scuffing the floor with her boots.

"What was the last insight?" Max asked. "Do you remember what you were doing and where you were?"

"Fighting against the Outsiders when the barrier broke," she said. "I swore I would fight to protect others, even if it costs me my life."

"Kat the Noble," Max mused. She punched him in the shoulder.

"Well, which one of those feels like it hit closer to home?" Max asked after a good chuckle.

"Which one of what?"

More muffled noise came from Maverick.

Max smiled. "Maverick wants you to know that he appreciates the superior prowess your mind is capable of."

Kat flipped Maverick the finger.

"Do you think the insight was profound and meaningful because you swore to offer your life, or because you swore to fight?"

Kat was silent for a while as she mulled it over. Then her eyes went wide, and she looked up. "Oh. OHHHHHHH! So that's how it works?"

Maverick struggled to let himself be known. Max decided not to convey the message.

"It's about fighting," Kat said, excitement mounting in her voice. She got up and nodded to herself as she balanced on her heels. "Oh, shit. I get it now. I think . . . I gotta go."

"Glad I could help," Max said and smiled.

"You're the best," Kat said. "I'll come check up on you here later, to make sure you're alright."

"I'll be fine," Max said. "You better not come back before some major-league breakthroughs."

"You got it. Watch me surpass you."

Max laughed and nodded in encouragement. Kat flashed him a rare smile back before waving and going off on her way. Max let his smile linger for a moment before he was brought back to his usual focused state. It was time to research.

CHAPTER EIGHTEEN

Studying Intent

Max started grabbing books from the library shelves through **[Telekinesis]**. Their topics included meditation techniques, preparing Cultivation food, appreciating the philosophy and existentialism of following one's Dao, and more. None of that interested Max. What he wanted was to have a better understanding of what he had done. How he had managed to destroy Spiritual Power itself. He was sure that if he could figure it out, it was a technique he could develop further.

Eventually he found a heavy leather tome. On the cover was a title etched in the most perfect cursive Max had ever seen: *The Basics of Super-mortal Cultivation: Dao, Karma, and Intent.*

Max opened the book with his **[Telekinesis]**, then using it to leaf through the pages, and skipping sections dedicated to understanding one's Dao or accruing and developing Karma. He had a basic understanding of these concepts already. He was rather driven to learn more about Intent, for he was fairly certain this book could answer his burning questions.

Finally, he landed on what he was looking for, and he started reading with great gusto:

When pursuing the art of Cultivation, one will find themselves wanting to exert their power in a more profound and pure way, possible through the means of enacting the abilities the Framework has granted us. The Framework is a wonderful weapon, giving us specific tools for our needs. These form the basis of our abilities.

But as one develops into the higher echelons of the super-mortal stages, they will find themselves wanting to break free from the boundaries set by the Framework. Their will could challenge Heavens themselves, but they find their abilities lacking. For that, we must find a channel through which we can influence the world around us.

While raw power in terms of the dantian's ability to hold Spiritual Power, and the meridians' ability to conduct it, is certainly a way to measure strength between Cultivators of the Diamond stage, Intent is another.

It is a subtle art—the act of transforming pure willpower into Cultivation power. Let us look at an example of the power that Intent might hold: Take Durian Stormundo, one of the few people who managed to crystallize their Diamond-stage Cultivation; he was almost able to ascend to the Celestial stage in the year 12055 after the Outsiders entered our reality. The Framework had granted him a [**Beastmaster**] Class, and he could command all manner of animal. Of course, he also had an ability called [**Dominate Animal**]. The basic spell granted the user the ability to control a wild animal with ease. However, by using his Intent infused with his Dao of Command, Durian managed to spread his will across a whole planet and engage thousands of beasts in the land and the sea to aid him in a valiant last stand against the onslaught of the Outsiders as they descended on his home planet.

As you may have gleaned from this anecdote, it is indeed our Dao which defines our Intent. This is why developing one's Dao through their Karmic actions will inadvertently strengthen Intent. Think of it this way: developing his Dao granted Durian Stormundo the ability to spread his will across the continent, engaging the minds of thousands of beasts. But practicing the application of his Intent gave him the ability to give further instructions, sometimes very intricate ones. This allowed the beasts to form tactics and formations, instead of just mindlessly attacking in a single horde.

The moral of the story is that it pays dividends to practice both. Many Cultivators will neglect the practice of their Intent. Of course, how powerful one's Intent may be is dependent on one's Dao. If one's Dao simply isn't suitable for Intent training, it is better to find strength in simply bolstering one's Dao through Karmic actions. But this will grow difficult over time, and it isn't difficult to pick up the low-hanging fruits of Intent training.

So how does one go about increasing their command over their Intent? This is an apt question and one that is easy to answer. The beginning of a Cultivator's Intent training is simple. One begins via the Framework.

Once Durian Stormundo reached a bottleneck in his training in the Diamond stage, he stopped for five decades to hone his Intent. The principles are described in better detail in the man's memoirs, from which these notes have been taken.

Durian Stormundo started with a very specific practice to start applying his Intent. He picked a single beast of the forest and used the most basic ability granted to him through the Framework, [**Dominate Animal**], on it.

The details of how to infuse a spell with Intent are obscure and difficult to articulate. It is best for the Cultivator to discover it themselves and follow their instincts. But here is a basic principle: pick the most-simple or most-used spell or ability in your *arsenal granted by the Framework. Learn to infuse it with your Intent, drawn from your Dao. It will change the nature of the spell or ability or grant it additional effects.*

The additional benefit of developing one's Intent is that it is seen as a Karmic action by the Framework. It is theorized that whatever system governs Cultivation understands that developing one's Intent is done to live in accordance with one's Dao. It is impossible to invoke one's Intent if it does not happen through a Cultivator's Dao. This is why it is impossible to change the nature of one's Intent. If you have a Dao of Creation, you are limited to only doing creative things with your Intent. If you possess a Dao of Trickery, you can only use it for such purposes. But when you do, your Karma increases. Not always, but enough to make the training of Intent worthwhile simply to increase the raw power of a Cultivator.

"Alright," Max said slowly as he put the book away. He undid the **[Telekinesis]**, and the heavy tome thudded to the floor with a resounding smack. "That's enough theory for me, so I know for certain that it was more than enough for you, Mav."

Maverick said nothing as he was busying himself with sulking. Max was fairly sure Twozerofive's muting spell had worn off by now, but Max's buddy was in the mood for silence. Max was careful not to say, think, or feel anything, lest that silence be broken.

"Hey!" Maverick exclaimed. "Where is my sympathy?!"

Damn it.

"Have you considered that you get muted by our great and benevolent instructor because you are insufferable?" Max suggested.

"They hate me, cause they ain't me," Maverick said.

"The Dao of Arrogance is strong in this one," Max said. "You would have made a great rap artist on Earth."

"Speaking of Dao," Maverick said, "how do we go about this Intent business?"

"I think it's fairly simple," Max said. "I use **[Telekinesis]** to get a feel for it, and you use your cannon blasts and infuse that with the Intent of Destruction."

"That sounds about right," Maverick said. "Only one problem, though. We have these blast-darned, gosh-damned, stupid limiters on us."

"We do," Max admitted. "That is kind of a problem. I wonder if we can take them off. I feel like I'm completely fine."

"Uh huh," Maverick said. "You sure?"

Max channeled his spirit, his meridians, his dantian. They were still kind of beat up. "Eh, I'm fine."

"Damn straight," Maverick said. "Me too. And I want to move."

"I know, right?" Max said.

"But Twozerofive probably won't see it that way," Maverick said and grumbled. "I feel like the old grouch is trying to teach us a lesson here."

"We can't have you learning common decency," Max said and shook his head gravely. "That means we only have one option left."

"For shame," Maverick said with faux regret. "We are truly unruly, never learning from our mistakes."

"Self-awareness is overrated."

"Truer words have never been spoken," Maverick said solemnly. "Now Karen this shit up."

Max did. He called the Zoos Collective.

CHAPTER NINETEEN

Negotiations and Debts

It wasn't long before the Zoos Collective jellyfish arrived, bobbing up and down in the air as per usual.

[**How may we assist you, Max?**]

"Our instructor put these limiters on us. We can't train."

The Zoos jellyfish stood still for a moment, most likely assessing the situation and possibly contacting Twozerofive and having a brief discussion. Finally, the avatar spoke again.

[**It seems you two have exerted yourselves to the point where your bodies need time to rest and heal.**]

"That is out of the question," Max said immediately. "There is no time for that. There has to be a spell or an ability or some Item that we can use to recover faster."

[**There are potential methods, but you have to understand that we have already poured a considerable amount of resources into developing you, and using more will result in weakening some other process involved in our galaxy-spanning line of defense against the Outsiders.**]

"I know," Maverick said. "Just put it on our tab."

"Our what?" Max asked.

"Our tab," Maverick repeated. "You're going to weigh us down with some bullshit contract that makes us a debt-slave for a few hundred years, right? Just make the debt that much larger."

The plastic jellyfish hummed, clearly considering the idea. Max knew that some part of the collective was engaged in a vote right now, to decide whether or not it was a viable option.

Max was worried about this tab thing, and Max asked Maverick what he was up to through their [**Divine Soulbond**]. In response, Maverick sent a pulse of emotion that was effectively the equivalent of slapping Max's across the cheek. Maverick told him that had no intention of being indebted to the Zoos Collective or ICCB. They would simply take advantage of the fools now and figure it out later when they were strong enough to negotiate on better terms. They hadn't signed anything just yet.

Maverick, you sly bastard. Remind me to never get on your bad side.

Then the jellyfish spoke again:

[**We find this acceptable. However, it is our prerogative to include a running interest on any and all Items that you deem necessary to purchase through the debt contract like this. Additionally, we will have to enforce a preliminary contract that will bind you to pay for this Item and the interest on it. As per our previous agreement, we will not enforce a fully binding contract before the threat on Alpha Ludus is resolved but consider this a pre-contract. For now, it will only include the incurred costs by teleportation and use of [Karmic Restoration Crystal]. Do you find this acceptable? If you do, simply say the words "I accept," and the contract will be effectively signed by you.**]

Max thought about it for a long time, staring at the floor tiles in front of him in silence. He had no intention of spending a few hundred years indebted as a mercenary in the ICCB's stupid wars. He wanted to help them, but he would do it on his own terms. He and Maverick would not be slaves.

However, in order to have a say in such things, Max needed to be powerful. If you didn't have the strength to negotiate, you had no business dictating your fate. You would only be tossed around by the mighty. Signing this deal might be risky. It *was* risky. Max didn't even know how expensive this Item would be. But he didn't want to stop. He wanted to train and practice his Intent. He needed to be as strong as possible, and he would do what it took. He would find a way to pay off the debt. He asked Maverick once more, but his buddy had already decided. He wanted to scam the Zoos Collective and the ICCB.

Run a scam on the single most powerful entity in the universe? Sounds just up our alley.

"I accept," Max said.

The plastic jellyfish hummed, and Max got the impression that they were pleased with the decision. A green floating screen appeared in front of Max with the contents of the contract.

[We hereby acknowledge the pact that Maximilian Cromwell has formed with us, incurring a debt of 21,500 official ICCB credits. This amount and any amount added will accrue an annual interest of 16%. The default—]

"Sixteen percent?!" Max asked in shock. "That's preposterous."

[It is the wartime standard. As we were saying. The default method of payment for this debt is work as a contracted mercenary for the war effort, but other methods of payment can be discussed and agreed on upon request.]

The Zoos Collective jellyfish droned on for a while. Max wasn't interested in listening. The short of it was that he was getting royally screwed, and if he didn't figure something out or straight-up scam the ICCB, the interest would ruin them. The Zoos sure were done with running Max on charity. They wanted him in a binding contract.

I will not be anyone's property. But for now, I'll play along.

It only took a few seconds for Max and Maverick to be healed. First the Zoos jellyfish removed the limiters on their bodies, then a floating white crystal appeared and flashed, enveloping them in a warm, bright light. Max felt his meridians starting to heal, the aching pain lessening with each second. His dantian, the well of his power, was being cleansed. It was like a full factory reset on his body and spirit. The medicine, **[Karmic Restoration Crystal]**, might have been expensive, but it sure as hell was effective. It didn't only recover his exhausted spirit. He was completely healed. Any residual fatigue in his mind and body was now fully gone. And that fatigue sure accrued fast as hell when one Cultivated. This was a huge boon. Now Max wouldn't have to strain his willpower to push further. He had reserves again.

It was just what he needed right now.

Yeah . . . This was worth it.

[This concludes our business here. We are sorry to not provide further company or instruction, but right now, as we are the head of the ICCB, we are excessively busy. The path you are taking is the correct one, and we look forward to watching you achieve great progress in training your Intent. Your instructor, Twozerofive, has been informed of the discussion we

have had, and we have instructed them to aid you in any way necessary for you to enjoy the maximum benefit of your healed body. Now, proceed. Goodbye.]

Max nodded and cracked his knuckles. Maverick jolted up from the ground. It was time to go hard again. Time to practice destructive Intent.

CHAPTER TWENTY

Practice Makes Perfect

Max emerged from the compound to get some fresh air. On his way, he met with both of the vulpines. The woman was still full of pride and didn't want to speak, but the male was enthusiastic and eager to learn from Max.

"How should we train?" Kerro asked. "It feels like training for meridians isn't getting us fast-enough results."

Max brushed at the vulpine's spirit. Low Ruby stage. Was there really no one stronger out of his whole species?

"You should look into the Insights. There are several to be found, and they are free progress. You also need them when you get to Diamond stage, because they're directly related to your Dao."

"My Dao?" Kerro asked.

"It's essentially the reason you're a Cultivator," Max said. "But don't focus on that for now."

"Just find your Insights," Maverick said impatiently. "Nothing more, nothing less. Focus on finding them and work your way toward the [**Breakthrough Insight**]. I don't know if you rabble have entered the simulation yet, but you're basically useless to us if you don't break into Diamond."

Kerro's face fell, but he nodded solemnly at Maverick. The female growled. A bright orange fireball started swirling in her hand, but Kerro went over to her and grabbed her wrist, sharply hissing something.

"I apologize for Rakii's uncouth behavior."

"Don't tell them my name," she snapped.

Max waved a hand. "It's nothing."

"Yeah," Maverick said. "We don't care. She can't hurt us anyway."

Max gave Maverick a look and said nothing.

Kerro heaved a sigh of relief while Rakii looked more livid than ever. The fireball in her hand flared up violently for a second, but then she snuffed it out.

"Let me know if you need any more pointers," Max called out as he walked away. "But focus on Insights."

"Will do!" Kerro called out. "Thank you."

Max and Maverick walked away at a leisurely pace.

"Why aren't we hurrying to train?" Maverick asked. "If your results didn't speak for themselves, I'd be asking what this time-wasting is about. You always do this."

"It's mental preparation," Max said. "I'm taking in a moment of peace."

"Does that help?" Maverick asked. "Wouldn't it be better to just focus on a life of training and fighting?"

Max mulled it over as they walked. The compound was on the southern end of the planet, and it seemed that they were at the edge of a savannah. There were short trees in a sea of dry, yellow ground, with small patches of grass here and there, and a pond whose waters gently rolled in the soft winds of Alpha Ludus. A pack of tiny zebra-like creatures with green bodies and yellow stripes were drinking from the pond, swishing their tails at the insects flying about them.

"No, it's better this way," Max said. "These little moments before a plunge into a battle are kind of like checkpoints in a game, I guess," Max said.

"That sounds extremely stupid," Maverick said.

"I've come a long way," Max said and stopped to watch the zebra's drink. "I like to think about how far I've come without quitting. Always pushing forward. Always making sure I can do my best to win."

"Yeah?"

"I enjoy these moments because they bolster my pride and sense of achievement. They help me appreciate how powerful I've become."

"Damn straight," Maverick said. "I suppose that makes sense. I do that too."

"You do that every waking moment of your life, you little shit."

"Hey now!" Maverick said, offended. "Pride is a powerful thing, and it needs to be cherished."

"You're right on that," Max said. "It's something I've only recently come to appreciate. Through pride, one can keep their head high and face whatever comes. Having growing pride in yourself makes all the struggle worth it."

"So, you finally admit you're doing all this Cultivation for yourself and not to protect anyone."

Max chuckled. "There's a saying on my planet. It goes something like this: Everyone has two reasons for doing a thing. The noble reason and the *real* reason."

Maverick hooted. "I like that! But I'm not one to fool myself. My reasons are noble and true. Nothing is more noble than aspiring to becoming the most powerful being in the universe."

Max shook his head and laughed. "Never change, Mav. But come on now. Let's go figure this Intent business out."

Max concentrated on the subtle feeling of his Dao. It was all about him, of course, an integral part of his being. But calling on it at will was quite a different thing.

A broken stump of a tree lay before him, cracked from the base by wind or lightning. Max had a clear memory of how he had managed to wipe out the excess Spiritual Energy from his body by calling upon his Intent. But now he didn't seem able to get it back. He tried reaching for it forcefully, commanding his Dao and his very being to manifest that destructive Intent again.

Nothing happened.

Max turned to Maverick. "What should we do?"

"You're asking me for advice?" Maverick said in mock shock. "Why, I'm honored."

"Shut up and be useful."

"Well . . ." Maverick said, dragging the word out. "I have a theory."

"I'm listening."

"The Intent needs to be destructive, so it needs to destroy, right? So, when you were struggling with the Cultivation array and the energy flooding into your body, you *needed* to destroy it. If you hadn't, you would have lost. But here you are trying to attack this poor old tree stump. You don't *need* to destroy it, you just *want* to."

A revelation hit Max. This dumb little disc could be onto something. Maverick picked up on the vibe through their bond.

"Of course I'm on to something," he said haughtily. "You can't use Intent here because you're you. You need intensity. You need competition. You need stakes. This is just too boring for you."

"Damn it, Mav," Max said. "You might be right."

"I'm always right. So, what do you want to do next?"

"Well, it's a stupid idea, but I have one," Max said.

"Ooh, I love stupid ideas. Let's do it."

"Alright," Max said. "We need to talk to Twozerofive."

CHAPTER TWENTY-ONE

Practice Bout

Y ou want to do what?" Twozerofive asked skeptically.

"Fight against all the other strike force members," Max said. "I need them attacking me, putting me in danger."

"It is more likely you will put them in danger," Twozerofive said. "But I do think this is a good idea. It is simply . . . unorthodox."

"That's how we like it, baby," Maverick said and excitedly spun around in the air.

"This is a good opportunity for the strike force to practice real combat," Twozerofive said. "But you have to feel real threat. I assume you mean to engage your Intent. That is why I won't be allowing you to fly in this module."

"Wait . . . what?" Maverick asked. "What am I supposed to do, then?"

Twozerofive shrugged, and a mean little smile tugged at his thin, gray lips. "Figure it out."

Twozerofive left a thoughtful Max and a grumbling Maverick to their devices.

"How the hell am I going to do anything if I can't fly?" Maverick asked, fuming.

"I can use [Telekinesis] on you," Max said.

"You can, but it's so . . . demeaning!"

"You'd rather lay on the ground like a piece of junk metal?"

"No . . ." Maverick muttered. "But this is beneath my station."

"He's doing it on purpose, cause you're a jerk," Max said.

"While true," Maverick admitted, "this limitation does make sense. We would wipe the floor with them if we were able to fly."

"True," Max said. "Which means they couldn't put us in any meaningful danger, and we would obliterate them, giving them no chance to grow and learn."

"I hate to admit it, but that Twozeroguy knows what he's doing," Maverick said.

"Sure looks like it," Max said distractedly. His mind was running through plans for how to engage in battle without flying.

It had been a long time since Max wasn't able to use flight as an advantage in fights. At least he could still maneuver deftly and quickly with [Tether] and [Telekinesis]. Those two abilities would be the basis of his strategy. They would give him the mobility he needed. It was probably best to keep Maverick on the ground most of the time and have him come up at opportune moments to shoot a few blasts of destructive energy at their opponents.

Opponents, huh. Feels weird. I've only had enemies until now.

Max didn't know the full extent of the abilities the other strike force members had, but it didn't matter. They would put pressure on him, and he would attempt to strike them down using his Intent. Now it would be harder. The battle situation would be more hectic and chaotic than his solitary tests. Additionally, now the destructive Intent would have to leave his body instead of swirling inside of him, looking for targets.

If this doesn't work out, I'll just ask Twozerofive to kill me. I'm sure he'd gladly oblige.

Maverick let him think and floated along until the two of them reached the edge of the sand pit. There would be nowhere for the two of them to escape or hide. It would be a full-on fight-to-the-"death" until there was only one side left standing.

Seven against one. But most of them are only at Ruby stage.

Max jumped down. He landed softly. The arena reminded him of all the gladiator movies he had ever seen. He explored the area, enjoying the chance to know the terrain before the battle for once. However, there were no tricks or secrets to be found. Max wondered if this bout would be enough of a challenge. Maybe he should have asked Twozerofive directly. It would have been bold, bordering on arrogant. But if this match turned out to be a wash . . .

Max looked up and found that it might not have been as boring as he had initially predicted.

All of the strike force members gathered at the edge of the arena. All of them were wearing strange blue attire that clung to the contours of their bodies like wetsuits. They gleamed with light and rippled softly as if small waves were cresting up and down under the sleek material. Max brushed his spirit at Kat who grinned triumphantly down at him.

She was at Diamond stage.

Surely not.

"Oh shit," Maverick said quietly. "You're really gonna need to pull a rabbit out of your ass with this one."

"Rabbit out of my hat," Max corrected.

"Nah, this situation won't be resolved with a mere hat-rabbit. You're gonna need an ass-rabbit."

Max brushed against all of the other strike force members' spirits. Losshnak was Diamond stage too, almost as strong as him. But the rest of them . . . the peak of Ruby. All of them full to the absolute brim. But the other five were not at super-mortal Cultivation.

Max could work with this.

Fighting against two Diamond-stage Cultivators and five at the peak of Ruby stage.

"This is gonna be fun!" Maverick exclaimed.

Twozerofive floated above the arena. He seemed as bored as ever, but there was an ever-so-slight note of interest in his voice.

"We will hold a practice bout. The purpose of this match is to test your skill. To even out the odds, Max and Maverick have been forbidden to use flight, and additionally the rest of the strike force has been equipped with Version 2 of the standard-issue ICCB battle-uniform. It will add a force multiplier to your existing Cultivation. You will most likely be able to use these uniforms when you engage in real battle against the Outsiders, but do not grow too accustomed to these. They are expensive, so they're no guarantee."

Twozerofive flicked his hand, and all of the seven strike force members floated down into the arena. They brought out their weapons. Kat brandished her [Unique]-Class shield and a nasty barbed spear. Ashkarassa had a bundle of throwing spears, wrapped in a cloth. Losshnak used sword and shield. Kerro had a long, thin scimitar, while Rakii scowled at Max and flashed a swirl of fire in her hands. The two insectoids looked around and nodded in Max's direction. They were unarmed, and Max had no idea what sort of abilities they had.

"You are permitted to use lethal force. I have full confidence that your bodies, especially when protected by the battle-uniform, can take a full blow from Max or Maverick. Additionally, if you are able to land a fatal blow on a Cultivator of Max's caliber, you shall receive accolades and rewards beyond your wildest dreams."

"Pah," Rakii said. "I will accept that challenge."

"I won't go easy on you," Kat said and grinned.

"It will be an honor to exchange blows with you again, Master Warrior."

Max nodded at each of the strike force members and lifted Maverick off the ground with [Telekinesis].

"I'm going to use you as a throwing weapon," Max said. "You just blast at them as you see fit."

"Simple man, simple plan," Maverick mused.

"I don't think we need anything more complicated."

Ashkarassa stirred at that. "Such arrogance. There are seven of us."

"There could be twenty," Maverick said. "And only your hunky hubby and the human would be a threat."

"Hunky hubby?" Max asked.

"I don't know. I'm still figuring out how to get under her skin. That fox girl is too easy, anyway."

"I heard that," Rakii said and glared at Maverick.

"I'm glad you at least have adequate hearing, darling," Maverick said in his most condescending tone.

"Begin," Twozerofive said.

Immediately a golden barrier of light sprung up around the strike force members. Max threw Maverick spinning like a massive frisbee, and the disc crashed into the barrier, immediately shattering it.

Blasts of yellow and gray energy shot in every direction. A stray fireball and a spear flew at Max, but he dodged them easily. He cast a [**Gravity Storm**] in the area as soon as the barrier shattered. Grunts and gasps of pain filled the air. A lance of light sent by Losshnak tried to pierce Max, but he used [**Tether**] on the ground behind him to dance away from the energy beam.

Then he flicked his hand and halted Maverick's flight, moving the disc above the strike force, from where he rained down destructive beams. When the strike force members were struck, Twozerofive placed a stasis on them, encasing them in a block made up of a light gray substance.

Only Losshnak and Kat remained. They were barely able to stand after having taken a few shots from Maverick and weathering Max's storm.

As weak and limp as they were, they charged at Max. He didn't want to waste anyone's time, and so he didn't do anything fancy. He used [**Tether**] on both of his opponents and then locked them down with [**Gravity Storm**]. Then he lifted Maverick once more to float above them and rain down hell until Twozerofive put a stasis on both of them. It was like fighting children. Max barely had to move.

"Stop," Twozerofive called. His voice was dripping with utter disgust.

The stasis was released, and the strike force members limped toward each other to form a line. They were all dejected, especially Rakii, who didn't even have enough pride left to glare at Max.

"What an absolute disappointment," Twozerofive said. "You are woefully unprepared to be anything but chum for the Outsiders. Do you have the faintest idea of how powerful the enemy is? A sorcerer will strike you down with more ease than Max did here. If they decide not to play with their food first. Pathetic."

The rest of the strike force assembled themselves into a formation and waited for further instruction. Twozerofive sighed.

"Maverick, you are out for this round," their instructor said.

"Excuse me?" Maverick said with mounting indignation. "You wouldn't dare! I'm as much a part of this strike force as Max. In fact, it's widely known that he's the sidekick and I—"

Maverick was cut short as Twozerofive put him in stasis. Max could feel his buddy's building wrath through their bond, as he used [Telekinesis] to move him to the side of the arena.

"Quite the handicap," Max said.

"They need it," Twozerofive said. "As do you, if you are to engage your Intent."

"Fair point," Max said, and [Scythe of Oblivion] appeared, floating behind him in the air. Twozerofive glanced at the large black weapon but said nothing.

"Begin!" the Gray said in a sharp voice, bolstered by Cultivation.

The strike force's assault this time was ferocious. They still operated from behind Losshnak's shimmering golden barrier, but when Max's scythe cleaved into the barrier and didn't immediately break it, it gave Max's opponents enough time to attack.

Two large fireballs flew at him, as well as a fusillade of spears and a strange cloud of purple and pink . . . insects?

Max managed to dodge the spears and the fireballs fairly easily, but the swarm of insects seemingly made of pure energy quickly surrounded him and started to . . . drain his Cultivation?

What a powerful technique.

As a reasonably powerful Diamond-stage Cultivator, the drain on Max was relatively light, but someone at the Ruby stage would have definitely felt threatened. However, this was good. If the fight dragged on, Max would start to feel the pressure.

Kat and Kerro surged out of the formation when the next strike of the scythe broke Losshnak's barrier. The paladin Ishkarassi also charged at him, quickly catching up to his two comrades.

Another set of fireballs and spears attacked him, and the strange swarm of energy insects followed Max, sapping his power with every passing moment.

The strike force's three melee fighters then engaged and exchanged serious blows with him. Max called back the scythe and wielded it in melee range, swinging the large weapon in large cleaves right and left, keeping his enemies at bay.

Sometimes he would use [Tether] to obstruct movement and attempt to lock down his opponents, but it seemed Kerro had some Skill that made it hard for Max to use his control abilities on anyone.

Max raised his eyebrows and the male vulpine grinned. He lunged recklessly and almost cut Max with his strange scimitar. Max dodged backward, but Kat slammed him with her shield. *Hard.* The pain was significant. Kat had to have used some Skill as well.

Losshnak pierced Max's shoulder with a [**Light Lance**] and the swarm of insects swooped down, enveloping him.

Okay, I'm in trouble.

Max dodged around, using [**Tether**] to keep himself moving, but he was slowing down. One of the orange fireballs struck Max and he was thrown to the ground. Two spears flew at him, and he called on something inside him. The energy flared from his dantian to his meridians, and they were instantly infused with it. Max directed the energy toward the spears. They shattered in the air.

But immediately after that happened, a lance of light pierced his throat, and a heavy shield struck his midsection. The pain flared up to maximum intensity for a second, before it was cut off by a stasis being placed on him.

"Much better," Twozerofive said. "Now that the enemy was not coming at you with oppressive force, you managed to actually cooperate and approach the situation tactically. Commendable."

Then their instructor turned to Max. "You managed to call upon your Intent and destroy those spears. Was it an accident or can you replicate this?"

The stasis was released, and Max found he had no wounds on his body. "It was intended, but everything I do, I do instinctually. Give me enough repetition, and I can do it on demand."

"Very good. Then we shall go again," Twozerofive said. "Get back in formation and we start."

They fought through the afternoon well into the night. The bouts were fairly even. Max found that if he attacked the backline and took out the ranged support, he could win rather easily, but he only resorted to that until he felt he could not carry on. He wasn't in it to win it, anyway. He was doing this to develop his Intent.

And that he did. Match by match, he managed to call upon his destructive Intent more and more. It felt great to hone a weapon like this with methodical practice. At first, he was able to use it here and there when the situation called for it. Even by the end of the sparring session, Max wasn't yet fluent in using his Intent but could still call for it on demand. When he had started, it had only been reactive, something he could do under duress.

Now, he could lash out with his Intent, destroying weapons and causing damage to his enemies. It wasn't precise, but it was effective. Using his Intent, Max could immediately disable his opponents; soon their bodies would start to disintegrate. Each time that happened in these battles, Twozerofive would put them in immediate stasis and heal them.

By the end of the day, Max was tired beyond comprehension. But he would have kept going. They only eventually stopped for the day because the rest of the strike force was breaking down. They were mindless zombies on their feet now, pushed to their very limit.

Max could sympathize. He could barely string two thoughts together. But he was happy—very happy. Now he could call on his Intent when the situation demanded it. It was slow, it was clunky, but he could do it. Through this rigorous training, he had formed a baseline that he could develop at will. Now it would only take time and intense practice.

Twozerofive berated them as he dismissed them to eat, wash, and rest. But that was just his style. The Gray was an asshole, that was certain, but Max had to admit that he had started to develop some begrudging respect for him. The Gray had pushed them and thus given them all a chance to ascend. Now that each member of the strike force dragged themselves into bed after a meal and shower, they were all stronger Cultivators than they had been in the morning.

Twozerofive knew his shit.

CHAPTER TWENTY-TWO

Prepare for War

Max spent the next few days purely honing his Intent. He argued for a while with Twozerofive for the freedom to do so, and eventually the Gray instructor relented, begrudgingly. Max suspected it was mostly because he knew Max would go Karen-mode again and talk to the Zoos Collective to get what he wanted, anyway.

That saved time, which was good. Max wanted to spend it optimally.

After having sparred with the strike force, Max could now call on his Intent at will. The training had worked. But he still needed to refine his ability. Even after one achieves the ability to perform a technique, one needs to master it. What about speed? What about efficiency? He would need to have maximum efficiency in the use of his Spiritual Energy, lest he run out in a fight.

I can't be doing that anymore. The kid gloves are off.

He would soon be fighting toe-to-toe against the real enemy. The Outsider horde was bad enough, but there would be sorcerers too. If Max lost against them, there would be no safety net. It would mean his death. But he needed to do this. His Dao would advance through the warfare, he knew it.

Max was outside now, trying to get the practice he needed, flying about and destroying the enemies on Alpha Ludus that were connected to the Framework. Even though he could no longer get any Experience points from them, he could feel the Framework infusing his dantian ever so slightly every time he used his Intent to explode a three-headed demon dog or giant acid-spitting dragon.

These beasts were nothing compared to the horror that was the Outsiders. Especially the sorcerers.

Max wondered if the sorcerers had any weapons against Intent. They had to. There were enough Diamond-stage Cultivators in the employ of the ICCB for a good portion of them to develop their Intents, whatever their Daos were.

"But they sure as hell haven't faced anything like you and me, buddy," Maverick said cheerfully.

"You think we'll be able to fight them?"

"*Pffft.* Of course not. We'll get swatted like flies and die horribly," Maverick said.

Max grumbled. "I don't know what I was expecting from you."

"Of course we'll be able to fight them, idiot. What do you take me for? I am Maverick, Master of Magnificence."

"Please never call yourself that," Max said.

"Bah," Maverick said and huffed. "My point stands, regardless. We won't only fight them—we're gonna defeat them. I don't know why you're even considering the possibility of any other outcome. It is not like you."

"We haven't been able to do it in the simulations," Max said.

"Who cares about that?" Maverick said. "Besides, you've gotten stronger. That Intent business is serious. I say we go have a spin in the ol' green portal and see what's what."

"Yeah, let's go do that. I feel like doing this isn't refining my skills enough."

"That's cause it's too easy for you," Maverick said. "You're so boneheaded the only way you learn is when in significant danger."

"Funny."

"I wish I was joking . . ."

Max found himself once again in a simulation of frozen waste. There were other options, but this one was his favorite. It was the hardest, with the densest number of sorcerers on the battlefield. It was a guarantee that if he fought long enough, he would attract one. It didn't take longer than a few minutes of using his Intent to explode the mantabats in the sky for him to see a tall humanoid with eight arms waving about, and a white mask, smiling maliciously.

Max ran it over and over again for the next few days. Nothing but simulations, day and night. Two meals in between and sometimes two or three hours of sleep to replenish his spent Spiritual Energy, then back again. The other members of the strike force and even Twozerofive could hardly believe it. Max only smiled and pushed forward. Every moment of his waking life was now dedicated to mastering Intent. Sure, he honed his skills against the sorcerers in other ways too. He learned to pick up patterns in the way they moved in the air and the timings of their attacks. He and Maverick even got pretty good at dodging them.

But it was the grind for mastering his destructive Intent that really wore him out. After a total of five days of Max pushing himself to the absolute brink, he finally couldn't take it anymore.

When he finally sat down for a big meal at the end of that day to replenish both his Spiritual Power and his fighting spirit, he ate like a horse. The other members of the strike force tried to engage him in conversation, but he didn't have the energy to respond. Mostly they wanted to know how to push themselves as hard as he did. Max mostly communicated through grunting and shrugging as he savored the avocado and chicken pasta with cream sauce.

What surprised everyone was that not even Maverick was willing to talk. The otherwise-insufferable piece of weaponry had some small amount of energy left in him, but his insults were strangely listless and lethargic.

Still, Max felt good, and he knew Maverick felt good too. They had worked hard. And hard work, as it often does, had paid off. They had clearly spent the past week living according to their Dao.

It made sense to Max. His was the Dao of Destruction. He was honing his skills for a very singular cause: to destroy his enemies. Whatever Powers That Be decided who got to advance to super-mortal Cultivation was clearly pleased. Max brought up his status screen and enjoyed the view before he slumped off to sleep.

CHAPTER TWENTY-THREE

Dog Fights

The next day Max asked the Zoos Collective to transfer him to the battlefield. There was some negotiation, but they ultimately agreed. Max and Maverick were teleported there almost instantly.

He was given rations that boosted his Spiritual Energy. Additionally, he was given one of the special battle-uniforms, which bolstered his Cultivation and shielded him from attacks. Maverick got nothing, but the force multiplier from the suit worked through their [**Divine Soulbond**].

Now, Max watched the battlefield from a holographic screen on an ICCB spaceship, watching the Outsiders and the sorcerers waging war against the ICCB Cultivators.

Max breathed in deeply. There was a calm inside of him. This was what he was meant to do after all. But he was still afraid. Fear could be a powerful thing when kept under control. Max wasn't sure how well he was doing in that regard, but he was trying his best. He checked his equipment. He brushed his spirit sense at the [**Scythe of Oblivion**] hovering behind him. It *thrum*med with his will. It wasn't sentient, but it mirrored Max's impulses. And while Max was scared, he was also excited.

[**We have to reiterate that, while we understand that you need to destroy the enemy in order to grow, we beseech you to put your safety first. You are an extremely valuable asset to the ICCB, and if you behave recklessly here, Alpha Ludus will likely be doomed.**]

Max nodded grimly. He was sick and tired of these crazy stakes. It was never just him and Maverick. It was always the worst-case scenario.

"You ready?" Max asked Maverick. The large disc under him only sent a pulse through their bond. It was focused, but there was also trepidation.

That's just part of the meal.

"Send us in," Max said.

They vanished and everything went black for a moment before they reappeared at the edge of the battlefield. The fighting was fierce. The desert sand was flying up in great geysers as relentless explosions threw it up from the ground.

This was easier terrain than the Himalayan-like mountain range, for sure, but it also came with some disadvantages. The enemy could swarm in a way that was impossible on an uneven battlefield.

Thousands of the doglike creatures, the shambling zombies with long tongues, the giants, and the spiders were attacking in waves against the Cultivators, and while the latter's powerful attacks were doing some damage to the charging Outsider lines, the black ooze started to get sucked into the remaining forces and they grew stronger. Whenever a wave of enemies crashed against the Cultivators' lines, flying Cultivators focused fire at the pooling sludge that would rejuvenate the Outsiders.

Max felt his Cultivation weakening. He could feel it clearly now—something heavy pressing down on his spirit. He wondered how someone with only Ruby Cultivation would feel the pressure. It must be crushing. For him it was uncomfortable, and it clearly weakened him. But he would muster on.

It doesn't look as bad as in the simulation.

The horde of the Outsiders was large. Massive, even. From high up in the air, it looked like the ground was crawling with black insects. But the sky wasn't darkened by their flying forces. There were hundreds of those mantabats that rained down their corrosive acid, as well as swarms of horned dragonflies. One such swarm seemed to have noticed Max and Maverick. Max breathed in and let his meridians fill with Spiritual Energy.

The buzzing sound got stronger, and a swarm of the dragonflies surged toward them. Maverick fired his cannon. A few of them were struck. Max took another breath.

I am Destruction.

Then he extended his hands and slammed them together. A crushing **[Gravity Well]** appeared in the midst of the swarm. A dozen dragonflies got sucked into the veritable white dwarf in the air. They slammed into each other and turned into black oily paste. The **[Scythe of Oblivion]** sliced through them to finish what was left.

But many of the dragonflies only had their flight path distorted and carried on their buzzing charge. Maverick fired another shot, taking down two of the insectoid enemies. Max swiped his hands upward in a violent motion. The concentrated **[Gravity Well]** moved.

It hit the enemy swarm again. This time it was more dispersed, but it still sucked in four more and crushed them into ichor and mush in seconds. Maverick hooted and fired off his gun a few more times, finishing off the stragglers with the explosive energy of his.

+1 Karma point

"Hell yeah!" Maverick exclaimed. "This shit is easy. What did you do with that **[Gravity Well]**? That was new!"

"It was," Max said as he looked around. He was wary. Yeah, it seemed like things were going well. They might go well for a while longer. Until the sorcerers took notice.

"Peh!" Maverick said. "Stop being such a worrywart. Let's kill another swarm of those things."

Max nodded and started cycling the Spiritual Energy inside himself. He wanted to be ready. Sooner or later, they would have to fight the sorcerers. But before that, Maverick was flying them toward another swarm currently attacking a Cultivator in the sky.

She was a beautiful blue woman, seven feet tall, lithe and graceful. She was standing on top of a large flying sword, hands weaving wildly in the air, as a dozen more swords surged and sliced around her in a wild and violent dance.

Max brushed at her spirit and saw that she was very powerful, but also at the end of her rope. Who knew how long she had been fighting here? *Days?*

A few of the mantabats took notice and started lobbing their acid at Max and Maverick. Their attacks were *much* faster than those that Max had fought in the Deathmatch. Maverick weaved and dodged while Max distorted space and gravity around them, making the projectiles miss. A few would have struck, but Max's scythe blocked them and dispersed the globs harmlessly.

"Why are we helping her?" Maverick asked as they approached the woman fighting the swarm.

"We might as well," Max said.

Maverick said nothing, but Max could feel his Intent through their bond. He was not happy about this.

"Our attacks are not conducive to having allies nearby," Maverick said finally.

"She can take care of herself," Max said. "Since when do you use fancy words like conducive?"

"Shut up and focus," Maverick said. "If we die because you wanted to help this stupid woman, I'm going to kill you."

They flew in the midst of the swarm. The swords were keeping the black dragonflies spread out around the woman in a sphere. Sometimes a few of the enemies would surge toward the woman in an attack, which led her to dodge and counter, often slicing through a dragonfly cleanly, turning it into black sludge that fell down into the battlefield below.

I want to try something.

"You got it," Maverick said, understanding instantly through their bond what Max intended to do.

Maverick surged into the fray. Max pushed and pulled on reality, feeling it bend under his will. He sent a wave of Spatial Energy toward the dragonflies where the swarm was thickest. They were all instantly pushed back. Then, he used a **[Gravity Well]** which clumped them together.

The blue woman only gave him a sharp glance and switched her swords from defense to offense, sending five of them to lance through Max's spell. All of the dragonflies then exploded into black sludge. Max kept the gravity spell going, Maverick moving around, dodging and shooting as he concentrated on the sludge. If he let it go, it would fall down to the battlefield and feed the Outsider infantry.

So, Max called on his Spiritual Power to try to crush the swirling sludge. It was resilient. Max pushed further, feeling a slight strain in his meridians. Maverick kept shooting and the woman returned her swords to spin around her in a defensive formation as they sliced at the remaining dragonflies in the swarm.

Then she stopped, her eyes going wide with horror.

"No! You idiot! What are you doing?!"

Max turned to look at her, but she was already sending a sword surging toward them. Maverick yelped and dodged. The sword followed, and Max steered it away with his powers. But he lost control of the **[Gravity Well]** and the black sludge fell down.

"You fool!" the woman screeched. Then she flew straight toward Max and grabbed him.

"W-what?" Max spluttered as she hoisted him up on her shoulder like a sack and started speeding away to the edge of the battlefield.

"Hey!" Maverick yelled from behind them as he tried to follow. The woman was too fast, and his shouts were sounding thinner. "What's the big deal?!"

"Maybe they didn't . . . If there is only one . . . We might be able to . . ."

The woman muttered manically to herself. Max looked at her. She was beautiful, with perfect marble skin, full lips, and wide blue eyes. She looked a little bit like those creatures from that *Avatar* movie. Only without the tails, fur, and animalistic features.

She was more like a statue, crafted with delicacy and grace.

They dodged between the acid globs thrown by the mantabats. The woman was slowing down, and Max could feel Maverick catching up.

"What's wrong?"

The woman cast him a nasty glare. "We might be dead."

"Huh?"

"You tried to destroy the Tar," the woman said. "That will draw the attention of the sorcerers."

"The what?" Maverick asked.

"Oh crap," Max said.

"Yep," the woman said.

Indeed, a few seconds later, as if from nowhere, a large black creature levitated upward in front of them and stopped, hovering. It had eight arms and a white mask sporting a malevolent grin. It was forty feet away from them when the woman skidded to a halt with her flying sword. The rest of her swords started swirling violently around them.

Maverick caught up, and Max flew up, landing on top of his friend.

"Oh-ho," Maverick said. "No destroying gloop. Got it."

"It was incredibly foolish," the woman hissed. "What are you guys? Barely Diamond? Why in the name of oblivion would you try something like that?"

"What should we do?" Max asked as he looked at the sorcerer. It was clearly waiting, , watching them intently.

"We will die gloriously," the woman said quietly. "Steel yourself. It will not let us go."

Max swallowed. He had fought these things and perished many times in simulations. The sensation of dying was rather real in a simulation, but it wasn't the real thing. But if this was it, then this was it. Max would give it his best.

"Listen, lady," Maverick said. "We are destined for great things, so we can't die here. How about we kill this thing and then you tell us more."

"The device is sapient?" the woman asked.

Maverick huffed.

Max shrugged. "We share a Cultivation bond."

"Interesting," the woman said. "You have gravity powers?"

"Close enough for this situation," Max said, his eyes never leaving the sorcerer. But the monster seemed to be content waiting.

"You try to pin it down, I will attack."

"No," Max said, earning a violent glare from the tall woman. "I control, you defend. Maverick here will be in charge of the firepower."

"Don't breathe in the purple gas," the woman said.

"I know."

"Then may the Heavens watch over us," the woman said in grim determination. "Perhaps we can bring it down before we are both destroyed."

They both surged forward. The grin on the sorcerer's mask widened and four of its hands lit aflame. Then it threw fireballs, which exploded behind them as they dodged. Maverick shot a missile of gray and yellow energy at the sorcerer, but the red bubble came up immediately and blocked the shot. Maverick growled in frustration and fired again.

The sorcerer flew around and cackled in a creepy, hollow voice as it continued to aim fireballs at them. A few plumes of purple smoke billowed around them, but they were moving fast enough to escape.

The four extremely powerful beings flew around like jets in a dogfight. Max did his best to slow down the sorcerer by increasing gravity's pull on it and distorting space around it, making reality more viscous around the sorcerer. The effect was as if it was attempting to swim through oil or tar.

Unfortunately, however, with a number of complex flourishes with its hands, the sorcerer stopped the effects of Max's powers on him almost instantaneously.

Sometimes the monster would turn in the air and flash a quick grin at Max. It seemed to be toying with them, having fun. Max didn't like that. The sorcerer was fast. It sometimes sprinted in the air so quickly that it looked like it had vanished for a moment, leaving behind an afterimage that only a Cultivator could see.

With that speed it could crush us in moments.

The blue woman growled with frustration. She made a hand sign and called all her swords back to her, where they started swirling around her in a dome formation. Max stopped.

The sorcerer did too, again opting to hover near them some forty feet away, watching and grinning.

"It's waiting for us to get exhausted," Max said.

"Of course it is," the woman said.

Max breathed and felt for his soul and his meridians. He still had a pretty full tank. But the sorcerer was *powerful*. Why did they play these games? Were they just creatures of pure malevolence? They wanted to watch them struggle in vain and then squash them like bugs.

Max shook his head and gritted his teeth. He would have none of that. There had to be a way. The sorcerers could be hurt, and they could be killed. Maybe he could weaken them somehow, overwhelm the shield, and apply gravitational pressure to crush them. Surely there was a point at which their healing factor would not be enough.

"What's the general protocol for fighting these things?" Max asked.

The woman looked at him and scoffed. She handed him two pills that swirled with blue smoke inside of them. "This will recharge your Spiritual Energy."

Max didn't question; he simply popped one of the pills in his mouth and flicked the other to Maverick's open compartments with **[Telekinesis]**.

The pill tasted like the ocean breeze and mint.

"The plan?" Max insisted.

The woman let out a dry chuckle.

"Hope for someone powerful enough to save you. Have you not fought these things before?"

"I have in simulations," Max said. "I almost got one."

"You—" the woman choked. "You WHAT?"

"I had teamed up with an ally. We wounded one severely, almost destroying it, but its brothers and sisters came in to save it."

"You managed to wound one?"

"It was weaker than this," Max said. "It couldn't fly, and it wasn't this fast."

"No," the woman said. "They are all one and the same. Just a single entity with a million ugly faces."

"I wonder about that . . ." Max muttered.

Max's mind raced as he considered the implications of the woman's words. Could the sorcerers really be a single, unified entity? And if so, what did that mean for their chances of victory?

He didn't have long to ponder, as the sorcerer suddenly sprang into action. It vanished from sight, only to reappear directly in front of them, its grin widening maniacally.

Max reacted on instinct, throwing up a [Gravity Well] between them and the sorcerer. The creature slammed into the invisible barrier, its momentum arrested by the sudden increase in localized gravity.

But it wasn't enough. The sorcerer's hands moved in a blur, weaving intricate patterns in the air. A wave of force erupted from its palms, shattering Max's [Gravity Well] like glass.

The woman's swords surged forward, a whirling storm of flashing metal. They sliced at the sorcerer from every angle, seeking to overwhelm its defenses.

For a moment, it seemed to work. The sorcerer's shield flickered under the onslaught, its grin faltering. But then, with a casual flick of its wrist, it sent the swords flying, scattering them like leaves in the wind.

Maverick opened fire, his cannon roaring as it spat bolt after bolt of searing energy. The sorcerer danced between the shots, its movements a blur of inhuman speed and grace.

Max gritted his teeth, pouring more power into his gravitational manipulation. He focused on the sorcerer's feet, trying to root it in place, to create an opening for Maverick and the woman to exploit.

The sorcerer stumbled, its movements slowing as the invisible chains of increased gravity wrapped around its legs. The woman saw her chance and pressed the attack, her swords converging on the creature from all sides.

But even as the blades struck home, piercing the sorcerer's flesh in a dozen places, Max felt a sense of unease. This was too simple. The sorcerer was toying with them, letting them think they had a chance.

And then, it revealed its true power, which Max had seen once before in a simulation . . .

The sorcerer's body began to shift and change, its wounds knitting closed as luminescent white tendrils erupted outwards from its frame. They lashed out like whips, seizing the woman's swords and shattering them to pieces.

The woman cried out in pain and shock, her face going pale. Max and Maverick could only watch in horror as the tendrils surged toward them, their tips glinting with malevolent purpose.

Max threw up another **[Gravity Well]**, trying to deflect the tendrils. But they slipped through his grasp like water through a sieve, their form insubstantial and elusive.

One of the tendrils struck Maverick, wrapping around his metallic form. The gun let out a scream of static and feedback, his systems overloading under the sorcerer's assault.

"Maverick!" Max cried out, his heart seizing with fear for his friend. He could feel Maverick's pain through their bond, a searing agony that threatened to consume them both.

But even as despair threatened to overwhelm him, Max felt a surge of determination. He would not let this monster take his friend, his partner. He would not let it win.

"I WILL DESTROY YOU FOR THIS!" Max roared.

+3 Karma points

With a roar of defiance, Max unleashed the full might of his Cultivation. Gravity warped and twisted around him, space itself bending to his will. He seized the tendrils with invisible hands, tearing at them with all the force he could muster. He summoned the full extent of his destructive Intent and surged it at the enemy with all of his might.

The sorcerer recoiled, its grin twisting into a snarl of pain and rage. It redoubled its assault, pouring more of its dark power into the tendrils.

But Max wouldn't yield. He pushed himself to the brink, his meridians burning with the strain of channeling so much Spiritual Energy. He could feel Maverick's presence in his mind. He was still in the fight, his cannon firing at the enemy, but his mind . . . It was dwindling.

Max lashed out again with his destructive Intent, and the sorcerer was clearly taken aback by it. Max tore through its slick flesh, but it kept reknitting itself.

But Max and Maverick pushed back against the sorcerer's onslaught. Inch by inch, they forced the tendrils back, severing them from the creature's body with blades of concentrated destruction.

The sorcerer let out a howl of fury and pain, its form writhing as it sought to regenerate its lost appendages. Max and Maverick pressed their advantage, however, Maverick's cannon flaring as it fired shot after shot into the creature's body.

The woman joined the fray, her own Cultivation flaring to life as she wove barriers of shimmering force around them. Her swords may have been destroyed, but she was far from helpless.

Under their combined assault, the sorcerer began to falter. Its movements grew sluggish, its attacks less precise. Black ichor oozed from a dozen wounds, its regeneration struggling to keep pace with the damage.

But even as victory seemed within reach, the sorcerer played its final card. Its mouth opened wide—far wider than any natural creature's should. And from that gaping maw poured a torrent of purple gas, a noxious miasma that engulfed them in an instant.

Max held his breath, his lungs burning as he fought the urge to inhale the poisonous fumes. Beside him, Maverick wavered, his form flickering as the gas seeped into his systems.

The woman's barriers shattered, her own breathing growing labored as she succumbed to the sorcerer's vile breath.

Max knew they had only moments before they'd be overwhelmed. With a final, desperate surge of power, he seized the sorcerer in a gravitational vice, pouring every ounce of his remaining strength into crushing the creature with a concentrated **[Gravity Storm]**. It writhed within it, but it was fully enclosed, its tentacles cut off; it couldn't resist any longer.

Max started feeding pure destructive Intent into the creature.

+1 Karma point

The sorcerer's body broke under the pressure, its bones snapping and its organs rupturing. Max roared a final time, and then, it exploded.

As it did, one last, long luminescent white tendril struck out and flicked Maverick. Maverick immediately fell to the ground.

Max cried out, reaching for his friend with his hands and mind. But the gun-disc did not respond. Max surged toward the ground and picked his friend up. Max tried to reach Maverick through their bond, but there was nothing but weak static. It was as if Maverick's mind had been wiped.

Max pushed away grief and anger. He had to focus. From what he knew of the sorcerers, more would come immediately after one of them was killed.

"Can you fly?" Max asked as the blue woman descended. She was clearly beaten down, and a brief brush at her spirit told Max that she was on her last legs.

The woman nodded weakly, her eyes glazed over with pain and fatigue. "For a while."

Warrior, this one.

The two of them flew away from the battlefield until they reached a small oasis. There were no sorcerers following them, which was extremely fortunate. Had there been, they wouldn't have made it out alive.

They will likely search for us. We need to recuperate for a day or two before any chance of fighting . . . And that's only if . . .

Only if Maverick bounced back. As insufferable as his little buddy was, the overwhelming silence coming from him worried Max.

But now was not the time to worry. It was time to secure survival. Max surveyed his surroundings.

There was a pond of clear water and sparse trees here and there. Palm trees with coconuts. Cultivators of their Level didn't need food to sustain themselves, but it would help them recover.

Stonework of some long-lost civilization surrounded the oasis; it looked as old as the sky, weathered as it was from the winds and sand. Crumbling walls and statues. There was a doorway half covered in sand, leading down somewhere. Max wondered who had built all this.

When they reached the oasis, the woman fell on her hands and knees. Max called to her, but she had already passed out, her sword thudding on the soft, yellow sand before it vanished into a green glimmer.

Maverick didn't respond when Max called to him. He hadn't expected his buddy to answer, but it still pained him.

Max sighed wearily and looked around. He saw the entrance of what must have been a cave and made a quick decision before the sorcerers came seeking revenge. He took hold of both his companions and carried them into the cave.

CHAPTER TWENTY-FOUR

Favani

Max limped toward the woman. She seemed to still be unconscious, only muttering an incoherent whisper now and then. Maverick, on the other hand, was in the corner of the cave. Max tried to reach out through their bond, but it was still full of static.

Max cursed the sorcerers and the Outsiders. Max looked at his comrades. One of them unconscious, another driven insane. He himself limping around with a quarter of his strength left.

And that was just one sorcerer. Even two would have utterly annihilated us.

Max knelt down next to the woman and started dabbing her forehead with a wet rag. She mumbled in her sleep and tried to swat away his hand, but the movement was too weak to accomplish anything. Max grabbed her hand and squeezed.

"Thanks for saving my life."

Maybe he was imagining it, but she might have squeezed back weakly.

Max produced the tub of green gel that he had been given with his survival supplies. It was a healing concoction. He coated her body with it, trying not to be weird about it. Her skin was smooth as marble and her body battle-hardened and beautiful.

Afterward, he lathered himself with the gel and then Maverick, whose disc-shaped body flinched like an abused cat when he touched him but eventually allowed himself to be gelled-up.

Even after using what must have been a gallon of the gel, the tub remained just as full.

"Huh," Max said to himself. "Pocket dimension Tupperware?"

Then he sat down. He wasn't sure what to do next. He could meditate, but his instincts told him that wasn't a good idea. He needed to let his soul rest. He would recover, he was fairly sure. And with the advancement in their Dao, he would come back stronger. He looked at Maverick.

I just hope it didn't come at too great a cost.

There was something off about the way the sorcerers fought. They were clearly rational individuals. This one seemed to enjoy playing with its food. But what he had been told about the Outsiders was that it was a hive mind, a swarm that was practically mindless and working with a single objective: Consume.

"So why do they act like people?"

It seemed that the only reason why they had been able to defeat this sorcerer was because of the arrogance of the creature and their luck at having experienced an ascension in their Dao. Before that, this sorcerer could have just squashed them like bugs.

"Can we use this to our advantage? I have so many questions."

Max wanted to contact the Zoos Collective, but when he tried, there had been no response. They were most likely too busy. But right now, Max was in way over his head, not sure what to do, except to wait.

He looked at the woman and his friend. Both were wiped out.

Max got up and limped to the opening of the cave. He flicked his hand and the water from the oasis pond started streaming toward him and formed a bubble on his hand. The bubble was unstable and wobbled, but Max would be damned if he couldn't manage a single party trick, as powerful as he was.

He drank from the bubble, and it shrank in size. The water was sweet. He limped back to the woman and brought the bubble to her lips and lifted her head with the other hand.

She murmured and her eyes flickered, but she did drink. Barely, but it was something.

Max got up, took another drink from his bubble, and tossed it at Maverick, who, to Max's surprise, responded this time. Maverick seemed to be slowly regaining consciousness. But his mind was broken. When the bubble struck Maverick, the disc flinched in the air and spoke utter gibberish. Then Maverick settled down and went back to its muttering.

Max sighed.

What am I supposed to do?

He decided to try the Zoos Collective yet again.

"Uh, hey," Max called out. His voice echoed faintly in the cave. "Zoos? It's Max. I need help."

After a moment the familiar plastic jellyfish appeared in front of Max. This time, there wasn't any static, the steady hum emitted by the Zoos' avatar crystal-clear.

[Greetings, Max. It is most excellent that you have survived your first battle. We are looking at the recording. Please hold.]

And then, a few moments later:

[**Astounding. Simply Astounding. The blunder you made almost cost you everything. But you managed to turn it into a win and advance your Dao. To think that at your Level you managed to defeat a sorcerer is . . . unheard of. How do you feel?**]

Max mulled over the question. He shrugged.

"Truth be told, I haven't had a chance to interact with the Framework. I've been worried about my friends. But since you asked, I think I feel more . . . clear. Everything feels clear. My body, my mind, my spirit. Even the Spiritual Energy within me feels less muddy and vague. It has a certain sharpness to it."

[**Yes. This is the result of your Dao becoming more defined. This has happened mostly due to your diligent practice of your destructive Intent. Your Spiritual Energy is starting to take on a unique aspect. Your Cultivation is finally in the middle of the Diamond realm. This gambit of yours seems to have paid off.**]

"It has," Max said. "But it came with a steep price."

Max gestured behind him with a thumb at the blue girl and Maverick, who was softly banging himself against the wall of the cave.

The Zoos jellyfish blinked next to them and Max walked over.

[**The Jianari woman will be fine. You did well to ally yourself with such an experienced warrior.**]

"What about Maverick?" Max asked impatiently.

[**He was struck by one of the sorcerer's spells. It is their most horrible weapon, designed to permanently damage Cultivation.**]

Max felt as if a cold rock had dropped down to the pit of his stomach. Immediately he reached for the bond he shared with Maverick. It was hard to navigate and fuzzy, but Max pushed through. Maverick's soul was a cacophony of mess and chaos, with barely a coherent thought or emotion. It was like he had lost his mind. But the power was there.

"I think he's just out of it," Max said. "I can sense him through our bond. He's just insane."

[Interesting. It seems to our sensors that he is weakened. We have a spell to restore minds, but we do not know how it will work for an animated object.]

"Please just try," Max said.

The jellyfish did something and the air rippled, but to no avail. Max sighed in disappointment. The avatar froze for a while and then spoke:

[That did not work. The damage is far more extensive than we thought. We do have a solution, but it will cost you.]

"Added debt with that sweet sixteen percent annual interest rate?"

[We are afraid so. The treatment will take time and resources, and we have to ask for recompense.]

"Fine," Max said. This wasn't a decision he needed to mull over. "Just do it fast."

[Very well. We will adjust the contract we have with you. We will start fixing him and return him when appropriate. The teleportation costs of his deposit and withdrawal will also be added to the debt.]

Max waved a dismissive hand. He wondered if this debt was something he was ever going to get out of. It didn't matter, though. He needed Maverick.

The Zoos jellyfish blinked away, as did Maverick. Max was left alone with the large blue woman lying on the cave floor. He approached her.

She stirred when he got closer and weakly opened her eyes.

"Hey," she said.

"Glad to have you back," Max said and smiled.

She looked him up and down and groaned. "So, it wasn't a bad dream."

"Come on, I'm not that bad."

"I don't know how you had enough power to fight against a sorcerer at your Level. No, wait . . ."

Max felt a light touch on his spirit. The woman's eyes went wide.

"You weren't this strong when we met."

"I suppose I advanced a bit when we fought."

"To advance that fast . . ." the woman muttered to herself. Then she looked up at Max. "I am Favani, the first crown princess of the Jianari Empire."

"I'm Max," he said, nodding and smiling.

"I am here to secure an artifact for my people," Favani said with an imperious voice, only betrayed by a weak cough. "You will assist me in finding the secret tomb in which this artifact is buried."

"Sorry, lady, but I have my own plans."

"I see. You are the ICCB's slave. Their plans are your plans."

"Hey now," Max said irritated. "I am just trying to help everyone deal with the Outsiders."

Favani looked at him appraisingly. "If that is your goal, then help me. I am a princess of a powerful empire. Help me and I will make sure you are rewarded. We could use an ally like you."

"How big a reward are we talking?" Max asked.

Favani said nothing, but Max could feel her brushing against his spirit again.

"More wealth than you can carry," Favani said.

CHAPTER TWENTY-FIVE

Ancestral Ruins

Max did a little flourish as they arrived at the doorway half-covered in white sand. Only the archway and the upper half of the door were still clear. There were two statues of snarling beasts on both sides of the door. Their eyes were rubies, and their teeth made of gold only slightly weathered by the sands of time. The stone gateway was covered in carvings from what appeared to be a myriad of different writing systems.

"Ta-da!" he said. "Here is your secret tomb."

"It was here all along?" Favani said, in a dubious tone of voice.

She brushed pashed Max and started sliding her hand across the glyphs etched into the doorway. The doors looked heavy and unmoving.

"The doors are heavily enchanted," Favani said. "There's no way two Diamond stage Cultivators can break them."

"Yeah, I thought so," Max said.

"We have to find a switch, password, or key," Favani said.

"Any ideas?"

"About how a culture thousands of years gone locked their warehouses?" Favani said and raised a sardonic eyebrow.

Max chuckled and found he liked this woman. He came up next to her. She took a wary step sideways to maintain a bit of personal space. Her shoulders were tense, but Max ignored that.

"It could take days of trying to get in," Favani said. "It's better if you return to the battle against the Outsiders and leave me here."

"You said you'd reward me if I helped you, didn't you?" Max said.

"Beyond your wildest imagination, slave."

"Stop calling me that," Max said.

Favani scoffed.

Max looked at the glyphs. They told of an old war and how this tomb contained the weapons that had been used to win it. Most important was the mention of an opening mechanism buried three feet below the sand at the feet of the guardian beast statues. Opening both mechanisms would unlock the door.

She can't read the glyphs. I can because of the skill those ICCB guys gave me. Even after the Framework got upgraded, I can still understand any language.

"Tsk," Favani said in frustration. "At least the cave is nearby. I should be able to uncover the secret of this door in a few days."

Max simply gave her a look and started to use his **[Telekinesis]** to move the sand at the feet of the guardian beast statues.

It was always a little tricky to move a mass of very small objects, like water or sand, versus something like rocks, but at this point Max's Cultivation was at a Level where he could do it with a modicum of focus.

"What are you doing?" Favani asked.

Max didn't answer. He simply sifted away the sand with sweeps of his hands and shooed her away whenever she was standing in the way. Huffing indignantly, she still allowed Max to move her with his ability.

"Answer me, slave."

"Call me that one more time and you're on your own."

"I told you to go fight your war," Favani said.

Max found the glyph and pressed a hand to it. It didn't seem to do anything. Breathing out, he let the Spiritual Power from his meridians flood his hand and exude out of it, filling the glyph with light.

Favani's eyes went wide with surprise. Max only gave her a deadpan look and nudged his head toward the other beast statue. Favani got the message, uncovered the other glyph and placed a hand on it.

The large double doors clunked as the lock mechanism was released, and they groaned like bending metal as they opened outward, causing the ground around them to rumble. Finally, they locked in place with another clunk and Max and Favani were left standing in front of the doors, staring into pitch-black darkness.

"After you," Max said.

Favani gave him a look. Less hostile and untrusting this time. More like appraising. "How did you know how to do that?"

"If I tell you, are you going to finally accept my help?"

"Maybe."

"Maybe you need to start thinking of a way to reward me," Max said and flicked a hand at the darkness ahead of them. "After you."

* * *

"So, what is it that you're looking for here?" Max asked. Their steps echoed faintly in the dark corridors. Favani had a gemstone on her wrist that was emitting a soft red light. It illuminated the dark hallways.

The walls were high and the pathways narrow. On the walls were strange alien pictures depicting large-scale battles between various alien races with massive machines shooting fire and energy beams. Most prominent amongst the races were the tall blue humanoids, clearly the ancestors of Favani's people.

Favani didn't answer Max's question right away. Instead, she spent time analyzing the pictures as they walked deeper into the ruins.

"My people Cultivate in a very specific way," Favani finally said. "We use a technology called metagems. I am looking for an ancient treasure that could enhance the way we use them."

"So vague," Max said.

"You don't need to know more, sl— lackey."

"Slackey, huh?" Max said and laughed. "Better than a slave. I told you, I'm not contracted."

"You are a mercenary for the ICCB," Favani said. "You are clearly contracted."

"Technically I am still playing the Cosmic Games," Max said.

Favani stopped walking and fixed a suspicious gaze on Max. "That is a lie."

Max shrugged.

"Why would you tell such a blatant lie?" Favani demanded. "You are a Diamond-stage Cultivator, as weak as you are. This is the result of years of Cultivation. The Games rarely last that long."

"I guess I've been lucky along the way," Max said and started walking.

Favani followed, and they ventured deeper and lower into the tomb.

"Lucky . . ." she muttered to herself. But the echoing from the high walls and Max's Cultivator senses made her words clear. "I've never seen such raw talent . . ."

Max grinned to himself, finding himself feeling surprisingly smug. Now that Maverick was out of the picture, it seemed like Max was taking over some of his regular roles.

"How old is this tomb?" Max said after they had walked another ten minutes. The corridor had ended in a large round room with a ceiling so high even with his heightened Cultivator senses, Max couldn't see the end of it. They must have ventured miles deep.

"Eighteen thousand years, give or take," Favani said absently. She lifted her ruby gemstone to take a better look at one of the murals. "It was created when my ancestors were still craftsmen, not warriors."

"What changed?" Max asked.

"The ICCB," Favani said bitterly. "They started a war."

"With the Outsiders?" Max asked.

Favani only grunted.

"I thought the Outsiders came here and started attacking things, eating planets, and whatnot," Max said.

"I bet they like that story better," Favani said.

"So what's your side of the story?"

Favani sighed. "Two of the ICCB races were collaborating on a science project a very long time ago. This was back when your patron race still had physical forms. Look."

Favani shone the light at a mural where two forces were fighting side by side against the onslaught of a black swarm. The Grays were depicted the same as they ever were: short and monochrome. But there was a species next to them. Floating white and purple jellyfish, large and queued up as a front line against the Outsiders' assault.

"But they were greedy," Favani said. "And tried to tap into a power beyond this reality to another dimension. They figured that if they could route energy from another realm into this, they could have infinite energy. Turns out the Outsiders were waiting behind the door."

"So that's what started the war?" Max asked.

Favani nodded. "Could have been worse. My father said his great-grandfather got intel from the Grays. There was a creature there, behind the veil. Something so monstrous, it made the Zoos immediately turn to making their existence virtual."

"What kind of creature?" Max asked.

"The accounts are unclear and very, very old. I only know that there is something inside the realm the Great Enemy comes from, and their king is vast in power and cruelty. It is a creature of death and madness. Something that feasts on life-energy itself."

"I suppose it never got inside our reality?"

"My great-grandfather said that it could have. It simply did not."

That didn't sound good. That basically meant that the war that had been waged for thousands of years could tilt at any point if the Big Bad suddenly decided to emerge.

Thousands of years . . . ?

Favani laughed. It was a throaty, low thing and it seemed to relax her a bit. Max's anger receded. "Perhaps it is good that you joined me in this, Max. You will find I am generous to my friends."

Max shook his head as he admired the murals. "You don't need to keep mentioning bribes. You helped me out, I helped you out. We're friends."

"Friends . . ." Favani said thoughtfully, as if tasting the word.

"Yeah," Max said. "I don't have many of those either."

After a pause, Favani gave Max a look he couldn't quite read. "I doubt we will be friends, Max."

Max shrugged. "We'll see."

"Indeed." Favani said with a mysterious smile tugging at her blue lips.

CHAPTER TWENTY-SIX

Inside the Tomb

S top!" Favani hissed. "From hereon, it will be dangerous."

"Dangerous how?" Max asked, lowering himself to a more ready stance, letting the Spiritual Energy flow through his meridians in a controlled trickle. He had to admit he was nervous. He was not used to fighting without Maverick. Max sent out an exploratory pulse of emotion through the bond. It was dull, but he could feel his friend. His mind was still jumbled, but he was resting, still in the cave.

"There are guardian constructs protecting the crafts of my ancestors," Favani said. "I do not know what will trigger them to attack us, but it will happen, heed my word."

"Heeded," Max said.

Favani turned to look at him and narrowed her eyes, unsure if she was being made fun of. Max only smiled genially.

They ventured deeper into the tomb and soon they noticed heavy footprints on the dust-covered floor. Bipedal. Large.

Constructs, huh?

"What kinds of abilities are we to expect of them?"

"They are designed specifically to fight against Cultivators," Favani said. "If there are enough of them, I am sure they can overpower two Diamond-stage warriors, weak as you are."

"I thought you just called me talented earlier," Max said.

"Potential is not might, you young fool," Favani said haughtily.

Well, beats being called a slave.

They crossed a room that looked like a great observatory. Why there would be one inside a tomb miles beneath the surface of the planet was a great mystery to Max.

Favani explained that the equipment had been used to observe realities beyond this one, something that was no longer practiced under penalty of death. One of the rare few things the ICCB and the empire of Jianari agreed upon.

Another room looked like a giant laboratory, completely round with seats of varying sizes at the sides. In the middle was some sort of a Cultivation array.

"An attempt at copying the technique with which the Zoos Collective transcended their physical forms. It never succeeded as well as their technique, but my father has records of this method. This test was useful. Knowing your begrudging allies is sometimes more important than knowing your enemies."

"What exactly is the relationship between your people and the ICCB?" Max asked.

Favani spat on the ground. There was no further answer.

Finally they heard heavy, steady footsteps in the darkness somewhere nearby. Two sets of feet. Max extended his Spiritual Sense to brush against anything that might have Spiritual Power. As he did that, he gathered power from his dantian and sent it softly surging around his meridians.

"Do not try to sense them," Favani said, and Max immediately retracted his Spiritual Sense. "They might notice, and we may need the element of surprise."

"Then why are you talking?" Max said.

"They're constructs, I doubt they can hear us."

"Alright, smart girl," Max said and enjoyed watching Favani's eyes flash dangerously "What's the plan of action?"

"You can fly, yes?" Favani said and waited for Max to nod. "Give me air support and distract them while I attack with my sword."

Without further elaboration, Favani moved forward, smoothly flourishing a sword. It started glowing green and then magically multiplied silently in the air around her.

Meanwhile Max flew up to the ceiling and started floating above Favani. Even though they were Cultivators, there was something *dense* about this darkness. Max couldn't see much further than he could when he had been a regular human. It was a strange feeling, reminding him of how far he had come.

Feels like a lifetime ago.

But when Favani turned off the light that had been emitting from the red gemstone, it became pitch black. That wouldn't do. Max assumed the tall blue woman had a plan and didn't intend to fight in complete darkness. Or maybe she could see perfectly. Max didn't want to ask stupid questions, as some part of him wanted to impress this woman.

So instead, he did what came naturally to him. He gathered a trickle of Spiritual Energy and routed it from his meridians into his eyes. It was a subtle thing at first. Shapes in the shadows gently came into focus. Max could hear the clunking movements of something heavy walking, and as his eyes were infused with more power, he found himself able to connect the sounds to movement.

It wasn't perfect. But he could clearly see outlines in the darkness. There were four of them and they were large—fifteen feet each, eight feet wide at the shoulders. They seemed clunky, in construction. Max assumed them to be enchanted stone golems. Each of them carried a strange club. He would have liked to know more about the weapons, but he couldn't see well enough, so he flew closer, past Favani, and noticed that the corridor opened up higher in the air, giving him more room to move through the dome-like room. That was good, he could use the bird's-eye perspective. He flew high enough to see all of the four idly moving shapes in the darkness. If they had noticed him flying by, there was no indication.

They're terrible guardians if they didn't notice me. Most likely they're triggered by some event, such as opening a door.

"Max," Favani called out, "begin."

Max looked at the faint outline of a tall woman with a regal build. That was all he could see, as the sword was no longer glowing green. There was a slight glint of metal reflecting from what little light there was in the room, but only a Cultivator could notice it. Max wondered if the golems could see it.

A thought for another time.

He swooped down toward the nearest golem and pushed pure gravity against the enemy. He infused the gravitational force with flickers and specks of his destructive Intent, causing some splints of stone to cut off from the golem as it struggled against its invisible restraint.

The golems all groaned in strange, low voices, like heavy metal doors slowly turning on their hinges. They spoke in unison in a language long forgotten, but Max understood them.

"Leave, intruders. You are being given a single warning. Heed it or be neutralized."

Max was not deterred. He caught the other four in gravity lock-holds, letting the full power of his Spiritual Energy flood through his being. While he was actually attempting to only hold the constructs in place, he was infusing the gravitational energy with his destructive energy in order to crush his enemies into fine sand.

This infused his Cultivation with his Dao and made the spells he wove that much stronger.

But it wasn't enough. The golems groaned and started shrugging off the oppressive weight Max was trying to pin them down under. Favani attacked them with flying swords, but soft blue fields of energy appeared around them when the swords came slicing.

Max strained to keep the enemies held in place. But managing four of them was beyond his power. They were too strong.

"I'm going to release one of them," Max called. "I can't hold them all."

"No! Max!" Favani cried, but it was too late.

Max let go of one of them, and it immediately attacked.

There was a crack in the darkness, and something flew toward Max. It was fast. Max reacted on instinct and accelerated to move away from the threat. An object whizzed past him—a stone sphere. He felt it with his Cultivator senses. It missed him by a yard, but it still managed to rip up Max's clothes with the force of its attack.

It also jumbled up his Spiritual Energy. Max fell to the ground, and the other three golems were released.

Crack. Crack. Crack.

Three spheres shot out of the massive clubs the golems were wielding. Two headed for Favani, one for Max, who was in a freefall. He had no defenses.

Max could sense the sphere coming. His first hope was to use a **[Tether]** technique and thus repel himself from the assailing object. But his meridians weren't responding.

Max needed to call on a higher power. A more primal power. And so he sent out his Intent toward the object speeding toward him—a full blast of it, which enveloped the sphere. It started to crumble and break.

But it moved so fast, and Max's Intent was only able to affect it for so long. The crumbling sphere struck Max straight in the shoulder, crushing it, and sending him flying toward a wall.

Max's world filled with pain as he blacked out and woke up face down on the ground a moment later.

Crack.

Another sphere was coming. Max refused to let this one hit him. He gathered his Intent and infused the floor with it. The floor cracked and crumbled beneath him, and Max sank into the stone as if it were quicksand. The sphere crashed into the seam connecting the floor and the wall behind Max.

Despite the pain and disorientation, Max was a warrior, and he had a job to do. He shrugged and focused on the sphere behind him with his Spiritual Sense. It was the size of a basketball, and it was brimming with Intent. The same Intent as his. *Destruction.*

Oh . . .

"I have a plan," Max said to Maverick, before he realized his buddy wasn't there.

"Then act on it!" Favani snapped from close by. She was using a storm of her swords to slice and stab at the closest construct, which was charging another shot with its club. The stone orb floated in midair as the golem prepared to strike it with his club. It was a lumbering movement, but full of taut strength.

This time Max was ready. He flew up in the air, above the hulking structure. His meridians were clearing, and Max accessed his power again with full gusto.

[Alter Gravity]

Max pushed all of his Spiritual Energy into a single point in space. The stone sphere weapon of the construct.

Crack. Another swing of a club from the darkness. Max dodged and found himself directly in front of the golem that was preparing to hit them with the stone sphere point-blank.

Max wouldn't let it. He intensified the gravitational power with all of the might of a Diamond Cultivator. The Outsiders' suppression field affected them even inside of the tomb, but the effect was lessened. Max was *powerful*.

The stone sphere crashed into the ground, grinding its way through the floor, eating it up. The great golem swung its club, but it whiffed and unbalanced the construct. Favani struck it with a dozen swords, stabbing into its every limb.

"Good plan," Favani said.

"That wasn't the plan," Max said and flew off, leaving a confused Favani to fight with the construct, who was now taking swings at her with the club.

Crack.

Max dodged. A great stone orb flew past him. Its speed and power ripped into him, the air current cutting into his skin, slicing thin wounds into his arm and side. His crushed shoulder throbbed with pain, but Max ignored it the best he could. He was no physical fighter; he could make do with an injured shoulder.

Meanwhile, another golem was preparing to launch one of its high-speed projectiles at Favani. This was more dangerous, as her mobility was much more limited than Max, as agile and fast as she was.

It was a shoddy plan; it hardly made any sense. But it made sense to him. It was a flash of intuition. A sort of foolish genius allowed by circumstance.

Max and Maverick had learned they could transfer Spiritual Energy between each other through their [Divine Soulbond]. Max could give it to Maverick, and vice versa. But Max also knew that one could attempt to take it from another. Of course they wouldn't do this, as they were partners. But technically it was possible. Either party would of course resist, and it would result in a stalemate, if such betrayal ever happened. But what if Max could form this into a technique?

Max reached for the floating sphere with his Spiritual Sense. The moment he sensed it, he charged it with his Intent. Connected with it. Then he opened up his Soulbond with Maverick. He was still there, dull and mindless. Max wrested control of the bond and connected it with the lifeless sphere.

It worked.

Max could sense its thoughts and reserves of Spiritual Energy. As it was a lifeless sphere made of stone, it had very little going for it in terms of mental activity. But it was brimming with destructive power. Max tapped into that, gripping that power. He started pulling it from the sphere and into him through the bond.

There was no resistance.

All of the destructive energy flowed from the sphere into Max, invigorating him, making his whole being *thrum*. He felt the pain recede and energy flowing through his meridians.

Crack.

The golem launched the sphere anyway. Batting it straight at Favani. But the orb was bereft of its power. It struck Favani and she gasped. But it only toppled her. Max paid her no further heed. He was sure she could take a punch.

"What the—" she muttered, her voice echoing in the wide darkness.

Crack.

Max immediately used **[Tether]** to slam himself to the ground, making the great destructive orb fly past him. Infused with destructive power as it was, it felt like it was going to rip Max's scalp from his head as it flew past, even though it was at least four feet away.

It disoriented his Spiritual Energy but not enough to deter him. He surged after the sphere, dodging another one flying at him. It seemed like the golems were now much more interested in him than Favani.

Max arrived at the orb, but it was already levitating and getting ready to return to its owner. Max pushed it down with gravitational energy.

"Favani," Max called, "attack the one in the middle."

While their teamwork wasn't as seamless as his with Maverick, it was good. Favani acted instantly, without hesitation, leaving the target she was attacking. She roared and lashed out at the golem that was trying to call its sphere back. She cut into its arm with her sword, making the great construct stumble and groan. Her swarm of flying swords followed, striking it here and there, slicing little cuts into the stone.

It was enough for Max to wrest control of the stone sphere completely. He tapped into it, bonding with it. It felt wrong to share a bond with anyone but Maverick, but now was not a good time for foolish sentimentality.

Through the bond, Max reached and found that this orb was also *thrum*ming with destructive power. He drained it, letting it flood into his spirit. It made him stronger. This wasn't only power that he could steal and reuse; it was a form of energy so natural to Max's body and spirit, that he could infuse his dantian with it. And since they were already winning the fight, he took a moment to do so.

+1 Karma point

The orb went dim as Max drained it fully, reveling in the heady feeling of growing even more powerful. Once the sphere was spent, Max crushed it with a stomp, sending fragments of stone scattering to the winds.

Two more to go . . .

Infused with an excess of raw power, Max didn't even bother to use his **[Telekinesis]** to make himself fly. He twisted his leg and kicked at the ground, sending himself speeding toward one of the golems preparing to take a shot.

The great stone construct was done with its backward motion and struck at the floating orb. Max surged forward with the pure power of Cultivation infusing his body, seeping into every limb. He tackled the giant golem just as it struck.

Cra— hhh . . .

The strike had been aimed straight at Favani, who was busy fighting with two of the golems now bereft of their orbs. They were swinging their massive clubs at the graceful blue Cultivator, but she was dodging and dancing around them with relative ease.

The club didn't properly connect, and it only glanced at the orb, sending it flying violently into the corner of the wide room at a diagonal angle.

Max used a **[Tether]** to bind the construct's legs together, and flew toward the orb. He would drain all of them and become that much stronger.

More. I want more.

Reveling in his greed, Max landed next to the orb. It was *thrum*ming like a rocket ready to take off. When it finally managed to lift off the ground, Max slammed it back into the floor with heavy gravity. He now had energy to spare, and he kept the orb still. He reached into the core of the sphere and drained it.

There was no notification from the Framework, but he could again feel himself getting instantly stronger. His well-trained meridians let the power of the orb surge through them effortlessly as Max guided his new strength into his dantian, where it settled and was infused into his very being. A permanent power increase.

There was a heavy explosion which was followed by a rain of rocks and pebbles, as one of the construct giants was destroyed by Favani's attack.

One more to go.

Max wasted no time; he let his Spiritual Sense scan the room and locate the final orb infused with power. It was just about to launch at Favani.

Crack.

Max reacted instantly. He yanked on Favani. Max felt her spirit flutter and she didn't resist. She sped toward Max and crashed into him. They toppled and fell and Favani landed on top of Max, their faces inches from each other. She looked at him with shock, confusion, and embarrassment.

"I . . . I" Favani stammered.

"Move," Max said and brushed her off. "Keep the golems busy."

Not waiting for a response, Max flew toward the final stone orb.

It was already midair and flying back to its owner.

"Favani, this one!" Max called out.

The final golem was already waiting like a baseball player at the batting area. It swung immediately when the orb came back to it. The swing wasn't as hard, but it still sent the orb flying at a speed that would have been impossible for a non-Cultivator to even see.

Max dodged and tethered himself to the golem. He flew toward it, kicking it in the chest, toppling it. Afterward he used [Tether] to bind the great guardian on the floor.

"Favani!" Max called. He jumped out of the way as a storm of swords cut into the golem.

Max went after the sphere. It turned out the other golems were interested in it as well. Max was bound in battle by two of them, as they swung and tried to grab him as he went for the orb. He attacked them with gravity, slowing them down, and taking distance in the air. But the moment he did that, the golems started moving toward the stone sphere. Max could sense the destructive energy it emitted, and he yearned for it.

CHAPTER TWENTY-SEVEN

Exploration

Max and Favani both closed their eyes and leaned against the wall behind them. Max felt spent. Despite having acquired all this new power from the orbs, his meridians were throbbing with exertion.

"I need a break," Max said.

"Yes," Favani said between labored breaths. "We will camp here tonight."

"Do you need to sleep?" Max asked.

Cultivators of the Diamond stage needed very little sleep. It could still be a good idea if one had expended too much energy—it was invigorating and sped up the recovery of Spiritual Power, but it wasn't strictly necessary. Even without it, Max would be back in fighting form in two or three hours. But Favani looked like she could use a rest.

She didn't say anything, though. Instead, Max felt her spirit brush against his. It was a cool and graceful thing, with a softness hidden underneath. Favani's spirit touched his dantian briefly, then retreated.

"So much . . ." she said.

"I absorbed a lot of power from those orbs."

"How is that possible?" Favani asked.

"They were compatible with my Dao," Max said and shrugged.

"Even still," Favani said, her brows furrowing. "Absorbing power without technology like metagems . . . I do not understand."

Max explained to her the whole extent of his technique, utilizing the now-hollow bond he shared with Maverick.

"Why would you trust me with this secret?" Favani said warily.

"I thought we were allies," Max said. "Why wouldn't I tell you? You've told me stuff too."

"Nothing you can use against me," Favani said bluntly. "I could harm you with this information or use it against you in battle."

"Why would we be battling each other?" Max asked.

He could sense Favani being taken aback by his question. She was a strange woman. But eh, different cultures and all that. He wouldn't judge. This woman was a fine warrior and collaborating with her would likely yield great rewards, as she had promised.

"You are a sl— a servant of the ICCB," Favani said, her voice suddenly becoming colder. "It is only natural that we should be rivals. Perhaps even enemies."

"I don't really care about all that," Max said. "How about I just help you clear this tomb, you get what you're looking for, reward me, and we see where we go from there?"

"I would like that." Favani said in a soft voice. "You are an unusual man, Max. Are all humans like this?"

"There aren't any other humans like me," Max said.

Favani turned her head to look at him, but he refused to elaborate further.

"Let's rest," Max said. "I'll stay awake and guard you. You need the rest more than I do."

"There is no need," Favani said and produced a small blue gemstone in a metal casing, crisscrossing along the surface.

Favani tossed it in the air, and when it reached two yards above them, an umbrella of energy bloomed out of it, encasing the two of them in a dome.

"This will give us enough time to prepare for an ambush if there are threats around," Favani said. "Now, let us sleep."

Max nodded, thinking he needed one of those.

Max woke up feeling refreshed. He must have slept for three or even four hours. It was more than enough. His meridians were stable and there wasn't a hint of a throb of pain or exhaustion. His dantian, the well of his Spiritual Energy was still as a pond. The darkness around them was peaceful.

Max looked at Favani. She was in the fetal position, her hands tucked under her cheek, snoring. He had to admit she was beautiful, her features feminine, graceful, and soft—in sharp contrast to the hideous noises she was making. This girl didn't just snore, she practically shook reality itself.

It was a small wonder they didn't have a pack of monsters prowling around the protective blue array. Max didn't know how strong it was, but it felt safe.

Max tried to Cultivate. Just for fun and to keep up the habit. He let energy fill his meridians and he cycled it around for a while. But the violence of Favani's snoring was too much for Max's feeble spirit to withstand.

So he got up. He wondered if the protection array would alert Favani should he try to leave it, but he wasn't about to stay huddled up in there for hours, able to do nothing but to suffer through that cacophony.

Max pushed against the array and passed through, relieved to note that it didn't react in any way and Favani didn't stir. Max figured that she was tired enough to sleep for a while, so he might as well explore the ruins.

Dangerous? Maybe. But Max was bored.

Favani had been stingy on the details of the ICCB's origins, her people's involvement in it, and the nature of the Outsiders. Since the walls here were full of murals, Max figured they might be able to help him piece something together. With some luck, he might even find a stone tablet or something featuring a bit of history. Having the ability to understand every language was really handy. *Thanks, Ugly Space Flies.*

Max wandered around the ruins, backtracking a few corridors. He was a bit worried he might get lost, but he kept extending his Spiritual Sense periodically until he could feel Favani's spirit in the distance. Finding her was easy when you knew what you were looking for.

"I wish I had a torch," Max said to himself. "Not because I need it. I just feel the situation calls for a torch."

Talking to ourselves now, are we? Damn, I miss him.

Experimentally, Max reached into his **[Divine Soulbond]**. He found Maverick instantly. He was there but only a hollow echo. Max sat down and just stayed there a while, keeping the bond connected. Maverick was conceited, arrogant, boastful, ridiculous, bombastic, and downright insufferable. But he was Max's best buddy. And Max had to admit that he was feeling a bit lonely. Begrudgingly he admitted to himself that he missed Maverick.

"Hopefully he'll be alright soon."

The Zoos had said that they would fix him. But there seemed to be conditions and stipulations left unmentioned. *Don't trust Favani and don't ally yourself with her.*

"Why?" he asked himself aloud. "She seems alright."

There was some kind of a schism between the two factions. The last thing Max wanted was to get in between the two forces. He sighed. Knowing his luck and fate, that was exactly what was going to happen.

Max got up. There was no good reason to keep worrying. Whatever happened, happened. But right now, torch or no, he would explore the ruins and look at the murals.

Nearly every wall was covered with them. Most of them were generic and didn't seem to have much to tell. They were just depictions of battles that had transpired in the early days of the war. It was hard to imagine that a war that started eighteen thousand years ago was still ongoing. Despite all of their power, the ICCB could not stop the Outsiders.

Having spent time with Favani, and gleaning some information from the simulations and the war zone he had been in, had revealed something to Max: the ICCB were not as powerful and godlike as they had let on.

Everyone having trouble with the sorcerers was a telltale sign. If there were Cultivators indentured to the ICCB for hundreds of years, there should be those among them strong enough to take on the sorcerers. Okay, granted, there were *some*, as Max had observed from the simulations and the real fights. However, considering his own fast progress, it was unfathomable to think that if he was given even ten more years to train, that he couldn't crush a horde of the Outsider sorcerers. That is why it was strange that there were no such warriors employed.

Which led him to believe that he was already one of the strongest warriors at the ICCB's disposal. There were likely no warriors currently even at the Celestial stage. Max wondered if the leadership themselves were at that stage or if their great power was only the result of being at high-tier Diamond. Most likely so.

Max was fairly certain that a great amount of them weren't even at the Celestial stage of Cultivation. Twozerofive was most likely a Diamond-stage Cultivator. But Diamond was a vast stage. The difference between Quartz and Ruby-stage was nothing but a speck in the width of early-stage Diamond and mid-stage Diamond.

Favani is two hundred years old and only a mid-tier Diamond. And from the looks of it, she is some kind of royalty. Which means she has the resources needed.

That was slow progress. Was Max truly so talented? But Losshnak had kept up with him in Cultivation through the Games until Max had broken through to Diamond. The bold lizard had been lagging behind him but was still hanging in there. Perhaps he was similarly talented.

I hope the strike force guys are doing alright . . .

Max wandered into a room that looked like a study hall from a university—an amphitheater of benches descending down into a platform and a podium.

Had people lived here?

There were no murals on these walls, only empty cold stone. Max infused some more Spiritual Energy into his eyes, letting himself see more clearly. The floors were covered with crumbled stone. But when Max got down to the podium, his heart jumped with excitement. There were stone tablets on the floor! Mostly intact, even.

CHAPTER TWENTY-EIGHT

A History Lesson

M ax looked at the stone tablets. They were all filled with text—small but perfectly legible. Only a Cultivator or a high-powered laser could produce such clean work on hard stone. Max took a quick look at the tablets and could see they were meant to be assembled to tell a story. So he organized them accordingly and sat down to read:

The exact details of how the species known as the Outsiders came into existence are unknown. There was scant communication with them after they were identified as being extremely hostile. But the individuals who discovered them claim that they are intelligent.

There are three identified subspecies of the Outsiders and one which has not been verified.

When the explorers of the Zoos and the Kiritus Corporation first entered the Outside, they discovered it was a universe very identical to theirs—other than being completely overwhelmed by the Tar, a substance which seems to be the basis of Outsider existence. This discovery was very unsettling, as the Anti-Spiritual Power emitted by the Tar was evident to the explorers. However, in their greed for knowledge, they decided to venture further into the new universe they had just discovered.

It is unclear whether this new universe was the only one that the Outsiders had conquered or consumed. It might have been their original reality, or it might have been one of many. It is generally believed that the Outsiders destroyed and consumed multiple realities before entering ours. It was almost as if they were simply waiting to be discovered.

The explorers didn't initially visit star systems that were consumed by the Tar, which was wise of them. Had they had any more sense, they would have simply returned all together. But their thirst for knowledge made them finally visit one of the planets despite the warning signs.

This is where they discovered the Outsiders' baseline species. It is not important which form they took in the reality in which they were discovered. They are shape-shifters, which is what is crucial. The Outsiders' way of life is to assimilate material, especially biomass. They will eventually turn unliving material to their own ends, given enough time and no other options, but it is biomass through which they gain their endless power.

They assimilate DNA into themselves and evolve through it. The baseline species consists of two major variants: the creatures that absorb, assimilate, and transform the biomass, and the warrior species.

It is clear that the Outsiders are hostile by nature, and they will take a myriad of forms in attempts to optimize their combat skills. Why they choose the specific forms that they do remains a mystery, as they don't seem to be the most efficient forms possible. But don't mistake our luck of understanding as a lack of logic on their parts. They work from an entirely different frame of reference.

A notable feature present in this group is their ability to reuse their biomass and the Tar. When they're destroyed, they release their essence into their immediate surroundings. This essence is called the Tar. The Tar is a protogenic biomass with some form of consciousness. Very little research has been able to be conducted, for the Tar needs to be utterly destroyed in order to fully neutralize the Outsider threat. But observation has shown that, when they release their Tar, others of their kind will absorb it and strengthen themselves, which means that the strength of their forces is not diminished if combat is handled in the traditional way.

That is why the destruction of the Tar is pivotal to fighting their forces, but this is something that they have developed strategies against. This is why the enemy deploys Sorcerers. They are the battles' overseers. They seem to be connected to a hive mind like the Outsiders' infantry units, but they also possess some manner of autonomy. They seem to have preferences. Some are cowardly, some are cruel, some are smart, and some are stupid. It is unclear why this is, for their abilities and combat capabilities are uniform. Specific manuals for battling these creatures have been written, so we will refrain from providing an overview of their abilities here. This memo is an exploration of the nature of these creatures and how they connect to the Outsider threat as a whole.

In addition to being the overseers, they are also commanders. They are designed to take out the most prominent threats to their advance and to assimilate the resources, as well as protect their process of absorbing biomass.

There are two particularly noteworthy things about their strategies. Firstly, when you attack the Tar directly, you will summon a sorcerer. They fiercely attack anyone who attempts to diminish the power of their collective.

Secondly, when a sorcerer's life is threatened, they will call others of their kin to defend them. And they are very hard to kill. Even if you manage to fatally wound one, you will have a difficult time finishing it off when you're being forced to fight many of them at once.

Some diplomatic communication attempts have been made with the sorcerers. They seem to be able to understand spoken language to a degree. They are intelligent enough to realize they are being spoken to. But it is likely that they simply refuse to communicate back. Even though the sorcerers have traits that would seem to require personhood, they are not people. The Outsiders are creatures who only seek one thing: to assimilate biomass. And these sorcerers are the overseers of that process. If you are of middling Cultivation, it is best to ally yourself with other Cultivators or run. They are merciless and your death will result in your essence being assimilated into their biomass and thus weakening our force and strengthening theirs.

This is why they pose such a profoundly existential threat. Every single loss is a costly one for us and a boon for them. It is a phenomenon that in some cultures is called a "snowball effect." No efficient strategy to mitigate this effect has been devised, and we urge every single strategist to spend most of their time considering this lopsided mechanic in the battle against our enemy.

We will proceed to provide an overall view of the threat shortly, but first, it is important to consider the Outsiders' other two classifications.

The third classification is common. They are the transportation methods. The Outsiders have been able to create rifts from their reality into ours ever since they first took note of us. It seems that in some way they have imprinted unto our universe, and now they can create gateways. We cannot study these gateways because they appear at random and disappear immediately afterward, leaving zero residual energy or radiation or anything to suggest a space-time anomaly had even happened there.

The transport class has two functions. It will carry a so-called "seed" biomass which is used to establish all the necessary elements on a planet or a moon to start the assimilation process. But there is another stranger, more sinister function: they can generate widespread suppression fields. For some reason the Outsider threat has evolved to counteract the effects of Cultivation. This is most likely the result of extensive combat with species that have engaged with them before, namely the master-species that visited our universe at some point. It is almost certain that our universe is not the first ever to be threatened by this creature.

This suppression field will affect Cultivators of every level, and it can span millions of miles in space. There are a few rare Cultivators with very specific Daos that can engage combat in space, and thus it is crucial that these individuals are used to disrupt the transportation class creatures. Additionally, it is of paramount importance to develop technologies which allow for fast space travel as well as combat, and potentially technology that can disrupt the Cultivation suppression fields. The transport class creatures are not hostile in and of themselves, but they are able to defend themselves and counterattack if threatened. They're big and sturdy, so preparing an assault against them is not simple. Preparation is key.

The Outsiders' fourth classification is elusive. Only a few sparse reports of its existence are available. This creature has a nightmarish aspect. The reports about its form *vary, but it is said to be enormous—on a planetary scale. Report #201 left by the old Zoos faction described a solar system within which all of the planets had been assimilated—dead rock covered in Tar. And rather than orbiting a star, they orbited a monster of horrific size and aspects.*

The postulation is that these creatures are the hive minds of the Outsiders. Whether they are many of them, acting as nodes or clusters to an even-larger super-organism, such as a neural network or a field of fungus, it is difficult to say.

But the power and vastness of these creatures was described as so preposterously large that it would take several Celestial-stage Cultivators to even attempt to approach them.

These creatures do not Cultivate, but they do clearly understand the concept and even have their own bastardized version of it. The Sorcerers are a prime example of this, emitting power very similar to Spiritual Energy and possessing abilities that someone with an advanced Dao could command.

But these creatures that were encountered in expeditions which spawned reports #201 and #218 emit a very specific kind of energy. It could almost be considered Anti-Cultivation or Anti-Life Force. It is very fitting, for the sole purpose of the Outsiders seems to revolve around destruction. Perhaps it is more complicated than that from their perspective, and it is known that there is always a seed of creation in every destruction. However, we refuse to be destroyed.

Whether the ICCB's plan to form an army of slave warriors can be seen as ethical or not is outside the scope of this essay. Sometimes desperate times require desperate measures. And there should be no mistake about the gravity of the existential threat that the Outsider threat poses.

However, we are not alone in our plight. It is clear that just as there is something so profoundly sinister as to be singularly concentrated on the destruction of all life force other than itself, there are forces of equal benignity in this universe or some other reality.

Because it is clear that we have been visited. And we were visited precisely because of the Outsider threat. The Framework had of course been utilized for eons by every sentient species that has attempted to Cultivate ever since it was discovered. However, it was truly activated only once the Outsider threat first entered our reality. This confirms that the master-species that designed the Framework knew that this threat was out there. Had they escaped into this reality from the Outsider threat from somewhere else? It is impossible to know. Why are there no records, archeological findings or other technology left behind by this master-species? The prevailing theory is that these creatures are a wandering civilization of altruistic disposition. It is likely that they travel between realities and infuse them with the Framework, giving emergent species the chance to fight the Outsiders, if they are unfortunate enough to encounter them.

Max leaned back and sighed. His heart was pounding as he read. It had felt revelatory.

This threat—these Outsiders—had been a pestilence on the whole universe for over eighteen thousand years. While humans had busied themselves with inventing sticks and the wheel, the ICCB and the Jianari as well as most likely many other species had been waging a war for their very existence. Max couldn't help but feel a flash of gratitude toward the ICCB. As much as he found their practices distasteful, they had done what they had seen necessary.

I'm still not about to become their little servant. But I get it. And I want to fight.

Max read through the tablets again. He could feel his resolve strengthening. He squeezed a fist and destructive Intent surged through him.

I will destroy this threat.

Then he suddenly picked up on something. Something eerie and sinister. Just a faint feeling in the back of his mind. A sense of danger. Dread. A very specific dread.

Surely not.

But Max had to act on it. His intuition had been his lifeline ever since arriving at Alpha Ludus. He was not about to stop listening to it right now.

Something had stirred the old, stale air of these ruins. Something had followed them.

CHAPTER TWENTY-NINE

Fight for Survival

Max ran through the corridors back to Favani. To his frustration, he realized he had ventured far into the ruins. He focused on his Spiritual Sense to find her. Her spirit was still; she was clearly still asleep. Then Max flared out his senses, trying to verify whether his ill feeling had been accurate.

He found it. Something was approaching. Something bad. It could only mean one thing: somehow the Outsiders had picked up their scent and followed them into the tomb.

Max pushed Spiritual Energy into his legs and lungs and blasted through the corridors with explosive speed, barely touching the floor, using [Tether] and [Telekinesis] to bounce himself off of walls at the corners.

Max was getting close to the large room with the destroyed golems and Favani when he heard chittering and a large, encroaching mass. He looked behind him into the dark corridor and enhanced his eyesight to penetrate the darkness.

A mass of black sludge came sloshing his way. All sorts of monstrosities were emerging and dissipating into it, as if the Tar wasn't sure which forms it wanted to animate. But above them floated something fully formed and terrifying.

It was tall with eight arms hanging down loosely by its sides. It wore a white mask with a malicious grin spanning cheek to cheek.

Max could feel the sorcerer noticing him.

Great . . . Doing this without Maverick is gonna be just great.

A purple cloud of smoke billowed around Max. But he had expected this and held his breath. He blasted off and away from the miasma, using his Cultivation to enhance his speed. He got twenty yards away when a black fireball connected with the purple smoke and the corridor exploded, making everything tremor. Stone began to fall from the walls and ceiling.

I sure hope that woke Favani up.

Max sped through the corridors, setting off a local **[Gravity Storm]** here and there.

When he finally arrived at the large room, he noticed that the blue barrier was already turned off. That was good. It meant Favani was awake.

Max kicked off the ground and landed in front of her.

"Situation?" she asked immediately in a clipped tone.

"One sorcerer," Max said between breaths. "Brought friends."

"Cursed creatures," she muttered.

"Can you fight?" Max asked. "Recovered enough?"

"And if I couldn't?" Favani asked. "Where would we escape to?"

"Back to the surface?" Max asked.

"Absolutely not possible," Favani said. "They're a hive mind, you know. If we manage to get away from this sorcerer, you can be sure another will follow."

Max brushed against Favani's spirit in an attempt to gauge her strength. She sensed it, of course, and swatted him away.

"Rude," Favani said.

"I need to be in the know."

"We will perish here if we fight, Max," Favani said solemnly.

"So what do we do?"

Favani was silent for a moment. Max immediately extended his Spiritual Senses. The Outsiders were getting close. They had a minute to spare, at best.

"Do you trust me, Max?" Favani asked suddenly.

"Kind of?"

"It is up to you to judge whether that is enough or not," Favani said. "Here is what I suggest. In the next room I suspect is the treasure we are seeking. A technology to harness the metagems in a fashion my people have lost. But I will need time to figure out how the technology works."

"You want me to hold them off until you can come on the first light of the fifth day?" Max asked and gave a little smirk.

"Fifth day?" Favani asked, confused. "I do not think it will take—"

"Forget it," Max said. "I'll trust you on this. You seem honorable. But if we make it out of this, you owe me big time."

"I already do," Favani said quietly.

"Then get a move on, Princess," Max said.

Favani nodded, her face etched with worry and solemnity. But there was no fear. That was good. Max knew this was not the time for fear.

He breathed in deep, gathering his Spiritual Energy into his meridians as Favani ran toward the large double doors on the other side of the room.

Max lifted up in the air and flew toward the corridor. He could see the outline of the encroaching horde rushing toward him.

[Gravity Storm]

Max didn't use only his Spiritual Energy or the gravitational force. He infused the storm with his destructive Intent, so that the black biomass writhed, becoming singed as the pressure assaulted it. The sorcerer kept grinning despite that, but that was fine with Max. He summoned **[Scythe of Oblivion]**.

The large scythe cut through the air in a wide arc, spinning violently as it sliced into the sorcerer, who weaved its many hands and erected a red bubble of energy. Max infused the scythe's blade with his destructive Intent, however, and it cut through the barrier. The weapon struck true, cutting a deep gash into the sorcerer from shoulder to navel.

The creature screeched, its white masked grin turning into a grimace of fury. It hurled fireballs of black flame at Max, but he flew out of their range and recalled his scythe. It flew smoothly toward him and Max grabbed it and flourished it like a samurai's sword, sending the tar-like blood of the sorcerer dripping to the floor, where it hissed and writhed.

Max released the **[Gravity Storm]** holding back the horde, for it took too much of his energy and focus. The horde started morphing into more distinct shapes—mostly dragonflies and mantabats.

The sorcerer is directing the growth. It's making air units, because of my ability to fly.

Max infused the scythe with his destructive Intent and made it *thrum* with power. He hurled it to the center of the biomass that was now flooding from the corridor into the large room. It cut through the creatures like a hot knife into butter. But the creatures only broke and dissipated back into Tar, which was absorbed by the other emergent forms. Max would only tire himself out like this. His real fight was with the sorcerer.

Max flew out of a blooming purple cloud of Cultivation-sapping miasma and saw that a sorcerer was preparing a fireball for him. This time, Max tried something different. Max concentrated on the center of the flame and tethered it ever so slightly to the sorcerer's mask. But it was a very subtle thing, with no tug. Yet.

Then he concentrated on the purple miasma. Some of the Outsiders had already taken form; two mantabats had already started lobbing their corrosive blobs at him. He dodged with ease and concentrated his destructive Intent on the purple cloud. The fireball was ready, and the sorcerer pulled back its hand to throw it. Max then focused all of his concentration on the **[Tether]**, and the sorcerer was instantly absorbed in an explosion of black flames. The corridor rumbled and some of the brickwork from the ceiling fell upon the black mass of Tar, smashing emerging forms to pieces, buying Max more time.

The sorcerer screeched in anger. Max sent the scythe out to cleave through the two mantabats and an emerging swarm of the horned dragonflies. They were all cut down and fell to the floor of the tomb in a dark puddle. Some of the shambling humanoid forms with their long tongues lolling out of their mouths emerged from the biomass and ran toward the puddles of Tar left by the flying units. They absorbed it and grew larger. Max gained greater altitude until he was almost at the ceiling.

No room to escape any further upward. The sorcerer will most likely notice and try to force me into a checkmate.

But all the while this was happening, Max was extending his destructive Intent. His meridians were strained. Right now his Intent required intense control. Some of it was in the [**Scythe of Oblivion**], which was keeping the biomass at bay, preventing most of it from taking form. Some of it was gathering on a particular shambler. Just a fleck. Just a molecule's worth of Intent. But Max's Dao was strong. It should be enough.

But most of it was on the purple miasma. It floated in the air, thick as smoke but completely unthreatening. Max was infusing it with destructive Intent.

Will the sorcerer bloom another? If it forces me to dodge downward with another one of those purple smoke clouds, it might get a direct hit with a fireball.

The sorcerer attempted just that. Max, having anticipated the move, dodged backward, toward the door where Favani had entered.

That girl sure is taking her sweet time.

Max focused his Intent. His meridians were aching; he had to release it. The shambler down on the floor exploded. The Tar flew out in every direction. The sorcerer cried out in fury and started peppering Max with small black fireballs, to inflict any amount of damage it could.

The miasma didn't explode. But some of it did dissipate, the ominous cloud getting thinner and smaller. It had been a waste of energy but worth a try.

However . . .

Quickly, Max directed the scythe to pester the sorcerer, flying toward it and slicing at it from every angle. In response, the sorcerer sprouted those horrid white tentacles to attack the scythe.

Max, for his part, now charged a speck of his Intent against a number of the Outsiders: a shambler, a mantabat, and two dragonflies, and then dodged out of the way.

As he did, he pressed on the Intent, snapping his fingers. All four targets exploded, the Tar that had been animating them turning into a ruined, burnt crisp.

The sorcerer charged at him, the tentacles flaring violently around. One slapped Max on the arm, and a penetrating pain entered his mind, causing his vision to go blank for a moment.

He instinctively flew away, infusing the sorcerer with the full weight of his ability to alter gravity. The sorcerer was taken by surprise, and slapped to the floor like a wet rock.

That gave Max enough time to recover enough to get out of the way of another cloud of purple miasma. But as disoriented by pain as he was, he accidentally inhaled and cursed himself for it. Immediately it started taking effect, sapping the flow of his meridians.

I'm on borrowed time now. Don't get too comfortable, Favani.

The sorcerer stopped and the mask that had mostly been furious before now sported a malicious, victorious grin. Max didn't think the creature had that much to gloat about. Just a whiff of the purple cloud wasn't fatal, even though it would hinder him.

But then Max realized something and extended his spiritual sense.

"Oh . . ."

The sorcerer had called for reinforcements. Two more were on their way.

CHAPTER THIRTY

Jianari Legacy

The room Favani was currently in was a masterwork of craftsmanship. The floors were made of the purest clear glass, below which an endless abyss of darkness swallowed all light. The walls were studded with gemstones that glowed faintly. Metagems. The legacy of her people. In the middle of the room was something that had to be a Cultivation array, although it was of a kind Favani had never seen before.

It was a strange contraption made of glass, whose swirling tubes ended in vials, sometimes after fusing together to create specific mixtures of the liquids within. On the other side of the room were concoctions of various colors and viscosities encased in sealed glass jars. Favani went up to them, took pictures of them with a memory crystal, unsealed all of the jars, and took samples in small crystal boxes, which she then stored in a storage ring. Then she moved on, trying to keep up a fast pace.

There was a set of instructions written on stone slabs. For a moment, Favani feared she wouldn't be able to read them but found that with a translation manual, she was able to get the job done. It would be slow, but this was the only way.

Max could have read them in an instant, but he was fighting.

Favani worked frantically. The mechanisms were designed to be simple, and she had well-written instructions, but she was still working with technology that was thousands of years old. This would take time. Time that they had only a limited amount of.

"Will he be alright?" she found herself asking no one in particular.

She shook her head. Wrong place, wrong time for these kinds of thoughts. She needed to focus as a warrior should. She wished she could fight, but the reality had to be faced as it was. This was the best course of action.

She started by documenting everything onto a memory crystal. She was going to set up a teleportation array here, but whether they could use it wasn't guaranteed. The Outsiders could destroy the contraption if they overwhelmed Max and forced Favani to escape.

She could teleport away at any point with a very expensive device given to her by her father, the king. But she had too much honor to even consider using it, unless it was the absolute last resort. This man she had met was . . . special.

The fighting outside sounded fierce. That was the only way she had ever seen Max fight. With all of his heart, holding nothing back. It was a beautiful thing, the hallmark of a true warrior.

Yes. I think he is worthy.

It was exceedingly rare to see such prowess, especially at such an age.

And he is fairly handsome, if a bit short. But that could be fixed . . .

This always happened to Favani. When she was nervous and under pressure, her mind wandered. As powerful a warrior as she was in her own right, she couldn't maintain her focus. Her brother and father both had their theories as to why that was.

Favani knew the real reason. Whenever she was afraid, her mind wandered in order to escape. She feared the responsibility. The failure of not being able to meet expectations.

Being the crown princess of her father's galaxy-spanning empire of course was a big burden to shoulder. She knew she was remarkable, but would that be enough?

The strange glass contraption chimed, and a thick glowing liquid started pumping through the translucent tube.

"It's chock full of Spiritual Energy . . ."

Favani moved with the grace of a high-level Cultivator and collected the liquid in a crystal container. It was hot as lava and shone brightly.

This is a melted metagem. This device . . . It can create metagems from scratch.

It was just like his father had told her. The old technology was here, buried on this strange barren planet on the edge of the Milky Way. The difference between a natural gem and a synthetically made one was groundbreaking. The metagems, which were the basis of Favani's people's cultivation, were these days crafted from gemstones created in pressurized conditions deep underground on planets with sufficient carbon.

That came with limitations. Favani was no expert in metagem crafting, but it had something to do with the density of the gem and the potential amount of facets one could create. They all played a part in aiding Cultivation. And most importantly, only diamonds could be naturally formed . . .

It hadn't been the ICCB but the Jianari who had discovered Cultivation eons ago. And along with that, their practice of using gemstones for their Cultivation. The power varied from the lowly quartz to the dense, beautiful diamond. That is how the stages had been named—after a Cultivator's ability to craft and use certain gemstones to aid their Cultivation.

That is why Favani's people thought Celestial-stage Cultivators were nigh-impossible to produce these days. There were no known methods to create Celestial-stage gemstones.

But now . . .

My father could use this to leapfrog the Cultivation level of our whole civilization . . .

The gem she had just produced was bright red. It was beautiful, dense, and of an extremely high quality. But small.

I can only produce Ruby-grade metagems for now . . .

She cut herself some slack. It had been a first attempt, hastily made. She might be able to even create Diamond-stage metagems. A fitting reward for the unlikely hero she had just met.

She started creating another metagem. This one would make a difference. She reread the instructions and realized this would be risky. She would be all but spent after using her own Spiritual Energy to create this metagem.

I won't have enough power left to activate the emergency teleport . . .

Was this man trustworthy enough? Would she risk her life and the future of her people for him? That sounded preposterous. But the potential of this Cultivator, Max, was astounding. If she could . . . Yes, she would have to. It was bold, but if she was right, Max could be an asset to the family even beyond this metagem discovery . . .

She decided to take the plunge. Max was worth the risk. She started crafting the metagem and poured her very essence into it.

CHAPTER THIRTY-ONE

The Last Stand

Max was gassing out. When fighting the sorcerers with their tendrils out, he had learned that not getting hit by them was a winning strategy. He had been struck twice. The pain and fatigue were mounting. And that was not all. He was clearly doing a great job fighting against this sorcerer. In fact, under normal circumstances he would have been thrilled. He was doing this without the aid of Maverick, who possessed basically half of their combined power. He was holding his own. He had clearly advanced enormously in his Cultivation.

But despite that, any joy he might have made from progress turned to ash in his mouth. Two more sorcerers were watching the fight with particularly malicious grins on their faces. Max had managed to severely wound the sorcerer with its tentacles out twice—exactly the number of times he had been struck by the white pain of its weapon.

But every time he had gained a chance to make a fatal strike, the two other sorcerers had interjected and forced Max to retreat and take a breath.

Now, despite the fact that the sorcerer Max was fighting was clearly tired, it was sporting a nasty grin on its mask.

They're toying with me.

Max gritted his teeth. Even if this was his last stand, he would give it his all. He gathered up his destructive Intent, pushing his meridians to the brink. He considered using [**Scythe of Oblivion**] for the attack, but it was risky. Right now, it was cutting down the emerging creatures from the Tar which covered the floor. No, he didn't want any extra distractions; the scythe was where it should be.

Max focused on the Intent. He could do nothing but place tiny specks of it around his immediate vicinity. But they were potent. They flared up as subtle sensations all over the sorcerer's body. The sorcerer seemed to sense it, because it immediately launched to attack Max again, its white tentacles whipping wildly.

Max created a powerful [Tether] between himself and the sorcerer. It repelled the attack, stopping the enemy mid-flight, leaving the fiend stunned as it almost fell out of the air. Max ignited his Intent, and its body exploded.

A great screech of anger and pain sliced through the air as the sorcerer's black body burst, pieces erupting this way and that. The two other sorcerers immediately rushed to their ally's mangled torso and started aiding it in regeneration. Max placed a concentrated [Gravity Storm] on them and started infusing it with the power of his destructive Intent. The [Scythe of Oblivion] then arced in the air and crashed into the cluster of sorcerers, slicing and spinning up and down, attempting to create as much mayhem as possible.

Max exerted himself to his fullest. His dantian was getting empty. His meridians were aching with a throbbing, insistent pain. But he would not let up. And the sorcerers were disrupted. After a few seconds, they fled from the body of their defeated comrade and menacingly rose up in the air.

Max had defeated a sorcerer.

The two remaining sorcerers attacked with a viciousness Max had no stamina left to repel. They chased him, giving him no space to attack. The other sorcerer made the purple toxic miasma plume up around Max, and he managed to fly out of the way just as the other sorcerer lobbed a fireball at him. At the same time, Max had to dodge globs of corrosive acid from the mantabats and the shamblers' long tongues.

While Max ran and dodged, he tried to attack and disrupt the enemy with his [Scythe of Oblivion] but both of the sorcerers had their tentacles out and, with their help in addition to the red barriers, the scythe couldn't get in through.

And he was way too tired for that.

He took in huffs of the purple toxic miasma. A fireball singed his skin here and there, and when he flew too close to a wall, an explosion of black and purple made him crash into it, causing unpleasant crunches in his shoulders and sides.

The sorcerer's furious visages were turning gleeful and malevolent again.

I'm going to die.

Max's mind wasn't filled with horror at the thought. It was only a statement. There was no way he could keep this up, and even if he could, the enemy wouldn't ever back down. It was only a matter of time.

But time is what I'm trying to buy here.

Max's mind felt like it was being sapped. His dodges got less and less sharp. His body was aching, suffering from exertion, spiritual exhaustion, and physical damage. The toxic fumes of the sorcerer's purple clouds were seeping into his spirit, slowly paralyzing his meridians, and fogging his mind.

A distant whisper in the back of Max's mind asked him why he didn't just give up.

That angered him. Max Cromwell didn't give up. He didn't yield. It didn't matter if it would take him two more minutes or twenty: he would fight and he would endure.

He spun around and summoned his scythe to reach him. He grabbed it and sped through the air as the sorcerers aimed their next projectiles. He flew right toward one of them, infusing the [**Scythe of Oblivion**] with the last dregs of his destructive Intent. Flying as fast as a suicide drone, he shot past one of his enemies, cutting in a perfect horizontal line.

The tentacles lashed; the red energy bubble flared. But they were both cut, and the sorcerer's legs were separated from its torso.

Angry screeches. But as one sorcerer fell, the other crashed into Max, filled with unadulterated fury.

The tentacles latched onto him. The slick white things wrapped around his hands, legs, and neck. They *squeezed*. Max tried to breathe in, but only a cough of blood came out as the enemy tried to crush his throat. He struggled and tried to call on power from his dantian. There was hardly a trickle left. Max was barely conscious, so spent was his power and will.

He started blacking out as the sorcerer pulled him in closer. His body was going limp, and consciousness was leaving him.

As his vision dimmed, the last thing he saw was a powerful vibrant flash of green and a sword decapitating the sorcerer holding him.

CHAPTER THIRTY-TWO

Plan Assessment

The atmosphere in the ICCB Council Room could have been described as restless. That was a feature of creatures with corporeal existence. The Zoos Collective felt no restlessness. There were only probabilities and outcomes. The probable outcomes for this particular scenario were of course predetermined.

The faculty that was in charge of managing the council meetings was issued a reprimand, which had been voted on. The plans were set and the ICCB leadership had been acquired in accordance with the collective vision, but this was not the time to be arrogant.

This was a time to manage politics and buy time. Maximillian Cromwell would deliver. The asset's companion would, of course, be repaired. They didn't fully understand what the asset's [**Divine Soulbond**] meant, but that was unlikely to affect their ultimate plans. What mattered was that Maximillian Cromwell kept advancing.

His talent as a Cultivator was absolute. There might not have been a more suitable individual in existence, and to have him emerge at such an opportune time . . . The plans had been set in motion, and then this human appeared!

It was just so perfect. All of the Collective agreed. And "perfect" was not a word that the Zoos used lightly.

"So, are you saying that the asset is damaged and lost?" Azzzhtik'Likzirrruk, the Swarm's spokesperson, asked in an unforgiving tone.

[As we stated before, the asset, also known as Maximillian Cromwell, is not damaged. He uses a sapient device called the Maverick through a very interesting Cultivation method called [Divine Soulbond]. This Maverick has been damaged by an Outsider Sorcerer using something very specific. It was so specific that it caught our attention.]

"You have not addressed the fact that you have lost the asset!" one of the Grays standing on their floating platform said sharply.

"What was this specific thing?" Azzzhtik'Likzirrruk asked.

The Zoos Collective had already voted to disclose the information. It was very likely that the Swarm already knew. They were powerful sorcerers and most likely had the right people scrying the planet where the asset had been placed to develop himself. There was a high probability that this was a test to see if the Zoos would be willing to share information. Of course, the Swarm knew that the Collective knew. Divulging the information for the Kiritus Corporation or the Z'var was not an issue nor out of accord with the Zoos' plans.

[The Outsiders are very aware of the asset as an entity. Both his strengths and weaknesses are known, and for some reason the enemy is very interested in Maximillian Cromwell. The tentacle attack is something that is generally only deployed against higher-tier Cultivators to disable their Dao weapons, mostly Intent. However, the sorcerer's hidden weapon was augmented to also attack a Soulbonded creature. This is unprecedented, which verifies the suspicion that the Outsiders attacking Alpha Ludus is not an accident. They knew of this human, and they want to stop him before he grows too powerful.]

"And now he has escaped your clutches," one of the Grays said, angrily swatting at the air. "We should be pumping the asset with Cultivation supplies and preparing him."

[And why do you think the asset is with Princess Favani of the Jianari Empire? We made a strategic play on the Jianari Empire taking interest in the asset. They will fund his advancement.]

"And attempt to forge an alliance. You have delivered the asset into the hands of our rivals," Azzzhtik'Likzirrruk said, and his accompanying metallic screech bore an intense undertone of anger.

[We still have custody of Maverick, and the Collective intends to use its repair as a bargaining chip. We recognize the risk we have taken, but if the gamble pays off, we will have the asset back, and we will have cut a significant amount of expenses in advancing his Cultivation. Need I remind the Council that the asset is no longer able to benefit from the Framework, as he has recalibrated it. Advancing his power is becoming exponentially expensive. Alling our rivals to deplete their resources in order to increase his power is a wise course of action on our parts.]

"The Kiritus Corporation does not approve," the leader of the Grays said from his floating platform. "We are ready to use a considerable amount of veto power to force you to return the asset into our custody. We believe this is too large a risk to take."

"Why not?" the leader of the frog-people spoke from the green gel in which his retinue resided. "Alpha Ludus is not more valuable than any other habitable planet. It is true that we have set it up as a perfect environment to use the Framework to find powerful individuals, but ultimately it is expendable if push comes to shove."

"This is not about the planet," Azzzhtik'Likzirrruk said and buzzed higher above the table to regard them all imperiously. "This is about the Zoos- Collective taking undue risks with an asset that is all of ours."

[We must remind you that humans are a species that was specifically selected by the Zoos Collective. If the Cosmic Games had proceeded as planned, he would have certainly prevailed and thus been in a contract with the Zoos Collective, not the ICCB. You have no stake or ownership in Maximillian Cromwell.]

"The situation has changed," Azzzhtik'Likzirrruk said. "The asset is too powerful to be held by your faction."

[According to what stipulation? We are allowing you to have a voice in the matter, because we recognize the uniqueness of the asset's talent. But make no mistake, he is the property of the Collective.]

"Seems to me that he will likely be property of the Jianari Empire," one of the frogs said, and they all laughed, a burbling sound.

[That will remain to be seen. It will be difficult to acquire the asset after the empire gets a hold of it, but not impossible. His Cultivation is so extraordinary that it is worth taking risks for. Especially since the Outsiders have taken interest in him.]

"Could he truly be talented enough to warrant the interest of the Outsiders?" the leader of the frogs asked.

"His growth is unprecedented," one of the Grays said. "We would like to once again offer a joint contract with the Zoos Collective if—"

[Denied.]

"The attack on Alpha Ludus worries the Kiritus Corporation," one of the Grays admitted. "It is uncharacteristic. Could there be more to this?"

"There is nothing out of the ordinary with regards to the scouting and assault party that the enemy is deploying. It is being monitored and attacked as we speak," the leader of the frogs said.

"Should we expend teleportation resources and outright destroy it?" one of the Grays asked.

[The Collective wishes to observe the asset in action. His Dao is unique, and it will certainly further develop in battle. It is more beneficial for us to let him struggle against the Outsiders, even if the end result is having to evacuate him and relinquish the planet.]

"Has there been any further inquiry into his Dao?" Azzzhtik'Likzirrruk asked, the buzzing soft and alluring.

Another question. The Swarm was so insistent on an answer to this one that they placed a subtle spell on the Zoos to the point that most of their voting system was scrambled in favor of answering the question. The Swarm had kept this spell a secret for a long time, so revealing it now was a testament to how important this asset indeed was. Once their minds had been broken from the charm, the Zoos Collective rejoiced.

Maximillian Cromwell seemed to have one of the absolute Daos, in other words one of the ones with a counterpart. The further a Dao was diluted from the absolute, the weaker it innately was. It could be said that the perfect Dao was *Dao* itself—a paradox, impossible to achieve. So the absolute Daos were the next best thing.

The Collective possessed a very powerful Dao that they had Cultivated for eons: The Dao of the Many. It was very versatile but also too specific for their purposes. Even with countless time and endless resources, there was only so much it could be developed. The Kiritus Corporation had an individual called Zerozerothree, one of the council members, who was in possession of the Dao of Wrath, which was equally powerful to that of the emperor of Jianari Empire, King Valdemar III, who was in possession of the Dao of Tyranny.

But none of these were absolute. They had no counterpart. They were derived from more powerful concepts. But Maximillian Cromwell was absolute: *Destruction*.

Its counterpart was Creation. Just like Life and Death were counterparts, as well as Order and Chaos. There had been a Cultivator with Dao of Chaos, but the Collective had had to assassinate him for their plans to succeed. Now that another holder of an absolute Dao had emerged, the timing was ripe—nay, perfect. The Zoos only needed to make sure to thwart any ideas or plans of neutralizing the asset.

So obviously, the Collective would not divulge any of this information. The Swarm was too rich and powerful. They might even attempt to assassinate Maximillan Cromwell in a dire situation, if they saw it as the only option. The collective therefore had to provide a situation with probabilities that would steer toward a peaceful reacquisition of the asset. They would, of course, be willing to lend the power of the asset to any willing party, however—for a price.

[There is little to add. You have already been informed of his ability to use his Intent as well as the extent of its power. Needless to say, being able to target individual cells and destroy them at will is the mark of an extremely powerful Dao. But we shall learn more when the asset develops his Cultivation further and tests it in battle.]

"We should not let Alpha Ludus fall so easily," the Grays demanded angrily. "We shall veto—"

"With what veto points?" Azzzhtik'Likzirrruk said with a sharp screech. "After you foolishly spent most of them in your quarrel against the Zoos over a pittance of a matter, we no longer have enough combined veto points to force action. If we had, the asset would be back on Alpha Ludus and preparing under his strike force instructor."

Publicly acknowledging the alliance between the Swarm and the Kiritus Corporation was an interesting move. It could have been an honest slip of the tongue, of course, but it did not matter much, as things stood. It was common knowledge that the two factions had allied themselves soon after the Zoos had taken charge.

But it was, indeed, a shame that the Kiritus Corporation did not have enough veto points to affect outcomes. The Zoos Collective had amassed veto points and expended resources at just the right times, taken the correct calculated risks to reach this position. They would hold this position and use their wisdom for the betterment of the universe.

They were the stewards of reality now. And Maximillian Cromwell would be *the* asset to watch. With his involvement, the Collective could rule reality for the foreseeable future, and all would benefit.

CHAPTER THIRTY-THREE

At the Estate

Max woke up in an unfamiliar place. For one thing, he woke up in an actual, honest-to-goodness bed, which he definitely wasn't used to any time recently. To call it exquisite would have been an understatement. Soft, but firm mattress, the pillow just right, and the blanket on him heavy and comforting. He was warm but not hot, and the air in the room was pleasant to breathe.

There was no pain. Max recalled the last of his feverish memories. He looked around the room. It was ornate and stylish. The wall panels and roof were a fine dark wood, decorated with paintings of red, blue and purple hues. In the corners of the room were statues carved out of gemstone. They shone brightly, clearly infused with some sort of magic.

His bed had four posts with bed curtains made of white silk and embroidered with gold.

It's like the guest room in a billionaire's summer home.

Max reasoned that he had to have been saved by Favani and transported to one of her people's abodes. That was good. Max would have to thank her for it. That also meant that he would get the compensation that he was promised.

Max tried to move but found he wasn't able. All he could do was turn his head—slightly. Max's eyes dashed around frantically. He didn't seem to be restrained. No—he wasn't. Or if he was, they had restrained him with a paralyzing agent, as he couldn't lift so much as a finger.

Still, Max refused to panic. He didn't seem to have been drugged, nor was he likely paralyzed, and even if he was, it probably wouldn't be permanent. The most likely explanation was exhaustion. He had never fought so hard in his life.

Max's mind went back to the fight.

There had been no Level Up, no Karma points, no advancements in any of his abilities.

But damn, had he grown in just that single fight. It had been defining. He had put himself in absolute danger, due to a promise he had made to someone, and he had not quit. He had given his *all* to fight the enemy and that had changed him. Something had changed in his mind and soul. He could feel it. He had discovered a new sort of strength. It was as if a limiter had been removed from his mind.

I had no idea how capable I actually was.

Max was snapped out of his thoughts when something strange entered the room—a little person, flying on hummingbird wings.

He was rather ugly, with large eyes wide apart, a soft round face, and a potato nose. He was dressed in a simple blue tunic and carrying a glass of some liquid and a syringe.

He saw Max was awake, gasped, turned, and left the room. A few moments later, Favani entered.

She looked *very* different.

Dressed in a long gown of deep purple, free-flowing and loose, yet also managing to cling to the athletic curves of her body. Her shoulders were bare, tasteful laces of small glowing gemstones wrapped around her arms. Her luxurious white hair was cascading down one of her shoulders, like a waterfall of pure silver. Her lips were painted deep purple, and her bright eyes looked at Max with a mixture of concern and joy. Max felt his heart skip a beat as she rushed to his bedside.

"Finally!" she gasped and grabbed him into a hug. "You've been unconscious for three days!"

"Thank you for helping me," Max rasped. His throat was raw and only a weak whisper came out.

"To battle against three sorcerers . . ." Favani said. "I have clearly chosen correctly."

"Favani . . . You're hurting me."

"Oh!" she said and untangled herself, her face flushing purple in embarrassment. She straightened her dress.

"I can't move," Max said after a moment of silence.

"That's nothing for you to worry about," Favani said and smiled. "My medical team has placed your body in a resting state through the careful use of our herbal medicine."

"So, easily fixed?" Max asked.

Favani let out a little laugh and nodded. Then she reached for somewhere inside her dress and took out a small, round, forest-green pill. She placed it in Max's mouth, an action that felt strangely intimate. Max felt Favani's fingers linger on his lips for a moment longer than was strictly necessary.

"I would still suggest you do not move much," Favani said. "You pushed yourself beyond my comprehension. It was only because of my mother's healing arts that you were able to recover as quickly as you did."

The pill took effect immediately. A fresh, minty feeling started spreading throughout Max's body, a cool breeze that infused him with energy. He found he could move his fingers again. Favani was right, though. He shouldn't move. Even that tiny motion had been excruciating.

"Where are we?" Max asked.

"At one of my family estates on the planet Niaran," Favani said. "It was the closest planet to our capital that I could teleport to. It cost me dearly, but it is nothing compared to the boons you shall receive."

Max grinned. "I'm glad I could be of help."

"To put it mildly," Favani said. "They are preparing a show of gratitude from me and my people to you. It will be ready in a day or two. Until then, I suggest that you rest. I am at your call in any way you require."

"Thank you, Favani," Max said. "Glad to have made a friend in you."

"Oh, I wonder about that," Favani said.

"What?"

"I am a princess," she said and gave him a mysterious little smile. "We don't make friends."

"Well, I do," Max said.

Favani laughed and placed a hand on Max's arm. She said nothing more and neither did he. They just enjoyed the serenity. They were fighters, both of them— warriors of the highest order. But Max couldn't deny that these moments of peace after an arduous battle were precious to him. He was glad he could share this with Favani. She was a good ally, a good friend to have.

Their reverie was then abruptly interrupted by a floating object appearing inside the room. It was the Zoos jellyfish.

Favani stood up immediately, clenching her fists.

"How in the dead hells did you find us?"

[**Algorithm. And a location spell.**]

"You are breaching the Unecala Treaty," Favani said in a low, dangerous voice.

[**It can be construed that way. However, according to Clause 227, Section D 1.1, paragraph 3, the Unecala Treaty does not hold if the other party is in illegal custody of the other party's assets. We are merely here to negotiate and to be informed.**]

"He is not your asset," Favani growled. "He is not a slave."

[We do not have slaves. We have contractors. And it is our prerogative to make sure those contracts are in accordance with our agreements. We are merely checking up on our asset.]

Favani looked unsure. Her gaze flicked to Max. "Last I checked, he is not under contract."

There was a moment of silence, and the jellyfish avatar froze in midair for a few seconds. Then the self-assured monotone robotic voice continued:

[According to the ICCB Self-Defense Declaration, page 114, paragraph 7—]

"Can you just get to the damn point?" Max asked and sighed.

Another moment of silence.

[Certainly. In the aforementioned document, it is stated that if both parties act over a certain period of time as if a contract is already in place, the contract is interpreted to have started from the point that such behavior began. This is actually beneficial to the contractee, as their indenture is shortened by that length of time. We thought it humane.]

"There is nothing humane about your contracts," Favani hissed. Then she relaxed. "However, all I am hearing is that there is no binding contract between you two, not by law, nor by spirit. All I am hearing is a bunch of assumptions and politicking."

[Do not test our patience in this matter.]

"We both know you can't afford to start another war, especially not with us," Favani said.

Another moment of silence. Max only watched, enrapt. He wasn't sure what he was learning, but he was learning a lot.

[This individual, Max Cromwell, is extraordinary. We need him in the war effort. Perhaps a negotiation between the ICCB and the Jianari would lead to an ideal outcome. We commend you on your deft acquisition of this asset and will not pursue the implications of such an act. We are willing to negotiate and pay recompense, if you return the asset to our custody.]

Anger flared up inside Max. He tried to get up, winced with pain, but did it anyway. Favani pushed him down firmly. Max looked up. Cold fury was written on her face. She was done playing nice.

"Call him an asset one more time, and I swear to Heavens the whole ICCB will tremble before the might of our kingdom."

[And what do you have to say in all of this, Max? We made an agreement.]

Max let his anger wash over him. Favani cast him a look. She still clearly had a lot to say, but Max shook his head. Slowly he got up, his face twisting with discomfort. The Zoos jellyfish bobbed up and down slowly.

"I want to honor my agreement with you," Max said. "It's the right thing to do. And despite your methods being questionable, I think you guys are doing the right thing. The Outsiders are beyond horrible, and we need to work together to stop them."

[So, you will return and sign a contract with us, we assume. We are most thrilled to hear this. Additionally, congratulations for successfully accruing more strength and Experience through battle! This will be most valuable in leading the strike force.]

"Hold your horses for just a minute," Max said.

"What is a horse?" Favani asked.

"I'm not signing anything with you. I am definitely coming back and defending Alpha Ludus when the attack arrives. But I don't owe you anything, and I am not your property. Favani and I have a deal of our own. She has promised me a lot of resources for helping her. My staying here and receiving the fruits of my labor will be the most beneficial course of action for all parties involved. I'm not certain on the details of the feud between your people, but I'd rather make my own decisions instead of being a pawn in some game of Chess I don't even understand. All I care about is stopping the Outsider threat. For me to play my part in that, I want to get as strong as possible, as fast as possible."

[At this juncture, we must remind you that we are in custody of your companion, Maverick.]

Max's heart dropped to his stomach. *Crap.* They had him there.

"Excuse me?!" Favani shot up. "You will return my . . . my friend's companion instantly, with his mind fixed, or you will find yourself in a very unfortunate political situation."

The Zoos jellyfish froze. This time, the pause was long. So long that Max and Favani had a chance to glance at each other.

"Before you say anything, know that they are listening," Favani said.

"I know," Max said. "Looks like they needed to involve other parties."

"You're pretty valuable, you know." Favani said.

"Makes it sound like I'm some prized farm animal for auction."

"It's not like that for me," Favani said softly.

Max felt his cheeks go warm and red. "I, uh . . . Thanks for sticking up for me."

Favani let out a throaty laugh. "A strong warrior you might be, but when it comes to politics, you're a novice. It is in this arena that I can return some of the favors you have done for me and my people."

"Seems like you figured out something with the metagems?"

A wide, toothy grin spread across Favani's face. She turned to Max, eyes twinkling, and placed an index finger on her lips to symbolize silence. "I'll give you the full scoop later."

"Why do you think it's taking them so long?" Max asked.

"Oh, they probably called my father and are not getting the answer they wanted."

"Your father is kind of a big shot, I've come to learn."

"Well, he is one of the few Celestial-stage Cultivators in the universe," Favani said nonchalantly, but she did glance at Max to check his reaction.

His eyes went wide. "I want to talk to him."

Favani laughed. "You will."

The Zoos jellyfish started bobbing again, and soon the robotic monotone voice was droning on:

[We accept these terms. We will return Maverick to you and pay half of the teleportation expenses. Additionally, we renounce our right to form a contract with Max Cromwell. However, in exchange it has been agreed that Max Cromwell will assist in the full defense of Alpha Ludus. Not just the scouting phase but also in the case of a full assault of the Outsiders. Additionally, he will be expected to aid the ICCB until the resources used on him are recompensed, including the reparation of the mind and body of his companion, Maverick. Additionally, we suggest a preliminary contract to pay off the debt. Perhaps fifty years would be—]

"Dead hells, no," Favani cut in. "We accept everything except the preliminary contract. The Empire is willing to pay off Max's debt. Goodbye."

With that, Favani flicked a hand, and a ring with a green gemstone on one of her fingers flared up with light. The plastic jellyfish in the air froze, then became static and finally vanished.

"That felt good," Favani said and grinned. "I've never had a chance to dismiss them before like that."

"I'm getting Maverick back," Max said and sighed contently.

"I look forward to getting to know him," Favani said.

Max laughed. It hurt a bit, but everything else was going so right in his life that he really didn't care. "I'll remind you of those words in your darkest hour, when you think you can't possibly be more annoyed."

Favani only laughed, oblivious to the horrid fate of having to get to know Maverick that awaited her.

CHAPTER THIRTY-FOUR

Filials and the Jianari

A few hours later, Max was on his feet, thanks to Favani's herbs and medicines, as well as a strange infusion from one of her metagems.

It was a weird sensation—sort of similar to a Cultivation array infusing him, but instead of having to sit down and Cultivate, the energy simply flowed into his dantian in a gentle stream, replacing his spent power.

As they were walking in the estate gardens, Max asked about what happened after he passed out and Favani immediately brightened and started blabbing.

"After destroying those sorcerers, we were able to teleport all of the useful items from the tomb to here. That doesn't only mean the equipment to create synthetic metagems but also a vast amount of information and recordings."

"That's amazing," Max said.

"You are amazing," Favani said and blushed a slight purple. "You will be rewarded by the king himself. Even with the ridiculous expense the teleports ended up costing, this discovery will pay for itself tenfold, and your bravery is what made it possible. You are an outstanding warrior, Max."

Max didn't know what to say, but his heart swelled with pride. They continued walking side by side through the garden whose yellow grass was vibrant and shining like gold. Bushes of red berries and tall trees with dark ebony bark were dotted across the landscape. They flowered with large violet and purple petals. Strange animals resembling deer and rabbits went about their business in the garden, completely undeterred by their presence. One of the rabbits even came up to Favani, and she fed it with some seeds from the pockets of her dress.

Max was then treated to a delicious meal full of exotic flavors. The Jianari's palate was close to that of humans; their meats were savory and their sauces rich. Most dishes were purple, red, and blue. It was a little disconcerting eating a haunch of blue meat, but Favani assured him the food was good for him and that he needed to eat.

Max was slowly gathering his powers back. It was nice, spending time with Favani, just taking slow strolls in the gardens.

Max was especially fond of the estate's luxurious bathhouse. He bathed a lot, at the insistence of Favani and her friend Havairi, their medical master, a short woman for a Jianari, and a stout one. Older than Favani and with the motherly aura of a born caretaker about her.

Sometimes Favani would join him in the baths, and while that was exciting, it was also awkward. Max couldn't help but steal glances at her when she was shuffling in or out of the bath, tall, beautiful and athletic as she was. She would always quickly clad herself in towels, but she did it in a way that made sure Max was within eye range. She noticed him looking every time and blushed a slight purple as he did. It was a strange game they played but one Max found himself enjoying.

Finally, after two days, Maverick was teleported to the estate. When Max heard the news, he instantly reached into their [**Divine Soulbond**]. Instead of the faint silence he had received recently, he got a pulse of the emotional equivalent of "I'm back, bitches!"

To say Maverick was buzzing with excitement would be an understatement. He flew around in his disc form, changing sizes for the heck of it and barraging both Max and Favani with questions of their adventures. He was also even more insufferable than usual, but Max was too glad to have him back to complain. Maverick picked up on this emotion through their bond and resolved to make every awkward comment possible the next time Max and Favani were sharing a bath together.

"So, what's going to happen next?" Maverick asked Max when they were sharing an evening meal. "And who are these creepy little guys?"

One of the flying gnomes who was picking up Max's finished plate at the time shot a disgruntled glance at Maverick but said nothing.

"They're Filials," Favani said. "They are our servant people, a bond thousands of years old."

The Filials were flying around, filling cups and cleaning up finished plates. None of them seemed angry or upset about their position as servants.

"Are they slaves?" Max asked.

Favani was quiet for a while as she slowly chewed on a piece of a blue fruit she had just popped in her mouth.

"You could argue that, but I wouldn't consider that a fair assessment," she said. Max turned to her to hear the rest of her answer, and she swallowed her fruit.

"They look like humanoids, but they are not as sapient as you and me," Favani said. "My grandfather found them on a planet whose atmosphere had been ravaged by a massive meteor strike. There were only a few thousand of them left, going extinct, freezing and starving in caves. We took them with us and trained them to serve us."

"You didn't release them somewhere with a healthy atmosphere?" Max asked.

"Give them a whole planet?" Favani asked incredulously.

"More like a continent?" Max suggested. "A sanctuary?"

"No," Favani said. "I don't see a problem with this. We saved their species. We offer them a clean, healthy, and safe environment, and free time. Something that they would have had to struggle for tens, if not hundreds of thousands of years without us."

"Doesn't sound much different from the ICCB and their contracts," Maverick said. "You sure know how to pick 'em, Max."

"Pick what?"

Favani clobbered Maverick on his dome with the butt of her sword. It was a deft and powerful strike, well-practiced. Her mouth twitched a little, but she maintained a neutral expression as Maverick slammed the ground.

He proceeded to instantly challenge Favani to a duel, to which she enthusiastically agreed. The people of the estate cleared from the table, and a swarm of Filials swooped the tables away at the command of Favani's personal manservant, Jiefran.

Max watched two of his closest allies facing off against each other. Favani was skilled and graceful, but Maverick was holding out well. Really well.

Have we truly grown this strong so fast?

Max got a quick pulse of emotion through the bond he shared with Maverick. It was a strong affirmative. Yes, they had. There was also a request. Maverick wanted Max to give him some of his energy.

While he was still recovering, his dantian was again a deep well of energy, even if Max was not in his best fighting form. He grinned devilishly as he watched Maverick dodging around Favani's flying swords and firing off small, yellow and gray energy bullets at her.

He let the energy flow from his dantian to cycle in his meridians as he slowly fed it destructive Intent before guiding it through the [**Divine Soulbond**].

Every second that it happened, Maverick got slightly faster, slightly more agile, and his shots got slightly more devastating.

However, Favani was not to be outdone. She dodged a shot from Maverick and turned to Max in confusion. She narrowed her eyes and gave him an ugly look. Max only responded by smiling sheepishly.

She extended her hand and let one of her rings flare up with red energy. The crowd around Max *ooh*ed. Max didn't know much about the customs and powers of these strange people, but if he had to guess, he would say Favani had just drained a metagem.

Max sent a pulse of warning through the Soulbond. It was too late.

Favani blasted forward in a blur, slamming into Maverick. She climbed on top of him, and they went up, down, and sideways as Maverick tried to buck her off like a rampaging bull, all the while exclaiming expletives.

She didn't fall, instead calling all of the swords to float above her, before slamming her fist down, dropping Maverick like a rock. When the sapient disc hit the ground, all the swords came down as well, forming a neat circle around him. Favani huffed triumphantly and stood tall, receiving cheers from the crowd. Max joined in, and Maverick cursed up a storm.

"Some friend you are," Maverick muttered after the tables were returned to their places. "Cheering at my unjust defeat."

"I gave you all the Spiritual Power I could in my state," Max whispered.

"Wasn't much," Maverick said. "You have grown lax in my absence. Next time I demand to siphon more."

"I knew it!" Favani hissed and turned to Max, glaring at him. Her cheeks were flushed with wine and victory, and despite the intensity of her glare, she was grinning. "You aided him with some trick."

"Maybe," Max said and grinned back. "He is my buddy."

"That's right!" Maverick said, getting his bravado back. "Bros before ho— *ooofff*."

Favani slapped him with her sword again.

Maverick didn't stop bickering and sulking that night, but Max only drank wine, jested with Favani and some of her closer friends, and enjoyed himself. He had earned this, and he would enjoy it.

CHAPTER THIRTY-FIVE

Metagems

After the enjoyable party and a hearty night of sleep, Max felt fully regenerated. Maybe it was the wine and food infused with Spiritual Energy. Maybe it was the excessive amount of sleep for someone of his Cultivation Level. Maybe it was getting his buddy back, or just having a few days to himself where he didn't need to push himself to his fullest and fight tooth and nail for his life.

Whatever it was, Max felt great. When he shared this news with Favani over a breakfast of fruit and nuts, she grinned widely.

"Shut up, you rabble," she snapped at the other people sitting at the table.

Maverick hooted and laughed at that.

"Rabble?" Max said, quirking an eyebrow.

"What did you say?"

"I'm fully recovered."

"So fast . . ." Favani said, more to herself than to Max. "That is fantastic news. Finally."

"I was thinking I could look into the many rewards you promised me."

Favani laughed and lifted her head in the air. "Listen to this, you rabble. This is the intensity of greed that a Cultivator needs. I have kept our guest fed and warm, but he demands more!"

Favani started enthusiastically gobbling up the food on her plate, calling a Filial over to fly by and pick up her plate as soon as she was done. Max had barely set down his fork when Favani clapped her hands, and a gnome flew by to pick up his plate too. It seemed she was in a hurry.

"There isn't much time," Favani blabbed on, as she dragged Max by the arm through the luxuriously decorated corridors. "You must prepare for the audience with my father."

"The king of like half the galaxy?" Max asked and couldn't help but feel nervous.

"Finally, an audience befitting our grand stature," Maverick said gleefully.

Favani cast him a narrow-eyed glare, but said nothing.

"If I am to bring you to my father in his court, we must prepare you."

"Prepare me for what?" Max said and swallowed. The lump didn't go away. "Why must I meet him?"

Favani only cast a mysterious, demure glance at him. "Come on," she said and squeezed his hand harder.

Max was confused and felt for the bond which he shared with Maverick. There was mirth there—great mirth that Max didn't understand.

"What's this about?" Max asked.

"Part of our reward, I'm sure," Maverick said, barely containing laughter.

Max didn't like being the only one not in on the joke, but that didn't matter now. What mattered was getting stronger.

They arrived at a great underground room full of Favani's people. They were all tall and blue with hair ranging from dark gray to pure pearly white. Most of them kept it long, just like Favani.

They were greeted by the Jelidi, Favani's stout medical master.

"How good of you to have come, mistress," she said and bowed. "The preparations are ready."

"Very good, Jelidi," Favani said with her patented regal grace, head held high. "We will start with the Ruby-grade pills."

Jelidi bowed and called some of her underlings to listen to her instructions. Favani walked further into the compound like she owned the place. Which, Max supposed, she did.

The room was a large laboratory, like a Cultivator workshop. The flying gnomes zipped here and there, carrying bottles of varying sizes containing liquid.

Max took a gander at one of the tables where a young Jianari boy was working. His face was scrunched up in concentration as he carefully used a pipette to administer a drop of yellow serum onto an onyx-black pill. He took a glance up and looked at Max. He was startled, eyes going wide with recognition. The yellow drop missed its intended spot, landing on the young Jianari's hand, and burning him. He dropped the pill, which rolled toward Max and their little retinue.

Max flicked a finger and used [Telekinesis] to pick it up and send it flying toward the young alchemist. He grabbed it and bowed deeply. Max smiled and nodded.

Favani turned and fluttered her eyelashes. "As gracious as he is powerful."

Max only chuckled, but he flushed slightly.

"What manner of power up are you going to give us?" Maverick demanded. "I am sick and tired of drudging along in lower Diamond stage."

That made a few more heads turn. Every alchemist in their close vicinity looked at Maverick in utter shock.

"I have to agree," Max said. "If you can help us reach the middle of the Diamond stage, we would be eternally grateful. Or, well, I would be. Maverick . . . would be less of an asshole. Maybe."

"Maybe," Maverick said. "Depends on how much you people are willing to spend on us."

Favani shook her head. "You two are completely ridiculous."

"Ridiculously awesome," Maverick said.

"What do you mean?"

"This greed of yours . . . No, I don't even think it's greed. But it is some strange sense of assured privilege that you should be able to reach the top of Cultivation in mere months when it usually takes centuries to even get where you are now."

"It got us this far," Max said and shrugged.

"Indeed, it did," Favani said as they reached an ornate table, studded with glowing gemstones under a thick layer of glass. Lying on the table was a red handkerchief on which sat four pills, glowing ruby red, with swirls of yellow and orange shifting inside like heavy clouds of magma.

"Depending on how you look at it," Favani started and picked up one of the pills. "These are quite the gift all on their own. A single [**Pure Ruby Pill**] contains the Spiritual Energy of a single Ruby-stage Cultivator. They are designed to increase pure power, and are crafted using the arts we developed eons ago in perfecting the metagems."

"That means the energy will flow straight to my dantian?" Max asked.

"You pick up on things remarkably fast," Jelidi said and came to stand next to Favani. "You have chosen well, Princess."

"You don't even begin to know the half of it," Favani said and smiled. Jelidi grinned in return. Despite their difference in status, Max noticed the two of them were clearly friends.

The stout blue woman turned to look at Max. Her eyes were friendly, but there was a hard intelligence behind them. "You will ingest one of these pills, let the energy settle inside you, and immediately consume another. The process must be repeated until you are unable to take more energy into your dantian. After that, we will have you take an [**Obsidian Core Expansion Elixir**]. You will be consuming quite a lot of pills today, great warrior."

"That is fine," Max said. "Whatever it takes to get me stronger."

"I like him," Jelidi said to Favani.

"Me too," she whispered before extending the hand holding the pill to Max.

He didn't hesitate, swallowing it down immediately. Then he went up to the table with the handkerchief and took another pill.

"Not so fast!" Jelidi said, worry lacing her voice.

"It's for Maverick," Max said as his buddy floated behind him and opened up a compartment.

"This device . . . It Cultivates?"

Maverick sniffed haughtily but didn't deign to answer. Favani smirked at the sapient weapon.

"We're a team," Max said. "More than that, actually. But it's complicated."

"Bring four more pills," Favani said. The medicine master bowed and went up to a nearby table.

Max sat down cross-legged, feeling a warmth spread throughout his body. Through power of habit, he tried to engage the emerging energy spreading from his stomach with his meridians, but instead it flowed straight into the well of his spirit, the dantian.

It was as easy as Cultivation had ever been. Since he didn't need to focus on circulating and controlling the energy intake, Max focused on the nature of this energy. It was soft and warm, like a lagoon on the shores of a tropical ocean.

There wasn't that much energy in the pill, all things considered. Max soon found it had ingested had exhausted itself and settled smoothly into his dantian.

This is the extent of power a Ruby-stage Cultivator has? How paltry.

Max hadn't considered the power difference. He had known he was much more powerful than Kat or any of the other members of the strike force. They had seemed like veritable children compared to his power. Having achieved a super-mortal stage in Cultivation was the difference between an ocean and a lake. But this pill felt like a puddle. He was far from being full.

"Another one!" Maverick demanded.

Favani grinned and handed Max two more pills.

Max popped both of them in his mouth to Favani's mild shock. She chuckled and Maverick started bickering until Jelidi brought six more Ruby pills. Max took two and placed them inside Maverick. The two of them focused on the feeling, letting the Spiritual Energy flow into them.

+1 Power

"How do you feel?" Jelidi asked, taking out a slab of thin stone upon which she was making notes with a bright blue pen that seemed to be made of gemstone.

Max shrugged. "Nothing much. It's nice."

"Would you venture to guess how valuable and sought after each of those pills is?" Favani asked, smirking.

"You know," Max said. "I haven't thought about the monetary value of this or that for months. What can you buy with these pills?"

"Let me put it in a way you can appreciate," Favani said. "Each of these pills sold to the ICCB would shorten the contracted years of indenture by four years."

"No way," Max said. "These little things?"

"Little?!" Jelidi asked, slightly offended. Only years of disciplined upbringing stilled her tongue.

"If this is all the reward we are getting, none of us is going to have a good time," Maverick said loudly.

"You weren't even there to earn the rewards," Max reminded him.

"If I had been, I would have helped, and it would have been epic," Maverick countered.

"See?" Max said, turning to Favani. "This is the kind of bullshit I have to deal with daily."

Favani laughed and offered the last pills to Max. "It is only natural to have high pride as a warrior of your caliber. Worry not. This is not the extent of your rewards. It would hurt my pride as a fellow warrior, as a princess of my people, and as your friend."

In the next moment, the Filials flew overhead in a small swarm and placed bottles with clear liquid on the purple silk handkerchiefs spread out on the table.

"How did you like that warm-up?" Favani asked, a slight smirk playing on her purple lips. Max could see she was excited by all of this.

"Warm-up?" Maverick asked, perking up.

"The [**Obsidian Core Expansion Elixir**]," Favani said and waved a hand at the table with the liquid and the black pill. "Made using our metagem technology on a very rare substance. Obsidian is hard. It is not part of the core of our science, but it is valuable."

"What does it do?" Max asked, eyeing the liquid, as Jelidi dropped a pill into it, causing it to instantly throw up a coal-black cloud above the bottle.

"It forces your dantian to expand," Favani said. "It artificially enhances your capacity to absorb and contain Spiritual Energy within yourself. However, the process is rather . . . intense."

"Intense how?" Max asked.

"The dantian is essentially stretched open. Violently. I will be very interested to see how much you can handle."

"Ha," Maverick said. "You dare doubt us?"

"Even as talented as you are," Favani said, "some of the elixir's power will be wasted. When you feel the dantian stretching too much, you need to release the extra energy through your meridians. Please aim the energy at the metagem over there.

A large, dark-blue sapphire was gleaming dimly on a pedestal that looked like a golden chalice, upon which the giant, egg-shaped gemstone rested. Some glyphs were arrayed around the pedestal in a circular formation.

Max scoffed. He had an idea of how to take advantage of this situation.

You know, Maverick. I learned a few tricks while you were sleeping.

Maverick sent a pulse of gleeful emotion through their bond. He already knew what Max was thinking.

Max walked up to the table and took the liquid. The bottle was scalding hot, but nothing a Diamond-stage Cultivator couldn't handle.

"Bottoms up," Max said.

CHAPTER THIRTY-SIX

Rapid-Fire Improvement

When Max chugged down the [**Obsidian Core Expansion Elixir**], it took about two seconds for the magical liquid to reach his dantian. The alchemical concoction hit him like a freight train.

Max gasped and fell on his knees. Favani crouched and, with her wrists on her knees, observed Max. Her eyes were restful as was her smile.

"You can do it, My Prince," Favani said. "My father will be quite impressed."

"Prince? Wh— Aargh . . ."

Max was forced onto his hands and knees as the magic potion *exploded* inside his dantian, forcing it open with violent insistence. It was like having stomach cramps cranked to eleven. Like his whole torso was being sucked into a black hole, the pressure mounting. The sweat was flowing off his face to form a small puddle beneath his nose tip.

Max collected himself. Got a good deep breath in and mastered his mind under the duress of pain. He reached for the [**Divine Soulbond**] and pushed the storming energy ravaging inside his dantian through the bond between him and Maverick.

Maverick went instantly stiff in the air and fell on the ground with a clunk. There, the two of them lay and writhed in agony, gasping and grunting. Favani watched, and the rest of the room was as quiet as a grave.

But now the discomfort lessened by half. Max could endure this. Hell, he had endured worse when fighting the three sorcerers in the darkness of that old tomb. They had brought him to his most extreme. Max recalled the fatigue, the despair, the pain. How he had been brought to the brink. Brought to death's door, yet he had fought on.

This? This is nothing.

He lifted his gaze from the puddle of sweat dripping from his face. Favani's eyebrows shot up, but she was still crouching before Max, quietly examining him.

Maverick also rose up in the air.

There was still a storm full of turmoil attacking Max's dantian. It made his muscles twitch, and his whole body was flushed with heat and sweat. Oh, there was pain. There was discomfort. But having been able to halve the intensity to share it with Maverick had done the trick. Now both of their dantians were expanding.

+1 Power
+1 Control
+1 Speed

"Max!" Favani said after a while, concern starting to etch itself into her beautiful features. "Discharge the energy. You might cripple your Cultivation if you aren't careful."

"Make . . . another . . . batch," Max managed to spit out. Despite sharing the load with Maverick, the strain on his spirit was still bordering on overwhelming. This method of training was clearly not meant to be fully absorbed.

"Only one batch?" Maverick said. His voice was strained, but he managed to maintain his usual boastful tone.

"This is impossible," Jelidi said.

The room was dead silent as Max rose. Sweat was still pouring from his every pore, but he held his head high. The storm in his dantian was calming. He had conquered this battle. His near-death experience against the three sorcerers had tempered him. Pain and discomfort were inconsequential now. They were only something to endure, something to conquer. The swirling black mass of energy attacking the edges of his spirit, pushing it violently to the very edge of its existence, settled down.

+1 Power
+1 Control

"Another one," both Max and Maverick said in unison.

Favani and Jelidi looked at each other in a mixture of shock and awe. The room was still dead silent and Favani had to bark orders twice before she got the Filials and the alchemists moving so the two of them could have another elixir.

The second one was a harder beast to tame. Despite the alchemical concoction not exactly damaging his dantian, it still put a strain on it, just like circulating Spiritual Energy did to his meridians. Discomfort became pain. Pain became agony. Maverick couldn't move at all. Max was reduced to a fetal position. It took a long while this time. However, Max realized that there was not much that he could actually do. It was more of a test of endurance.

He felt the mounting urge to discharge the energy toward the sapphire meta-gem a few feet away. Favani and Jelidi had urged him to do it multiple times, to the point where Max had to snap at them to shut the hell up. He needed to focus. He would not listen to any naysaying. He would do this. He would conquer himself. He would become as strong a being as he could.

+1 Power
+1 Control
+2 Karma points
[Greater Diamond Stage Achieved]

CHAPTER THIRTY-SEVEN

Princess-Minded

Favani let her eyes rest on the beauty of the courtyard garden. She was with Max on the balcony, just the two of them, which was a rare treat. She had grown used to his stoic silence.

"What's it like to eat?" Maverick asked in the background. "Shove one of those scones into my compartment. No . . . not that one."

Mostly just the two of them . . .

Favani threw a side glance at Max, who was arguing whether it mattered which of Maverick's compartments the scone should be placed in. She wondered how Max could be like that. So normal, so down to earth.

And yet he was also a Cultivator of a caliber that she had never before seen. Not even her father was this talented. She had tried asking Max how exactly he could accomplish these feats. His ability to withstand not one, but two **[Obsidian Core Expansion Elixirs]** was nothing short of astounding.

She sipped her tea and Max noticed her staring. He threw an easy smile at her, and she blushed. He turned before he could see if she returned it.

Max had no answers. Maverick kept calling her stupid and Max even stupider every time she brought up the topic. The weapon knew something. No, it probably didn't know anything Max didn't. But it had *some* kind of understanding Max didn't.

Idiot savant, huh?

Favani didn't think it was so simple. You could spin it that way, but at the end of the day, what Max had was heart and grit. Loads and loads of it. It hadn't taken a long time for Favani to notice. And the fight against three sorcerers had cemented that truth.

Max was unyielding to his very core.

Maverick had said Max had no ability to quit in him. He simply didn't think about it. The way Maverick spoke of it, it was as if Max *wasn't physically capable* of considering quitting. Or stopping for that matter. Only the assurance from her that they would soon leave the estate and arrive at the king's palace was enough to satisfy him for now. He had just kept pestering her for more pills.

Favani sipped the tea and enjoyed the salty taste, infused with the Intent of heat. She admired people with Daos of utility. Hers was a sharp Intent. Perfect for swords, perfect for weapons. That was, at the end of the day, what she was. A weapon.

Even my relationship with Max is defined by that fact.

Princess, warrior, politician. Many hats to wear, but none of them seemed to fit quite right.

She finished her tea and a Filiial brought her another. The ceramic cup was so hot, the little gnome had trouble holding it, but for Favani it felt only slightly warm. Filials could not Cultivate. They had tried over the years but failed due to lack of understanding.

Only so much could be conveyed about Cultivation. It was mostly an inner art. Favani loved it. She had had the best background imaginable. The daughter of the single-most powerful entity in the world. Well, she guessed it was up for debate whether her father was the strongest. Top five? Absolutely certain.

Yet, she seemed to lack . . . *something*. All of the best teachers, all of the most expensive elixirs, even the requisite bravery to always be willing to throw herself into danger in order to advance. Two hundred years of single-minded focus.

Yet, here stood Max Cromwell. A human of twenty-something years. No background. Fighting for scraps in the barbaric arena of the ICCB war machine meatgrinder.

The Framework may be barbaric, but it is certainly efficient . . .

The Framework was the ICCB's bread and butter, and it was completely alien to Favani, who had been brought up Cultivating through her people's metagem science. Both styles of Cultivation had a lot of commonalities. With resources, you could reach Ruby almost immediately. If your Insights held you back, you could still master them in a few years. Diamond was the great bottleneck. How well one assimilated the Framework limited talent. Favani wondered if Max knew that.

There was also one other thing. A secret about the Framework which the majority of the Jianari population didn't know. Her father knew, and so she and the rest of the royal family knew. It ignited a burning hatred in Favani's just and gentle heart. She wondered if the ICCB's corruption had spread to her friend . . .

It does not seem like it has, which is strange . . .

She wasn't sure, but every time she had brushed at Max's spirit, it had felt pure. *Seamless.* Favani was fairly certain that assimilating the Framework had gone perfectly for Max. It didn't go perfectly for anyone. But it was as if the Framework favored Max like he was its own child. Blessed by the Heavens?

One thing was for certain, however. Yesterday, Max Cromwell, a twenty-year-old human with no remarkable background, had surpassed Favani, the two-hundred-year-old princess of the mightiest empire in the known universe.

"Talent" just doesn't begin to describe it.

It was hard to not feel jealousy. It was a strange emotion for her, she who had never wanted for anything. Fortunate beyond belief. Blessed by the Heavens a thousand-fold. There had never been a need in her life that had been left unfulfilled.

But there it was. An ugly snake slithering in the shadows of her mind. Poisoning it.

How can I not feel it?

She sighed in exasperation and threw away her tea, cup and all. Max noticed it, but she waved a hand, signaling for him to leave her alone. In his infinite grace, he did.

He is perfect.

Favani barely noticed the Filials swooping down with silk rags to clean up the spilled tea and picking up the plate and cup.

Favani understood perfectly well why the ICCB was so keen to have him. This kid could change the outcome of the war in several solar systems.

By himself.

Their family needed him. She would have to pull every trick in the book to convince him to stay. She wanted him in her life as well. She would have him. Her father's opinion, be damned. She would go to him of course and seek the appropriate blessings.

But if he does not consent, I will take Max anyway.

Her father would be a fool of the greatest order, the greatest buffoon in the universe, if he did not see Max's ridiculous potential. But in the case he didn't see them, Favani would have to act of her own accord, for the benefit of their empire.

Sure, she felt jealousy. But that was thwarted by a more intense feeling. What she felt toward Max was *awe*.

My, my, Favani. You have a crush, don't you?

She blushed and snappily ordered another cup of tea.

CHAPTER THIRTY-EIGHT

The Ascent of the Mighty

After another day passed, it was time to move out. Max had not only fully recovered but he had grown in strength. He had never felt so powerful. With a swoop of his hands, he could cleave mountainsides.

Meanwhile, Maverick was more than thrilled to have his mind back and to find himself in a body that was even more powerful than before. He flew around and hooted excitedly, blasting destructive energy this way and that, much to the chagrin of Max and the excitement of their retinue.

They were traveling in palanquins of gold and gemstone, carried in the air by Filials, hanging from great golden rods.

This morning, they had teleported to a garrison city below a gigantic mountain. This planet was the Jianari's original home world. Max had wanted to fly and explore the planet, but Favani had told him to save his strength. He did. Not that he minded chatting idly with Favani about this and that—well, mostly Cultivation, but what was better than to discuss your passions with an attractive woman?

Their retinue stopped at the base of the most massive set of stairs Max had ever seen. Each one spanned a hundred feet in length; one would need to take a few steps forward before ascending to the next step with the lift of a leg that would certainly require stretching beforehand.

"Behold," Favani said. "The Ascent of the Mighty."

"Did you really just say 'Behold?'" Max said and smirked.

"Shut up," Favani hissed. "I need to put on a show for the rabble."

"I can't believe you keep calling them rabble," Max said.

"She's right," Maverick said and sniffed. "Look at them. Most of them aren't even in the Diamond stage."

"Neither were we a month ago," Max said.

"Pfft, stop dwelling in the past, Max."

The giant steps seemed to go on forever until they vanished into soft white clouds. Beautiful trees and bushes grew alongside the regal staircase. The air felt rich with Spiritual Energy.

"So, what's the deal here?" Max asked Favani, but she ignored him, instead walking toward her subjects.

"Max here is mighty, and he has promised to challenge the steps."

Their retinue cheered and waved at Max, who gave them an awkward smile and a wave.

"Promised what?" Max mouthed to Maverick. The floating disc only bobbed up and down and chuckled.

"I don't know, but it sounds like there's going to be some fun."

"Should he succeed, I will grant him an audience with my father, the king. The day of my choosing may have finally arrived!"

Another cheer. Max wondered idly what choice was being talked about as he looked up at the steps. If he wasn't allowed to fly, this would suck. He probably wasn't allowed to fly . . .

"And of course, as anyone wanting to prove themselves mighty, Max will proudly wear our legendary cursed artifact on his head," Favani pronounced.

"Huh?" Max asked.

One of the gnome servants flew to Favani holding a box. It opened silently with a commanding swish of a hand from Favani. From inside, she picked up a crown made of silver, black onyx gems studded to its sides. It shone with an eerie, sickly green light.

"Behold," Favani said. [**The Crown of Blighted Fatigue**]!"

The crowd oohed and turned to look at Max. He did his best to look unphased, because he knew this was something important for Favani and she appreciated the decorum. Inside, however, he was freaking out.

"As you all know," Favani said, "the crown will sap a person's Cultivation the longer it is worn. Many have perished attempting this challenge, but I have great faith in Max's abilities!"

The crowd cheered and clapped.

"Of course, the Filaoi people respect potential and do not want to destroy it. This is why I have brought Max here. He is my choice. He is nothing if not full of potential. This is why the crown has been designed to count the steps it is worn for. If Max can wear the accursed crown for twenty thousand steps, I shall grant him an audience with my father, so that his strength may be further tested!"

"Max! Max! Max!" the crowd cheered.

Favani turned to Max and with practiced moves, she inclined her head and offered him the crown.

"How many steps are in this climb?" Max quietly asked as he took the crown. It was *heavy*. His hands dipped down before he reinforced them with Spiritual Energy.

Favani only smiled. "You are not to know."

"Great."

"But I have absolute faith in you," Favani said. "The further you can get with the crown on your head the better as far as my father is concerned."

Then she smiled slightly and added, "And that goes for me, too."

"I'll do my best," Max said.

A moment of weakness flashed across Favani's face. It was rather endearing, Max thought.

"Please don't die, Max."

Max barked out a laugh. "If the sorcerers couldn't get me, I sure as hell won't die walking up a set of stairs."

"Damn straight!" Maverick shouted. "We've been kicking ass for so long, I'm numb to it. This ain't nothing but a day's work."

"Easy for you to say," Favani said. "You don't have legs."

"Right," Max said. "How's this work, considering me and Maverick share a bond?"

Favani thought for a while. Then she shrugged. "He can tag along to keep you company for all I care. I'm not interested in him. It is you that I have chosen."

Max nodded slowly, still trying to understand this "choice" business. Favani blushed and quickly turned.

"To the elevators!" she commanded the retinue who started moving instantly.

"We will be watching your progress, Max," Favani called. "Don't die."

"I won't," Max said. "See you up there."

Max looked at the massive staircase. Then he shook his head. Of all the crazy things he'd been roped into . . .

"A journey of a thousand miles starts with a single step, right?" Max said and placed the crown on his head.

As the crown settled there, he felt an immediate drain on his Spiritual Energy. It was like a leech, sucking away at his vitality with every passing second.

He gritted his teeth, his mind already beginning to fog with the insidious fatigue the artifact induced.

"Alright," he said, squaring his shoulders. "Let's do this. Step one . . ."

He lifted his foot, the motion feeling unnaturally heavy and labored. As his boot came down on the first stair, a glowing number appeared in the air before him.

"One," Maverick read aloud. "Only 9,999 to go!"

Max shot the disc a glare, but Maverick just chuckled. Together, they began the ascent, Max's steps slow but steady as he fought against the constant, draining pull of the crown.

The higher they climbed, the thicker the mist became. It swirled around Max's legs, cool and clammy against his skin. The wind picked up, howling through the trees and buffeting Max's body with sudden, unpredictable gusts.

"Two fifty-six . . ." Max grunted, his breath coming in labored pants. "Two fifty-seven . . ."

"You're doing great, buddy," Maverick encouraged. "Just keep putting one foot in front of the other. Or, you know, on top of the other. Stairs are weird like that."

Max managed a strained chuckle, but it quickly turned into a grimace as a particularly strong gust of wind nearly knocked him off-balance. He caught himself on the step, his fingers digging into the stone as he fought to maintain his footing.

The numbers kept ticking up, each one a hard-won victory against the relentless pull of the crown.

"Four hundred twelve . . ."

". . . Seven eighty-nine . . ."

". . . Twelve forty-three . . ."

Max's legs were burning, his lungs screaming for air. The mist had soaked through his clothes, chilling him to the bone. The wind was a constant, battering force, threatening to tear him away from the steps and send him tumbling down into the abyss below.

But still, he climbed. One step at a time, one after another. He focused on the count, using it as an anchor, a lifeline to keep him tethered to reality as the crown's insidious magic sought to unravel his mind.

"Fifteen sixty-eight . . ." Max panted, his vision blurring at the edges. "Fifteen sixty-nine . . ."

Maverick hovered beside him, the gun-disc's presence a constant, reassuring warmth amidst the cold and the mist. But even Maverick's indomitable spirit seemed to be flagging under the relentless assault of the elements and the crown's draining power.

"Max," Maverick said, his voice strained. "I hate to say it, but I don't think you're gonna make it."

Max shook his head, the motion sending a wave of dizziness washing over him. "No," he said, his voice a hoarse rasp. "We can do this. We have one trick up our sleeve. We can use the [**Divine Soulbond**]."

Maverick was silent for a moment, and Max could feel the gun-disc's hesitation, his reluctance to admit weakness. But finally, with a sigh that sounded almost like the wind itself, Maverick relented.

"Alright," he said. "But don't go spreading this around, yeah? I've got a reputation to maintain."

Max felt a surge of warmth, a trickle of Spiritual Energy flowing from Maverick into his own battered body. It wasn't much, but it was enough to clear the fog from his mind, to ease the burning in his muscles.

"Thanks, Mav," he said, a tired smile tugging at his lips. "I owe you one."

"Damn right, you do," Maverick grumbled. "Now, what number were you on again?"

Max blinked, his count suddenly eluding him. The numbers seemed to blur and shift in his mind, dancing just out of reach.

"I . . . I don't know," he admitted, a flicker of panic rising in his chest. "Damn it, Mav, I think we're going to have to start over."

Maverick let out a groan that was half-frustration, half-exhaustion. "Seriously? After all that? We're going to have to keep this blasted crown on for the whole climb? You're gonna suck me dry."

Max set his jaw, a new determination burning through the fatigue and the pain. "Looks like it," he said. "But we can do this. In a way it's better."

"Better how?!" Maverick demanded.

Max didn't answer. Instead, he took another step.

"One," he said, his voice grim and low with resolve. "Two. Three."

And so they climbed, the count starting anew, the journey stretching out before them like an endless road. The mist swirled, the wind howled, the crown drained. But Max and Maverick pressed on, their bond a shining beacon amidst the darkness, their shared strength a bulwark against the trials that sought to break them.

They had faced worse than this, had stared down the very maw of oblivion and emerged victorious. A few thousand steps, a cursed crown, a mountain of mist and wind—these were just more obstacles to overcome, more challenges to conquer.

Max was a Cultivator. This came with a certain sense of pride. Besides, there was loot to win. If he could impress Favani and her king, the rewards would be worth it. So, Max would take another step.

To reach the top. To prove their worth. He would show everyone he was the top dog here.

One step at a time.

CHAPTER THIRTY-NINE

King of the Jianari

Max looked up at the giant red temple at the top of the stairs. Even as a Cultivator of a fairly high Level, the steps and the crown had taken almost everything out of him. He wiped a sheen of sweat off his brow and looked questioningly at Favani who was gazing at him with wide eyes.

Max turned to look at the rest of the retinue. Half of them were gaping and the other half were whispering urgently to one another and subtly pointing at him.

Max walked up to them. "What's the big deal?"

"You—" Favani said and blinked dumbly. "You're still in the Diamond stage, aren't you?"

"Well, yeah," Max said and shrugged.

Before Favani could say anything else, a tall man stepped forward wearing an ostentatious robe and jewelry on his wrists, chest, and neck.

"That is so ridiculous," Max muttered to Maverick.

"That is *so* cool!" Maverick exclaimed. "Why don't we have anything like that?"

Max snorted and watched as the man approached with long strides to stand before Max. He loomed over him like all of Favani's people did. He had similarly sharp features to her and similar eyes. This had to be one of her brothers. His nostrils flared.

"He smells weak, sister," the man said in a loud voice, clearly intended for the whole court to hear. "This Cultivator is barely super-mortal, isn't he?"

"He just rose the steps, Falrid," Favani said coming up next to them and idly brushing a hand at Max's arm. "Wearing the [**Crown of Blighted Fatigue**]."

"There is no way!" the brother exclaimed and turned back to look at Max, a snarl of thinly veiled contempt marring his beautiful features. "You cheated!"

Max only raised an eyebrow and shrugged, as if to suggest that he did and what are you going to do about it? Maverick sniggered, as he sensed what Max was doing through the bond.

"Sister," Falrid said, "as your elder brother, I detest this choice. Surely Father will—"

"Father will run the trials and make his decision. You have no say in this."

"Tsk," Falrid said and turned. He cast one more baleful glare at Max before he harrumphed, turned his heavy cloak in a flourish, and stormed away, glinting like a disco ball.

"Choice?" Max said. "What choice?"

"Oh," Favani said, and her blue cheeks turned a shade of purple. "Let's talk about that later. Come, follow me, the two of you. It's time to see the king."

Max nodded and idly gave the crown to one of the nearby servants. Her eyes went wide, and another servant rushed to help her.

They both slammed into the ground so violently that the marbled platform cracked, sending tiny scraps of rock flying here and there.

Maverick burst out laughing. Favani turned and let out something between a sigh and a chuckle.

She took the crown, pinning the two servants down. Max noticed her hand trembling.

She set the crown down and helped the two servants up. They were pained and dazed.

"Go to the druids to be healed. Free of charge. After it is done, go to my cousin, Diemetra, to receive fifty drakmi in compensation, both of you."

The pained expressions on the servant's faces mellowed into relieved smiles. They steadied each other and started limping toward the left, where a path of bright, white marble was laid to pass through a garden of tropical plants.

"I think my father will like this side of you," Favani said and smiled as she grabbed Max's hand to lead him inside.

They rose a few more steps between massive marble pillars full of a bright red substance that seemed to move like flowing lava was captured under glass. Max brushed against them with his Spiritual Sense and saw that they were brimming with Spiritual Energy.

Favani turned to see if Max had noticed, and smirked.

Two doors made of solid gold opened smoothly to the sides, revealing a long hall. There were more pillars on both sides, and a line of black marble dotted with shining white specks, like stars. The line led toward a dais a quarter of a mile away, on which a giant man sat on a giant throne.

Between the pillars sat guards in meditation. They all wore tight, white outfits that accentuated their athletic forms. Their blue faces were scrunched up in concentration, and their eyes were closed. Before each of them was an open scroll with runes and writing that glowed faintly blue.

Guided by instinct, Max looked above him. Hundreds of shining swords flew around like a swarm of bees. Max brushed lightly against one of the guards' spirits. Greater Diamond stage.

Their steps echoed in the wide hall as they approached the dais. Upon it was a throne towering toward the high ceiling, made of a metal that looked like the fabric of space itself. It was black and speckled with a few stray stars here and there like the marble Max was walking on.

It was as if the Milky Way had been captured in all of its glory and placed inside the throne. It glowed majestically as slowly swirling shapes moved within.

And then there was the king himself. While all of Favani's people were larger than humans, their king was so enormous, it would have been comical, if he weren't so majestic.

He sat with a straight back, his head eighteen feet in the air. Fully standing he must have been twenty feet tall. From his great height, he peered down at Max imperiously, seeming to judge his every movement. The king's eyes were the same light purple as Favani's and a short, immaculately cropped gray beard framed his handsome, angular face.

Upon his thick and massive fingers many rings shone with the same over-powering light as Falrid's jewelry had.

He didn't wear a crown in the traditional sense but had instead a halo that floated above his head, shining an angelic light. It was crafted from the same cosmic metal as the throne.

"Who dares seek an audience with me?" the king's voice boomed as Max and Favani approached.

Now, Max was no coward. He had faced insane odds and had always been the kind of person who jumped into the fray, trusting himself and his abilities.

But right now, standing before the gargantuan king, he felt very, very small.

He swallowed and looked up at him. Immediately the man's purple eyes flared. Max's every muscle tensed in response. He started cycling Spiritual Energy through his meridians and sent a pulse for help to Maverick through their bond. His buddy obliged and started sending his energy over, like they had done when Max was ascending the stairs.

The pressure only intensified, and one of Max's knees buckled. Favani took a sharp look at him and twisted her head subtly.

Show no weakness, huh?

Max breathed deeply and unfurled his bent back and neck, pushing himself to keep looking at the king squarely in his eyes.

If this impressed the king, it did not show. Instead, the pressure intensified, and Max started to feel pain in his meridians. He sent another request to Maverick, and instead of a trickle of energy, he was now receiving a full, steady flow.

This went on for several minutes, with Maverick pumping progressively more power into Max, and Max doing his best impression of a stone statue. He kept staring, and the king kept increasing the pressure.

"Father!" Favani demanded as Max's nostrils started spontaneously bleeding. "Do you intend to kill my guest?"

"Silence, Favani," the king boomed, his voice cutting through the air like a scythe through dry grass. "This is no mere guest you have brought before me. I know your intentions, and you know my duty."

The pressure was still intensifying, and Max felt another knee buckle. The king raised an eyebrow, and a subtle smirk spread across his mighty features. Max knew he wouldn't last long. He would collapse.

But he needed to win. There had to be *something* they could do. But his Dao was one that was mostly concerned with offense and destruction. Max felt a sense of foreboding. Failing this test would likely have grave, even fatal consequences. This was not a nice friendly visit. He was in a den of wolves and the biggest was looking hungry. Favani's people seemed to work independent of the ICCB and clearly had enough power that the Zoos could not simply zip in to interject. He was on his own.

And the situation required a solution. He could feel his vision dimming and a trickle of warm blood from his right eye starting to fall down his cheek.

Is he going to kill me?

Max felt for the energy the king was emitting. It was an unyielding blanket of pressure that enveloped him. Max stretched through the oppressive barrier. It was thin, like a cloak wrapped around him. Reaching outside of it with his spirit felt like a breath of fresh air. He had torn a hole in the pressure.

The king's eyes widened, and the pressure intensified again. This time it brought Max to his knees, and he coughed out blood.

Favani shot a look at Max—mostly filled with concern, but there was also reserved judgement there. Max let Maverick feed energy into him, but it wouldn't be enough.

How do I overcome this?

There was a surge in their bond. Maverick's trust. It was absolute. He knew as certain as the sun would rise that Max would overcome this. The pressure made his ribs and shoulders crack, and Max gasped out in pain.

Max waved his hand in a slow, steady movement, as if he were underwater. At that, the [Scythe of Oblivion] appeared behind him and struck at the cloak of pressure around Max. The pressure released, like a hole punctured into a balloon.

The king's purple eyes intensified yet again, and his mouth moved quietly, as if he was muttering to himself. His expression was regal, majestic, and unreadable. The whole court was quiet, with only Max's heavy breathing echoing through the high walls.

Max fell onto his hands and knees. But the scythe struck again, swinging in a black and silver arc.

I will destroy you.

The Intent released something inside Max. A new feeling blossomed, like a fire raging in his chest. He pushed that feeling forward at the blanket of pressure around him. It started to disintegrate, like thin paper over a candle. The king's eyes widened.

Slowly, coughing out a mouthful of blood, Max rose. The king struck again with his tyrannical pressure, but the scythe swung, and Max released another wave of that feeling inside of his chest. The pressure was parried.

+3 Karma points

"What is this?" the king asked, half-whispering, but it still carried through the halls. "Daughter, what creature have you brought here?"

"Just a man, Father. A human."

The king enveloped Max again. But this time the pressure wasn't violent. It was still oppressive and absolute, and the power of it lifted Max off his feet into the air. Max found he couldn't move. The scythe swung again, but with a flick of a finger, the king scattered Max's Intent, and the weapon clattered uselessly to the ground, with Max unable to reach it to command it again.

Limp and breathing heavily, he spat out a glob of blood and looked the king in the eyes with a weary gaze as the monarch lifted him to be level with his face.

"How did you find this jewel?" the king asked Max.

Favani chuckled. "He tried to get me killed by a sorcerer."

"Did he defeat one?"

"Yes, Father," Favani said. "We did it together."

"Ahem," Maverick said.

Favani shot the disc a glance, before turning back to the king. "Father, he is responsible for the recovery of the relic. He held off three sorcerers."

"Remarkable," the king said. "And yet he seems to be no more than a Diamond-stage Cultivator. How can this be?"

"I do not know, Father," Favani said. "But I want him."

"And you shall have him!" the king boomed. Max was only mildly aware of what was happening, as his head drooped in the air. He was concentrating on staying conscious. Maverick hooted and laughed, and Max wasn't sure why.

"Let it be known throughout the kingdom and all of its vassal planets that my daughter Favani has chosen a mate. A warrior of the highest order, and I, King Valdemar III, will bless this union with many a gift. Heavens know, a mere Diamond Cultivator is weak. But our people respect potential. We shall raise this human to our standards, and he shall be a stalwart defender of our virtues. Never have I witnessed such fighting spirit under my [**Tyrant's Wrath**]. This human shall be a prince among you, and you will do as he commands!"

Max blacked out to the sounds of cheers and claps along with Maverick's howling laughter echoing in his ears.

CHAPTER FORTY

Proposals of All Kinds

Max woke up in a bed. Again. It was soft, fluffy, and even larger than king-sized. It was basically the size of a living room unto itself. He was covered with the finest silks in a myriad of bright colors, and a tall blue woman was playing a harp with soft and gentle notes nearby—*Favani*!

She brightened and stopped playing when she realized Max had woken.

"Remarkable," she said and beamed. "Absolutely remarkable. Where have you been all my life?"

"Uh," Max said.

She rushed to his bedside, grabbed his wrist, and felt for his pulse, as he felt her spirit brush against his.

"So quick to recover. Your Dao must be immensely powerful."

"It kind of is, yeah," Max said.

"Max, you lovable fool," Maverick said as he burst into the room. The disc zipped into a smaller form the size of a dining plate and started zipping around Max's head. "Look at this, look at it!"

"That's convenient," Max said.

"Indeed," Maverick said proudly. "I tested it outside. I can get really big, too. I can carry twenty of those I deem worthy upon me."

"Who might those be?"

"Well, you, I suppose, although that would be a begrudging decision," Maverick said. "And I suppose Favani, by extension. Man! I get to design a bachelor party? That's amazing. I mean, surely I'm the best man, right? Not like you have any other friends anyway!"

"Ouch," Max said. "Hey, wait, what? Wedding?"

Favani blushed purple and cast her gaze down at the floor demurely as she started fiddling with the harp.

Maverick burst out laughing again as he zipped around the bed, alternating in size to the rhythm of his laughter.

"Oh, it's been a day for sure," Maverick said. Max could feel the impression of wiping away a tear of laughter through their bond. "I'm sure the two of you will be very happy together!"

"The two . . ." Max slowly started putting the pieces together. With wide eyes, he gaped at Favani. "That's what this was about?!"

"Look!" Favani said and rushed to his bedside. "I don't know what human customs are like, but I assure you, this will be mutually beneficial."

"You didn't even ask me?"

"I asked my father," Favani said.

"You mean you tried to get me killed by him?" Max said. "Shouldn't you have let me know what you were planning?"

"It was kinda obvious, Max," Maverick said.

Favani's face was full of pride. "I am a princess, some day to be queen. I do not need permission for my actions."

"But aren't I— What?"

Maverick laughed and hooted like a kid on Christmas morning. "Enjoy the rapid-fire wedding, Max!"

"You like me?" Max managed to sputter out.

"I have never seen a finer warrior," Favani said and blushed. "To think you are only at Diamond stage and this powerful. It bowls me over just to think about it."

Max sputtered in disbelief and Favani looked hurt at that.

"Do you not approve?" she asked, brushing a lock of white hair behind her ear.

"You roped me into a proposal without even asking me!" Max exclaimed. "You can't do that to people."

Favani stood up straight and regarded Max with imperious anger. "Do not presume to tell me what I can and cannot do. I will make you respect and love me, just you wait!"

Max was about to say something, but he only looked at Favani warily. Her eyes welled up with the beginnings of tears, and she sniffed and rushed out of the room. Maverick waited until she was out of earshot before he started laughing again.

"Asshole," Max muttered as he rubbed his head. He would need to go and placate her. And he would need to talk to someone who could give him some straight answers.

What in the hell kind of a mess did I get myself into?

He was betrothed to a princess of a powerful kingdom. Not a terrible prospect on paper. Even though all of these people were, to put it mildly, really damn weird.

Favani is pretty, though. Besides that ten-foot-tall-and-blue Avatar *vibe she's got going on.*

Max shook his head. These kinds of royal marriages generally had less to do with looks, affection, and romance. From the looks of it, Favani had wanted to marry him into the royal family for his strength. A very Tudor-Era kind of thing to do. Pragmatic.

But she did rush out with tears in her eyes. . . .

Max decided he wasn't going to outright reject her. Hell, he probably *couldn't* reject her. What was he to do? Escape? The king would flay him alive.

"I, for one, am quite thrilled by this turn of events," Maverick declared gleefully.

"Uh huh," Max said and rubbed his face. "And why is that, pray tell?"

"Two reasons. For one, the king promised to give us a shitload of resources to get us out of the Diamond stage. That's a huge win, no matter how you look at it."

Max mulled over that. He had received some kingly gifts before from Durum of the Obsidian dwarves. He was pretty sure these gifts would be even more amazing—on a goddamn galactic scale. "You're right about that. And the second reason?"

Maverick hooted. "This is going to be like my own personal reality TV show. *Max and His Clueless, Catastrophic Love Life*! A blockbuster in the making."

"I'm glad I'm a supply of endless entertainment for you . . ." Max said. "What should we do?"

"I'm not gonna do anything," Maverick said. "I am just gonna watch and enjoy myself as you flounder around as a member of the royal family of a culture you know nothing about."

Max groaned.

"But as for what you *should* do," Maverick said, a little bit more serious this time, "go along. Marry the girl. Favani's awesome. Much better than that Kat girl, who you didn't even really like. She just happened to be there."

"That's harsh."

"You didn't really respect her," Maverick said, sending a shrug through their bond. "Say what you will, but you and Favani have a lot in common. You both respect strength."

Max said nothing to that. He slid a hand across the bed's silk sheets. Smooth. Infused with Spiritual Energy that nourished his spent meridians. One might consider himself lucky to find himself marrying a beautiful princess.

"She's blue," Max said. "And taller than me."

"She probably has pills to turn you any color you prefer," Maverick said wistfully. "I wonder if they have any treasures to improve my form. Oh, I can't wait to be rewarded by the king!"

"You didn't even do anything," Max protested.

"I fed you energy," Maverick huffed. "Besides, the best meals are the free ones."

"What a terrible attitude," Max said.

"Eh," Maverick said, sending another shrug through their bond. "The way I see it, it's nice to get something for free, after we've had to fight for every scrap, tooth and nail."

Max had to admit, the little bastard was right. There would most likely be all kinds of terrible politicking and blunders in etiquette and dealing with Favani's asshole brother and a myriad of unpredictable problems to come. But he would also be married to a powerful princess of a Cultivator dynasty. This was a lucky break, and it should be viewed as such.

Max got out of bed and found himself to be naked. He quickly located a thin blue robe and a heavy bracelet under a black cloth. It was glimmering the intense green light of an enchanted emerald.

He put on the robe and ignored the bracelet.

Then something strange happened as he was heading out the door.

Reality blinked in and out of existence. The ornate hallway of marble and jewelry was turning black and white, then back to normal in rapid succession.

A familiar sight materialized. The Zoos Collective jellyfish. But this time there wasn't one but a whole school of them. They formed a loose circle around Max, and one of them took the front, bobbing up and down urgently in front of Max.

[Greetings, Max.]

"YOU DARE?!" a massive voice echoed through the hallway, making the whole palace tremor with its power. Then King Valdemar III appeared. His Intent flashed, flooding the room like a tidal wave. The circle of jellyfish erected a green energy barrier, and his tyrannical pressure cracked it until it was bolstered and smoothed out again.

Two dozen guards stormed into the room, sat down, and placed a scroll in front of them, and swords started emerging from the scroll and flying in formation.

Favani also arrived, a look of shock and fear on her face. But she was dressed in her battle attire, her swords buzzing around her in a circle. Max reached out and felt her Intent. She had come here to fight to the death against a superior enemy to get back what was hers. Max found him noticing how beautiful she looked.

[We have come to negotiate.]

"We have nothing to discuss," King Valdemar said. "You will leave without the prince."

[These terms are unfortunate. The Zoos Collective must ask, is he truly a prince yet? We did not know the ceremony with the princess had already happened.]

"You spying little viruses," Favani screeched. "It's none of your business!"

[Maximilian Cromwell is an asset that is currently under contract with the ICCB. We would view any attempt to remove him from our custody as a breach of that contract and an act of aggression against the coalition.]

"You have no right to claim him as your property," Favani said, her voice rising with anger. "He is a free man, and he has chosen to ally himself with the Jianari Empire."

[The terms of the contract are clear. Maximilian Cromwell owes a debt to the ICCB for the resources and training provided to him. Until that debt is paid, he is obligated to serve the coalition's interests.]

"That is not what I agreed to," Max said.
"The Empire will pay off the debt," Favani said. "Or you could improve your standing with the Jianari and consider it a dowry . . ."
"A dowry?" Max asked.

[That is a deft, if risky move, Princess. Note that if you plan on this course of action, you might hurt your already-strained relations with the ICCB.]

"I heard there was a leadership change in the organization," Favani said offhandedly, looking at her nails. "It sounds like a good time to renegotiate."

[You will find us more willing to negotiate if Maximillian Cromwell is not bound to your family.]

"Those wheels are already in motion, come what may," Favani said fiercely.
"What wheels?" Max asked. Maverick snorted.
"Shut up, Max," Favani said. "I was raised for this. Let me negotiate."

[Do you understand the implications of what you are saying, Princess?]

"I said," Favani said, glaring at the hologram, "Come. What. May."

It seemed like the hologram was stunned into silence for a moment. Eventually it spoke again.

[You would risk war with the ICCB? Over one man?]

"Over a principle," Favani said, her eyes flashing with resolve. "You will not take him. For you would not risk war either. Cease with the idle threats, you little virus."

The Zoos Collective was silent for a long moment, most likely engaged in rapid-fire voting inside the collective.

[We will consider your position, Princess Favani. For now and until the battle on Alpha Ludus, you can maintain custody of Maximillian Cromwell. We trust that he holds to that specific obligation and joins the battle. If this clause is breached, the ICCB *will* engage in an all-out war with you. We will not be slighted. But for now, we understand what is happening. There will be no dowry. Pay the debt. But know that the ICCB will not relinquish its claim on Maximilian Cromwell lightly in the future. There will be consequences, should you choose to defy us further.]

"Then let them come," Favani said, her chin held high.

The holographic jellyfish flickered and vanished, leaving Favani and Max alone in the room. They exchanged a long look, a silent acknowledgment of the mess Max was in.

"So . . ." Max said slowly. "About that dowry . . ."

CHAPTER FORTY-ONE

The King's Fault

The vault of King Valdemar III was a sight to behold. Ornate and sprawling, it was filled with treasures and artifacts that would make even the richest nobles of the Jianari Empire green with envy. Hell, it would probably make even the big wigs at the ICCB tremble with excitement.

The walls were adorned with intricate tapestries depicting great battles and the triumphs of the royal bloodline, while pedestals and glass cases displayed ancient weapons imbued with powerful enchantments and glittering metagems of every color and variety that captured and refracted the room's light.

At the center of the vault, on a raised dais of polished marble, rested the crown jewels themselves—a resplendent collection of shining gold and metagems that seemed to pulse with an inner radiance. This was armor for a Celestial Cultivator. Max wondered why the king didn't wear it.

He could feel the weight of history and power that permeated every inch of this chamber, a tangible aura that set his heart racing and his mind alight with the promise of untold potential. He would be getting some of this! Maverick was floating next to him and the disc-shaped gun could barely contain himself.

The king regarded Max with a smile. His purple eyes were still wide and intent, making him look slightly predatory.

"We have many things to offer to our prince."

I guess I'm really doing this.

"Father, might I make suggestions?" Favani asked.

"No," he said. "I am the king. This is my vault. Do you question my judgement in how I should reward those who I deem fit?"

The last part was said with a cutting edge of danger. Max swallowed. If this was how the king talked to his own daughter.

"No, Father," Favani said. Then she turned to Max and whispered sultrily, "Don't worry. I shall give you a special set of gifts from my own personal vault."

She grinned and bit her lip, utterly confusing Max.

Giving gifts to make me more powerful is foreplay? These people are completely nuts.

Maverick was hovering in the air above them, barely suppressing his laughter. Max shot a disapproving glance at him, but it only increased the little bastard's mirth.

"This scythe of yours is a remarkable treasure," the king said. "I would like to augment it. Give it to me."

Max felt an impatient presence suddenly looming over him. He nodded and willed the **[Scythe of Oblivion]** into existence. The king levitated it to himself. He pinched it between his fingers and examined it.

"Aspect of Destruction," King Valdemar mused. "Completely pure. This one might be even more powerful than your companion. It is no wonder that you managed to pique my Intent."

"Hey!" Maverick said, completely affronted. "What do you mean 'more powerful?!'"

All it took was an icy glance from the king aimed at Maverick and he yelped and fell down on the floor, clattering and cursing to himself.

"But you do not know how to wield this weapon," the king said. "I shall teach you and we shall do battle together, until you and your tools are strong enough to face the Outsiders and utterly destroy them."

The whole court oohed, aahed, and clapped. Even Favani looked shocked.

"Fight you?" Max said and swallowed.

The king shot an impatient glance first at him and then at Favani.

"You are a poor wife, Daughter," Valdemar said. "How is that he does not know of our Cultivation method?"

"We haven't had the chance to discuss such matters, as we have been otherwise occupied."

Titters and whispers rose among the crowd, especially the women. Max and Favani both blushed. The king looked pleased, however.

"It is good of you to immediately get set on providing our family an heir, Max," he said. "I am of a mind to reward you further!"

There were applause and cheers, and Max was definitely not going to correct the king on his assumptions on what had kept him and Favani busy.

"But to rectify my daughter's oversight," King Valdemar continued, "our people Cultivate through the intensity of combat. Those with weak Daos make up the servants and peasants. But those who have the right Daos can grow through combat. The more powerful your foe, the more potential for growth. As a wedding gift and for your show of loyalty to us in the negotiation with the ICCB, I have deigned to grant you personal duels with myself, in order for you to grow."

Max grinned. These people were so ridiculous. But he was sure that sparring with this absolute monster of a Cultivator would do him good, regardless. He could exercise his Intent to destroy without having to be careful. There was no way he could hurt the king, who had Cultivation of a Level Max couldn't fully comprehend.

"This shall be done later today, after you have ascended," the king said. "Preparations need to be made for our duels and you will need to reach the peak of the Diamond stage, lest I utterly destroy you."

Favani brought out an ornate box with glittering gems studded along its golden lid. Inside was a set of equally dazzling pills. They shone with a bright light, like tiny stars imprisoned within pearls.

"These are [**Divine Ascension Pills**]," Favani declared to the court, who responded with the requisite jubilation.

Max picked up one of the pills. He could feel it *thrum*ming with power. These were *potent*. Far more potent than anything he had held before. Even the resources he had received at the ICCB training camp were no match—not even close.

"Two shall be given to Max!" Favani said, her voice bolstered by Cultivation so that it boomed over the courtyard. "His potential as a warrior is exemplary, and we would be fools not to bind him to our family with gifts of great value. With these pills, he can advance to the peak of Diamond stage."

Maverick sent a pulse through their bond for Max to show him one of the pills. Max did so and Maverick bobbed up and down in the air as if nodding thoughtfully. Currently he was the size of a large dining plate.

"These feel special," Maverick said.

"That's putting it mildly," Max said. "I feel like this one has one of those Cultivation arrays inside it."

Favani came closer to Max and pressed her forehead against his. Max reciprocated, even though it felt awkward. Her forehead was cool and her scent spicy and sweet.

"These pills will make you stronger than me," she said quietly.

"Why don't you take them?"

"I have taken one," she said. "It helped me break through from the lower stage of Diamond into the greater realm."

"So, take another?"

She shook her head. "It doesn't work like that. They are only able to ascend you proportional to your potential."

"Why do I get two?" Max said.

"Mainly it is because of your [**Divine Soulbond**]. While Maverick is seen as an extension of your power—"

"Hey!" the disc exclaimed.

"—He still warrants a pill of his own. I want you to appreciate the magnitude of this gift, Max. These pills are worth the resources of a small planet."

Max's eyes went wide with shock.

"A planet?"

"Not a particularly powerful one, but yes."

"Sweet baby Jesus," Max muttered.

Favani quirked an eyebrow at that but didn't say anything. "These pills will increase your capacity and power significantly, most likely prompting you to ascend a stage. Additionally, they will send you on an internal journey. Your Dao will reveal itself to you. I want you to take these pills tonight. I will sit with you, guide and watch over you as you travel within, to find the key to the heavens."

Max nodded solemnly.

The ceremony went on, and Max received many more gifts, although of significantly lesser interest. He received an estate near the main complex of the courtyard. With that came a midsize palace, hunting grounds, and gardens for spiritual herbs and plants, a hundred servants, and tithes from the citizens of the nearby area. Max shook his head at the absurdity.

I guess I'm royalty now.

"It was about time we received at least as paltry a station as this," Maverick muttered. "I'm of the opinion we should be crowned King of the Universe, but I suppose I'll have to be patient."

"You, uh . . . do that," Max said and shook his head. Favani giggled.

Then Max had to receive various members of the court, each asking for him to visit their homes, where there would be promises of many rewards if he would deign to ally himself with their noble houses.

It was a long day, but after shaking countless hands and making many new friends, Max retreated with Favani into their new home. Tomorrow would be a big day. A day of gift-giving that was anticipated by everyone in the capital.

The new prince would duel with the king.

CHAPTER FORTY-TWO

A Royal Duel

King Valdemar III loomed over Max and looked at him with the impassive confidence of someone who hadn't faced a real challenge in the longest time. Max wished he could say he could give him one, but it honestly didn't seem likely.

"Is that doubt I detect?" Maverick asked. They were hovering in the midair, level with the king's gaze.

"Not really," Max said. He breathed out and let his shoulders relax. They were inside a pearly iridescent dome the size of a football field. Outside was a crowd eagerly waiting for this fight.

"I have no doubt the king is stronger than we are," Max said. "But we aren't fighting with life and death stakes here. It's different."

"I wonder . . ." Maverick said.

They would have three bouts. Max and Maverick were both wearing belts and bracelets of heavy gold, studded with those magical, brightly shining gems. A fist-sized emerald shone on each of Max's wrists, as well as on the two belts around his waist. He additionally wore a necklace with a large amethyst, and a crown studded with small, bright rubies on his head.

Max brushed at one of them with his spirit. It was empty for now. Max had earlier asked Favani about this Jianari custom. With a laugh of disbelief, she shook her head. "They aren't decorations. Sure, the richer you are, the more of them you have, but they're technology that lets us rival the ICCB and not be subsumed under their rule. Metagems are the pride of our people."

"What do they do?" Max had asked and tapped a fat ruby on Favani's necklace that was hanging low above her bosom.

She had blushed and swatted away his hand.

"They store fighting Intent," she had said and cast a lingering glance at the hand that had brushed at her. "Do you know the basic mechanics of Dao and Karma?"

"I know something of them," Max had said.

"When your actions are aligned with your Dao, you generate Karma. We call that Intent. An advanced super-mortal Cultivator such as my father, the king, can use pure Intent to fight, as he did with you in the throne room. He can determine reality."

"Damn," Maverick had called out and started spinning around them with excitement. "How do we learn to do that?"

"Not for a while," Favani had said. "It takes a long time before your Intent can be used without expending too much of your Spiritual Energy. But it is always present in your techniques. That is how you're able to make something out of nothing or bend the rules of physics. Because of Intent. It is the rule of the Heavens."

"So what do these gems have to do with it?"

"They store it. They are a defensive mechanism that allows you to dissipate techniques and keep the Intent that is used. That way later, after you have defeated your foe, you can use that stored Intent and transform it into Karma."

"That sounds convoluted," Max had said.

"It is very simple, really," Favani had explained, brushing a lock of hair behind a blue ear. "Say you're attacked with a technique that holds Intent. This Intent is the result of someone following their Dao. Then you store the technique within a metagem. After the death of your foe, you can then sit down and contemplate on your own Dao, using the energy that the metagem stored. There are a myriad of Daos and different ways to Cultivate, but ultimately, Spiritual Energy is the same. Think of the metagems as distillers."

Max came back from his memories to stare at the king, who was exuding an air of disdain. Max wondered how much stronger he was than he and Maverick.

That was why it was considered such a great boon for the king to have bouts with him. He had massive amounts of Spiritual Energy, and they had fitted Max with the metagems. He would get to keep the intense energy that the king released during the fight.

"Are you ready?" the king asked.

Max nodded grimly.

"Good," Valdemar III boomed. "Have your wits about you. This dome will protect your essence, for the most part, even if I release a technique too powerful for you. But it isn't foolproof, so I urge you to do your best, lest you be destroyed."

Max swallowed. Perhaps this was more serious than he had initially thought. Maverick sent a pulse through their bond saying, "Told you so."

"No one likes that, Mav," Max said between his teeth. He was breathing deeply through his nose, letting the Spiritual Energy start flooding his meridians.

"Bah," Maverick said. "If I stopped doing my thing just because people didn't like what I do, who would I be?"

"Nothing, or someone else than yourself," Max admitted.

"And if that is not the true essence of self-destruction, I don't know what is," Maverick said.

"I guess you have a point there."

"I *always* have a point," Maverick said. "Now, focus."

Max nodded.

"Ready yourself!" King Valdemar boomed.

The king lifted off his feet with a smooth wave of his hand, and a shower of purple laser bolts shot out at Max and Maverick.

They moved so fast that only their instincts saved them. Maverick instantly swerved and Max used his spatial abilities to divert the bolts' energy. The meta-gems glowed and hummed softly, and Max felt them becoming slightly heavier.

The new powers he gained for being at the peak of Diamond Cultivation allowed him to sense the next attack with a speed that bordered on precognition. Another fan of purple laser bolts spread out in his direction. Max and Maverick dodged, and then Maverick sent a bolt of yellow and gray energy directly at the king, but he swatted away the attack with a contemptuous flick of a wrist.

Meanwhile Max realized that the energy bolt that they had dodged by half a foot had done some serious damage.

The sleeve of Max's silky robe had burned off and his skin was a singed red. It throbbed with pain that seemed to seep inside him even deeper.

The king sent out another spreading fan of energy. Max dodged, but the king blinked out of existence, only to reappear right above Max and Maverick.

"Oh," Maverick managed to say, before they were punted to the ground by a heavy fist.

They fell from the air and crashed into the marble courtyard, utterly shattering it. It cracked open with the sound of thunder, and Max scuttled out of the hole they had created before a heavy blue foot could land on them.

Max flew through the air with his own power, while Maverick did his dogfight maneuvers, changing his size and the power of his cannon blasts. But even at their heaviest, they seemed to be merely annoying to the king, like flies or mosquitoes on a summer's day.

Max used the space Maverick had given him to prepare a spell. He knew he didn't need to hold back. He gathered the power in his meridians to the point that they were strained. Then he brought Spiritual Energy flowing into his hands and compressed it, until there was a veritable ocean of power *thrum*ming there, just waiting to be let go and burst. But Max didn't let it go. He pressed it deeper into itself, until it became *heavy*.

"Mav!" Max shouted, and the disc sped toward him, scooping him up. Their flight was wobbly due to the weight of Max's spell, but it was fast enough to dodge another volley of purple energy.

The king used the same technique again and blinked in and out of existence next to them, slamming a giant fist again. With a mighty roar, Max smashed the swirling mass of gravity into it.

They crashed together, and another thunderclap echoed through the dome. Max blacked out for a moment and then found himself crashing against the side of the dome on the other side of the field. He fell to the ground next to Maverick and groaned.

If I had still been at the early stages of Diamond Cultivation, that strike would've killed me.

The metagems on his body were getting heavier and brighter.

Max scrambled on top of Maverick to fly away from the next attack that was surely coming.

But it wasn't. Instead, when Max looked at King Valdemar III, he noticed that he was . . . *struggling.*

The spell that Max had created was still stuck in the king's hand. The way Max imagined it, it was like a white dwarf—a star collapsed unto itself. Of course, Max didn't have the power to infuse his spell with as much power as to rival the mass of a star, but he was pretty sure that the king had the weight of an ocean stuck to his hand.

The king snarled and tried to lift it. He *just* managed, but he was clearly thrown off-balance by it. Max's instincts told him it was time to attack.

The [Scythe of Oblivion] appeared behind him, and he threw it at the king's neck in a spinning arc. It struck true, and there was an exploding flash of silver and black energy. The king grunted. Meanwhile, Maverick was preparing a blast of energy from his cannon, and Max, while spent from his spell, started creating a field around the king, which distorted reality itself, making it harder for the monarch to move, to think, to simply exist.

The king's hard purple eyes shot at Max, and there was shock in them. Not fear. Not defeat. They were still the eyes of a person in absolute control of an outcome. But there was shock.

Max smirked as he intensified the reality-distortion field. Maverick let out the bolt of energy with a roar. It made ripples in the air as it smashed into the king's head.

The great blue giant of a king toppled, and the ground trembled as he hit it. The [Scythe of Oblivion] rose up in the air and sliced down like a guillotine, going in for the kill.

But just then, a great violet ring of energy flared out from the king's body. The scythe clattered to the ground and Max felt the reality-distortion field fade.

When the spell released, the arena's marble floor cracked again. Maverick shot another blast of energy, and Max charged his meridians with Spiritual Energy, in preparation.

The king was in no mood to play games. He came at them with a tall spear of purple energy, which he hurled at Max. It moved so fast, there was no dodging it, even with the senses and speed of a peak Diamond Cultivator.

With a gasp, Max felt the spear pierce his abdomen, and in the next moment an intense heat spread from within, and he looked down at his hands which had started to disintegrate into black ash that was even then scattering into the air.

CHAPTER FORTY-THREE

Metagem Cultivation

Max woke up in bed. . Favani was beside him, naked under the sheets. She sighed softly and snuggled into his side. Max looked at his hands. They were still there.

"Ugh," Maverick said with a groan. "Did you have to wake up already?"

"Sorry," Max said.

"I guess we're alive," Maverick said. "That king is such an asshole."

"Mmm," Favani moaned sleepily. "It is considered treason to slander my father."

"We'll just have to get stronger than him," Maverick said.

"He is halfway through Celestial stage," Favani said as she snuggled deeper into Max's side. "You'll need a few centuries to get stronger than him."

"Ain't nobody got time for that," Maverick said. He flew up in the air, shrinking himself to the size of a saucer, but the flight was wobbly and after a while, Maverick decided to land on the bedside table. "Uh, maybe another nap would not be a bad idea."

"Probably for the best," Favani said with a light chuckle and hummed contently as Max put an arm around her.

Max looked at Favani, his wife. It was a completely strange concept to him. He didn't love Favani. He liked her, sure. She was pretty, confident, powerful, and gentle in her own way. But she was still an alien princess who, as far as Max was concerned, had tricked him into marriage.

Still, feels good to have her here. I don't feel so alone anymore.

Maverick sent a pulse of annoyance through the bond. He was clearly miffed.

"What happened?" Max asked as he brushed Favani's luxurious hair.

Favani's hand slid up and down on Max's chest. "You're amazing."

Max let out a little confused chuckle. "Thanks?"

"No one has ever been able to give my father even a lick of struggle."

"I felt his Intent," Max said. "He really was trying to kill me, wasn't he?"

"He is a warrior first, a king and father second," Favani said. "He saw you as a foe to be vanquished. His pride was hurt, and when you hurt the pride of a warrior, you must bear the consequences."

"Why aren't I dead?"

"My mother is a great healing sage," Favani said. There was a flash of sadness in her eyes. "She saved you."

"I haven't even met her," Max said.

"I hope you will," Favani said and cast a warm smile at Max. "She's no warrior, but she's powerful in her own right. She expended some of her life force to restore you."

"Damn," Max said and looked at his hands again. "Remind me to thank her."

"She did it for me," Favani said. "And now she must slumber for at least a few years to restore herself."

"I'm sorry," Max said, shocked.

Favani got up and looked at him in utter confusion. "For what?"

"For making your mother sacrifice herself for me."

Favani said nothing, only looked at Max with incredulity. "You are so silly sometimes."

"What?"

"It was my father who lost control. It was my mother who saved you. You only did what you do. You followed your Dao and attempted to destroy your enemy. I have nothing but respect and love for you, Max. And so does the kingdom."

Max raised an eyebrow. "The kingdom?"

Favani laughed. "You were, of course, famous as my consort. The word was already spreading that I had found a warrior-mate to strengthen the dynasty. But to think that I had brought home a warrior that can challenge the king! You are revered as a god among men now, Max."

"FINALLY!" Maverick boomed. "If this was all we had to do, we should have done it ages ago!"

"Challenge someone vastly more powerful than us and die in the process of fighting them?"

"Max . . . Max . . . My foolish, simple Max," Maverick said and tutted. "If, by now, you haven't realized that I plan on eventually going out in a ridiculously glorious blaze of glory, I don't think you really know me at all."

Max knew that was a lie. Maverick was the type to seek immortality so that he could enjoy adulation for the rest of eternity. Maverick jabbed him through their bond, telling him to sod off, so he could show off to Favani. Max sighed but allowed it. It was cute hearing Favani giggle at Maverick's ridiculous antics. Strangely enough, it made Max enjoy this side of his sometimes-insufferable buddy more.

"So what happens now?" Max asked after Maverick was done ranting.

"You must rest," Favani said. "Your body was completely disintegrated. It's nothing short of a miracle that you were able to be restored."

"Fine," Max said. "But what comes after I've rested? I don't have much time before I have an obligation to fill for the ICCB."

Favani blushed a slight purple. "Our wedding ceremony must be done before you depart. And when you leave, I shall come with you."

Max nodded solemnly. "Thanks."

"I have to protect the assets I've acquired."

Max sighed wistfully. "You're such a romantic."

Favani grinned. "Big talk from someone who was the one being pursued in this relationship."

Max sucked in his lips. *Cultural differences, huh . . . ?*

"I don't know if I can ever learn to love you," he blurted out.

There was a flicker of disappointment in Favani's eyes, but Max could tell she was a big girl.

"I don't love you either," she said tentatively. "But I know I will. You're such a remarkable warrior, yet so gentle and thoughtful. And you fought for me without hesitation when I was a complete stranger, and you took care of me and saved me and—"

Max took her hand. It seemed like the right thing to do. She stopped blabbering and smiled.

"I'm royalty, Max," she said and squeezed his hand gently. "We don't marry for love. But it would definitely be a nice bonus."

"I like you, and you're really pretty," Max said. "But this is really weird for me. It might take time."

"We're super-mortal," Favani said, perking up. "We've got time. We just have to make sure you don't get killed fighting the Outsiders. That's why I'm coming to protect my assets and my husband, who might, maybe, perhaps, possibly, conditionally, perchance love me someday."

"I know, I'm such a catch," Max said with a grin.

"I don't need you to love me, but I am going to start seducing the hell out of you soon enough. I am a warrior, and warriors have large appetites."

It was Max's turn to blush, but he kept his eyes locked on Favani, who was smiling like a cat.

"Favani," Maverick said matter-of-factly. "Did you know that not only can I turn myself so small that even you'd have difficulty seeing me with a naked eye, but I can also sense Max's emotions and feelings through our bond, *and* see through his eyes at will?"

"You know," Favani said, blushing again. "I'm not sure I like you all the time."

Max chuckled. "Welcome to the family."

After Max got out of bed, he wasn't rushed to the wedding ceremony. Instead, he followed Favani to a Cultivation Room, where he could transfer the massive amounts of Intent stored in the metagems that Max had worn during his spar with King Valdemar. They were so heavy, dozens of the tiny servants were needed to pull them into the room on sleds. The gnomes were heaving and huffing by the end. Max had suggested that he could simply carry them, but Favani had stopped him, telling him that it was beneath his station as a prince.

Prince, huh . . . It is gonna take a while to get used to that.

Their retinue arrived at a courtyard further away from the main palace, inside the royal garden. Max had a hard time wrapping his head around the fact that there was another building complex hidden inside the garden of a building complex. The Jianari Empire never did anything on a small scale, it seemed.

The courtyard was compact, all things considered, clearly only designed for the metagem cultivation. There were some storage buildings to the sides, as well as a few living quarters and a mess hall. Additionally, everything was adorned with statues or beautifully painted murals on the walls, with rich, vibrant blues, reds, and purples. In the middle of it all was a Cultivation array, the likes of which Max had never seen.

It was a round depression in the ground with tall, arcing towers sloping to the middle, like a claw clutching something by the tip of its fingers. The towers were all made of pure gemstone: amethyst, ruby, sapphire, emerald, diamond, and even one finger made from that iridescent star-patterned gem used in the king's throne.

Where the fingers of the array met in the air fifty feet above the ground, there was a floating box made of the same star-material. Toward the box flew a group of gnome servants from their retinue, carrying one of Max's bracelets. Max watched their flight and Maverick snorted at them.

"This is one of our greatest treasures," Favani said, nodding at the array. "It was built by my great-grandfather, Valdermar I. He was the first high king of our people, and he built this and most of our kingdom on this planet eighteen thousand years ago."

"Wait," Max said trying to wrap his head around his wife's long-lived lineage. "How old is your father? No. How old are *you*?!"

Favani smiled cryptically. "A bit older than you."

"Like . . . how old, exactly?"

Maverick chuckled gleefully. "Are you sure you want to know?"

"Indeed," Favani said and fluttered her eyelids. "Do I not look fresh and young for a maiden of two hundred years?"

"You're gorgeous," Max said off-handedly. "But you're making me self-conscious."

"I'm still fairly young, especially by my people's yardstick," Favani said. "My father is twenty-two."

"Twenty-two . . . ?" Max asked warily.

"Twenty-two centuries old," Favani said.

"Yeah, sounds about right," Max said, shaking his head. He knew he was in a completely different world now. He was a Cultivator. A super-mortal Cultivator. He didn't need to eat, barely needed sleep, and no illness or aging or decay could touch him. The only way he would realistically die was through violence.

"Let's just say that, after a few centuries, our age difference will hardly matter," Favani said and gave Max a smirk before she turned to address the servants. "Initiate the array. My husband will soon step in to absorb the first gem."

A group of servants flew to each of the fingers of the array and started infusing them with blue energy, until they started to glow.

The rest of their retinue settled on the most comfortable benches Max had ever seen. The stone seemed to give like a featherbed when people sat on them, and armrests sprang up on command. They were scattered tastefully around the Cultivation array, and people started unpacking small picnics.

Max shook his head. "Why do you always have this swarm of onlookers with you?"

Favani looked at them and smiled. "Not always. But the court nobles are all super-mortal Cultivators and most of them aren't joining in the war effort for this reason or that. They're *bored*. You're the most interesting thing that has happened in our kingdom's court in a few hundred years."

"Will I ever get used to them?"

"Perhaps," Favani said. "Stop worrying about it for now! Focus. The king's Intent is no easy thing to absorb."

"So how do I do this?"

"It works like any other Cultivation array. It will feed energy to you. However, absorbing Intent is slightly different."

"Different how?"

"The metagems are wonderful at transforming Intent into pure Spiritual Energy," Favani said. "But they're not perfect. There are still remnants of my father's Intent. I wouldn't even have you attempt to absorb it, if you weren't, well . . . you."

Max couldn't help but grin at that. Being fawned over by other humans or even the strike force members, who were vastly beneath him in power, was one thing. But to have the princess of the mightiest king in the universe be impressed by him . . . That did things to the fragile and vain male ego.

"It will attack your spirit," Favani said. "And you need to conquer it."

"You're a warrior people," Max said. "And your Cultivation reflects that."

Favani clearly liked that. She leaned in for a chaste kiss. Max didn't resist and reciprocated. It felt less weird than before. Favani's presence made him feel . . . Calm? Sated? Content?

I had always figured love was something fiery and passionate. But perhaps when you're set to live with someone for eons, slow, steady, and calm is what you're looking for.

"You'll make a good king someday," Favani said.

Max sputtered. "Okay, let's not get ahead of ourselves."

Maverick perked up and flew out of Max's pocket and resized himself. "You do realize that it will be a joint rule?"

Favani glared at Maverick. "Yes, it will be a dyarchy under Max and me."

"I believe you mean a triarchy." Maverick said triumphantly. "For I know I will be a good and just king. As long as my loyal subjects show me the proper adoration."

Max and Favani shared a look that was equal parts exasperated and amused.

"Eventually of course, when I'm fully ready, I shall take over royal duties myself," Maverick went on. "But I will have you two as my loyal servants, sidekicks, and counselors to the throne. I do realize that, despite my endless magnificence, I might overlook some small details of my kingdom, the overseeing of which is appropriate for those of your intelligence and ability."

"Uh . . . thanks?" Max said offhandedly. "Anything else we need to know about Cultivating with the metagems?"

Favani considered it, tapping a finger on her delicate purple lips. "Be prepared for a fight."

"At this point," Max said and chuckled, "I don't expect it to go any other way."

Max took the initiative and pecked a kiss on Favani's cheek. She flinched and went rigid as a statue, blushing from neck to forehead into deep purple. She quickly covered her mouth and looked around at the idle court on their benches. They were, of course, watching the two of them intently as they snacked on nuts and wine.

Max smiled and went toward the Cultivation array, Maverick following him, still going on about how he would rule the kingdom one day.

They settled in the depression in the center of the array. Maverick returned to his default size and Max sat on top of him. The towering gemstone fingers hummed urgently, and their light started to slowly turn from gently shining to overwhelming.

Max started to feel the weight of a tyrannical energy from above. The box that housed the bracelet Max had worn shone with a bright white starlight. It hummed and crackled violently until suddenly, without any forewarning, lightning struck from the box.

It seared through Max's meridians like flowing lava. Max flinched and attacked the oppressive energy with his own energy. He guided it to disperse evenly into his body. And because there was too much of it, he diverted some of it to Maverick, who had been hit by less of the attack, since he was below Max when the lightning struck. The prideful king-to-be took in the energy without complaint.

Max felt his buddy's spirit. No glee, no bombastic, vainglory. Only focus and humility. Max smirked. Maverick sent a proverbial kick to the shin through their bond, with a side-dish of "mind your own business."

Max could clearly feel the energy had come from the king. The same sense of overpowering violence with a heavy underlying control. It tried to squeeze the life out of his spirit, as if the energy inside of him wanted to overthrow and replace him.

Max would have none of that. He pressed against the energy. This time, he wasn't guiding it gently. This wasn't a negotiation; this was a battle. With that realization something released inside of Max. An Intent of his own. Max could hear the crowd oohing, and another bolt of lightning struck him a few seconds after.

But this time, Max was ready. He filled himself with the Intent. It flooded out of his Spiritual Core in the bottom of his navel.

And it suppressed the king's tyrannical Intent, which struggled, but was ultimately subsumed and absorbed by Max's destructive will. The king's Intent disintegrated into pure energy and Max took it in, strengthening his own Intent.

+1 Karma point

After the tyrannical Intent was completely absorbed and taken in, Max's Intent spread throughout his body, into his meridians, and then, strangely enough, outside of him. It brushed past Maverick, who was unharmed by it, but when it touched the Cultivation array, it . . . *broke.*

"STOP!"

Favani crashed into him with great speed, grabbing Max by his robe and picking Maverick up in her other hand. A blink of an eye later, they were on the stone floor of the courtyard. Favani was breathing heavily and whimpering with pain from the exertion.

Max calmed his Intent down, and his flared-up spirit settled from the mental equivalent of stormy waves to still water.

He turned to his spouse. Favani was holding her hands and trembling. Max took them in his. The skin was charred. Max's eyes went wide with shock.

"Hey!" Maverick shouted to the crowd who had risen from their seats and gathered closer. "Is there a doctor in the house?"

The crowd only muttered to themselves and watched.

"THEN, GO GET ONE!" Max shouted and cradled Favani in his lap. Her eyelids fluttered and she tried to speak, but she was too weak.

"Goddamn it," Max muttered. "Why does something like this always happen?"

"Heavy is the head?" Maverick suggested.

"Not in the mood, Maverick," Max said grimly.

CHAPTER FORTY-FOUR

Bedside Manners

It was Max's turn to wait by the bedside. It only took an hour before Favani woke up. Her hands were wrapped with a blue silk cloth that slightly glowed.

"Hey," Max said.

"Hey," she croaked back. "You're such a troublemaker."

"Yeah, I heard what happened from your enthusiastic brother."

"He must have been so happy to be given a reason to berate you."

"I'm just happy it was him and not your father," Max said.

"Knowing my father, he was probably livid and impressed at the same time."

"Yeah, that seems to be the vibe he's going for."

She got up, propping herself on the pillows. "You sure are something else."

"They said your hands and side will be alright, but it's gonna be expensive," Max said.

"Nothing the royal coffers cannot afford, I am sure," Favani said and started reaching for the water on her bedside, but she almost toppled it over with her wrapped-up hands.

"Let me," Max said and flicked a finger. The glass lifted in the air and planted itself gently against Favani's lips and tilted to let her drink.

"Such a gentleman."

"Nothing that isn't expected from the husband of a princess."

"You're sweet," Favani said. "But soon you will have to harden yourself. I want you back in the array."

"Me too!" Maverick interjected. "That felt amazing! Was that our Intent? How do we harness it? I want more, more I tell you!"

"That was your Intent," Favani said. "Your Dao is amazing. It seems to be more than just pure Destruction. What is it?"

"No," Max said. "You misunderstand. It's just that."

"Just what?"

"*Pure* Destruction."

"Oh," Favani said and looked at her hands.

"Yeah," Max said. "But they said it will be alright."

"You really need to get that thing under control as fast as possible."

"We really do," Max admitted.

"I can't wait to infuse this with my cannon blast," Maverick said, completely disregarding the solemnity of the room. "Imagine the power. I think I'll be able to take out those sorcerers with a single shot."

"You know," Favani said, "I really wouldn't be surprised if you did."

"Could be," Max said.

"I remember when I met you. The first thing you did was try to destroy the Outsiders," Favani said and laughed. "You almost got us killed."

"Yeah, I didn't know anything back then."

"You didn't," Favani said. "But your impulse was right. That is why the Outsiders are so unbeatable. They simply re-form over and over again, and their essence cannot be destroyed. That is why fighting them feels so hopeless."

Max nodded, thinking on what Favani said.

"But your instincts were right. The problem was you simply didn't have the power to do what you wanted."

"You think now I might?" Max asked.

"I'm not sure, but you're definitely getting closer. I want to discuss this with my father. If you truly have the power to destroy the Outsiders, you won't only be able to push back the enemy's advance; you could single-handedly end the war."

Max sighed. Maverick hooted.

"Damn straight, we will! Do you think we came here just to screw around?"

Max said nothing. Maverick cooled down and stammered something that might have sounded like an apology. Max was probably imagining things.

"What's wrong?" Favani asked.

Max rubbed his neck and looked away.

"None of your business, lady," Maverick said.

"I'm not some lady," Favani said with haughty, mounting anger. "I'm his *wife.*"

Then she rose from the bed and sat next to Max, bringing her bandaged hands to his. "Talk to me."

Max looked her in the eyes. They were trusting and open right now. Soft. Something completely opposite to the pure warrior fervor they'd been infused with when Max first met her. He found he liked this hidden gentle side of his wife.

And so he told her. He told her of how he had just been some guy, practically a loser, on his home planet. How he had just wasted his time and potential, until the ICCB had taken his species. Max told her of his growth on Alpha Ludus. Of the constant challenges. Of relentlessly pushing forward. Cultivating a mind, body, and being that had started to surpass his peers. Slowly but surely making people count on him, in rapidly and vastly increasing numbers. He had just kept pushing, doing what he thought was necessary. And then the ICCB's interest in him increased. The deathmatch had put the fate of his whole species on his shoulders. And the next thing he knew, he was recruited to not only protect his species but the whole planet of Alpha Ludus.

And now Favani was telling him that the war that had been raging on for eons, threatening the very existence of the known universe in all of its glory and vastness. All of it, Max could potentially end.

Max vomited. It was very undignified, and Maverick made a gasp. He didn't laugh though. There was nothing funny about it.

Max floated the glass of water to his mouth and drank. Favani only watched him silently as Maverick went to the door, blasted a hole in it, and called on servants to clean up the mess and fix the door.

"Well," Max rasped, "there you have it. I just . . . think I could use a day off. It's all a bit much."

"This is something I have never had to contend with," Favani said. "I am sorry that I said that you might be able to end the war."

"You're not taking it back, though, are you?" Max said, with a wisp of hope in his voice.

"I cannot," Favani said. "I am only sorry that it has to be you."

Max sniffed and nodded. They were silent for a while before Max took a slow, deep breath. In and out. His spirit stirred. It ached with emotion, but Max knew the time for therapy and crying about it would be later. For now, he got up.

"Well, it had to be someone," Max said. "Might as well give it my best shot."

"Hell, yeah!" Maverick said as he hovered over the gnomes on their knees, cleaning the floor.

"Remarkable," Favani said.

Max sighed. He was enveloped by a heavy blanket of emotions. Max felt Favani's spirit brush against his. He flinched at it, suddenly feeling vulnerable. Favani came in closer, slowly circling her arms around Max in a hug.

"I think I understand," Favani said quietly and kissed him. Max wondered if she truly did.

"I've carried my own burdens as well," she continued. "Perhaps not as mighty as yours, but enough to know the weight of responsibility."

"I shouldn't have said anything."

"Shh," Favani said. "I vow to carry this burden with you. Whatever you must do, I will follow. I can't take the responsibility from you, and I can't fully understand it. But I will support you. I will always be by your side. What kind of a wife would I be if I didn't?"

Max flinched again and his eyes went wide open. The loneliness that had been clutching at his heart lessened its grip. It was still there, but it was no longer as painful. He untangled himself from Favani and gazed into her questioning eyes. Then he kissed her.

She melted into his kiss. Maverick groaned and left the room.

The next time Max and Maverick were using the Cultivation array with the metagems, the king himself was overseeing the procedure. He had said nothing of the incident that had almost cost his daughter her hands. Max had tentatively glanced at the king, but his purple eyes betrayed not much beneath the royal veneer. But there might have been something that Max hadn't seen there before. Curiosity? Doubt?

When the lightning struck Max and Maverick in the array, they had been ready. Now that they had a feel for their Intent, it was easy to attack and disintegrate Valdemar's own oppressive Intent. As Max Cultivated the energy and assimilated it into his spirit, he felt the king's spirit touch his with a soft probe. Max couldn't blame him.

The king's Intent was powerful. Ridiculously so. It might be that the millennia-old king had never faced a foe that could contend with his Intent. But Max had to admit, once he had gotten the knack of it, it was *easy* to deal with the energy. There didn't seem to be anything that Max couldn't destroy with his Intent. And that was a heady, powerful feeling.

+1 **Karma point**
+1 **Karma point**
+1 **Power**
+1 **Power**
+1 **Control**
+1 **Control**
+1 **Speed**

As the metagems were spent, Max and Maverick strengthened their Cultivation, and the control and intensity of their Intent grew stronger. Max couldn't wield it like he had felt the king do, but it was a magnificent feeling. He felt he could affect reality itself with just the flick of his mind. But like in the classic comic books, it was important to remind himself, and Maverick most of all, that with great power came great responsibility.

He had almost ruined his wife's hands in an accident, after all.

When Max had spent all of the metagems he had accrued in his spars with the king, he stepped away from the array and sat in meditation to transform his Karma into power.

CHAPTER FORTY-FIVE

The Wedding

It took two days to prepare the main courtyard for the wedding ceremony even with all the resources and all the servants the royal family had at their disposal. To call it ostentatious would have been an understatement.

The wedding party was a lavish and spectacular affair, a grand celebration befitting the union of a powerful warrior and a royal princess. The main courtyard had been transformed into a dazzling wonderland of color and light, awash in vibrant shades of purple, red, and blue.

Giant peacocks, resplendent with iridescent feathers studded with glittering metagems, strutted proudly through the crowd. Their magnificent tails fanned out behind them, creating a breathtaking display of shimmering hues that caught the light and cast a kaleidoscope of colors across the courtyard.

The air was filled with a mouthwatering aroma of exotic dishes, as servers wove through the throng of guests bearing trays laden with delicacies from across the empire. Jianari nobles, resplendent in their finest attire, sampled the fare with delight, their laughter and conversation mingling with the gentle strains of music that filled the air.

Filials flitted about, their tiny wings a blur of motion as they attended to the needs of the guests. Some carried goblets of sparkling wine, while others bore trays of glittering jewelry and precious gems, gifts for the newlyweds from the noble houses of the empire.

The decorations were a feast for the senses, with intricate tapestries of rich purple and blue adorning the walls, and cascades of fragrant red and violet flowers tumbling from every balcony and archway. Glowing orbs of light—each one a masterwork of Jianari craftsmanship—floated above the crowd, casting a warm and inviting glow over the proceedings.

As the celebration reached its crescendo, a hush fell over the crowd. All eyes turned to the center of the courtyard, where Max and Favani stood hand in hand, their faces alight with joy and love. The king himself presided over the ceremony, his deep voice resonating through the courtyard as he pronounced the couple husband and wife.

A cheer went up from the assembled guests, and the air was filled with a flurry of flower petals and glittering confetti. The Filials zipped about, their tiny voices raised in song as they showered the newlyweds with blessings and good wishes.

As the party resumed, the courtyard became a whirlwind of activity. Jianari dancers took to the floor, their lithe forms moving in perfect synchronicity to the pulsing beat of the music. Filials flitted among the guests, offering refreshments and small tokens of appreciation, their merry laughter adding to the festive atmosphere.

It was a celebration that the empire made sure would be remembered for generations, a shining moment of joy and unity in a universe fraught with darkness and uncertainty. For one glorious day, the troubles of the world were forgotten, and all that mattered was the love and happiness shared by Max and Favani, and the bonds of friendship and alliance forged among the guests.

So, no big deal, right?

Max found himself fidgeting nervously. He was sitting by himself. Well, technically Favani's brother was sitting next to him, but they didn't exactly have a lot to talk about. The king was in a place of high honor on a dais, enjoying a goblet of wine, the size of a sink. His imperious purple eyes roamed the party and were seemingly satisfied. The few times Max had thrown a glance at him, the king had given him a nod. Most likely a high honor in their society.

Maverick was in a fairly mellow mood. He had been mostly in high spirits, apart from an incident where a member of the court had mistaken him for a table to place a drink on. That person had soon found that drink dripping down their hair.

The heads of houses came to pay respect to Max and brought many gifts with them. Most were Cultivation materials but of such low quality, Max could barely get use out of them. Instead, they were offered as gifts for the next generation in Max's lineage. The first time such a gift was given, Max had coughed up a mouthful of wine.

Other gifts included beautiful jewelry made of metagems, expensive fabrics, and books on statecraft and Cultivation.

Max accepted them gracefully and asked for each one of the gift-givers' names, which seemed to put a smile on everyone's faces. Because of his Cultivation-enhanced mind, Max was able to commit most of them to memory.

After the gift-giving, an elaborate dance began, Cultivators moving together in a blurred sync to impress the audience with their supernatural athleticism. They twisted and turned, each wearing blue, red, and purple robes so that the colors blended together in a fast blur. The crowd started clapping in a rhythm and Max joined in. But he found himself missing Favani by his side.

After the dance number was over, the servants carried in tables with countless exotic foods, fragrant soups in mighty cauldrons, grilled fish the size of an SUV, a steamed bright red tuber that was completely alien to Max, and more.

And especially for Max, they brought something that he had specially requested as the man of the day. He sighed wistfully and could feel his mouth starting to water as he took in the sight and the sweet smell.

Not that Max hadn't eaten well during his stay at court. Even the food that had been served as part of the strike force had been top notch. But this . . . He almost got choked up.

"What's the big deal?" Maverick asked. "It's just a pizza."

"Just a *pizza*?!" Max asked aghast. He shook his head.

Only the force of will his super-mortal Cultivator provided him stayed Max's hand and prevented him from instantly devouring this delicacy on his plate. He had been told to wait. Favani would soon be brought out.

Indeed, the idle chatter and the bustle of the gnomes was stopped by a mighty fanfare.

"Rise!" King Valdemar III boomed from his dais, and Max felt a tug at his will that was not his own, as the king expanded his own will to dominate the crowd. Max could have resisted it and broken the command, but he saw no reason to, and thus he rose.

Favani entered the courtyard riding a giant peacock, with her legs gracefully hanging by the side. She was dressed in the lightest, most vibrant silks of blue, red, and purple. They clung to her body, revealing every contour of her lithe, athletic body. Max found he liked the view. She wore a shawl of blue silk, giving her the air of an Arabian princess. Her eyes were lined with black, lips fiery red, and her luxurious hair had been braided into a snake studded with delicately glowing metagems.

Despite the crowd oohing and aahing around her, she only had eyes for Max as she rode toward him.

Max just stood there stunned, looking at this alien beauty. He was only snapped out of his reverie by Favani's brother, who jabbed him with an elbow and growled. "Go."

Max got up and headed to the middle of the courtyard, where Favani stopped. He extended a hand, Favani took it, and he helped her down. The peacock was taken away by the servants, and Max and Favani stood in the middle of the party, holding each other's hands and looking each other in the eyes.

"You look beautiful," Max said.

"Only the best for you," Favani whispered and blushed purple under her shawl.

Holding hands, they walked slowly toward the king on his dais. King Valdemar looked down upon them with an imperious glare, and Max felt conflict as he ventured to brush the monarch's spirit with his own.

There were many emotions, only as complex as a king thousands of years old could have. Fatherly worry was foremost. Beneath the veneer of pomp and protocol, the king was still a father whose daughter was getting married. There was also contentment with things going according to plan. There was pleasure at Favani's choice of mate, at which Max felt himself swell with pride. He found he wanted to impress this man. Max didn't think of himself much of a lickspittle, and he certainly had had no need to get brownie points from anyone in the ICCB. But he wanted his father-in-law to look upon him fondly.

But as Max probed deeper into the king's spirit, he found a strange fear. No—not exactly a fear, for how a warrior experiences fear is very different from a civilian, this Max knew. But he had no better word for it. Worry for the future. The king looked upon him and wondered whether he should be destroyed, lest he threaten the throne's power. Max didn't like what he found there. The king pushed his probing spirit away, and Max earned a flash from his glaring purple eyes.

Oops.

The king made no further remark; instead, he continued the ceremony.

"We have all gathered here to witness the union of the crown princess, my daughter Favani, and her mate, the warrior Max. I have tried and tested her mate, for the royal lineage cannot accept anything but absolute strength. We are a warrior people, and we respect potential. I am impressed by this human, even though his race is generally considered weak, barely worthwhile to even consider. But even from the most unlikely circumstances, greatness can emerge."

The king paused and let the crowd cheer, clap, and whoop before he continued.

"I commend Favani for her wisdom and Max for his strength. This is a union that I deem worthy of acknowledgement, and thus I will bless it. Let it be known here that these two spirits are now one and will forever be inseparable. Let it be known that from henceforth Max shall be considered as a member of the royal family and be given the same rights and responsibilities as if he were my own son. All hail Crown Prince Max!"

"Hail!" the crowd intoned and cheered.

The king held out a hand to silence the crowd. A pulse of his Intent rang through and made everyone still.

"And with Favani finally choosing a mate, her status will be elevated to that of vice queen and she shall rule over our kingdom in the affairs that the royal family seems fit. You will henceforth address her as Vice Queen Favani. Let it be known that if failure to pay the proper respect to either the crown prince or the vice queen is witnessed, punishment shall be administered. Hail Vice Queen Favani!"

"Hail!" the crowd said.

"And with this, I bless this marriage, and take Max the Warrior into my family. May your union last until the end of times when there is nothing left but darkness and dust."

Max turned to Favani, who, with a trembling hand, removed the silk cloth covering her mouth. She stepped closer, squeezing Max's hand nervously as she gazed at him. Max took her chin gently and pulled her in for a kiss. The crowd cheered.

Once they sat down, Max *attacked* his pizza. It was a straightforward one. Crust made from flour and herbs. Tomato sauce. Cheese with bits of meat and pineapple scattered throughout. Max had made sure to relay to the chefs that they shouldn't skimp on the pineapple.

Yet to Max it tasted like manna falling from the Heavens. Max moaned in pleasure as he took the first bite, everyone at the table turning to look at him in bemusement.

This had, of course, prompted Favani to try a slice herself.

"What is this dish?" she asked and stuffed another slice in her mouth.

"It's a human food," Max had said, trying to pull the plate away from her, but she struck a knife at the plate, shattering it entirely, prompting a disgruntled swarm of servant gnomes to fly over and pick up the pieces.

"I need this whole thing!" Favani declared.

"Just have another one made by the chefs," Max said and swatted away her hand.

"Does a dish like this take long?"

"I don't know if they have any dough left. If they start from scratch, it'll probably take a little while."

"In that case, I demand two more slices," Favani said with a voice as hard as steel. Then she turned to a servant. "And you, tell the chefs to make two more of these . . . *peezas*. Make them your absolute priority. Actually, make enough for everyone here, so all can experience the greatness of my husband's culture!"

After Favani managed to wrangle two more slices out of Max, the king's Intent brushed at their table and suddenly Max's whole plate was in the air. Max reached out to fight for his dish, but the king's Intent attacked him with such ferocity that it sent the whole table flying and shattering into splinters of stone. The royal guard, which was scattered here and there in the crowd, shielded the guests with their Cultivation, producing faint purple bubbles around them to absorb the shrapnel, shards of dishes, and food.

Damn, the king could still squash me like a bug. And seems to be willing to do it for a slice of Hawaiian.

The king was so impressed with the pizza that he sent word to the chefs to make a giant pizza just for him with the utmost priority. Max grumbled to himself. It would take a while until his and Favani's would be ready.

"I can't believe you people get so worked up over some food," Maverick muttered, earning a ferocious glare from both Max and Favani.

The festivities carried on throughout the day and into the night, with more pizza for the whole court and wine so sweet and strong that even a Cultivator needed to watch their step. Servant gnomes waited on the sidelines with glasses of water to help people clear their heads.

Despite being a seemingly serious and ceremonial people, the Jianari really knew how to party. There was dance and drink and even games for the children. Max himself was decreed to be the judge of the tournament, which he of course accepted with a grin. It didn't feel too bad at all to be revered by a court and given high honors. Wine and laughter flowed as the children fought with various techniques. They were all still in the lower stages of Cultivation. Most fights were between Amethyst and Ruby practitioners. That was just enough. The party would have been obliterated and the tone and feel of it would have been much more intense had super-mortal Cultivators gotten involved. This was just the right amount of simple fun.

At some point in the evening, Favani had the genius idea of pouring wine into Maverick's compartments. It was wine infused with Spiritual Energy, so Maverick, greedy for power as he was, didn't refuse. Max wasn't sure what to expect, but Maverick got drunk fast. Soon enough he was flying around carrying children on his back. Once he got bored of that, he went up to various guests and started challenging them to duels. A few fools actually accepted, and it was such a novelty and the court so inebriated that the king decreed they must proceed.

Maverick preened at the attention, as he had been feeling slightly miffed at having been mostly ignored. The flying gun-saucer was so in his cups that he could barely fly straight around Max and Favani as the servants prepared a proper arena in the middle of the. The tables had been pushed back several yards to make enough room for the Diamond-stage Cultivator fights.

"How drunk are you, exactly?" Max asked.

"Not drunk enough!" Maverick declared, earning titters and giggles from the table.

"Are you sure it's going to be alright?" Favani asked Max.

Max felt at Maverick through his bond. His buddy was drunk as a skunk, there was no doubt. But there was still some clarity in there underneath the haze. Max started feeding in his own power to Maverick. It was time to return some favors.

"Yeah," Max said and smiled conspiratorially. "I think he'll be fine."

"Fine?" Maverick said. "Bah. I will not be fine. I will be *excellent*. They will write songs about this fight!"

Max laughed. "Go get 'em."

The fights were short and decisive. Unfortunately, Maverick was really bad at holding back, even when he was sober. He ended the first fight instantly with a shot of yellow and gray energy from his cannon. It wasn't the sort of full-blown blast that would take out an Outsider sorcerer. More of a flick of power, a bolt the size of a baseball. It struck the first contender straight in the chest, and she cried out and toppled over immediately. Maverick hooted gleefully and flew circles around the woman until she was helped out of the ring.

The second fight lasted a little longer, now that the contender had seen Maverick's primary method of attack. This combatant used the flying sword technique that was customary to the royal court and its guards, but Maverick was too fast and could alternate his size, so none of the swords could touch him. He kept laughing as he flew in the air and blasted tiny bolts of pure destruction at his enemy until the sword movements got sluggish and some of them even scattered to the ground to give power to the rest. Maverick grew bored of that and blasted his opponent out of the arena.

"How does he not tire?" Favani asked.

Max gave her a side eye and Favani made a face.

"What are you guys doing? Are you somehow participating?"

Max only grinned and planted a kiss on Favani's cheek. She leaned into it. "Just let my buddy have his fun."

Then he called out a servant to bring him another cup of wine and he enjoyed the show.

CHAPTER FORTY-SIX

Ultimatum

After the wedding, it was finally time to go. They had spent two idle days after their big night, and Max found that he was falling for Favani. Her fierce warrior spirit combined with her femininity made her more than a fitting mate for Max. He was glad she was coming with him.

There were no more gifts to give, no more Cultivation to be had. Max brought up the Framework to see how far he had come. He had a lot of Karma points and was happy to spend them. Power was the way to go, as always.

Maximilian Cromwell
Stage: Diamond (greater)
Dao: Destruction
Karma: 0
Speed: 32
Power: 44
Control: 38

That would be enough, Max thought. It had to be. He had taken out a sorcerer as a lowly early-Diamond-stage Cultivator. Now he was approaching the Celestial realm. The difference between someone who had just broken through to Diamond and one who was at the breakthrough point to Celestial was the difference between a puddle and an ocean.

Max was sitting at a breakfast table, chewing on a porridge made of nuts as he thought. Favani was sitting on the opposite side of the table, smiling at him every time he glanced at her fair blue face.

If it weren't for the resources he obtained from Favani's family, he would have never grown this strong. That was the only reason the ICCB had let this marriage go forth.

Will they release me after I've helped them? I have my doubts.

"Of course they won't," Maverick said and scoffed. "What are you, stupid?"

"What are you two talking about?" Favani asked.

"Max thinks the ICCB will let us go after we've fended off the Outsider attack."

Favani snorted porridge out of her nose and started laughing uncontrollably, pounding her fist on the table. Maverick joined in, hooting. Max realized he was blushing.

"Come on!" Max said exasperatedly. "They made a deal."

"Let you go?" Favani managed to ask before she burst out laughing again.

"Even after all this time, you never stop cracking me up with your nonsense," Maverick said and sighed wistfully as if wiping a tear of laughter from the corner of his eye.

Favani chuckled and contained a final burst of laughter, before turning her violet eyes on Max. She grabbed his hand and squeezed it compassionately.

"I'm not coming only because I want to protect and help you," Favani said. "I'm coming because of my status."

"What do you mean?" Max said.

Maverick groaned. "It's a good thing we pumped up the Intelligence Stat when we had the previous Framework. Imagine how dumb you'd be without it."

"Just tell me," Max said and flicked a wave of gravity at Maverick, making him flutter in the air. He ran himself into Max's forehead.

"She's a liaison, you dolt," Maverick said.

Max turned to Favani, who nodded.

"We needed to get married before we left," Favani explained. "You are now my mate and even if they capture only you, that is enough to start a war that the ICCB cannot afford."

"You would go to war for me?" Max asked and swallowed.

"Hell yeah, I would," Favani said. "And so would my father. He has not been as impressed with a young Cultivator in probably . . . well, *ever.*"

Sometimes it was hard to fathom that his father-in-law was thousands of years old, nor that his own wife was a couple of hundred years old as well. Favani had insisted that after a while the age gap would stop mattering. Max had his doubts, but that hardly mattered.

"Will they attempt anything if you're with me and they know we're married?" Max asked between spoonfuls of porridge.

"It is very likely," Favani said.

Max nodded grimly. "We'll cross that bridge when we come to it."

Favani nodded.

"I'm glad you're coming with me," Max said.

She smiled. "I would not have it any other way, Husband."

After they had eaten and received the travel packs kept in storage rings, they said their goodbyes to the court and the king. Then it was time for Max to contact the ICCB. He did it right there in the middle of the throne room. Not only was it Jianari custom to do their business in front of the nobles of the court, but it was also a strategic decision needed for the negotiations.

The jellyfish appeared immediately.

[Maximillian, we take it that you are ready to assist?]

"Yes," Max said. "I will need you to teleport me and my wife Favani to join the strike force."

The jellyfish was silent for a while.

[We see. A wife. Married to the royal family. We unfortunately do not have the capacity to provide a teleport.]

"You will provide it," Max said. "As well as teleportation for both of us back here after I have helped you."

[We see now that you have another hand that feeds you, you choose to bite ours. Teleportation is expensive. With that in mind, we believe it time to reconsider the negotiations. We will be blunt with you, Maximilian. Of the entirety of this iteration of the Cosmic Games, you were the single interesting specimen. Yes, there are some decently powerful warriors on the planet, mostly on the strike force, but we do not care about the planet nor its current inhabitants.]

"It's a bluff," Favani whispered in Max's ear. The Zoos Collective probably heard it, but that was neither here nor there. Perhaps Favani meant it to be heard. "Every planet is valuable. Terraforming and creating an atmosphere on a barren planet is far more expensive than a few teleports."

[We are willing to expend some resources to slow down the assault and create a cost-effective defense that will make further attacks from the Outsiders more expensive. However, if need be, we are willing to let Alpha Ludus be overtaken. There are 2,321,011 humans on the planet, for your information. The remainder of your species.]

"Oh," Max said silently.

So that was their game. They couldn't force Max or Favani to stay and comply. They couldn't use violence, lest they start a war they didn't desire. But they could play this card.

"What do you want?" Max asked.

[Indenture. **We are willing to accept the breach of our previous contract and respect your wishes to join the royal family of the Jianari Empire. However, since the previous contract was broken and, seeing as we have resources to save your species, we believe a new contract should be made.**]

"He will NOT become one of your slaves," Favani growled.

The Zoos jellyfish was quiet for a moment.

[**We see. Perhaps a more lenient contract is in order, then. A mercenary contract. You will be fairly compensated for your services, and the terms will be more agreeable than a standard indentured-servitude contract.**]

Max narrowed his eyes at the floating jellyfish avatar. "I'm listening."

[**You will be required to assist the ICCB in matters of galactic security and conflict resolution. In return, you will receive access to advanced Cultivation resources and techniques, as well as a generous stipend. The contract will be for a set term, rather than an indefinite period of servitude.**]

Favani stepped forward, her voice firm. "And what of Max's autonomy? You're saying he'll be a contracted mercenary, but I know how your agreements go."

[**His freedom will be within reason. His primary obligation will be to the ICCB, but we understand the importance of personal growth and development. Allowances can be made for independent Cultivation and exploration, provided it does not interfere with his duties.**]

Max considered the offer. It was a far cry from the virtual enslavement the ICCB had initially proposed, but still, the idea of being beholden to the ICCB and Zoos Collective left a bitter taste in his mouth.

I don't owe them a goddamn thing.

"What about my relationship with Favani and the Jianari Empire?" Max asked, his hand finding his wife's and intertwining their fingers. "I'm allied with them. That was all well and good, since we didn't have a contract."

[Your marriage to Princess Favani will be recognized and respected. In fact, we see it as an opportunity for greater cooperation between the ICCB and the Jianari Empire. A symbol of unity in the face of the Outsider threat.]

Max was fairly certain there was a trap hidden somewhere in there.

Favani's eyes narrowed. "Pretty words, but what guarantee do we have that you won't try to undermine our union or use Max to gain leverage over my people?"

The Zoos jellyfish was still for a moment before they answered:

[We are prepared to sign a non-interference agreement. A legally binding contract that prohibits the ICCB from meddling in your relationship or using Max's position to influence Jianari politics. In return, we ask that the Jianari Empire refrain from obstructing Max's duties to the ICCB.]

Max and Favani exchanged a long look, a silent conversation passing between them. They both knew that the Zoos Collective was not to be trusted, but the offer on the table was far more palatable than the alternative.

"I'll be working as a liaison?" Max asked. "An in-between for two superpowers?"

[That is the essence of it.]

"We'll need time to review the specifics of the contract," Max said at last, his voice measured. "And we reserve the right to negotiate the specific terms before signing anything."

The plastic jellyfish bobbed in the air in a way that seemed to indicate that the collective was pleased. But there was no way the Zoos would reveal to him anything they didn't want him to see.

[We will draft the necessary documents and send them to you for review. However, none of this matters if the battle on Alpha Ludus is not successful. The Outsiders arrive within days. Are you ready?]

Max nodded curtly. "Give us a few hours."

[Call upon us when you are ready to depart. We will teleport you back to the strike-force headquarters immediately. Goodbye and good luck.]

With that, the holographic jellyfish flickered and vanished, leaving Max and Favani alone in the room. Favani let out a long breath, her shoulders slumping slightly.

"Do you think we can trust them?" Max asked.

Favani shook her head. "No. But they're right. You have to survive the fight. I mean, that should be fine, though . . . With as strong as you've become . . ."

Favani leaned into Max's side, drawing strength from his presence. "You're a terrible negotiator."

"That's why I have you, right?" Max asked.

Favani chuckled at that but said nothing more. She leaned into Max, smelling like lavender. Max found he liked her there.

They stood there for a long moment, drawing comfort from each other's warmth and solidity. Then Max stirred, as his nature was not to stand idly by.

"Come on," Max said at last, pressing a soft kiss to Favani's forehead. "Let's get ready and deal with this. The sooner we are done with Alpha Ludus and the ICCB, the better for everyone."

CHAPTER FORTY-SEVEN

Back with the Strike Force

Max, Maverick, and Favani were teleported directly into the strike force's training facility. Favani looked around, clearly displeased, but Max was happy to be back. Especially for Losshnak and Kat.

The whole strike force was meditating near the Cultivation array. Twozerofive was floating above and turned to them. His eyes went wide.

Max chuckled.

"What is it?" Favani said.

"He probably didn't expect to see the first princess of the Jianari Empire here," Max said.

Favani raised a quizzical eyebrow. "It is almost certain he knew."

"Then why is he shocked?"

Favani laughed. Maverick joined in.

"See?" Maverick said.

"I see it," Favani said between chuckles.

"See what?" Max asked with mounting indignation.

"Idiot savant," Maverick said smugly and Favani burst out into full laughter.

"What are you two talking about?" Max asked.

"Inspect his spirit," Favani said, suppressing a smile.

Max did, extending his Spiritual Sense to brush against Twozerofive's dantian. It was a shallow puddle. Max could absolutely crush him if he wanted to.

"How is he so weak?" Max asked aghast.

"He is stronger than me . . ." Favani said, suddenly not laughing.

"I didn't mean it like that."

Favani only cast a sulking glare at Max and said nothing.

The three of them went up to the strike force, and Max greeted Twozerofive. The Gray was not sure how to respond at first but eventually, he made a stiff bow in the air.

"This one greets his superiors."

"Well, well," Maverick said gleefully. "Could you say that again? I didn't quite hear it."

"Cut it out," Max said and shook his head. "Good to see you again, Twozerofive."

There was a moment of silence before the Gray answered, "Yes."

"How is the strike force coming along?"

Twozerofive's eyes flared up, almost as if in anger. "This one asks to speak directly."

"I like this!" Maverick said.

"Speak normally," Max said and nodded encouragingly at the Gray.

The small alien nodded and sighed, gathering strength for what was clearly an impending tirade.

"They are lazy, weak, and ungrateful. They cannot withstand even twelve hours of work per day, completely disregarding my instructions. My regimen is in shambles, my vision ruined. I was going to turn all of them into Diamond-stage Cultivators. But despite all of my instructions, all of the reading, all of the resources, half of them cannot even break through into the Greater-Ruby stage. Only the human, the female Vikirr, and the two Ishkarassi are on the lower end of Diamond stage."

"Nothing short of impressive to guide three individuals to Diamond stage so fast," Favani said diplomatically.

Twozerofive bowed stiffly again. "This one is humbled by the praise. But the truth of the matter is that these individuals just happen to be talented, like your husband."

Max still flinched at the word. But he snapped out of it and gave the Gray an easy smile. "Good work, Twozerofive."

Another bow. "Can this one be of any assistance to the three of you?"

"No," Max said. "Finish your training regime. We will help prepare supplies and a battle plan."

"A counterassault plan has been already issued. This one will not dare to question the machinations of greater minds, but he must remind you that my superiors also possess great minds with great plans."

"What a beautifully backhanded way of saying 'screw you,'" Maverick said and laughed. "I should strike you down for this impudence, worm."

Twozerofive immediately went into a full bow, his forehead touching his feet. "This one apologizes."

Max looked at him and wondered.

Fear. That is fear.

Twozerofive genuinely believed that Maverick would punish and even potentially destroy him for his slight. Max decided that he did not like the way the

ICCB handled things. He had chosen his side well. But in the end, there were only two sides to this war: the Outsiders, and those who wanted to live.

"Your plans did not involve me ascending as high as I did, nor did they consider Favani's strength," Max said. "Those plans are useless. We will make new ones. Make sure your superiors know."

"This one understands," Twozerofive said, still bowing. "They shall be informed."

"Good," Max said. "We'll be in the kitchen."

Max was fiddling with the chef robot's display panel. The AI was well equipped with a formidable amount of recipes from Earth but no burgers. After the great success of pizza at his wedding, Max felt it was his marital obligation to civilize Favani with a double bacon cheeseburger, but his prospects looked slim at the current moment.

"Perhaps I can verbally instruct it. Is there a command or a prompt or something . . . I'm so stupid with these things."

"I think you're stupid with most things, truth be told," Maverick said.

Max only grumbled.

"It's not a bad thing," Maverick continued. "In fact, I think it's one of your greatest strengths. Intellect is overrated."

"What are you doing?" Max said as he tapped the robot's touchscreen. It cracked at the force of his finger tap.

"Mostly educating Favani, I suppose,"

"I feel like I have a good idea of my husband's strengths and weaknesses," Favani said coldly.

"Oh yes," Maverick said sarcastically. "With your Dao of People Skills, I'm sure you've learned all that is essential in the two weeks you two have known each other."

"Dao of People Skills?" Max said and chuckled. "That's rich coming from you."

"You're both idiots," Favani said and buried her head in her hands.

CHAPTER FORTY-EIGHT

Catching Up

Max finally got the AI to produce burgers, and the robot attached to it started churning them out en masse—most of them double bacon cheeseburgers, like God intended, but there were some other variations. All five species involved had the ability to consume meat, but Max wasn't sure how insectoids would handle cheese. Cheeseless burgers were of course a crime against humanity, but in times of duress and war, concessions had to be made.

The burgers were a hit. The strike force came to the kitchen area absolutely drenched in their own sweat. It was lunchtime, and Max knew the strike force slept four hours every day, which was massive amounts of rest for a Diamond-stage Cultivator and more than enough even for the higher echelons of Greater Ruby.

Only Losshnak wasn't completely spent, even if he was tired, and he attacked the burgers with the gusto appropriate for a seasoned warrior.

"You return to us, Master Warrior," Losshnak said. "And I see you have found a mate."

"How do you know she's not just a friend?" Max said.

"We can smell it, you fool human," Ashkarassa said. Losshnak punched her in the shoulder, but it was light, almost playful in Ishkarassi terms.

"Quiet, you fool," Losshnak said. "Can you not see how powerful these three are?"

"You know I struggle with that technique," Ashkarassa said and snarled.

"Max is stronger than Twozerofive," Kat said quietly.

"As am I," Maverick said. "Isn't that amazing?"

"We would love to hear the tale of your exploits," Slargi said, his mouth and mandibles clicking as he spoke.

"Yes, tell us, so that we might learn to get stronger," the male vulpine said. The female cast an annoyed glance at him but said nothing. Instead, she turned to Max, ready to listen.

Max told them the story from the beginning, starting from the moment he decided that, in order to develop, even the strike force would not be enough. Everyone looked blankly at him and each other when he said this. Favani chuckled and Maverick had a hard time holding his tongue.

"See what I mean, Favani? He doesn't think about it at all. He just *knew* that the strike force wouldn't be enough. He can't understand why he makes these decisions. It's just instinct. Good luck to you dolts thinking Max can actually teach you anything useful."

Max cast an angry glance at his buddy, but he couldn't help but start to think that maybe Maverick had a point.

He carried on with the story, stopping to describe how he fought the sorcerers, in as much detail as possible about what they were like and how they were likely to act. Mostly he did it to make sure the strike force was as informed on the capabilities of the sorcerers as possible but some part of him also wanted to prove Maverick wrong. He could explain stuff! Sometimes.

The audience was rapt, as their lives and future depended on their performance against the sorcerers.

"A whole kingdom?" Plarag, the female insectoid, said in awe, her mouth clicking excitedly. "You are a princess, then, Favani? It is most humbling to meet you."

"Thank you," Favani said and graced the insectoid with a diplomatic smile.

"How powerful is this king you spoke of?" Losshnak asked.

Max nudged Favani who, at the time, had become completely enraptured by a double bacon cheeseburger.

She was startled from her reverie and answered the insectoid. "My father is a Celestial-stage Cultivator. He is the most powerful being in the universe."

"Is your kingdom part of the ICCB?" Rakii asked.

"No," Favani said curtly. "We recognize the coalition as an ally, but we consider their actions with the Cosmic Games a war crime."

"War crime?" Losshnak asked. "What does this mean? Perhaps my translator is misfiring."

"I think it means when you are very bad at warfare, constantly failing," Ashkarassa said.

It took a while to explain to Losshnak and Ashkarassa that some actions within war are unacceptable and considered inhumane. They laughed at the preposterous notion at first, but after having it further explained to them, they let Favani continue.

"My people will not align themselves with the ICCB as long as the Cosmic Games are in play and they so wantonly squeeze civilizations for a few strong individuals, causing the rest to go extinct or to be left fighting for scraps on their battle-arena planets."

"It has made us strong," Losshnak said. "That is good. I hold no grudge."

"Millions gave their lives in the gauntlet of the ICCB's sick games so that you could advance."

"How powerful are you?" Kerro asked.

"I am almost as strong as your instructor," Favani said. "But that is only a drop in the bucket compared to my father. I have only maybe a tenth of his might. Max here might have about half. Or perhaps a smidge more."

The strike force choked on their burgers.

"I knew you were mighty, but . . ." Ashkarassa said.

"How large is the gap between Diamond stage and Celestial?" Slargi asked and clicked his mandibles.

"Do you want an answer from me or Max?" Favani asked and smiled.

"Both," Slargi and Plarag said in unison.

Everyone at the table laughed and most of them returned to their burgers. Max considered the answer for a while.

"Oh, don't tell me you're actually going to attempt to answer," Maverick said and sighed theatrically. "When are you all going to learn that you should not listen to Max in anything related to Cultivation?"

Max groaned. "Go ahead, then."

Maverick flew over the table to bask in the attention. He started lecturing in a pompous voice. "It is hard to say because we are so insanely talented. We've fought numerous battles, mostly with sorcerers, but also with Favani's father, who is insanely powerful. He could have crushed us. The truth of the matter is that you are all very talented. I see three of you are already Diamond stage. Losshnak is half as powerful as Favani. Kat is maybe a fourth as powerful. Additionally, since Max and my power is split through [**Divine Soulbond**], it's difficult to assess just how strong we are. Although I do have an inkling how strong we could be together . . ."

Max looked at Maverick. There was something strange in the way his buddy had said that. Max probed through their bond, but Maverick refused to elaborate.

The strike force listened, but all of them were clearly confused. Favani cleared her throat.

"That was the worst explanation I have ever heard."

"I never tried to explain anything," Maverick said. "I just wanted people to know how awesome we are."

Max sighed and leaned on Favani's shoulder. She patted his head consolingly.

"It's difficult to explain to someone who has never known the power of a Celestial-stage Cultivator," Favani said, mulling over her words. "But I have seen over two hundred summers and two hundred winters. I reached super-mortal Cultivation when I had seen eighty winters and eighty summers."

"It takes that long?" Kat asked. "Why? You had all the resources, being a princess and all."

"Don't be rude," Max said.

"Well," Favani said, her tone darkened, "the Cosmic Games of the ICCB are a great breeding ground for warriors. I have nothing but praise for their efficiency, as inhumane as it is. The ICCB uses the Framework to artificially bolster people up to the Ruby stage fast. Without such training, it takes decades to reach."

"This one apologizes if it is a rude question, but why is it that you are not using the Framework in such a manner, if it is superior in efficiency?" Plarag asked.

"Fair question!" Maverick exclaimed. "Something I've wondered myself."

Favani cast a glance at Maverick and considered her answer. "My father, his father, and his father before him all disregarded the Framework. There are two very good reasons, and why normal Cultivation takes much longer. The first reason is that the Framework is a shortcut. Not using it forces a Cultivator to work on their meridians and dantian from the ground up, starting all the way from Quartz stage. It is a very different process, but it allows for more control and endurance, at the expense of raw power. You might be Diamond Cultivators, but your work is flimsy at best, and you could never challenge a sorcerer as you are."

The strike force members looked embarrassed. Only Rakii, Ashkarassa, and Losshnak kept their heads held high.

"The Diamond stage my mate and this human female are at is . . . fake?" Ashkarassa asked, her face scrunched up in anger and confusion, her lizard tongue flicking up a nostril so fast the eye could barely track it.

Favani imperiously crossed her arms as she answered. "Power is power, but mine is genuine. Yours is paid with blood."

"Wait, what?" Kat asked.

"Who cares how the power was acquired?" Rakii said and snarled, showing sharp white canines. "Power alone is not enough, anyway. It is the way we fight when we face our enemies that matters."

"Ah," Favani said softly, almost mournfully. She gave Max a side glance. He did not understand. "Who cares, indeed? We do. My people refuse to become like the enemies we fight. We must stand above them, lest we find ourselves contending with monsters of our own creation worse than the ones we are now fighting. And there's a second reason we don't use the Framework to Cultivate."

"What is it?" Max asked.

"I never told you," Favani said. She sounded embarrassed. "I didn't want to cause you any undue pain. Note that you are still talented beyond belief, a genius Cultivator the likes of which comes only once in ten thousand years."

"What are you talking about?" Max said, suddenly not liking where the conversation was going. "Do you know what this is about, Maverick?"

Maverick said nothing. Max probed at him through their bond. He didn't know, which was a relief. But suddenly Maverick became very serious.

"The Framework is a wonderful weapon," Favani said. "In the early stages of Cultivation, it will let you experience growth that is impossible without it. But there is nothing that comes from nothing."

"So, the energy comes from somewhere?" Ashkarassa asked. "Is it some sort of superstructure left behind by an old civilization? This is what our patrons, the Grays, told us."

"They didn't say more than they wanted you to know," Favani said grimly.

"Just cut to the chase," Kat said. Her voice had a sharp edge. She was clearly bracing herself; just like Maverick, Max was getting a bad feeling.

"Spiritual Energy is innate in all beings that achieve sapience," Favani said. "If you reach a certain point in consciousness, you are able to Cultivate. This means you have Spiritual Power. When I sit down and Cultivate the Spiritual Power of the universe without the Framework, it takes time to collect tiny motes of energy from the ether. That is why my people invented metagems."

"Excuse this one's ignorance, but what are metagems?" Slargi asked.

Maverick gave the table a very brief explanation of the way that the Jianari Cultivated, and Favani nodded in approval and continued, "But the ICCB uses a different method. They feed Spiritual Energy directly into the Framework. When you sat down and got your fancy little Level-Up notifications from the Framework, it was because the ICCB was artificially pumping you with Spiritual Energy. Care to wager where this energy was acquired from?"

The strike force was silent for a moment. Finally, Kat spoke: "From the people killed in the Games."

Favani didn't say anything. She didn't have to.

CHAPTER FORTY-NINE

Rallying the Troops

H alt!" Twozerofive said as he appeared above the table, placing everyone under stasis, including Max, Maverick, and Favani.

Max found himself completely frozen, but he quickly dissipated the stasis by hitting it with his destructive Intent. Favani and Maverick broke out of theirs soon after.

"You dare attack a delegate?" Favani asked furiously.

"The information you have shared is classified," Twozerofive said. "On behalf of ICCB, I must implore you to conduct appropriate diplomacy."

"They deserve to know how they got their power!" Favani said.

"It is not your business to determine what the assets of ICCB do and do not deserve to know," Twozerofive said coldly.

"Is this true?" Max asked.

Favani nodded. Maverick was quiet but attentive. Through their bond, Max could sense a weight bearing down on his buddy. Twozerofive looked at Max with black eyes devoid of pity.

"Is this true?!" Max asked, taking to flight, sending tables and chairs flying.

"You owe the ICCB," Twozerofive said. "We invested a great deal of energy in you."

"You injected me with the power extracted from the dead?!" Max asked.

Twozerofive didn't answer. He only fixed Max with a cold glare. "You will fight the Outsiders, as you promised."

Max gathered up his destructive Intent until it was a sharp, deadly spear in his hands.

Twozerofive only looked at him impassively. "If you kill me, no one wins."

Max roared. He aimed his spear at a wall, and it exploded against it in his rage. The whole massive training facility roof came crashing down in great chunks of metal and stone. The four of them ignored the debris as it fell.

"I am but a functionary doing my job," Twozerofive said. "Take it up with your precious Zoos Collective if you are so enraged. If you ask me, you are but a petulant child. Have you not enjoyed the strength we have given you? Is it not necessary to deal with the threat facing us?"

When the building was done crashing around them, Twozerofive released the stasis on the rest of the strike force. Then he rose a few feet higher and addressed them.

"The weak perished to bolster the strong. Their lives were not meaningless, unless you make it so by squandering their sacrifice. You all show great promise, and that is why you were chosen. What is a few billion lives if they are used to protect a zillion souls?"

"Monsters," Favani hissed.

Losshnak shook his head in slow solemnity. "We understand. Their lives will not be spent in vain."

Ashkarassa nodded. The rest of the strike force was stunned into silence. Kat and Rakii were bristling at the Gray.

"Calm yourselves and make peace," Twozerofive said. "Or do not. I believe I have done all I can with you. I will now leave and return soon to teleport you to the battlefield when the Outsiders arrive. Until then, you will report to Maximillian Cromwell." Then the Gray turned to Max. "Any questions?"

"None," Max grunted. Twozerofive nodded and blinked away.

The strike force was left to stand there in the ruins, filled with anger and confusion. Favani looked sad. Max and Maverick were quiet, huddling together on a piece of rock debris. Only Losshnak and Ashkarassa seemed to be unaffected.

They are the true warriors here.

Maverick gave Max a hard—practically violent—nudge through their bond.

"Idiot," the disc muttered next to him.

"Asshole," Max said. "What was that for?"

"We're way more awesome than anyone else here," Maverick said. "Nothing wrong with feeling like shit after what we just heard. Accept it and move on."

"I suppose that's how we do it," Max said. Then he turned to Favani. "Thanks for telling me."

"Should have done it sooner," Maverick said.

"I apologize," Favani said. "However, Maverick is right. Even worse, he is right on both accounts."

"When are you pitiful creatures going to learn that is always the case?"

"I should have told you sooner," Favani said. "But you also need to accept this and move on. You have a strike force to lead and an enemy to defeat."

"Right," Max said and stood up. The strike force was still stewing in their thoughts, but all of their heads turned when Max rose.

Before he said anything, however, he looked within. All of this power . . . It was built on the corpses of billions of humans—extracted from them and recycled into him. Max shuddered. It was disgusting, reprehensible beyond comprehension. Bile rose in his throat, but he swallowed it. If he had to deal with this later, he would. But one thing was for certain. He owed not a single thing to the ICCB. He did owe humanity a damn good fight, however. And once he was done, he would rebuild. The two million souls that were left on Alpha Ludus would be protected and nurtured; they would build the human race back up again.

This time we'll do it right. With less nukes and more meditation.

That was a thought for another time. But it gave Max solace. He couldn't change the past. He was the product of billions of dead people. Like Losshnak said, he had to honor them and make sure they had not died in vain.

Max nodded and gathered his resolve.

"Listen up," Max said, bolstering his voice with Cultivation. "I know you must be feeling pain. Sadness. Remorse. Disgust. I'm feeling all of those myself. But we have to live with that for now. Take a note from the Ishkarassi. They don't disregard the dead. They revere them."

"That is right, Master Warrior," Ashkarassa said.

Max turned to look at the female Ishkarassi. This was the first time she had acknowledged him. Losshnak whispered something in her ear, and she grinned.

"It is our duty to make sure we use every ounce of this power that was taken from the fallen," Losshnak said. "Make sure it counts."

"Yes," Max said. "We need to make sure *we* count. There are only nine of us and—"

"Ahem," Maverick said.

"There are only *ten* of us, and there will be thousands, perhaps even millions of Outsiders attacking us. Let us take inventory. Our melee fighters are Kat and Kerro, correct? Losshnak and Ashkarassa are hybrids. The rest of you are strictly ranged fighters."

There were nods and murmurs of assent.

"The most optimal course of action is for all of you to stay on Maverick, behind Losshnak's barrier."

"I'm to be reduced to a *bus?*"

"It will be a good plan," Losshnak said. "But what happens when chaos ensues?"

"If you are faced with a sorcerer or overwhelming numbers, you gather up and play defense," Max said. "Escape to a defensible spot if you can. I don't know how busy I'll be, but if you're in a pickle, I'll help you out if I can."

"I'm super strong. I can keep them safe as long as they don't do anything stupid," Maverick said. "But they probably will."

"We probably will," Kat said and smirked. "But what will us melee fighters do?"

"I think I can give you [Telekinesis]," Max said and rubbed his chin. "I'm not a hundred percent sure on it yet, but we'll test that after we are done talking."

"So, we will be able to fly?" Kat said, hiding her excitement poorly. She looked at Kerro and they both grinned at each other.

"Yeah," Max said. "The idea is that you two will be able to swat away any ranged threats putting stress on Losshnak's defensive barrier."

"We will be completely airborne?" Ashkarassa asked.

"Of course," Maverick said. "What kind of idiot would land among millions of Outsiders? As long as I fly high enough, none of the nasties on the ground will be able to do anything about it."

"Exactly," Max said. "But if you are forced to the ground by a sorcerer attack or something unexpected, stick together, find a defensible area, and wait for the cavalry to arrive."

"That mean the Big Guy or the Blue Chick?"

"Terrible codenames," Kat said.

"Yeah, we'll work on those," Max said distractedly. "Anything else?"

"Why are we only getting to act as backup or support?" Rakii asked and looked at Max fiercely. "I want to fight the sorcerers. Why is it that you get all of the glory?"

"You're all too weak," Maverick said simply. Rakii snarled at him, baring her teeth.

Favani turned to the vulpine woman. "We cannot have you fighting the sorcerers. They can wipe any one of you out in seconds."

Rakii looked frustrated and cast a nasty glance at Favani, but she said nothing.

"We know this, Warrior Princess," Losshnak said. "We have fought the enemy in simulations and none of us can match them."

"That's fine," Max said. "There will be lots more than sorcerers there to fight. Let Favani, Maverick, and me worry about them."

"We'll need to adjust our tactics, now that you three are here," Kat said.

Max nodded. "That's true. Now that all of you have eaten, let's get down to business. We'll go through the tactics we have discussed here and practice them in simulation before we go."

"Not only have you become a magnificent warrior," Losshnak said. "But a fine leader too."

CHAPTER FIFTY

Tactics and Preparation

After Max was done talking, they went up to the simulator. It took some time for them to figure out how to operate it without Twozerofive, but they eventually got it to work. All of them, other than Favani, entered.

They spent hours going over the battle tactics. Mostly it was Max observing the rest of the group riding Maverick through the air and dealing with threats. Together they could even fend off sorcerers, as their suits brought most of them up to the level of a super-mortal Cultivator. With Losshnak being fairly strong in his own right, his barrier could hold a couple of direct attacks from the sorcerers as well.

They worked until the end of the evening, when they sat together in meditation, led by Favani. All of them strengthened their meridians and made sure they were in peak condition for the upcoming fight. The Outsiders would soon enter the atmosphere and then the ICCB would know where they were about to strike.

The next day was just like the last one. But this time it was Favani who spent most of the time inside the portal simulation. Her fighting style was best suited for solo heroics, so it was good for her to grow accustomed to how the strike force moved and fought in combat, in case she needed to cooperate with them at some point during an actual battle.

Max watched them through the video feed and felt proud. The strike force was handling themselves well. As a group, they were even able to fend off two sorcerers attacking them directly for a decent while, before the ferocity of the attacks eventually forced them to scatter on the ground.

This was good, as it gave Max feedback on his tactics; he could see how the strike force would act when forced to the ground in various situations. When they managed to keep together and under Losshnak's barrier, they fared well. When they didn't . . . Well, truth be told, none of them expected for all of them to survive the assault.

That wasn't mentioned, however, and they kept up their high spirits. But as they ate, rested, and jested afterward, Max could feel it. They all could. The fight would be *bad*. And the brunt of the responsibility for success or failure lay on Max and Maverick.

Just like it always is, isn't it?

But Max realized that he wasn't feeling bitter about it. It was just the way of things. For some reason the universe or whatever had placed him into this situation. And as dire as it was, he would give it his best. He didn't want anyone else to die in vain on his watch.

And finally, the day came when Twozerofive returned. His tone was clipped but polite, and Max wondered what kinds of discussions had happened behind the closed doors of the ICCB elite regarding them. He knew that with his level of strength, he was most likely being observed by them every moment of his waking life.

It feels so weird being special.

His relationship with the ICCB had become complicated to say the least. But, on some level, he understood the actions of the ancient organization. As callous and horrible as they might seem, the threat of the Outsiders was so dire that it required extreme action.

If Max worked hard enough, improved himself relentlessly, maybe he could reach Celestial Stage. And if he did, it might be enough to tilt the scales to the point where they could drive the Outsiders back to their own damned reality. Max would give them no quarter.

Soon afterward they all assembled around Twozerofive, who gave them a boring speech about how this was an opportunity to serve the universe and all of them would receive great resources and shortened indentures if they survived and triumphed. Max barely listened. He wanted to just gather up their gear and go.

Shortly afterward, they were all suited up in the best attire that the ICCB had to offer. Even Favani relented at Max's insistence and donned the battle-uniform of the ICCB, as it gave a force multiplier on anyone's Cultivation. It was a nifty piece of technology, and they needed every advantage they could get.

They also gathered Spirit bombs, shield devices, and other gadgets. Max paid little heed to them, but the rest of the strike force was enthused, and Max agreed that they should take every advantage they could. Max was going to fight the sorcerers en masse, and little gadgets would do him little good when they dashed at him full-speed with their horrible white tentacles whipping.

The strike force also had four days of rations gathered up. Max doubted they would need any of it.

One way or another, this will be over fast.

CHAPTER FIFTY-ONE

The Noose Tightens

After thousands of years of planning, the Zoos Collective had everything it wanted. They had amassed a ridiculous amount of wealth and developed technology that rivaled the most powerful Cultivators.

Cultivators could do amazing things. They could alter reality itself. But technology was needed as well—teleportation, weapons of mass destruction, and Spiritual technology, which allowed the members of the ICCB to cast a myriad of spells that were beyond their Cultivation.

The Zoos Collective as a whole could be considered a Celestial-stage Cultivator. The details got complicated because they were a collective entity with millions of individual Cultivators. On average, the individuals would most likely be at high-Ruby tier. But together, they had enough Spiritual Energy to be a relatively high-tier Celestial Cultivator, perhaps even the strongest in existence.

Meanwhile, all member species of the ICCB had one Celestial Cultivator. It was a prerequisite to join the table. But such creatures were rare indeed. The king of the Jianari Empire was one, of course. He was an especially high-tier one, perhaps the strongest single individual in the universe. It was good that he participated in the war effort, but he could not be controlled.

And now there was a new player. The Zoos Collective had run a large number of simulations and used a vast amount of resources on predicting future outcomes. The end result was clear: Maximilian Cromwell would ascend to become a Celestial-stage Cultivator.

[What course of action does the ICCB want to take regarding this new power?]

The Swarm buzzed loudly, and their head spokesman responded in a metallic screeching voice: "You have attempted to lock this individual down with a contract, have you not?"

[Of course we have. We already have a preliminary contract with him that has a fast-accruing debt. But if Max Cromwell ascends to Celestial, he will have no reason to comply. Especially so if he is allied with the Jianari Empire.]

"Not only allied," the leader of the Grays spoke in a quiet, dangerous voice. Everyone in the room could sense his Intent brewing like a building volcano. This one was called Zerozerothree, and he was the first and only Gray to have reached Celestial-stage Cultivation through the Dao of Wrath. "But he is now married to the royal bloodline. Why the Zoos Collective has been so devastatingly lackadaisical about this matter is beyond my comprehension."

"Is it even a certainty that the human boy will become so powerful?" the leader of the frogs asked. The rest of their envoy chittered fast in their green gel. They were not happy. None of the members of ICCB were happy with how the Zoos Collective had handled this. It was understandable. The Collective had just recently taken charge, and Max, who had been their personal asset, was now untouchable. It was a failure, but something that could be remedied.

"Have you fool frogs no eyes in your heads?" Azzzhtik'Likzirrruk said and buzzed about, violently. "The human Cultivator is extraordinary. It is not unheard of for someone with the right background and resources to ascend to Diamond relatively fast . . . But Diamond stage is a long journey which takes centuries to understand and master. This human, barely an adult by their species' standards, has surpassed any expectation one could place upon raw talent. This human has shattered our worldview of how the Framework and Cultivation work. This is no minor thing. This is a matter of such great importance that we might have to start a war against King Valdemar III and his people."

"Do not speak so lightly of war," Zerozerothree hissed. "We do not have the resources, especially if the asset is close to the Celestial stage."

[There is other news to consider. While we thought the attack on Alpha Ludus was odd to begin with, our researchers have noticed something even stranger in the Outsiders' carrier-type vessels. It seems like they are transporting something massive. Something they haven't transported before— much less in an initial scouting assault.]

Azzzhtik'Likzirrruk of the Swarm replied immediately, "Is this related to the asset?"

The Zoos Collective was silent for a while, as they negotiated and voted amongst themselves as to how much was appropriate to divulge. But the fact was that this situation was beyond them. The Zoos Collective would need the full input of the ICCB for this.

[**Most likely. The portal through which the Outsiders prepared their assault appeared the moment Maximillian Cromwell attained Diamond stage. We know that both manufactured and simulated Outsiders are an information security risk. How they're able to spy through Outsider copies that we ourselves have manufactured is still being researched. However, one thing is for certain. They knew. They knew as soon as Maximillian Cromwell started fighting them that he was a threat that required an immediate answer. They knew where he was, as well, which is how Alpha Ludus was discovered.**]

"That is troublesome," the frog leader croaked thoughtfully. "But you must be more forthright. What are the carrier-class Outsiders transporting?"

"A portal," Zerozerothree said bluntly. The whole ICCB council was silent. The Grays smiled ominously. "It is not only the Zoos Collective that can see and hear."

This was a clear attack on the Zoos Collective's leadership. It was done at an opportune time, as they were currently at their weakest position as leaders in their history. And now the Grays had proven that they indeed could crack into the Zoos' well-encrypted data stores. Additionally, they knew the Zoos had no resources to investigate the matter and plug any leaking holes. It was a perfect move from the Grays, something that they must have planned for a while now. They calculated that there was over an 80 percent chance that the Grays had predicted the Zoos Collective taking over the leadership of the ICCB and had orchestrated a multistage plan to undermine their authority in order to strengthen the Grays' position in the organization. It was all much craftier and more cunning than the Zoos Collective had anticipated from them.

[**We believe it is a portal formation. It is difficult to be certain in these matters, as the technology that the Outsiders use is completely alien to us and does not work on the ruleset through which we understand the physical universe. But for them to have brought anything giving off this kind of radiation to a battle is unprecedented. It is almost certainly a portal.**]

"Why would the enemy bring a portal to Alpha Ludus?" one of the frogs asked.

Silence hung heavily throughout the Council Room. Every one of them was thinking the same thing.

"They're bringing in the fourth class . . ." Zerozerothree said in a whisper.

"That is a preposterous idea," Azzzhtik'Likzirrruk said, and the Swarm vociferously agreed, their buzzing sounding like creaking old metal being ripped apart. "They have never done anything like that before in eighteen thousand years. Why is this one human so important that they must destroy him?"

"Are other humans special like this Maximillian Cromwell?" one of the frogpeople asked.

[We ran several tests and did extensive research on the remaining human population on Alpha Ludus. This species is very well attuned to the Framework and can indeed increase their Cultivation surprisingly quickly with it. Humans are definitely an outlier species, and it is fortunate that we have found and claimed this asset. However, Maximilian Cromwell is an outlier among outliers. No individual, not even King Valdemar III has experienced such growth in such a stupendously short amount of time.]

"What is done with the rest of the humans is of no importance to us currently," Zerozerothree said, and the two other Gray stooges at his sides nodded. "What is important is how we respond to the threat of a potential fourth-class Outsider emerging."

"Do we have an estimate of how powerful a threat this will be?" Azzzhtik'Likzirrruk asked.

[We must be ready to immediately employ our highest-tier Cultivators. It is unlikely that this can be defeated with merely Diamond-stage warriors. At least two Celestial-stage Cultivators must be deployed and an agreement with King Valdemar must be reached, so that he will also engage in battle if deemed necessary, which it most assuredly will be.]

"King Valdemar will surely comply," one of the Grays said. "He grows bored sitting on his throne. He will come if properly enticed. The fourth-class Outsider could be a threat that rivals even his strength."

[We are working with scant information, which is unfortunate. It is important that we plan contingencies as we cannot lose Maximillian Cromwell as an asset, no matter which side he chooses. **Right now, it seems that the side he will ultimately land on is King Valdemar's, but that doesn't mean he cannot become a Celestial Cultivator—which will be important to the well-being of the whole universe.]**

"We place troops in reserve and send them in if the fourth class emerges," Zerozerothree said. "If the planet is lost, we secure the asset and destroy the planet. The use of atomic weapons enhanced with Spiritual Energy should be allowed in the case of the fourth-class Outsider emerging and establishing itself in our reality."

The members of the council considered this suggestion silently. They were considering obliterating four species, snuffing out over ten million souls, and destroying a completely habitable planet. It was *barbaric*. But if the fourth-class Outsider emerged, it would be necessary. That creature could grow to the size of a sun. At least. From what information on it they could glean, it was most likely some sort of focal point for the Outsider hive mind. There were currently none in this known reality, even though the Outsiders held a sizable percentage of the local galaxy. But the implications of it arriving and establishing here were . . . unthinkable. But what role could this one human play?

[We agree. The idea of eradicating these species that we ourselves placed on the planet is . . . unsavory, but the safety of trillions more is more important. What is a relative handful of lives when weighed against all sapient beings in the known universe? If required, we will use Spiritually-enhanced weapons of mass destruction to atomize the planet.]

"Hear, hear," the frog-people said in unison from their green gel.

"Then, it is decided," Azzzhtik'Likzirrruk said. "We shall prepare an armada of high-tier ICCB Cultivators to contend with the potential emergent fourth-class Outsider threat. We shall extend an offer to King Valdemar, and we will prepare atomization weapons in the event of the worst-case scenario, and extract Max Cromwell if he is still alive at the point we are forced to evacuate and retreat."

"It is decided, then," Zerozerothree said. "We trust that there are no further topics of importance to discuss?"

[Nothing that compares to the attention required by the situation on Alpha Ludus. But if the situation is resolved and Maximillian Cromwell ascends to Celestial stage, we must discuss our diplomatic relations with King Valdemar's empire. The ICCB must reign supreme. Any challenge to

our rule has to be considered a threat to the universe as we know it and all
the sapient species within.]

"So even the ever-so-graceful Zoos Collective is pining for a war," one of the
Grays said and grinned in satisfaction.

[We will do what is necessary. Meeting adjourned.]

CHAPTER FIFTY-TWO

The Final Battle

Max stood on Maverick—who had stretched himself to the size of a tennis court—along with Favani and the rest of the strike force. They were watching the sky. The orange sun cast a soft light on the world, a sharp contrast to the thick dark clouds being burst by black comets streaking down.

The Outsiders had finally come.

They were landing all over the horizon. Their strategy was clear: spread out, start consuming and assimilating biomass immediately in order to build too many fires for their enemies to control.

Maverick could fly fast, though. And Max was able to use gravity to hold all of the strike force members on the platform so that they didn't fall. And if needed, Max could ask the ICCB for teleportation, especially intercontinentally, as local teleportation wasn't prohibitively expensive.

A whining sound of gathering energy filled their ears as Maverick charged a blast of pure destructive energy in his massive cannon. When he was ready, the platform tilted upward slightly, and Maverick let it rip: a massive blast that tore through the air and rocked the platform to the point that Kat yelped and Favani had to grab her so she wouldn't fall. Kat begrudgingly thanked her and ripped her hand away once the platform stabilized.

Maverick's aim was true. He struck one of the comets far off in the distance, and it instantly exploded. Max had high Cultivation, and his eyes could see far. The comet was made of the black goopy substance that seemed to be the basis for all Outsider life, the Tar. It scattered to the four winds, turning into black smoke.

That's going to piss off the sorcerers!

Max wondered how many there would be. This was just a scouting force. But he only had a handful of his people there—as powerful as he, Maverick, and Favani were. And, to be fair, Losshnak had gained substantial power in his own right. He was at the cusp of the Greater Diamond realm, which was no small feat in such a short amount of time with the resources ICCB had available. Max trusted him. The rest of the strike force, he wasn't so sure of. They would most likely get in the way or die. Maverick had made Max promise that he wouldn't try to play the hero and attempt to save everyone, and Max had agreed. He would fill his end of the contract, do his best to save the humans on this planet, and then eventually move to a vassal planet of the Jianari and rule it with Favani.

Starting over with two million humans on a fresh planet. Favani and me as rulers. Lofty dreams.

King Valdemar III liked the idea. While the king wanted both of them to advance in their Cultivation to at least Celestial stage, he also decided that it was about time his daughter learned to rule.

As long as they won, everything would click into place beautifully.

We will. We have to.

There would be sorcerers, though. And they would be focusing on Max. Thankfully, Max was strong now.

Maverick fired off another shot. This one only clipped one of the comets, which seemed to swerve to the side to dodge the shot. Still, it managed to singe off some of the black goop and the comet seemed to sway off of its originally intended course.

"They're landing," Max said. "Prepare yourselves!"

"We will stand behind you," Losshnak said. "And perish at your command if it is required."

"I like this guy," Favani said and turned to smile at Losshnak, who barked out a laugh.

"Do not dare to presume to smile at my mate," Ashkarassa said and took a step forward.

Favani gave her a cold stare. "I'm sorted on that front myself, thanks."

Ashkarassa glowered but Losshnak put a hand on her shoulder in a calming gesture.

"She must be a powerful woman," Losshnak said to Max. "For you to choose her as a mate."

"You'll see soon enough, my friend."

Losshnak flinched but then smiled a toothy grin. "I hope you do not throw these words out casually."

Max shook his head. "After this is over, I want to take you to the planet that Favani and I own. You will be the duke, and lord of all the Ishkarassi. We have a lot to teach one another."

Losshnak considered it. "Hm. I like this, but we would be forever guests and secondary citizens of this planet, for you are human and it is your nature to ensure the wellbeing of other humans at the expense of other species. This is how it is and how it shall always be. I cannot accept."

Max was disappointed, but he nodded, turning to Favani. "Is there a star system your family owns with two planets that can sustain life?"

"Of course," Favani said. "In Proxima 5. The fourth planet is very similar to this one, if a bit warmer. The star of that system is very active. But the third planet from the star is close, and the climate is hot—scorchingly so. There is a mining colony there, and it is mostly a prison planet."

"We shall oversee this prison planet," Losshnak declared. "After my people are saved, we shall pledge allegiance to Max."

"You would bow your head so easily?!" Ashkarassa hissed.

"Silence," Losshnak said. "Do you not realize how powerful they are?"

"You know I am still having trouble extending my spirit like this," Ashkarassa muttered.

Max extended his destructive Intent at Ashkarassa. He was careful not to attack her with it, but the impression she received was not that of someone pointing a gun at her. It was someone pointing all the weapons of an *armada* at her. She flinched and her eyes went wide with shock.

"It seems I have been the fool," she said. "I thought you two were all mostly bluster . . ."

"You felt it?" Losshnak asked.

"He touched me with his strength," Ashkarassa said and gave another glance of disbelief at Max.

Losshnak chuckled and shared a look with Max. "Forgive her. She is of a fiery nature and will only listen to force."

"That's why I did it," Max said. "I need you all to be focused and listening to me. I'm in charge. Stick to the formation. Stay on Maverick and inside Losshnak's barrier. If anything gets into melee range, Kat will spring into action. You will defend the barrier. I will fly nearby to make sure you guys can stay airborne. Are you confident in your ability to fly?"

The male vulpine and the human female shared a look and nodded to one another. Kat looked at Max with a level stare. "We'll do what's required."

Max nodded. "Good."

The first black comets in the vicinity crashed to the ground. The battle would be fought on an ocean shore surrounded by rocky, grassy hills reminiscent of Ireland. Maverick sped toward the crash site, and Losshnak erected his golden barrier. Meanwhile, the two insectoids drew a circle of ritual magic and sat down inside it, starting a chittering chant. Around them in the air bloomed tiny insects like stars popping up at dusk.

They flew above the crash site and saw that the Outsiders weren't idle. Immediately upon crashing, the goopy substance flew this way and that, and horrid shapes emerged from it. They looked like crabs and lobsters, and they immediately burrowed into the grass and started seeping some sort of corrosive poison which withered the grass and turned it black, as its life force was drained.

Maverick fired a blast of pure energy at a cluster of the monstrous crabs. They exploded into the black tarry goop and flew this way and that. Swarms of crabs clustered around the scattered mass and absorbed it.

Max flew out of the bubble to attack the crabs and was instantly attacked by a plume of black fire whizzing toward him. He made a fist and pushed forward his destructive Intent at the fireball, extinguishing it.

Max looked up to find a sorcerer floating in the air, its many hands weaving around in patterns, and a malicious leer shining on its white mask.

"Only one of you?" Max called out to it. It said nothing, but Max could feel a malicious force pulsing toward him. "That won't be enough, bastard."

Max snapped his fingers and flicked a blast of concussive energy at his foe, who erected a red barrier. Maverick, however, was already firing a blast of gray and yellow energy at it. The disruptive spatial energy struck the barrier, making it flicker and falter, and the blast struck the fiend straight in its torso.

The sorcerer fell, a trail of black smoke emanating from its scorched body. It thudded to the ground, and Max sent his scythe to finish it off. The sorcerer erected another barrier of red energy, but the scythe cleaved through so smoothly, it was as if it wasn't there. The malicious grin on the mask's face turned to one of shock, finally confirming to Max that this was indeed no mask but its actual face.

While the sorcerer's body was already beginning to heal, the **[Scythe of Oblivion]** cut off its head. The body started to evaporate in a cloud of nasty black vapors.

+1 Karma point

But before Max could turn to attack the crab monsters already assimilating the biomass, he noticed a myriad of monsters had sprouted from now-blackened acres amidst the bright green grass of the rocky shores. A swarm of dragonflies had emerged, now circling Maverick's platform, crashing into Losshnak's golden barrier, trying to break into it. But as far as Max could see, the barrier was holding strong. That was good; he had no time right now to babysit. Another sorcerer had emerged.

This one was different, Max could tell. To his surprise, it didn't have the malicious grin he had been accustomed to seeing plastered on the faces of the others. While the eyes were nothing but black and emotionless holes, its mouth was a thin line that seemed to speak of focus and disapproval.

Max heard a discordant whisper, as if it was attempting to communicate. He couldn't understand the words, but the intent was clear: *Surrender and I will grant you a clean death.*

"Come and get it," Max said and flicked another wave of gravitational energy at his foe, who was forced to erect a red barrier.

This sorcerer was stronger than the others. Or at least smarter. The barrier flickered from Max's attack and Maverick fired off a blast. But the sorcerer dodged. A hint of a smile started forming on its mask. Max sped up as a plume of purple smoke erupted around him. He took in a whiff of it, but it only sapped his strength by a negligible amount. There would be trouble when the purple clouds started attacking Maverick and the people on his platform, though.

That's why Max had to attack ferociously and keep the sorcerers busy. This time instead of a flick of his fingers, trying to destroy the barrier in a delicate, controlled burst, Max released a blast of pure destructive energy, attempting to rip space-time itself around the sorcerer. It escaped, but the **[Scythe of Oblivion]** cleaved at the sorcerer's arms just as it was weaving a fireball. The fiend sent a pulse of wrathful Intent at Max, but he could care less. He only attacked more ferociously, sending out another pulse of destruction.

But now the sorcerer was clearly playing for time. Max realized that they knew. They knew that the planet was mostly undefended. Every second this sorcerer managed to waste was a second that all the other clusters of Outsiders would be able to further consume biomass and replicate. It was only a matter of time before the encroaching mass of monsters reached the innocent races of this planet and consumed them too.

Max flew straight ahead at the sorcerer, gripping his scythe with all his might. Breaking the sound barrier, Max *sliced* through the sorcerer, infusing his enormous weapon's black and silver blade with pure destructive Intent. There was a flicker of a red barrier around the sorcerer, but it was nothing but a weak blink. It was torn in half with the same expression of mute shock on its mask as the first one had.

Max then came to a halt and turned to look. The sorcerer's form was dissipating in the air, its healing only making its inevitable death last longer. It couldn't handle the onslaught of pure destruction that was spreading through its wretched body. As it disintegrated, Max was already speeding toward the ground.

"**[Gravity Storm]**."

Max blanketed the whole seashore that had now turned black with the swarming horde of the Outsiders. The massive blanket of gravity crushed hundreds of monstrous enemies to the ground. They writhed, groaned, and burst into a black goop. Meanwhile, Maverick fired a fusillade of gray and yellow energy at them, tossing up the sand and the Tar.

After a minute, when Max was already blanketing another field of enemies with his **[Gravity Storm]**, two sorcerers emerged. Max only smirked.

"Took you long enough to realize you can't deal with me alone, did it?"

The sorcerers said nothing. They only stared him in the eyes as their hands weaved black fireballs, sending out pulses of murderous Intent. They were not grinning.

Max extended his arms to his side and brought them together in front of him in a massive *clap*.

Energy burst forth and Max guided it toward the enemy. They dodged out of the way of this massive gravitational energy, strong enough to distort space itself. Maverick unfortunately couldn't shoot a blast of energy at either of them, as he was busy maneuvering around in the air, dodging the corrosive blobs of the mantabats and the wanton charges of the dragonflies.

We are the only adversary for the enemy here, so their attacks are concentrated.

Max took a moment to observe his allies.

Losshnak's barrier was still holding, and his skill was so developed that it let his allies' attacks pass through without interruption while his lances of light energy zapped some of the dragonflies that got too close. Meanwhile, Ashkarassa threw spears at the mantabats with reckless abandon. The spears always boomeranged back to her after flying a hundred yards or so, sometimes skewering a dragonfly or two on the way.

The two insectoid warriors' iridescent butterflies and bees were flying around in artful swarms, crashing into the enemies and setting them on fire. Their wings were singed, they fell to the ground, and splattered.

However, the mantabats were gathering. They were lobbing their green corrosive energy at the barrier, which sizzled away at the energy, causing noxious vapors to rise. Max extended his Spiritual Sense toward Losshnak and the barrier. Both needed a break. Despite Losshnak being a powerful Cultivator in his own right, his was not a vast ocean of power like Max's was. He was still closer to mortal than god. The barrier wouldn't hold forever and was already starting to show slight fractures.

Max noticed a particularly large mantabat circling around and dodging a shot from Maverick. A spear from Ashkarassa struck it in the shoulder, and it groaned. But it kept charging. Kat jumped out of the protective barrier with a war cry, a spear and shield hoisted high.

Max watched in awe at her bravery. He cast a levitation spell on her as well as the two vulpines who also then jumped out of the barrier.

They maneuvered smoothly in the air, having practiced this move thoroughly in the last two days of simulations.

Kat especially . . . She's taken to it like a fish to water.

"Hey," Favani called as she circled next to Max flying on a large sword, "how are we doing?

Favani, who had been on containment duty, avoiding sorcerers and simply doing her best to prevent the corrosive consumption of the Outsiders from spreading, looked disheveled but still as glorious as any warrior princess. Max found he enjoyed the view.

"They're getting tired," Max said. "Especially Losshnak."

"He's the powerful one, yes?" Favani asked. "The one with the barrier?"

"Yes. They can't keep fighting without it."

"They will have to eventually," Favani said. "And some may perish."

Max disliked the thought. Maverick sent a pulse through their bond. It was the same old message: Focus, stop trying to save everyone, live according to your Dao.

"Yeah," Max said. "I know. I just don't like it."

"This is warfare," Favani said. "And you need to focus."

"Yes," Max said. "Help me take down a sorcerer or two before you go while you're here."

"Yes, my prince," Favani said and shot him a look. Max chuckled and tried not to blush too badly.

They smashed through a bunch of the mantabats, making them explode. It was better that the black tar-like substance on the ground, feeding the other creatures.

Max smashed a few massive **[Gravity Wells]** into the midst of the enemy ground forces and watched them turn into crunchy paste below him. That was enough to prompt the two sorcerers to attack again. They were strangely watchful.

It really seems like they don't want to get hurt. That or they're trying to learn . . .

The sorcerers started tossing black fireballs at them, but Max dodged them with ease. They realized this and started targeting Favani instead. Her storm of swords sliced and blocked most of the energy as she flew around, but some of the fire still singed her. Despite the welts on her cheeks, her eyes were fierce and focused.

Max flew straight toward the sorcerers. He was gathering a mass of heavy gravity in his hands. Maverick shot an explosion of yellow and gray energy at one of them, forcing it to dodge downward. Max nosedived and struck it in the chest with his gravity-infused hand. A purple cloud of deadly vapors bloomed around them, but Max was too fast. They plummeted to the ground like missiles and crashed.

The swarm of Outsiders was immediately upon them, trying to protect their leaders. Max sent out a pulse of spatial energy into every direction around him. It crushed the onslaught, causing the enemy to be tossed back hundreds of feet, black goop flying out in every direction.

The other sorcerer attempted to come to help, but Favani was keeping it busy. She could barely go toe-to-toe with them, but the distraction would have to do.

The sorcerer beneath Max struggled against the hand pressed against its chest. It felt slick, slimy, and cold; the sensation disgusted Max, but he pushed more energy into the gravity spell.

White, luminescent tendrils sprouted from all over its body and struck like snakes, trying to wrap around Max.

"Oh no, you don't."

Max sent out another blast of spatial energy from his core, spreading out in every direction. It was an overpowering force that managed to squish the tentacles. The sorcerer's face went from an angry sneer to a look of pure shock. Max gathered energy into his other fist and smashed it in the face. There was a flicker of red energy, desperately trying to shield against the strike, but Max infused his fist with pure destructive Intent and it crashed through, utterly bashing the sorcerer's head to a pulp.

The healing factor started to work, apparently able to even restore a sorcerer who had lost its head, but Max placed his hands on its body and infused it full of destructive power and let it rip. It burst into a thousand bits of black goop, scattering this way and that. The other sorcerer in the sky paused in its fight against Favani and screeched.

Favani attacked it with a swarm of swords, but it revealed its tentacles and swatted them away. In a furious frenzy of attacks, the sorcerer sent a flurry of tentacles, purple clouds, and fireballs against Favani, who was forced to retreat. Max could feel her two hundred yards away, her energy coursing through her meridians, as she took a much-needed break.

The sorcerer let out an ear-piercing screech. Something very bad was happening, Max could tell. He flicked a slicing cut of destructive energy at the sorcerer, but the red shield emerged and blocked the attack. Max had been expecting that, which was why the [Scythe of Oblivion] rose up from behind the sorcerer, in an attempt to slice up its spine.

The tendrils glowed white hot as if they were burning at five thousand degrees. It screeched again, and Max felt his spirit tremble. Something was ripping open in the space behind it. A pitch-black darkness omitting some kind of sinister energy.

"What's happening?" Maverick asked as he circled up to fly next to Max.

"Nothing good," Max said.

Maverick said nothing, only charged a massive blast of energy, which whined in its containment.

He released it, and Max infused it with spatial energy, making it blast forward even faster. But a shadowy, inky tentacle emerged from the black rift in the air, slapping away the energy blast. Max watched it streak into the distance, until it hit a hill, reducing it to a crater.

What the hell is happening here?

Max didn't want to attack again before knowing what was happening. But he feared that might be too late. So he called up his Spiritual Energy and released a [Gravity Storm], concentrated on the sorcerer and the rift behind it.

The distortion of space made everything heavy. The sorcerer flinched and tried to bring up a red bubble of energy to protect itself, but the shadowy tentacle emerged from the rift again and weaved a black sign in the air. It was alien and intricate but clearly some kind of language. It emitted a field of energy which *ate* the gravitational energy Max was exerting.

It's absorbing my technique.

Then the tentacle pierced the sorcerer, which let out a screech that was somewhere between pleasure and pain. It started to wither away, red veins streaking on its black, slick skin, until there was nothing left but a skeleton, arteries, and the face. The arteries and face crumbled into dust and the rift flared out wider, and now two tentacles managed to squeeze out of it.

More sorcerers were flying toward them.

"Maverick," Max said. "This could be really bad."

"Master Warrior!" Losshnak called. "What do we do?"

Max brushed at Losshnak's spirit. He was exhausted. While they had been fighting a winning battle so far, it had come with the price of him exerting his strength to the fullest. If he couldn't keep his barrier up, all of the other strike force members would be in danger. But right now, they seemed to be facing a foe unlike any they'd ever seen before. Max seriously did not like the energy emitted by the black rift. There was something very, very bad in there.

"Flee!" Max said. "You will only get in the way. This foe is too strong."

"No!" Kat said and flew next to Max. "I am not a coward."

"Can you not feel its power brewing?" Max asked.

The sorcerers in the sky were gathering. Four, then six, now eight. They were flying toward them from other crash sites, being called by whatever was in the rift, trying to break into this reality.

Even Max couldn't fight eight sorcerers.

Before he could argue with Kat further, the creature in the rift struck out. A lance of pitch-black energy shot toward Max with a speed he could barely react against. He dodged and diverted the energy with his spatial abilities. But it was like a mortal trying to bend hardened steel with bare hands.

The beam grazed Max on his shoulder and a brutal pain ripped through his whole body. He started falling to the ground where a swarm of Outsiders waited. Max pushed Spiritual Energy into his meridians. It was like trying to push the earth itself down. Nothing happened. His Cultivation was cut off.

He fell.

"Max!" Maverick shouted and dodged another black beam. He shrugged off his platform shape and reverted to his normal size, a tractor-tire-sized disc.

Everyone in the strike force fell off. Losshnak activated his bubble, which popped when they hit the ground, splattering black goop everywhere as they crushed into a handful of Outsiders. The swarm attacked them immediately. Favani flew downward to help, with her swords swirling around her.

Maverick scooped up Max and fired a blast of yellow and gray energy at the black rift in the air. It waved a tentacle and shot another black beam at them. It was fast, but they had seen it before and Maverick dodged it.

The eight sorcerers stopped to float in the air, four on each side of the rift. They all grinned widely.

Max and Maverick stopped, and the rift opened further. Tentacles pushed out and an eye appeared. It was pure white with only a single black dot as a pupil. A single thought, a single impulse, seemed to be emanating from that eye.

Greed.

It was overwhelming. It was like King Valdemar's tyrannical Intent, but tenfold. Max, who was slowly getting control of his Cultivation back, had to push with all his might, lest his mind, body, and spirit be overwhelmed by the pure oppressive hunger to own and consume *everything*.

"We need to run!" Maverick said.

Max let out a weak scoff. "To where?"

Maverick had no answer. Max, who was still lying against Maverick's cool platform, tried to extend his Spiritual Sense downward to see how his comrades were doing. The dark Intent of pure greed would not let him do that. The primal eye kept staring at Max. A mounting fear started to creep up in his mind.

It's overwhelming.

With Valdemar, Max had felt he stood a chance. He could fight back. But this Intent was beyond anything he had ever imagined. His own power level was at the peak of Diamond, Valdemar was a Celestial-stage Cultivator. But this . . . In terms of the Framework, this beast must have had a power level of one hundred.

But it only waited and watched. No more black beams were shooting out of it. The sorcerers weren't attacking, either. And it seemed like they could care less about the battle going on below them.

Max could see why. It required the keen senses of a Cultivator, but by a fraction of an inch at a time, the rift was widening. Whatever gargantuan monstrosity of immense power was inside of it wanted *out*.

"We have to destroy it," Max said.

"Haha," Maverick said with a trembling voice. "How about you manage to get back on your feet first."

Max tried, but the immense greed pushed harder down on him. The creature in the rift sensed his struggle and wanted to toy with him.

That's when an armada appeared before Max, with the ICCB jellyfish right in the middle of it, directly in front of Max. A group of Grays were standing on a floating platform similar to Maverick. A small battleship that looked like a submarine was hovering nearby. Max extended his Spiritual Sense and saw that it was full of the strange frog-people. They were preparing various weapons, mostly tridents brimming with blue energy.

Lastly, a swarm of extremely ugly flies buzzed in the air, dense as smoke, metallic screeches resonating in the air as they spoke to one another. A firestorm was burning above them and growing in size as their buzzing intensified.

The monstrosity inside the rift didn't waste a moment; a great black fusillade of dark tendrils struck out against all of its enemies, but just then, a great green forcefield sprung around the armada and deflected the attack. A copy of the Zoos jellyfish appeared in front of Max and Maverick.

[Maximillian, despite our previous disagreements, we are all as one now, fighting against this encroaching monstrosity seeking to consume us all. You have fought valiantly, and even managed to somehow fend off against this threat.]

"What is it?" Max asked, as he struggled under the pressure being exerted by the creature in the rift.

[It is best not to say too much. Know only this: It is the Outside. The end-less void that seeks to consume everything in this universe. It has done this for longer than life has existed. And it seeks to consume this universe as well. Has any universe ever managed to resist the inevitable? We do not know.]

The magnitude of it was overwhelming. The concept of something so horrible, enormous, and relentless attacking reality itself was making Max's head swim.

Max struggled against the power. The creature in the rift was hitting the armada with countless attacks—dark purple clouds and energy beams in addition to its lashing tentacles. But all of the magic and technology of the ICCB combined was able to fend it off. For now.

Max understood now. He understood the Cosmic Games. He understood their necessity. Their brutality. The need for a gladiator planet. The need for draconian contracts to recruit slave-warriors. It was brutal and inhuman.

But it was necessary.

There was no other way to fight against this threat than with absolute brutal efficiency. It wasn't about the ends justifying the means. It was pure survival. Humans had fought against nature for thousands of years, and each other in forms of competing tribes and oppressing tyrannies for thousands of years after that. Not to mention the fight against the self which every conscious soul had to contend with.

But it was nothing compared against this foe.

The creature in the rift let out a terrible scream. It ripped through the air and Max had to push with all his might against the oppressive *greed* which wanted to consume everything and anything in its wake. The armada that defended the line and attempted to attack the rift recoiled and reshaped its lines. But it wasn't enough. This was only a part of the ICCB going up against the single-minded Intent of anti-life itself.

Max realized something. A new fire kindled inside of him. An understanding of being part of the continuity. Part of the fight. He was the culmination of thousands of years of evolution which had happened through endless combat.

And he would do his part.

Something began to stir inside of Max, but then he was startled by more people teleporting in front of the rift.

King Valdemar III appeared along with twenty of his personal guards, as well as Favani's brother and other relatives.

"Father!" Favani cried out. The royal guard flew down immediately and started destroying the swarm of Outsiders.

"Favani," the king boomed. "Get out of here."

Favani hesitated but flew behind toward Max, pushing Maverick away from the rift by twenty yards.

"Are you alright?" she asked Max.

"I'll manage," Max said. Now that the creature had other fish to fry, the pressure on Max eased. He got up, and power started flowing through his meridians again. "What is that thing?"

Favani said nothing, only looked at the rift.

"Max, I don't like this," Maverick said. "Can we bail?"

Max recalled that feeling he had just felt. He nudged Maverick through their bond. Maverick groaned.

"We will fight," Max said grimly.

Favani cried out desperately. "Max, please reconsider."

"No," Max said, his voice full of steel. "You have to go, Favani."

"We cannot fight this," Favani said.

"We *must* fight this," Max said.

"Favani makes sense," Maverick said. "I know what you're thinking, Max. You know I do. But I vote live today, fight another day."

"If this thing rips out of that rift, there might not be another day. It might *all* end," Max said. "I won't let that happen. I will destroy Destruction itself."

Dao Breakthrough Activated

With that, he shrugged off the blanketing Intent of the creature in the rift. His meridians were filled with a bright power, like light and fire turned liquid, which coursed through his whole body and gave him strength. He summoned the [Scythe of Oblivion]. It shone in the evening light as it floated next to him. He breathed in, and all of the power in the universe seemed to converge inside of him in that single breath. He struck and smote the creature in the rift. The scythe shot forward, a black streak faster than thought.

The creature inside turned its wild, hungry eye toward Max. It screeched again and started gathering the black energy on the tip of its tentacles. Already, six had emerged from the rift, which was growing larger by the minute.

"Defensive formation A-12!" one of the Grays shouted and the ICCB armada took their positions, a great shimmering barrier of pearly white enveloping them.

"Mass Sword Deflection!" Valdemar commanded, and hundreds of swords shot up in the air to swirl in a dome around the king and his retinue with blinding speed.

Swords and balls of energy flew against the rift. Maverick pulled a deft fly-by and shot a blast of destructive energy at it as well. They were all stopped by a round matrix of red and purple spiderweb that appeared before the rift. The attacks couldn't pass it.

Max felt a terrible Intent coming from it, but it was different than before. This wasn't the Intent of a Cultivator exerting their Spiritual Energy. This was an . . . attempt at communication. Something akin to emotion sent across the field in some form of alien telepathy. But it was so strange, so eerie, so disturbing, that Max's mind rejected it. But from the garble of thoughts, emotions, and will, one thought rang out:

WE WILL TAKE EVERYTHING.

The energy from the six tentacles converged in the middle. The sorcerers flew into a formation near the rift, and they all died with a wail as their essence was absorbed into the attack—a great crackling ball of black energy that grew bigger and more unstable as the creature fed energy into it. Finally, it was released just as the ICCB and the king of the Jianari prepared their defenses.

Max knew he had to dodge. By half a mile at least. He, Favani, and Maverick were already flying downward, grabbing the fighting strike force on the ground.

When the creature released the blast of energy, there came a mighty crack so loud it seemed a that the world itself had broken. It rippled through the whole planet, and everything turned black and white. Then there was silence, as complete and eerie as one can only experience in a dream. A total void of sound, like a silence that *consumed.*

Max felt his mind weaken and his Cultivation drain, as it was forced to transform Spiritual Power into life force. He sensed Maverick weaken too, and saw that Favani, who was flying next to him on a large sword, was wobbling. She had a look of utter horror on her face. They had all been significantly weakened, their energy destroyed or stolen.

Without the surge of power that the Dao Breakthrough had bestowed upon him, he would not have been able to fend off this attack. Max was wobbly in the air, but he would manage.

But the strike force huddling under Losshnak's shield on Maverick's platform had taken the worst of it.

They had grown *old*.

Max was astonished. Losshnak and Ashkarassa's shiny scales had turned gray and mottled. The insectoids' carapace had gone pale, and their forms had shriveled. The vulpine people, so athletic and virile before, were bent over, their fur now gray, a look of stunned horror on their emaciated faces.

And Kat had withered into an old woman.

Her hair had gone thin, her face wrinkled and skin now pale and thin as paper, with blue veins jutting from her skeletal hands. She looked at them in disbelief. Her eyes were still young, fresh, and blue, but everything else about her had aged sixty years in an instant.

The world was still black and white. Sound was returning, but the only thing Max could hear was a soft but insistent whining in the back of his skull, like the aftermath of an explosion.

Max turned to see what was happening. The ICCB was launching a series of ferocious attacks, blasts of energy of every color of the rainbow swirling into each other. Great plumes of toxic smoke, fire that burned so intensely they were pure white. Despite his weakened state, Max sent a pulse of destructive Intent at the rift for all he was worth.

But the terrible monster—Max could somehow tell its name was Sinside—only screeched and raised a barrier. It was damaged by the myriad of attacks, but the sorcerers beside it absorbed most of them, sacrificing their lives to protect the abomination as it finally fully pushed itself out of the rift.

Its form was as eerie and alien as Max had imagined. It consisted mostly of tentacles. They were black and dark purple with tiny obsidian barbs. They waved and swirled around the monster's hideous form, as if tasting the air. The tentacles surrounded a horrifying mouth like that of a dried-up mummy with an eye in the center, unblinking, inhuman, bestial, yet gleaming with intense purpose and a cold, predatory intellect.

It was enormous. The tentacles unfurled, seeming to fill the entire sky. There were *hundreds* of them, swirling around hypnotically. Meanwhile, the creature's body was obscured by shadows that shifted and billowed and withdrew like inky smoke.

[Do not let it exit the portal. Call in an emergency teleport for reinforcements. The Swarm will need to bring in a power array to counteract the suppression field it is emitting.]

Oh.

Max realized his weakened state wasn't the result of the creature expressing some kind of interest in him and pushing him down personally, as he had first thought. The creature simply did not regard him at all. The effect was passive. It had locked out Max's Cultivation almost completely simply just by *existing*. Now the creature floated in the air, with its countless tentacles swirling around it like a flock of synchronous birds. It looked like a cold black, monstrous sun, a true blasphemy. An anti-star emitting anti-light. This creature was Anti-Life.

"Max," Maverick said. "We aren't going to escape, are we?"

Favani looked at Max with unbending resolve in her eyes. Max knew she would die here if need be. Max shared the sentiment.

"We aren't going anywhere."

"In that case," Maverick said, "I think we have a lot to learn from this big bastard."

"What do you mean?" Max asked as he stifled a cough. The toxic plumes from the ICCB's attack were being blasted in their direction by a firestorm explosion from the Grays.

"If this thing had a Dao, it would be to eradicate all of existence, right?"

"Yeah?" Max said.

"It's pretty similar to the very essence of Destruction, wouldn't you think?"

"Oh," Max said.

"Yeah," Maverick said.

"Okay, sure. But what are we going to do about that?"

"Well, I've got a crazy idea," Maverick said.

"I think we are going to need one to win this fight," Favani said.

"So, we have this Soulbond, yeah?" Maverick said. "We can feel what we're each thinking . . ."

"I'm not sure I like where this is going, but go on," Max said.

"And you're getting really good at directing your Intent. Could you attempt to take the energy and form of our Soulbond and direct it as Intent at the creature? Just like you joined with the Zoos guys to fix me in the cave?"

"You want us to *communicate* with it?"

"I want to learn from it," Maverick said. "Just like you could use King Valdemar's tyrannical Intent and Spiritual Energy and transform it into Destruction, you can use this creature's anti-life Intent and transform it."

"Do you have any idea how powerful it is, and how risky forming a bond with it could be?"

Maverick was quiet for a moment. "I think it came for us."

"No way," Max said.

"Never has the ICCB or anyone else mentioned a creature like this. A simple scouting mission warranting the whole-ass ICCB and the king of the Jianari making costly teleports just when this thing shows up? Not a coincidence."

"He has a point, Max."

"Why would this thing come for us?" Max said aghast, his voice half a whisper.

"Because it sees you as a threat," Favani said. "You are special, Max. It's not just that you're talented. You're the epitome of a great Cultivator with a perfect Dao to challenge the Outsiders."

Max was silent for a while. It was just too much. But when he looked at the great monster floating in the air before him, blasting beams of black light at the armada fighting it, Max knew Favani might be right.

"Okay . . . Okay." Max said and breathed. "We'll do it."

"Yeah?" Maverick said. "Well, better get on with it before I change my mind and chicken out."

CHAPTER FIFTY-THREE

The Sidekick

Maverick felt strange. There was some sort of constriction in the center of his disc. That's where his soul was. Well, technically, his soul was inside Max. Not that he would ever admit it. Max didn't know that. Max didn't know the truth. The bitter truth. That it was actually Maverick who was—Maverick sighed—He was . . . Was the . . .

Sidekick.

It had bothered him for the most of his existence. He was the perfect killing machine. He was confident, intelligent, powerful. His progress and relentless ability to focus during and withstand arduous Cultivation practice was unparalleled. But . . . He had eventually come to realize that it wasn't his own power.

He was a reflection of Max. His glorious, beautiful forms weren't fully his own. They had been what Max needed. Of course, Maverick was also his own person. And sometimes, nay, often—no, that was also too modest—he *always* knew best. He always knew what Max needed. But it was not because of their bond. Maverick barely bothered to use the bond. He knew Max fully, because he was a part of him.

It pained him. What was this existence? Why was it that he had been given a supporting role? He had never even been given a chance. He was a side character in his own story right from the get-go. It was unfair. He had tried to make himself important. But even that was a reflection of Max, who didn't think he wanted to feel important. On some level it was because he had wanted to be a normal person. On another level it was because he hadn't wanted to admit *wanting* to feel important.

Maverick embodied the part of Max that secretly did. He was what Max needed.

But that made him, by definition, a side character. It was insufferable.

That all had gradually changed as he watched over Max and eventually even watched *himself* grow as a result of his buddy's growth. Yeah, Maverick was the sidekick. He was a side character in his own life.

But at least he was the sidekick to the *main character*. This Max Cromwell who he had bonded with wasn't just extraordinary. He was the *most* extraordinary person in existence. The only person who could withstand the Outsiders and the Anti-Life.

How did Maverick know this?

He wasn't sure. This didn't come from Max. For he wasn't fully Max. He was also a representation. An avatar. A concept in a physical form.

He was from the Framework. In its infinite wisdom, it had given Maverick to Max. It had given Max what he had needed every step of the way. Maverick had thought it was his own power, but it wasn't. It was all Max and the rest of it was Framework.

But Maverick refused to wallow. Max would never wallow, and the Framework was infinitely wise. So, Maverick would execute what he knew was needed. He knew better than Max.

But, boy, does it suck. Why does it have to be me? What about my feelings—my wants and needs?

Maybe it wasn't so bad. Maybe it was just the next natural step. He knew what he needed to do, and he would do it. But that didn't mean he wanted to do it.

Maverick reached inside of himself. In that place where his soul was. It was ready. Ready for transformation. A final one. A complete merge. He had started out as a gun. Then he became a carrier. His final form would be *integration*. And it would be epic and heroic.

"Max," he said as he reached for the transformation inside himself, "I need you to hold still."

"Mav . . ." Max said. "What are you doing?"

"What needs to be done."

"This is something new, huh?" Max said. "You've been keeping an ace in the hole."

"I always have an ace in the hole!" Maverick boasted. It was an empty one. He was scared. Max sensed it, the bastard. He hated it when he did that.

"You're doing something bad," Max said slowly. "Something you don't want to."

"I think . . . I think it will be fine," Maverick said.

Then he released the transformation. Maverick's glorious, beautiful black-and-golden disc form started to melt into pure liquid, and he felt his consciousness dim. He used the dregs of his focus to keep the form floating and intact. He shaped black, golden swirls. Slowly it took form. Maverick felt the essence of his very own self start to dwindle. But the form was getting more powerful and fearsome. What a legacy to leave behind! The ultimate weapon.

The form finally solidified. Maverick could faintly feel Max floating close by to touch it reverently. Maverick could feel the touch. It soothed his fear. No matter what, no matter how this turned out, he knew he wouldn't be alone.

"You were never alone," Max said. "And you were never the sidekick. You needed me, and I needed you. We were, are, and always will be partners."

Something broke inside Maverick. He let go of his feelings. The pride, the smug joy of being better than everyone else. The safe confidence that he was smarter and wiser. The comforting feeling of being the most glorious and beautiful creature in the universe. All his most cherished feelings. And his love for his comrade, friend, and the mirror to himself. He let it slide away. And the fear. There was only peace, oblivion, and a white light.

"Thank you . . . for everything."

Max stepped into the armor. It was gold and black, and it *thrum*med with power. Exactly half of the power Max had already commanded. Maverick had always seemed like he had been in command of maybe 20 percent of the power Max had had. Either he had been obscuring the truth, or there was something else going on here.

It didn't matter. What mattered was that this had been necessary. With this, Max would have enough power to fight the Anti-Life.

The armor gleamed in the light of Alpha Ludus' setting sun. When Max had stepped into it, it had reacted. Now it was swirling around him, settling in to envelop his body. Tasteful black and gold metal blended together and enforced every muscle, feeding pure, raw destructive power into his spirit. Max felt the power as well as the pride.

He let that pride into his heart. He had been running from it. Running from being a protector and a savior. He now knew what needed to be done. And he would do it. He would not just fight this threat. He would *annihilate it.*

With that resolve, something burst open. The armor not only merged with his body but with his very soul.

STAGE BREAKTHROUGH ACHIEVED
YOU HAVE REACHED CELESTIAL STAGE
ADJUSTING POWER, CONTROL, AND SPEED

An unfathomable amount of power began rushing into Max. As if the armor was a conduit for something. *The Framework?*

Could be. There was no room to think. There was only intense focus and concentrated power of will as massive amounts of Spiritual Energy flowed into him, filling his very essence.

Max reached for the bond he had shared with Maverick. It connected to the armor, but there was only silence. A full ocean encompassing a world, completely still. It had no mind or will of its own—only raw energy.

"Are you . . . really not there anymore?" Max asked silently.

There was no answer. Max didn't know if Maverick was still there or not. His buddy had sacrificed himself. Subsumed himself completely to grant Max the power needed.

"I will never forget you," Max said.

The armor finished settling onto Max, and he extended himself to his full length. He felt taller. He *was* taller. Towering over Favani as if she were a child. Max summoned the **[Scythe of Oblivion]**. It was massive. It gleamed in the air like a black shadow, augmented by his Cultivation and the enhancements King Valdemar had given it. When Max grabbed it, it responded, flickering and materializing into reality as a swirl of edges and shadows.

Max realized something as he watched the scythe brimming with power, something new. The Framework had given him just the tools he needed. Instead of letting the scythe float, he took it in his hand and felt its weight. It was just right. Max fed destructive power into it. It could absorb an ocean, and Max gave it to it. It would not be enough to obliterate the Anti-Life, but it would damage its very existence.

But now was not yet the time. Despite having grown ten times in strength, he was still not ready to defeat this great foe. He would need to challenge it. He would need to *absorb* it.

Max looked at the battlefield. The Anti-Life was swelling. It was getting more and more powerful as it absorbed energy from all of the attacks on it. Max hadn't sensed it before. He wondered if anyone else could. He doubted it. They weren't like him. They couldn't even comprehend him.

The husk of his and Maverick's **[Divine Soulbond]** were still there. Max infused it with his own Intent. Not pure destruction. This was something else. It was meant to absorb life in order to acquire Destruction. It was all complicated and conceptual, and Max didn't fully understand it. He didn't need to. He only needed to wield it.

He directed the infused willpower and bonded his mind with the Anti-Life.

The great monstrous eye flared open and emitted a blast that broke the formation of the armada challenging him.

Max fell into the abyss of its mind.

CHAPTER FIFTY-FOUR

The Anti-Life

The scale of the Anti-Life was massive. Max's mind could barely withstand the vastness of it. But in the vast folds of oblivion, something lurked. Something that was beyond good and evil. Something with a terrible, endless intelligence, yet a simple mind, almost bestial. It only wanted one thing. For everything to be nothing.

And it noticed Max inside of the void.

It attacked with a ferocity that would have broken the mind of a sage. Max was plunged into a cacophony of madness, every dark vision imaginable assaulting his consciousness. He pushed against it, and the pain of it almost overwhelmed him. It tried to drive him to the edge of sanity, but the armor which enveloped Max protected him, absorbing the terrible Intent sent out by the madness.

It gave Max enough space to withstand. The intense Cultivation training he had done, all of the fights for life and death, all the tribulations—they had tempered his mind to hold its own against the Anti-Life. The great darkness beyond darkness which sought nothing but nothingness.

Max tapped into that power through the husk of a bond left from the [**Divine Soulbond**]. He merged with the Anti-Life. It tried to push its powerful destructive Intent at Max in order to crush him, but Max sent out his own destructive energy, destroying destruction itself, only allowing as much energy to pass as he could absorb.

And with every passing moment, he grew stronger and stronger, and despite the vastness of the void, it was dwindling.

An urgent rage, a truly desperate screech from the depths of the abyss that sent shivers through the ripples of reality itself, attacked Max. The intensity grew, but Max held steadfast. He pushed against the abyss and the void and the darkness. He would destroy the Anti-Life. He would destroy anything that threatened the balance.

He *was* the balance.

But the void was vast and endless, and while Max was getting stronger, he was also getting overwhelmed.

The visions of madness and darkness encroached on Max's mind again and distracted him. His flow of destructive energy short-circuited. The Anti-Life flooded into Max and started ripping apart the fabric of his very existence.

Max let out a fierce roar.

Then the armor sent out a surge of divine will. It was the will of the Framework. Something pure, something wild, but contained. Like the embrace of a lover, so fierce, so gentle.

It empowered Max, as a good lover does. It filled his soul with a bright light. The corrosive energy of the Anti-Life, which had been filling Max's soul with black sludge and corruption infused with madness, was receding.

Faintly, in the midst of chaos, dreams, and death, Max felt Maverick. It was a faint whisper from the other side of reality, but it empowered him. Maverick was taunting him, belittling him in his loveable way. He was challenging him into action, as the power of the Framework flooded into Max . . . And the corruption receded.

Max fought for freedom, like a drowning man fights to reach the surface.

The void burst open with light.

Max's spirit and soul heaved, and he pushed with the full force of his Intent at the Anti-Life. It took physical form in the pure void, and it was as hideous as its reason for existence: a blasphemous form of swirling tentacles greedily reaching out to snatch life, and the maw between them seeking to consume everything.

But it was not to be.

Max would be the one who consumed—the void, that is. He would take and destroy it completely. He would give it no quarter. Max used to be scrappy. Fighting tooth and nail for survival. Making sure if someone wanted a bite out of him, they would have to chew. Now, the situation had reversed. Max would be the one swallowing his enemy whole now.

And so he did. He reached out with the full Intent of his spirit, an absolute destructive power. Consuming the Anti-Life into his own spirit and transforming it into his own with the metagem techniques he'd learned. The void trembled. For the first time ever, it felt something other than oppressive greed.

It felt *fear*.

Max would give it no sympathy. He sucked in *everything*, even the creature's fear. He would take everything from it. He would not leave even a shred of a ghost left of this thing that had haunted reality for ages.

Reality was his to protect.

Max reached out and took in the rest of the monster's power. It screeched and writhed in the void. It pushed back and raged wildly in its last stand:

I AM THAT WHICH EATS LIGHT AND SHADOW. YOUR REALITY IS MY FOOD.

Max only scoffed.

"I am the predator here, and you are my food. I will take everything from you. I am Destruction. I am Oblivion. I am inevitable. You cannot escape."

There was no more discussion. Only rage. The creature tried to resist. It tried to break Max with its power, but it was dashed like ocean waves on rocks. The creature howled in frustration and escaped.

Kat coughed weakly on the ground. She felt *horrible.* Her life force had been drained. She was old. Her body was slow, muscles weak, joints stiff.

The charred remains of the Outsider force were all around her. A terrible smoking ruin. The strike force had fought hard. Kat herself had fought harder than she had ever thought herself capable of. Every breath, every swing of her shield had been painful. But she had kept fighting.

It hadn't mattered.

Max and his annoying blue wife had done the brunt of the work. Kat and the others' efforts had barely registered as a blip. And then that great monster had come—the ominous thing with the giant eye.

It had scared the shit out of Kat.

Now it was still. Enveloped in an inky black bubble, probably made of the same material as these other bastards. The menagerie of ICCB aliens had first tried to attack the creature's oily shell, but it had yielded nothing, so they were gathering strength and negotiating.

Max, on the other hand . . .

He was floating in the air with the gleaming gold and black armor. He had grown in size. He was *massive* now. He looked like a god.

Felt like one too.

Kat was never adept at extending her Spiritual Sense to suss out other people's power. And now she couldn't feel any of her Cultivation. It was as if it had been drained away. But she had always been able to sense Max, and he was a veritable fusion reactor of power now. She could sense it from a mile away. Max's Spirit was *massive.* And it was still swelling. Growing ever more powerful in unimaginable ways.

"Somehow it seems that he's fighting with *that* thing," Ashkarassa said and came to stand next to her. Her voice was ragged and sounded as old as Kat felt. Losshnak limped next to them.

"Such prowess," the tall warrior said. Now he was slouched over, and his scales were gray.

"He's just standing still," Kat said.

"So is that creature," Losshnak said. "I do not think it coincidence."

"Their smell has changed," Plarag said as she came close. Her carapace was dry and cracking on the edges. "If they're fighting, Max is winning."

"Of course he is," Rakii said. Her fur was falling off in a cascade as she walked toward them with a grace that surprised Kat. But when she looked closer, she noticed the vulpine woman grimacing with pain to keep up the facade. "That man does not know how to quit."

"Sure doesn't," Kat mused. "But can he really fight something like that?"

"He is a master warrior," Losshnak said. "We are fortunate to witness this fight."

"Only if he pulls through," Kerro said. "Otherwise, we'll be even more screwed than we are now."

Kat looked at the dark bubble the great monster was encased in. It was cracking.

"I think we're about to find out."

Max woke as if from a dream. He was back on Alpha Ludus. Back in reality. He could feel the weight of his new armor on his skin, but not Maverick. He wanted to lament, but now was not the time. He had a job to finish.

He no longer felt the suppression field the Anti-Life had been emitting. He hadn't been able to completely absorb the monstrosity from the other side, but he had absorbed a great deal of it. Max looked up at the monster on the horizon. It was encased in some sort of defensive bubble. Even from this distance, Max could feel how strong the shield was.

Not strong enough. He could break it. And he would. But there was no rush anymore.

Huh, that's strange. I didn't expect to get this powerful.

Out of curiosity, Max called for the Framework to see his Stats.

Maximilian Cromwell
Stage: Celestial
Dao: Destruction
Karma: +99
Speed: 80
Power: 112
Control: 100

"Holy shit," he whispered. "Maverick, I wish you could see this."

He liked to think his buddy could. While Max couldn't sense Maverick through their bond, he still existed in some form within the armor. Max wondered if he would ever get to hear that obnoxious, gleeful bastard again. He thought not.

I'll miss you, buddy.

Max looked down at the **[Scythe of Oblivion]** in his hand. It felt light and dainty. He remembered when he had seen it the first time; it had been obscenely large—unwieldy, even. Definitely a threatening weapon. It seemed like a child's toy now.

Max infused it, letting destructive energy flow into it. The scythe's handle got thicker and longer, the blade sharper, and it took on a pitch-black aspect, even the silver edge of the blade darkening. The scythe's blade also grew, elongating into a deadly crescent.

Max wasted no time. He gathered a flicker of power through his meridians and released it. The air rippled and burned around him as he moved faster than teleportation could manage, crashing into the black oily bubble protecting the Anti-Life.

The bubble cracked like an old eggshell.

The Anti-Life screeched with all of the power it had left, and it attacked Max with its pure adulterated Intent of greed for all that exists.

Max brushed it off as he pressed down on the creature with his own massive Intent. He swung the scythe, and it rippled through time and space, creating a rip in reality itself. Another rift was created. It crossed the massive, monstrous form of the Anti-Life, which instantly stopped moving, as if frozen in time.

Max pushed on the rift with his Intent, forcing it open wider and wider. He could feel the creature trying to struggle, but Max had absorbed most of its power. The rift grew wider still until it enveloped the giant monstrosity.

Then, Max *squeezed.*

The rift contracted, pushing into itself, contorting to fit a single pinpoint of gravity that ended in a black hole that flared up in the sky. The crushing weight of reality fell upon the Anti-Life, and it was too weak to resist. It was sucked into the singularity, utterly destroyed atom by atom as it hit the event horizon.

And beyond that event horizon? No wormholes. No other side of reality. Definitely not wherever the hell Anti-Life had come from. Only Destruction itself in its purest form. The Anti-Life was utterly obliterated so profoundly that even the concept of its existence became an impossibility. Max didn't simply destroy the Anti-Life. He permanently destroyed the very *idea* of Anti-Life existing. He ended the threat right here and now, once and for all.

Within a moment, the last dregs of the monstrous creature were sucked into the black hole. Max closed the swirling hole of nothingness and then silence fell.

Something rippled through the air. A final death rattle. It was not so much a sound as it was a feeling. An impression. It seeped into every heart and soul in the vicinity. A promise of return, a promise of devouring. The Anti-Life was something beyond life and death, and not even pure Destruction would hold it back.

Max felt the fear around him within the strike force members and the king's royal guard. The ICCB and King Valdemar were not impressed. Max only scoffed.

If that thing comes back into our reality again, I won't be so gentle.

Something stirred in the gleaming gold and black armor Max was wearing. A faint hint of emotion. Pride. Smugness.

"Are you there, buddy?" Max asked quietly.

There was no further answer. Maybe it had just been an echo of Max's own mind. But Max liked to think that Maverick was still there. Maybe reduced to fine dust for now. But if he knew his buddy, which he did, Max knew that Maverick would reemerge one day.

"I have all the time in the world, buddy."

Max breathed in the air of Alpha Ludus. The sun was setting, casting an orange cloak over the world. Below them, a ruined land and charred-black Tar. They would have to dispose of it. Max would see to it himself. It was possible that if the Anti-Life had any real plans of returning, it would happen through the material left by the Outsiders. There were complete solar systems full of the black sludge. The ICCB would make sure to deal with all infested planets.

And if they don't, they will have to deal with me.

CHAPTER FIFTY-FIVE

Plans Within Plans

"Your leadership has proven inadequate," Zerozerothree said as he floated above the council table. On the opposite side, the Zoos Collective's avatar slowly bobbed up and down.

"The Swarm agrees," Azzzhtik'Likzirrruk said.

[While not everything has gone according to plan, we refute the notion that we acted incorrectly. The Collective has run a vast number of computer simulations all of which verified that this was our best course of action. We have concluded that it was the ideal outcome.]

"Ideal?" Zerozerothree hissed. "How can it be ideal, when the boy is no longer our asset?"

"Calling him a 'boy' is truly bold," the leader of the frogs said from the confines of his green gel. "Maximillian Cromwell is a Celestial-stage Cultivator."

"As am I, and have been for eight hundred years," Zerozerothree hissed. "Do not presume to think he and I are the same. I could crush him like a bug."

[With that Dao of his? Would you like to see the numbers our computers have to say on the matter?]

The Gray grumbled and said nothing. Azzzhtik'Likzirrruk, spokesman of the Swarm, however, refused to relent.

"The Swarm doesn't care about your number-crunching. We only see results, or in this case, the lack of them. You held the fate of the asset in your proverbial fingertips and let him slip through them. You must have known that Princess Favani was on the planet where you sent the asset to train."

[We knew. But it was impossible to know the alliance would result in their marriage.]

"Oh, please! It was obvious that the Jianari Empire would immediately press for marriage when they realized what manner of creature Maximillian Cromwell was!" Zerozerothree hissed in pure anger.

The Zoos Collective, of course, knew this. The simulations that they had given the Council had been fabricated, but none of the other factions were able-enough statisticians to verify the falsity. This was definitely a loss for the Zoos Collective. But it wouldn't be enough to oust them from the coalition's leadership. Allowing Maximillian Cromwell to enter the other faction had been a worthy gamble and sacrifice.

In fact, it was necessary. The stability of the universe rested on it.

The Zoos Collective often wondered why other creatures hadn't attempted to discard their corporeal forms and adopt a digital existence as they had done. Even though it made Cultivation complicated, the other perks made up for it. One of those perks was clarity.

The Zoos Collective could see very clearly how future events would unfold. One thing was clear: the emergence of Maximillian Cromwell as a Celestial-stage Cultivator would mean that the sapient beings of this universe could finally break the deadlock against the Outsiders. They could drive the threat to extinction.

And what would have happened after that, if Maximillian Cromwell had stayed with the ICCB?

Nothing short of the full deterioration of the war effort.

No, it was clear what needed to happen next. The Zoos Collective had orchestrated it. The threat of the Outsiders would soon be snuffed out. Then, in a few thousand years, all the alliances, all the hard work that had been put together to drive away the threat, would start to dilapidate. No longer would strong Cultivators emerge. No longer would there be the Cosmic Games, driving the sapient beings of the universe forward.

With no common enemy, there would be strife. Then strife would lead to conflicts and unpredictable outcomes. The ICCB would disband and there would be war between the factions. There would be chaos.

The Zoos Collective did not care for chaos. If there was going to be conflict, they would make sure they were in control of it.

Achieving a situation like that would be easy. All it would require was a war against the Jianari Empire.

This would not be a war of destruction. Not a war of attrition. Not a war of faith or any of the other silly reasons corporeal life forms waged war.

No . . . This would be a war for excellence.

The Zoos Collective saw it so clearly. The threat the Outsiders posed was absolutely devastating. The Zoos Collective knew this, because, despite there only being two official reports of the fourth-class Outsider threat, there were several unofficial ones.

This universe wasn't the only reality that the Outsiders had attacked. They had consumed several other universes. And while the ICCB and the Jianari Empire could together push back the threat that was now attacking them, it was but a fraction of the horror that could be unleashed upon their universe.

Given enough time, misfortune was almost a certainty.

That is why war was needed. A controlled war. Just like a controlled forest fire will make the soil of a jungle more nutrient-rich, a controlled war would make a population stronger. The Zoos Collective could never allow the sapient creatures of this universe let their swords collect rust, a barely remembered vestige of the old days. They would not be weak of body, mind, and arsenal when a real threat came.

The Zoos Collective would be the steward of this reality. They would have to instigate war. Forever, if that was what it required. The Outsiders had consumed several realities, star systems upon star systems, overseen by the malignant greed of the Fourth Type, the Anti-Life.

Defeating just one of them had required special circumstances and several Celestial-stage Cultivators. And that one had been relatively *small*. Miniscule, even.

Warfare was the ultimate whetstone. There was nothing like it. When everyone had to come together to strive for survival against an enemy, everything aligned—the hierarchies, the priorities for labor and resources . . . Warfare created the most exemplary bodies and minds. Was Maximillian Cromwell not a prime example of that? His unparalleled talent for Cultivation had come from warfare. Strife. Conflict.

The worst thing a sapient species could experience was peace. Peace created weakness. It created soft, lax and stupid creatures. The Zoos Collective would not allow it.

They would make sure the universe would never know peace.

They had to.

They were the stewards of this reality.

CHAPTER FIFTY-SIX

Aftermath

Max sat lounging on a sofa of preposterous size. Well, he was twenty feet in height now, almost as tall as King Valdemar. It would take some getting used to. Favani was pissed about it, because at least for now, it meant that they were slightly . . . physically incompatible to fulfill their marital duties. Not that Max was keen to have any sort of offspring in the immediate future.

Max swirled a sweet drink in a golden goblet. He sipped it and sighed contently.

No more fighting, huh? That will take some getting used to.

"What are you thinking?" Favani asked and leaned her hands and head against Max's massive thigh.

"What is a warrior to do after peace is won?" Max asked.

Losshnak slapped his thigh and hooted. Ashkarassa chuckled next to him. They were back to normal, their life-force returned to them. Max had taken them into his court, as was his right as a prince.

"Peace is hard earned, Master Warrior," Losshnak said. "More wine!"

A flying gnome immediately complied and arrived with a jug to fill Losshnak's extended cup. Kat and Rakii were also quick to demand refills. Kat gave Max strange looks from time to time, but when Max looked back, she always averted her gaze.

Most likely doesn't quite see me as human anymore. Must be strange. I'm not sure I am human *anymore.*

Max felt powerful. Being a Celestial-stage Cultivator meant that he was one of the most powerful beings in the known universe. He was now a force unto himself that even the ICCB had to acknowledge. King Valdemar and Favani had been wise to bind him to their family. That meant that their empire had gone from an underdog to a force that needed to be respected. Especially with as powerful a Dao as Max commanded.

If the ICCB didn't want to play ball, Max could be teleported to any solar system and take over all of the habitable planets within hours. There would still be friction. There were still Outsiders to destroy. But now they could tilt the scales. Max could make a difference.

Friction was fine. Max would play hardball with the ICCB. For all their help, they still held thousands if not millions of slave contracts with Cultivator-warriors of middling tiers. The Outsiders were no longer a threat. The contracted Cultivators were purely on cleanup duty. But Max had his doubts as to whether or not the ICCB would dismantle their great galaxy-spanning war machine.

If they didn't do it of their own volition, Max could perhaps . . . encourage them.

He was interrupted by one of the servant gnomes flying up to his face.

"Urgent message from the king," the gnome peeped in a high voice.

Max groaned. "Not again."

"I want to go," Favani said. "You might have won us peace, but I am still at war."

Max chuckled.

Kat perked up from the sofa cushions. "What war?"

Favani cast a bashful glance at Max. "I have to reach the Celestial realm to access certain . . . benefits."

"Oh," Kat said and blushed.

Favani blushed a cute shade of purple as well, and Max chuckled and brushed a lock of hair gently behind her ear.

"I do not get it," Slargi said in his gently clicking voice.

Plarag shook her head slowly. "It means Max is too big for her."

"A true warrior!" Losshnak said and slapped his thigh.

Favani only blushed further.

"At the rate at which your father requests these bouts with me, I'll outgrow him," Max said.

Favani nodded. "You do know that in the case that happens, he expects you to challenge him and take his place as emperor."

"I'm not going to do that," Max said.

"You will," Favani said and slid her hand up and down Max's massive thigh. "But I hope not for a few centuries."

Max nodded. A few centuries. He would most likely live for a thousand—no, *thousands* of years. Would there be peace? Max very much doubted it. The Anti-Life had come. It had been hasty, most likely because it had noticed Max growing too fast. It had been taken by surprise.

But what Max understood of the Outsiders—and he understood a lot after pouring through hundreds of recordings from both the ICCB and the Jianari Empire—was that the threat was not over.

No new portals to their reality had opened for the last twelve days. The whole universe was holding its breath. Right now, it seemed like they had peace. But for how long? Max could only guess.

The Anti-Life had attacked him swiftly. It would not make that mistake again. This fourth classification, the dark star with tentacles and the harrowing pitiless eye, had only been one of many. There had to be thousands of them. One, according to the two reports about the Anti-Life, had been the size of a star. If that thing entered their reality, the whole universe would tremble.

And Max had to be ready for that. If the Diamond stage was a long road, the Celestial realm was something else entirely. It was a *world* of creation, something Max still didn't truly understand. He could now shape reality with his Intent. He cupped his hand and destroyed the golden goblet in his hand, wine included.

Then a tiny plant sprouted from his hand. It was vibrant green and reached out into the air, as if hungry for life.

On the other side of Destruction is Creation.

A difficult concept to understand through Cultivation. Something Valdemar had imparted to Max. His was the Dao of Ruling. The king's initial Intent was tyranny and oppression. But on the other side of that coin, when he had reached the Celestial realm, was love.

"They are the same thing," the king had boomed. "A tyranny too hard and love too soft both lead to the same place. And vice versa."

What this meant for Max and his Cultivation was still shrouded in the mists of the future. But he would find out. He had to be ready. For Max loved the universe. He loved life. He had finally found his place in it. He would be its stalwart protector. He would be the person reality needed. He would enjoy himself, train hard, and become ready.

For the Outsiders would come again. And Max would be prepared. Just as the other side of tyranny was love, just as the other side of Destruction was Creation. The other side of relentless war was peace. The peace would eventually end. In a week? A month? A century?

Eventually.

And Max would be ready.

"Let's go, Wife."

Max and Favani walked out of the chamber, leaving their friends to enjoy their wine. They went joyfully, excited about their next steps together. Life was good. Life was as it should be.

About the Author

Wilbur Woods is an entertainer, coffee drinker, and story eater, as well as the author of the Cosmic Games series, originally released on Royal Road. He has loved stories since he was a kid, and when he asked himself what he really wanted to do, the answer was simple: write.

Podium

DISCOVER MORE

STORIES
UNBOUND

PodiumEntertainment.com

www.ingramcontent.com/pod-product-compliance
Ingram Content Group UK Ltd.
Pitfield, Milton Keynes, MK11 3LW, UK
UKHW031106170325
456354UK00005B/386

9 781039 465763